I0763291

A Heart of Fire and Flame

Book One of the Fire and Flame Series

K.J. Johnson

K.J. Johnson Books

First published by K.J. Johnson Books 2024

ISBN: 978-1-7636825-2-8

Contents

Dedication	VII
Content Warning	VIII
Map of Aetherian	IX
Pronunciation Guide	X
Prologue	XI
Chapter One	1
Chapter Two	7
Chapter Three	12
Chapter Four	17
Chapter Five	23
Chapter Six	28
Chapter Seven	36
Chapter Eight	40
Chapter Nine	46
Chapter Ten	51

Chapter Eleven	55
Chapter Twelve	61
Chapter Thirteen	66
Chapter Fourteen	71
Chapter Fifteen	76
Chapter Sixteen	82
Chapter Seventeen	87
Chapter Eighteen	91
Chapter Nineteen	95
Chapter Twenty	102
Chapter Twenty-One	108
Chapter Twenty-Two	112
Chapter Twenty-Three	117
Chapter Twenty-Four	121
Chapter Twenty-Five	126
Chapter Twenty-Six	130
Chapter Twenty-Seven	136
Chapter Twenty-Eight	141
Chapter Twenty-Nine	145
Chapter Thirty	149
Chapter Thirty-One	154
Chapter Thirty-Two	160
Chapter Thirty-Three	166
Chapter Thirty-Four	171

Chapter Thirty-Five 176
Chapter Thirty-Six 181
Chapter Thirty-Seven 186
Chapter Thirty-Eight 190
Chapter Thirty-Nine 196
Chapter Forty 202
Chapter Forty-One 207
Chapter Forty-Two 212
Chapter Forty-Three 218
Chapter Forty-Four 223
Chapter Forty-Five 227
Chapter Forty-Six 231
Chapter Forty-Seven 235
Chapter Forty-Eight 240
Chapter Forty-Nine 245
Chapter Fifty 252
Chapter Fifty-One 259
Chapter Fifty-Two 265
Chapter Fifty-Three 271
Chapter Fifty-Four 277
Chapter Fifty-Five 282
Chapter Fifty-Six 288
Chapter Fifty-Seven 294
Chapter Fifty-Eight 299

Chapter Fifty-Nine 304

Acknowledgments 310

About the Author 312

Social Media Links 314

For Nannie,
Go raibh maith agat as a chreidiúint ionam.

Content Warning

This story is intended for mature readers only.

It contains controlling and possessive behavior by the MMC towards the FMC, explicit sexual content, dubious consent, sexual assault, kidnapping, profanity, depictions of violence, and other topics that may be triggering for some readers.

Reader discretion is advised.

Map of Aetherian

Pronunciation Guide

- Valoren: Val–or–ren
- Netheran: Neh–thuh-ran
- Pyrithia: Py–rith – ee-ah
- Vidyaa: Vid–ee-ah
- Zarinia: Zah–reen–ee-ah
- Elysara: Eh–lee–sah-rah
- Aetherian: Uh–thir–ee–an
- Cathal: Kah-hal
- Cian: Kee–an
- Cillian: Kill– ee– an
- Fionn: Fee-on
- Misneach: Mish–nahh
- Caolán: Kway–lawn
- Oisín: Uh–sheen
- Rónán: Roh-nawn
- Niamh: Neev
- Fiadh: Fee–ah
- Fórsa: Fohr-suh

Prologue

The heavy wooden door was slightly ajar, allowing the light from the lantern to spill into the hallway, illuminating the figures within. Their shadows reached high on the stone walls, making them appear ominous and imposing.

"The coin covered the first infantry, the maps the second. If you require further aid, you know my price," a crisp, deep voice announced from within the room.

I froze where I stood on the precipice of the threshold. I knew that voice. That voice always sent a shiver of fear racing down my spine.

"You're asking too much," the other man hissed.

My husband.

I inhaled a sharp breath and stepped closer, peering into the room. My Husband had his back to me, so I could see his broad shoulders heaving with the effort to contain his emotions. His long, copper hair hung in waves down his back, swaying as he shook his head in anger.

A pair of striking blue eyes met and locked with mine over his shoulder. "That is my price," he said coolly, without releasing me from his gaze. Tattoos snaked up his throat, disappearing into his shoulder-length, snow-colored hair. His face was a work of fine artistry, with his chiseled jaw and light stubble, a straight, symmetrical nose, and eyes so captivating you could lose yourself in their blue depths. When I looked into those eyes, however, I saw the blackened soul beneath. The promise of cruelty and suffering.

My husband curled his hands into fists at his side as he weighed his options. After a long pause, my husband exhaled a shaky breath and replied, "As you say." His shoulders slumped with his words, defeat evident in his tone.

Those blue eyes remained locked on me as they sparkled with victory, and a small smirk tipped up the corner of his mouth. Shadows began to swirl in the space between the men, and then, just like a whisper in the wind, he was gone, disappearing in the darkness. Dread settled in my stomach and the air in the room seemed suddenly stifling.

I rushed forward, grabbing my husband's arm and turning him to face me. His emerald green eyes widened in surprise and then narrowed in suspicion.

"Eavesdropping on your King are you, wife," he bit out in annoyance.

He scratched at his short beard, the same rich color as his hair, as he looked down at me. It was one of his tells, something he did often when trying to conceal his agitation. There was something else there, too. A weariness that crinkled the corner of his eyes and dipped his copper eyebrows. His head dropped, and my feeling of dread only intensified as it spread throughout my body.

"Atticus, what have you done?" I said in a strained whisper.

"What I had to," he replied, turning away from me, no longer willing to meet my gaze.

Dread turned to desperation as I shook his enormous frame and shouted, "Tell me!"

After a long pause, he looked back at me, his face reflecting his misery. I gasped, anticipating the blow he was about to deliver.

Atticus schooled his features, squared his shoulders, and took a steadying breath.

The King had returned.

"I have... arranged our daughter's betrothal, Clementine."

I felt the words like a physical blow, and I staggered back.

"Once she has come of age, Harlowe will wed the King of Netheran. In return, Kieran will continue to support our war effort, and through their union, we will achieve an unbreakable alliance between our kingdoms."

A strangled cry escaped my lips. I felt my stomach sinking, and my legs on the verge of collapsing.

Fear, grief, despair, and hopelessness slammed into me, overwhelming me all at once. My precious, tiny daughter. Only five days old and already I had failed to protect her. To keep her safe from harm.

He... he had promised my newborn daughter to that... to that monster.

Fury overtook me, and my hand darted out in front of me, slapping my husband across the face. Hard.

"HOW COULD YOU?" I roared.

My anger was a palpable energy as it filled the room. Before I registered he had even moved, Atticus had gripped both my hands in his and had pulled me flush against his broad, rigid chest.

"You want to strike me, Clementine? Go ahead. I understand you are upset, so hit me, scream at me, punish me if you must," he gritted out between clenched teeth. "But when you are done, it's over. We will not speak of this again. Some may seek to harm our daughter if they discover her role in the alliance."

We locked eyes, breathing heavily in the silence. Tears filled my vision and I let the sobs overtake me. His eyes softened, and he tucked me against his chest, patting my hair in a soothing gesture.

"I am King, Clementine," he whispered. "We cannot sustain an indefinite war on three fronts. It is what they are counting on. I bear the responsibility for every life in this kingdom. Kieran's alliance is crucial for our people's salvation."

I was unable to respond. Sobs continued to wrack my body. I had heard the stories about Kieran. Everyone had. He ruled his kingdom with an iron fist. Known to be cruel and abusive. Especially towards those who dared to share his bed.

I didn't want that life for my daughter.

Atticus continued speaking, but I heard none of it. My fear overpowered me; crippling me. As my sobs receded, he held me at arm's length to look me over. His brows furrowed for a moment and then smoothed. He gave a subtle nod as if acknowledging an unspoken question.

"You must not mention this to anyone, Clementine. Harlowe will not know she is betrothed. We will teach her what it means to be the heir to this kingdom. To be a ruler. With time, she will learn to prioritize her people's needs over her own. Only after that will we disclose to her what transpired tonight."

I was incapable of giving him the confirmation he was seeking, so I said nothing.

Sighing, Atticus straightened and turned towards the door.

"She will understand," he whispered to the silence enveloping the room as if begging it to whisper its agreement in return.

He turned and reached out his hand, saying, "Come, wife. Let us put this night behind us." Taking his hand, I let him lead me out of the room and down the darkened hallway.

Just as we rounded the corner, I peered back towards the open door, the light still glowing faintly from the lantern within. There would be no forgetting this night. Not for me. It would serve as a constant reminder that I failed in the one duty I swore to uphold above all others.

The duty of a mother.

Turning back towards my husband, I studied his profile in the small glimmer of moonlight sneaking in through the windows. He was deep in thought, his eyes strained as he battled his own thoughts within the confines of his mind.

No.

There would be no forgetting this night for either of us.

We were bound to this night and its consequences. The consequences that my precious infant daughter had been damned to pay in time.

Oh Harlowe, how will you ever forgive us?

Chapter One

I woke to a deafening screech filling the early morning air outside my open window. I sat bolt upright, trying to shake off the remnants of sleep. Another screech sounded, closer this time.

No, not a screech. A roar.

Dragons.

And if there were dragons in Valoren, then the Cathal were here too.

While dragons were not isolated to the Kingdom of Pyrithia, they were the only kingdom foolish enough to try to wield them as weapons.

Dragons were unpredictable, aggressive, and deadly by nature, and one could only become Cathal if they could forge a bond with a dragon. It was a deep mutual respect and trust between the two beings. A shared sense of purpose and understanding of the world around them.

Most kingdoms had abandoned the practice centuries ago, as warriors were more likely to be killed by a dragon than bond one.

But not Pyrithia.

Those who reigned over Pyrithia were ruthless enough to continue sacrificing their warriors for the chance to swell the number of dragons within their ranks.

Not only were the dragons formidable foes but the Cathal were similarly feared. They were taught the blade from a young age and endured the trial of monsters at age ten.

No one entered the Forest of Nightmares for fear of the monsters lurking within. Most didn't return, but that didn't deter Pyrithia from sending their children in to prove their worth.

Those who survived became the Cathal; the most lethal warriors of all Aetherian. Together with their dragons, they were all but unstoppable.

Our kingdom had plenty of cause to fear the incoming formation.

During the Skirmish of Power twenty-five years ago, the Kingdom of Pyrithia joined forces with the Kingdoms of Zarinia and Vidyaa, attempting to overthrow my father and take the Kingdom of Valoren. Each kingdom bordered our own and their aim had been to conquer our kingdom and divide our lands and resources among themselves.

Pyrithia, with their dragons and Cathal, had wrought the most devastation on our kingdom during this time.

The realm within which we lived, Aetherian, offered up power to all citizens of the realm. This power was known as fórsa, and every single person within the realm was connected to it. However, not everyone could draw on fórsa and manifest it into something tangible.

To wield it as a weapon.

Those who could pulled fórsa to themselves, generating orbs of energy. Some were small, while others were as large as a human head. But every single one of them was deadly.

In the past, the subjects of Valoren accounted for a significant portion of those able to manifest fórsa, leading some to believe the land itself played a role. Hence, the desire of rival kingdoms to extend their borders into our lands.

They would have succeeded too, if not for the aid provided by the Kingdom of Netheran. Their aid prevented the onslaught from overwhelming us. The attack was short-lived, only lasting some few months.

When the fighting ceased, each kingdom agreed to the accords. Trade opened up between the kingdoms and we have enjoyed relative peace since.

That was, until this morning.

Despite the peace treaty, no citizen of Pyrithia had entered the Kingdom of Valoren in almost twenty-five years, which is why their sudden appearance could only mean one thing; they were here for violence.

I ripped back my covers and dove out of bed, pulling on my sheaths and filling them with daggers as I went. I didn't bother to dress. We were already out of time.

Fear trickled down my spine as I flung my door open, and I raced out of my bedroom into the adjoining antechamber. My chambermaid, Louise, startled as she whirled around to face me. She was in the middle of plumping the cushions on my velvet emerald chaise and setting up my breakfast tray.

Did she not hear the incoming terror?

Her chocolate-colored eyes grew wide as she took me in, her hand flying to the base of her throat in fright. "What in the realm?" I didn't wait to hear her next words before I interrupted.

"Hide!" I barked at her, and I rushed to the door.

As I sprinted down the empty halls, I beseeched the gods, praying that the silence reverberating around me was a sign that my father's soldiers had been alerted and were now getting ready to defend the palace. I could see the main entryway ahead, down the stairs that protruded from the first floor. I took a leaping jump, clearing the stairs in three strides.

As I approached the entryway, I slowed my pace and unsheathed a dagger. Peering around the heavy wooden door, I took inventory of the enemy I would be facing, not wanting to run headfirst into a battle unprepared. I saw the first dragon and their Cathal land in the palace square.

I could not see the army... or anyone... preparing to meet the enemy on our doorstep. I slinked into the shadows by the palace entrance as the Cathal prepared to dismount. I counted ten Cathal in total. Not bad odds had the fighters been regular infantry rather than the gods of death I knew them to be. Despite being outnumbered, I was still a trained warrior dedicated to protecting my kingdom at all costs.

I would buy my father time if nothing else.

I steadied myself as the Cathal ascended the palace steps. Waiting until the first warrior was just about on top of me, I moved from the shadows concealing me and aimed my dagger for the side of my opponent's neck, which was bare of armor, just as Zeke had taught me.

Moving faster than my eyes could process, a large, calloused hand swung up and gripped my wrist before my dagger could hit home. A jolt ran up my arm at the point of contact. Another hand gripped my shoulder, and a foot swept my leg out from underneath me in a move so graceful it could be mistaken for a dance. My back hit the stone ground hard, knocking the wind out of me. Before my head could follow suit, a large palm darted up, cradling my skull, and absorbing the impact.

For a moment I couldn't breathe, and then oxygen filled my lungs so rapidly it burned. I looked up and blinked at the man, who was only inches from my face.

And then I blinked again.

He was the most beautiful male I had ever laid eyes on. His dark brown hair was cut short on the sides and back, while the top was longer, falling to one side and framing his gorgeous face. Set amongst his lightly tanned skin were dark brown eyes that simmered with intelligence; calculating and shrewd. He raised a perfectly arched eyebrow at me in amusement and pulled up his soft, sensual lips at the side in a seductive smirk. Glancing lower, I noticed he had large tattoos framing his neck, which disappeared under his fighting leathers at his collarbone, only to reappear on his forearms, which were exposed below the elbow.

Dragons, I realized. The many tattoos depicted dragons engaged in battle.

He was sexy as sin.

I could only gape at him, and his small smirk grew into a knowing grin, making him all the more enticing.

Everywhere his body touched mine, small sparks of lightning raced along my skin, making me acutely aware of the position I was in.

"Harlowe." I heard a soft feminine voice gasp behind me, accompanied by the sound of boots on stone.

The cavalry had arrived. Led by my mother, apparently.

I could only tilt my head to observe the approaching crowd as the godly figure held me tight. My mother stood at the threshold of the palace entryway, her long golden hair twisted into an elegant bun at her nape. Her sky-blue eyes were wide with shock, and her soft, creamy complexion was a shade paler than usual as she took in the sight before her. She had painted her lips a deep crimson to match the ruby red dress she wore, which was embroidered with intricate golden designs that matched her hair. My mother was a beautiful woman. There was no denying that.

Her eyes crept lower, and she hissed in a sharp tone, "Are those your nightclothes?"

I had forgotten that I fled my chambers without bothering to dress, assuming the palace was under attack. My cheeks heated, and I tried to scramble out of the arms that held me. The male above me only tightened his hold and then pulled me flush against his body as he straightened. I could feel his muscular chest flex beneath my hands. He was taller than I initially thought, with my head barely reaching his throat.

I fled to my mother's side the moment I was free.

And then he winked at me.

He. Fucking. Winked. At. Me.

The audacity of this man. Like my mortification was for his pure enjoyment.

My mother hastily wrestled the nearest soldier out of his cloak and flung it around my shoulders, shielding my indecency from further observation. My cheeks only heated further.

Turning back to the delegation before us, my mother squared her shoulders and raised her chin. "I am Queen Clementine of Valoren, and this is my daughter, Princess Harlowe of Valoren," she said, gesturing to me.

I whipped my head around to face her, confusion clear in my features. What was going on here? My mother welcomed the Cathal as if she had been expecting them!

Each of the Cathal lowered their heads in a bow, acknowledging our stations.

"My husband, King Atticus, will join us soon. Unfortunately, he was called away from the palace this morning, but I expect him to return shortly."

My head was reeling. I had no idea what was going on.

But my mother knew.

And from the demeanor of the soldiers surrounding her, so did they.

There was only one possible meaning for this. This visit was planned. And no one had bothered to inform me.

"You must be hungry," my mother said to the awaiting delegation smoothly. "Please, follow me into the dining hall and we can all enjoy a hot meal while we await the King's return."

"What the hell is going on?" I demanded in a coarse whisper.

"Harlowe, language," she chastised, but I was not in the mood.

"Why wasn't I informed about enemy forces from a rival kingdom coming to the palace?"

"They are not our enemies, not anymore," my mother responded coolly. "They are here under invitation to train our soldiers."

My eyes widened. There had been no joint military operations with Pyrithia since the Skirmish of Power.

My mother eyed me. "Return to your chambers, get dressed, and join us for breakfast. You will not embarrass me further, Harlowe."

Her eyebrow arched before she swept her gaze up and down my body, indicating her displeasure at my current state of dress, or undress, as it may be.

My mother turned to one of the kitchen staff waiting nearby and gave her quiet instructions to lay out the morning meal in the main dining hall. Recognizing a dismissal when I saw one, I mustered as much dignity as I could in my current state and headed toward my chambers.

If my mother wanted me to play nice, fine, I would play nice. But that wouldn't stop me from getting answers.

Chapter Two

Louise was still in my chambers when I returned. She was busy cleaning and hanging the laundered day dresses I had no intention of wearing to my closet. "There you are. You had me worried half to death," she said as she strode towards me.

Louise was a gentle woman, only a year or two older than me, yet she brought a distinct maternal quality to our relationship. Today, she had her long, brown hair swept back into a loose braid and her warm hazel eyes were full of concern.

"What had you running out of here like you had harpies on your tail?"

I cringed, imagining how I must have looked sprinting out of my chambers, armed to my teeth and in my nightclothes no less.

"We had some unexpected guests arrive this morning. I thought they were attacking," I finished sheepishly. Guilt crossed Louise's expression, and she averted her eyes.

"But I'm guessing you already knew that. The entire palace seems to have known they were coming. Well, except me, of course," I muttered.

Louise returned her gaze to mine. "I'm sorry Harlowe. The staff were all instructed not to tell you or discuss it where you could overhear. The King thought it would... distract you from your studies. He has been very insistent that you prioritize your education above all else." She gave me a sympathetic smile, knowing just how much I detested those lessons. It wasn't so much an education as it was a study of court etiquette. My father was determined to turn me into a proper lady of the Court.

"If you ask me," she continued, "it was a little short-sighted since there would be no hiding their presence once they arrived. However, the King decided news of the impending delegation would have led you to abandon your studies in favor of joining those intending to train with the Cathal." She cringed at that last statement.

As I suspected, my father wanted me to play the perfect princess instead of learning how to defend my kingdom. He always hated my mother's encouragement for my training. In fact, it had been my mother who had arranged for her own guard, Zeke, to become my combat instructor. While my father's assumptions were correct, that did not justify keeping something like this from me. Even instructing the staff to not so much as whisper about it in my direction!

He was being ridiculous.

While I still had reservations about the Cathal even being within the boundaries of Valoren, I wasn't one to pass up an opportunity to sharpen my skills. And training with the Cathal, that would be the ultimate test of my capabilities!

I was turning all of this over in my mind as Louise helped me dress for the day. She had picked a velvet green dress that matched my eyes, the same shade as my father's. I argued with her for twenty minutes about wearing the ghastly thing, but she insisted, stating that I needed to make the 'right' impression on the visiting delegation. Begrudgingly, I let her dress me in it and she started brushing my hair, which I also inherited from my father. The long, copper strands were hanging loose in waves to my waist. Louise pulled it back into an intricate braid that she adorned with gem-encrusted pins, leaving a few strands hanging loose to frame my face. I brushed her off when she attempted to start on my make-up. I rarely wore it, knowing I would sweat it off within the first five minutes of my training. Louise muttered something about a hopeless case, and I grinned at her musings.

Peering in the mirror, I took stock of the small scattering of freckles that adorned the bridge of my nose. I had the same creamy complexion as my mother, despite the hours I had spent outside training in the sun. My lips were cracked from the constant need to wet them when exposed to the elements, so I relented and let Louise apply a thin layer of paint to my lips; a pale pink that made them look fuller. Satisfied, Louise released me, and I stood from my chair before the vanity. Casting one last glance in the mirror, my reflection was a far cry from my normal leather-clad appearance, but I had to admit, I looked beautiful, regal even.

"Thank you, Louise," I said, as I made my way towards the door, and she inclined her head in acknowledgment.

Heading in the direction of the dining hall, I saw that the usual flurry of activity had returned to the palace and the soldiers had resumed their posts. As I approached the dining hall entrance, I could hear a loud ruckus of voices emanating from within. Peering inside, I was taken aback by how... ordinary... the scene before me appeared. Seated around one table was my mother, her lady's maids on either side of her. Four Cathal sat next to them, two on either side, followed by several soldiers who mingled with the remaining Cathal further down the table. Everyone was chatting and joking with each other as though they were long-acquainted friends.

"Harlowe," my mother called out when she noticed me. "Come, join us." The Cathal sitting closest to her turned towards me and I realized it was the man that had taken me to the ground earlier.

In nothing but my nightclothes.

I groaned internally. A coy smile played on his lips as though he, too, was remembering the events of earlier this morning.

Embarrassment flooded my cheeks, but I raised my chin and headed towards the table. He whispered something to his companion, who promptly picked up his breakfast and strode from his seat to join the other Cathal further down the table. With the seat beside him now vacant, he turned towards me and peered at me expectantly. Reluctantly, I slid into the spot beside him.

"Harlowe, this is Silas," my mother said, indicating the male next to me. "He is the Commanding General of the Cathal for the Kingdom of Pyrithia. He and his King have graciously agreed to train some of our forces in the way of dragon bonding."

"So, I've heard," I muttered as I reached for a bread roll and set it on my plate.

"It is a pleasure to meet you... officially," Silas said with a sparkle of amusement in his eyes that I pointedly ignored as I gathered meat and cheese onto my plate.

"Likewise," I said, although somewhat coolly, without looking back in his direction.

"Harlowe," — my mother continued, the note of warning unmistakable in her tone — "this is Cillian, Silas's second-in-command." She gestured to a man across from me. He had short, brown hair, which was slightly longer than Silas's, and he was constantly shaking it out of his brilliant aqua eyes. He, too, was a beautiful man with his golden, tanned skin and faint stubble decorating his chin. Cillian dipped his chin towards me, and I returned the gesture.

"And this is Cian, Silas's third-in-command," my mother finished, indicating the man next to Cillian. His mop of curly, blond hair was cut similar to Silas's. He had a sharp, angular jaw and rich brown eyes that seemed to assess me. He also sported an array of dragon tattoos running the length of his arms from his shoulders to his wrists. Returning my gaze to meet Cian's, I smiled and said, "It is lovely to meet you all."

I could feel Silas's eyes boring into the side of my face as I continued to place fruit on my plate, but I refused to look in his direction. The conversation resumed, and I learned that the King of Pyrithia had approached my father. He offered to trade the services of his General in exchange for the services of Jury, one of our kingdom's tutors. Jury would teach the citizens of Pyrithia how to channel fórsa from the realm. They hoped Jury's tutelage would lead to more people being able to manifest fórsa into a weapon.

Just as I was readying my excuse to leave, the dining hall doors swung open and my father, accompanied by Zeke, and a small retinue of soldiers entered. My mother rose to greet him, followed by swift introductions of the Cathal spread amongst our table.

I rose from my seat and sidled up next to Zeke, giving him a disapproving look from the corner of my eye. He pretended not to notice. The sides of his long, dark hair were pulled back and bound with a leather tie, while the rest hung freely passed his shoulders. He said nothing as I continued to stare at him.

Unable to contain my aggravation any longer, I hissed, "I can't believe you didn't tell me about this." He turned to face me, a slight smirk hinting at the corner of his mouth. He simply raised one shoulder and returned his attention to the gathering before us, running a hand over his chin as if he hadn't a care in the world.

That dick.

Forgetting all pretense of decorum, I pushed Zeke hard, and he stumbled a few steps before regaining his composure. A full grin spread across his face, and he barked out a laugh at my antics.

"Well, well, well, the harpy has raised her vicious little head this morning. Fangs and all. We are in a good mood today, aren't we, Princess," he crooned. I scowled at him. He knew just how much I detested him using my title. His grin grew wider, and I couldn't help myself. I dissolved into a fit of laughter.

Zeke always had that effect on me. He never took anything seriously, so it was impossible to stay mad at him for too long.

"Harlowe," a deep male voice barked at me. My eyes snapped to my father's emerald ones, and I realized we had garnered an audience with our antics. Again, I could feel those calculating eyes on me, assessing me.

Silas.

I didn't dare seek him out to confirm it.

My father stalked towards me and, gripping my elbow in his hand, he whispered, "Do not make a spectacle of yourself. I expect you to carry yourself in a manner fit for your position."

"Perhaps if you hadn't kept me in the dark about your little arrangement," — I gestured towards the Cathal — "I would have been better prepared," I hissed back.

"Do not start this here, Harlowe," my father warned, his voice a low growl. "And while we are discussing the Cathal, I will make this plain right now, you will not be joining their training. You have other things to which you are required to devote your time." He paused before continuing. "And your behavior just now only proves that." I opened my mouth to argue, but my father silenced me with a narrowed glare. He had made up his mind and nothing would sway him. It wasn't like that would deter me, however.

Pivoting on my heels, I left the dining hall without another glance behind me.

Hunting. I was going hunting.

Chapter Three

Thirty minutes later, I was dressed in my fighting leathers with my bow slung over my shoulder, racing down the front steps of the palace. Still fuming, I failed to take stock of my surroundings and realized too late that I had marched straight into the center of the dragons, who were nestled in a group in front of the forest.

I knew you weren't supposed to approach bonded dragons without their Cathal. Hell, I knew you weren't supposed to approach dragons, period. Our kingdom had abandoned the practice of dragon bonding centuries ago, and for good reason.

Yet, due to my foolishness, I now stood in the middle of ten dragons, all with their serpentine eyes trained straight on me.

If I get burned to death, I only have myself to blame.

I could almost hear the lecture Zeke would spew at me. How my lack of awareness would get me killed. That I needed to always maintain a vigilant eye on my surroundings. But in my simmering rage, I had blocked out everything except that one blinding feeling and walked headfirst into a clutch of dragons.

The dragon in front of me stood to its full height, shuddering its wings as it stretched them wide and then tucked them away at its sides.

Straining, I looked up, and up, and up. The beast was massive.

With each movement, its scales flickered between a captivating mix of gray and green. The colossal head had a mouth brimming with razor-sharp teeth and wicked-looking horns with vibrant red tips. Its long neck led into broad shoulders that supported the massive wings I had seen spread wide just moments ago. The creature's long tail coiled around its thick thighs and had a red tip that resembled its horns. Long talon-like claws peeked out from each paw and its scales glimmered in the sunlight like armor.

It was the most lethal creature I had ever laid eyes on.

Taking a quick glance around me, I could see the other dragons in varying shades of red, green, blue, amber, gray, and black. Sometimes a combination of colors like the beast before me. Another dragon rose to its feet — a vibrant blue color with a red underbelly — and cautiously made its way toward me. The remaining dragons quickly followed suit.

Panic flooded my veins, and I was seconds away from trying to make a run for it when a low, deadly voice sounded behind me.

"Do not move. If you run, they will take it as an invitation to chase and incinerate you where you stand."

Silas.

"What am I supposed to do?" I hissed through clenched teeth.

"Just stay still and wait to see if they lose interest in you. To be perfectly honest, I have never seen anyone act so recklessly that they would approach an entire clutch of dragons." I clenched my fists at my sides. Maybe I deserved that, but I wouldn't give him the satisfaction of knowing I agreed.

"Not helping," I gritted out through clenched teeth. If I were moments away from death, I would go out with dignity. So I raised my head and met the eyes of each dragon as they approached me. A red dragon came within inches of my head, and I felt a puff of hot breath against the side of my face.

Did it just... sniff me?

Another dragon, green this time, nudged its enormous head against my palm, and this time I knew it sniffed me. One by one, they crowded around me, nudging my hands, legs, and head, sniffing me all over like they were trying to place my scent. Or worse, trying to figure out if I would taste good enough to eat.

I stayed perfectly still throughout the interaction, training my eyes on the largest of the dragons, the gray-green one I first saw upon entering the clearing. It didn't approach me, it simply watched me with an inquisitive eye. The other dragons retreated slowly until the only dragon left was the one directly in front of me. Eyes locked for a silent heartbeat, it inclined its head, almost like a bow, and then strode aside, clearing the path to the forest before me.

I released a shuddering breath I didn't realize I was holding and cautiously made my way forward. I didn't stop until the thick trees of the forest obscured me. Placing my hands on my knees, I leaned forward and greedily gulped a lungful of air. When my breathing evened out, I straightened.

I had no idea what had just happened with those dragons, but I sure as shit would not be inviting further scrutiny. Steeling myself against the lingering trembling in my limbs, I continued into the dense forest.

After what felt like hours later, I stood concealed behind a tree, an arrow pulled taut against my cheek as I monitored the large mountain lion patrolling the forest floor twenty yards in front of me. I exhaled a controlled breath and released my arrow. I knew I had hit true when the golden beast thumped to the ground without so much as a sound of protest escaping it.

I moved to take a step towards my kill when a calloused hand covered my mouth, while another reached around my waist, securing me against a hard wall of muscle. The hand on my waist made its way towards my breast, and the smell of male, leather and early morning dew assaulted my senses. Zeke cupped my breast in his palm and squeezed. A small moan escaped my lips against the hand that still covered my mouth.

It was no secret that Zeke and I were close friends, and I am sure many suspected that there was more between us. Those suspicions likely led people to believe a romantic relationship existed between us, but they would be wrong. While our friendship was certainly strong, we simply shared a physical relationship untethered by romantic feelings.

Zeke lowered his hand from my mouth and moved further south until he gripped my sex above my leathers. I moaned again, louder this time. Zeke nipped at my earlobe and then placed a trail of kisses down my neck, his slight stubble grazing my skin as he went. I shivered at the sensation and arched into his touch.

I moved my hands behind me, gripping his hard length, and squeezed roughly. Zeke growled low in my ear and pushed me against the tree. I twisted in his grip and met his rich brown eyes as they darkened with need.

I made to untie the laces of his pants and Zeke moved to do the same with mine, both feeling the urgency and promise of exhilaration waiting beneath our leathers. Panting in between kisses, I struggled with his laces until frustration took control and I pulled furiously, eliciting a soft chuckle from Zeke. Finally free, I gripped Zeke's throbbing cock with my palm and stroked. A groan left Zeke, and a thrill coursed through me, knowing I controlled his pleasure.

The cracking of a branch sounded to the left of us, and we both froze as we surveyed our surroundings. I locked on piercing brown eyes a small distance away, and Silas raised a brow, taking in the scene before him. Zeke and I both turned away, fixing our clothes; Zeke adjusted himself in his pants before turning back to face Silas.

Silas just stood there, strong, corded forearms crossed against his chest, an amused smirk on his face. I could feel Zeke bristle beside me.

"Is there something I can help you with, General?" I asked, breaking the silence. He surveyed me, taking me in from head to toe, and for a moment his eyes flashed with some emotion I couldn't quite read. Hatred, disgust, or maybe even lust.

"Am I interrupting something?" he asked knowingly.

"No," Zeke and I both answered too quickly. Silas only grinned brighter. My cheeks flushed, confirming what he already knew.

Zeke cleared his throat and said, "Is there a reason you are here, General?"

Silas's gaze danced to Zeke, taking him in for the first time, assessing and cataloging.

"I came to check on the Princess after her encounter with the dragons," he said casually, shrugging a shoulder.

Zeke gave me a sidelong look, and I muttered "later" in response to his unasked question.

Zeke turned to face me. "I should get back. I have things I need to discuss with your father."

"No doubt," Silas chuckled across the way, his smirk back in full force.

Zeke inclined his head towards Silas, acknowledging him with a simple "General," before glancing back to me and giving a brief nod.

I waited until Zeke had disappeared amid the trees before returning my gaze to Silas; amusement still evident on his face.

Prick.

Dismissing him, I moved towards my kill. I could hear Silas approaching behind me, but still, I said nothing.

Reaching down, I plucked the arrow protruding from the lion's body and returned it to my quiver.

"You have a good aim," Silas observed from above me. Still, I said nothing. When I stood to face him, I found him already staring at me, eyes intent; searching.

"How did you make it through the dragons?" he asked, voice low and demanding.

"What do you mean? You told me to wait them out. Not to move until they lost interest in me. That's what I did."

"I've never seen them let someone walk away, so you must have done something," he stated.

My mouth dropped open, and I just gaped at him. "You just let me what, wing it?" I asked incredulously. He lifted one shoulder, shrugging casually like he hadn't just taken a tremendous gamble with my life.

Seething, I snapped my jaw shut as I picked up my kill and threw it across my shoulders. I stalked away from Silas, flinging a rude hand gesture back over my shoulder, and traipsed out of the forest.

Chapter Four

The next morning, I went to find Zeke for our daily training session and came across him, silently observing the Cathal as they set about preparing for their first lesson. There were ten in total. Nine men and one woman. She was a tall, dark-haired woman with caramel strands that framed her face. Her chocolate-brown eyes were large, and she had lashes so long, that every glance was unintentionally seductive. Her full, dark eyebrows, plump pink lips, and high cheekbones completed her look. She was absolutely breathtaking.

Gods, were all these people exceptionally good-looking? Was that some sort of entry requirement for the Cathal?

Falling in beside Zeke, I asked, "Will you be joining in the training?" He flicked a quick glance in my direction before returning his gaze to the Cathal.

"Yes," he answered simply. I had expected that. Zeke was a formidable warrior, and my father would not waste the opportunity to make him that bit more terrifying.

"What about our training?" I asked, folding my arms across my chest, taking in the pile of swords that continued to grow as the Cathal unloaded their weapons. "I thought they were here to teach us about bonding with a dragon. Why so much weaponry?" I asked, gesturing to the rapidly growing pile.

"They are," Zeke responded, "but they'll also train us in dragon-mounted warfare."

Huh.

I guess I'd assumed the dragons were the weapon; no further effort required.

"As for your training," Zeke said with crooked a grin, "don't think you'll be getting out of it that easily. I have to train with the Cathal, yes, but I will still be training you. Just not for as many hours as you're used to. You will need to make up the difference on your own, or I can get one of the other soldiers to practice with you if you need."

I grunted, not even bothering to hide my disdain at his suggestion.

While Zeke was my friend, the other soldiers barely tolerated my training. They believed I had no place training with weapons and that I should focus on learning to entertain foreign dignitaries or other such nonsense.

Not that they would admit that to me.

My mother had been the one who insisted I train from a very young age, and she appointed Zeke as my combat instructor just over five years ago. My father did not approve, but for whatever reason, he gave my mother this one small indulgence, despite constantly grumbling about the time I dedicated to it.

"Let's go," he inclined his head towards our usual sparring spot. "Where are all the dragons?" I mused, noticing they were absent from the fields.

"I think they patrol the neighboring mountains when they're not required," Zeke supplied.

As if summoned by mere thought alone, ten powerful sets of wings blasted overhead, creating a windstorm around us as they made their way to the open field. Landing with a grace I did not expect from such gigantic beasts, the dragons stood in formation with military precision. It was a stark contrast to the wild beasts I learned about growing up.

"I guess that answers that," I muttered as I hurried after Zeke. I caught Silas's eye as he made to greet the dragons. He gave me a sly wink, and I rolled my eyes in response.

A few hours later, under the powerful midday sun, I lay in a heaving mess, sweat covering every inch of my body, after Zeke had taken me to the ground in a new move he was trying to teach me. "You did well today, Harlowe," Zeke said, as he offered me his hand. I placed my hand in his much larger one and let him pull me to my feet.

"You know," I mused, "I can't stop thinking about the strangeness of the deal my father struck with Pyrithia. I mean, they literally tried to destroy our kingdom the year I was born and now, they're just... what... helping us learn how to bond dragons, re-learn, or whatever. The one weapon that gives them an enormous advantage on the battlefield... why the sudden change of heart?"

"We have had peace with Pyrithia for twenty-five years, Harlowe. It's not that strange. Plus, you're forgetting that Jury is in Pyrithia right now trying to teach their people to develop a deeper connection to the realm and the fórsa it offers. Don't forget that the Skirmish of Power was fought because the surrounding kingdoms saw how citizens of Valoren could harness the realm's fórsa on a far greater scale than any other kingdom. Many saw this as our weapon, our advantage on the battlefield."

He was right, of course, although a little exaggerated. While the Kingdom of Valoren had more citizens who could manifest fórsa, it wasn't on a scale so grand that we could consider it an advantage on the battlefield. Plus, there was a cost for using too much fórsa. The more someone drew upon it, the weaker they became.

Most citizens felt fórsa emerging within them from around age twenty, and by the time they were around my age, they either had the ability to manifest it, or they didn't. It was through this power, this connection to the realm, that our lifespans were extended. We weren't immortal exactly, but we did live very long lives. Zeke himself fought in the Skirmish of Power and yet, he looked no older than I did today. The eldest person in our kingdom was over eight hundred years old. The stronger the connection to the realm, the longer a person's lifespan. Those who could manifest fórsa naturally lived the longest.

Both of my parents could wield fórsa, but I had yet to feel any connection to the realm, let alone touch its power source. I'd had tutors all my life and even Zeke and Emmerson, my best friend since childhood, had tried to guide me in drawing fórsa from the realm. Each had been unsuccessful. Just shy of my twenty-fifth birthday, I knew some within the kingdom were concerned that the heir to the throne would not outlive the current monarchs.

"It still feels... wrong somehow. I can't explain it, but I don't trust them. I think they have hidden motives for being here."

"Well, even if that is the case, Harlowe, you can bet your perky ass I'm going to take the opportunity to bond with a dragon when the odds of not dying are drastically improved." I rolled my eyes at his 'perky' comment, but let it go.

"That's enough for today," Zeke announced. "I have training with the Cathal this afternoon and I'd like to grab some lunch before then." I nodded my agreement as Zeke leaned down to retrieve his tunic from where he had discarded it earlier in the day. Shrugging it over his head, he started towards the palace. He peered back over his shoulder at me and raised an eyebrow when he noticed I hadn't followed. Still lost in my thoughts, I jogged to catch up to him.

After lunch, I returned to my training, taking refuge in the shade of the stables as I practiced with my blades. I had two short swords that were strapped to my back and over a dozen daggers sheathed about my person. I was working with my daggers, perfecting the killing blows Zeke had taught me to use in close quarters. Handy, if I'm ever cornered in a fight.

I was so enthralled by the sight of the blade as I sliced it through the air, watching the sharp tip glinting in the afternoon sun with such controlled precision, that I didn't hear the male approaching me until I sensed him at my back. Whirling around, I struck hard and fast, only to have my wrist caged in a much larger, much stronger hand mid-strike. Before I could get my bearings, I was spun around so fast and flattened against the hard muscle of an unmistakably male chest.

"You're quite the Little Menace, aren't you, Princess?" Silas crooned in my ear. I made to step out of his grip for the second time in as many days, but my dagger was pressed gently into my exposed throat.

"Never make the mistake of trusting anyone, Princess. Everyone is a potential enemy, especially to you."

Swallowing hard, I said, "Is that what you are, my enemy?" He only chuckled darkly in response.

"I can be whatever you want me to be, Princess," he whispered seductively, and heat instantly lanced my cheeks.

"Let me go," I commanded. He immediately released me, taking several steps back. He held tight to my dagger as he did so.

"That," I said, pointing to it, "would be mine."

"Is that so?" he hummed.

"Yes," I said.

He took a predatory step towards me, and I was determined to stand my ground. So, crossing my arms over my chest, I locked eyes with him and continued to track his approach. He was so close now our boots were touching. Even so, he didn't stop his advance. To avoid being trampled, I took a reluctant step back, and then another, until I was pressed against the stable door and his arms were caging me in.

I licked my lips nervously and a half smirk pulled up one side of his mouth. He was trying to intimidate me, and the prick was enjoying it. I straightened and scowled at him. This only made him laugh. Pushing against his hard chest, I tried to free myself, but he grabbed both my hands in one of his and pulled me flush against him.

A small flush of heat ran through me at the contact, which only infuriated me more. "What do you want, General?" I had tried to sound firm, and demanding, but my voice came out breathless and husky. My eyes darted to the tattoos on his neck and an overwhelming desire to lick them flooded me. I blinked in surprise and tried to regain my focus.

Silas noticed the action and leaned in close to my ear, whispering, "Maybe I should be asking you the same thing," he simpered. I pushed against him again, and this time, he relented, releasing my hands.

I put distance between us and repeated, "Why are you here?"

He shrugged nonchalantly. "I guess you could say I'm having trouble keeping my distance." His gaze swept over my frame and a wicked smirk curved up at the corner of his mouth. "Especially after the show you put on for me yesterday. Tell me, Princess, did you know I was out there, watching you? Did you want me to see you?"

I scoffed, unconvinced by his attempt to disarm me, but I couldn't conceal the blush creeping up my cheeks.

A wide grin spread across Silas's face. It was all teeth, all predator.

I could feel moisture pooling between my thighs at the thought of this gorgeous man watching me, running his hands all over me. I clenched my thighs together to ease the growing tension at my apex. As gorgeous as Silas was, he was also dangerous, and I didn't trust him, not for a second.

He tossed my dagger in the air, flipping it over and catching it by the tip, offering the hilt to me. The casualness and skill with which he handled my weapon bespoke the lethal warrior lurking below the amused smirk.

"Train me," I blurted out. I wasn't sure who was more surprised by my demand, him, or me. While I didn't trust Silas or the rest of the Cathal, I would be foolish not to make use of his skill set.

He studied me for a moment and then growled, "I don't think your... combat instructor... would enjoy being replaced so easily. From what I saw in the woods, he takes his role very, very seriously."

Do not blush. Do not blush. Do not blush.

My traitorous body ignored me, and my cheeks flamed red hot in embarrassment.

Trying to maintain a semblance of dignity, I raised my chin and said, "I am not asking you to replace Zeke, merely complement his training by extending it with your own." His eyes darkened at my suggestion.

"That's not... I mean to say... that's," I spluttered, trying, and failing to correct his assumption. He quirked an eyebrow and watched me floundering as I tried to find the right words to say. Conceding defeat, I scowled at Silas and turned on my heels to leave.

"Tomorrow then."

I stopped dead.

"What?" I said, peering back at him over my shoulder.

"Tomorrow," he repeated.

Turning to face him, I questioned, "You mean you will train me?"

He nodded once, and I beamed at him.

He stalked forward, stopping right next to my ear. "You might not be so pleased when I have you panting and sweating beneath me. I don't play around Princess. I like to... train... hard."

His eyes smiled with wickedness before he purred, "Then again, you just might." He strode out of the stables without a single glance back my way.

Gulping, I tried to swallow the knot forming in my throat.

By the gods, I was in trouble.

Chapter Five

Zeke came to my chambers that night and helped soothe the ache Silas had created. His strong, muscular body fit against mine perfectly. Yet, every time he thrust into me, it was a different set of beautiful brown eyes I envisioned. A different name was on the tip of my tongue as I came undone.

It took me hours to fall asleep after Zeke left. Troubled by my burgeoning feelings. I tried to remind myself that I didn't trust the Cathal. Silas in particular. But it seemed my body didn't get the message.

I dragged myself out of bed the next morning, bleary-eyed and exhausted from my restless sleep. Louise was in my chamber, drawing back my curtains, and I flinched from the sudden onslaught of sunlight.

"Good morning Harlowe," she said. "This came for you this morning." Louise pointed towards a note on my side table. I examined the letter, not recognizing the handwriting. Opening it, I read:

Meet me at the lake adjacent to the west side of the palace. 8 am. Don't be late. Silas.

I glanced at the mantle, noting the time. 7:45 am. Shit.

Springing out of bed, I rushed to dress and almost knocked Louise over in my haste.

"What's wrong? Where are you going, Harlowe?" Louise inquired, confused by my sudden urgency.

"Training."

She opened her mouth as if to ask more questions, but I was already racing out of my chambers.

Sprinting towards the lake, I silently cursed Silas for besting me... again.

While the lake was adjacent to the west wing, it wasn't exactly close. My quarters were on the other side of the palace, which didn't help matters. I wondered if Silas knew that and was trying to be inconvenient. It seemed like something he would pull. Prick.

As I reached the lake, Silas came into view. He was crouched next to the water, concentrating on something I couldn't see.

He stood at my approach and barked, "Come here," pointing to the spot in front of him. When I reached him, he said, "There are consequences to every decision you make in battle, Princess. Every time you fail to follow an order, it could mean the difference between life and death. If you want to be a battle queen, best to learn that lesson now." He grinned viciously and scooped me up in his arms before tossing me unceremoniously into the lake. I breached the surface, sputtering the lungful of water I had inhaled in my surprise. This early in the morning, the water was freezing.

I glowered at Silas as I made my way towards the bank, and he smirked back at me.

"Still want to train with me?" he asked in a saccharine voice. So this was some little test, was it? Well, I wouldn't cower in front of him. Not now. Not ever.

I nodded once.

"Good." He reached out a hand to help me out of the frigid water. "But let's get one thing straight," he said in a low, dangerous tone. "When it comes to you and me," — he pointed his index finger between us — "I'm the one in charge. Me, Princess. Not you. You will follow every command that I give you without complaint." I opened my mouth to argue but closed it when Silas quirked a brow. Satisfied with my compliance, he instructed me to take my stance.

Several hours later, I was seriously considering my life choices as I lay on the grass straining for breath. We had been sparring for hours, and if I thought Zeke was a tough opponent, I was sorely mistaken. The Cathal were feared for a reason. I didn't connect a single hit the entire session. Meanwhile, Silas had taken me to the ground every time. He hadn't been kidding when he said he trained hard. He didn't pull his punches or take it easy on me. I was going to be stiff and sore tomorrow, but I appreciated that he wasn't coddling me. If I was ever going to excel in hand-to-hand, this would be how I did it.

A dark shadow appeared over me, and Silas stretched out his hand to me, saying, "Again," as he pulled me to my feet. I groaned, which earned me a chuckle from Silas in response.

We continued for another hour and Silas only called an end to training when I was throwing my guts up from the exertion.

We walked in silence towards the dining hall for lunch. Mostly because all my focus was going into keeping myself upright as my legs threatened to buckle with each step.

We joined the rest of the Cathal and the soldiers they were training as we ate our midday meal. Judging by the groans of protest as the soldiers massaged their aching joints and limbs, the rest of the Cathal trained just as hard as Silas.

Over lunch, I was introduced to the Cathal I hadn't met yet. The youngest member, Fionn, was twenty-three. It showed, too, with his mischievous personality and the mirth that twinkled in his hazel eyes. He was shorter than the rest, with dark skin and shoulder-length, curly brown hair. He wore his hair in a braid away from his face and he had a unique circular pattern painted on his forehead that stopped between his eyebrows. Fionn told me that the pattern symbolized prosperity and his mother had painted it to wish him well on his first journey away from the kingdom. Fionn had spent a good part of an hour persuading me to go drinking and dancing at the local village inn on their day off. I knew I liked him already.

The man sitting to Fionn's left, Teller, was just as entertaining. He was loud and commanded attention. And not just because of the long brown hair he also wore in a braid or the trimmed beard that gave him a masculine, sexy look. He was handsome to be sure, but it was his sense of humor that made him truly attractive. I was certain he enjoyed his jokes more than those around him. He had me blushing furiously a few times, which delighted him to no end.

Fionn and Teller could disarm the most skeptical with their sense of humor alone. I forgot my earlier suspicions about their intentions and their reasons for being in Valoren. I was starting to feel more comfortable around the Cathal when I noticed Sienna, the lone female among the group, glaring daggers at me over her water glass. I glanced away, unsure what to make of it. When I glanced back in her direction a few minutes later, I saw that she was still glaring at me. I shifted uncomfortably in my seat and Silas tracked the movement, glancing towards Sienna across the table. Whatever warning she saw in his eyes had her ripping her gaze from mine.

I was saved from my musings when the dining hall door swung open and a woman entered, screeching, "Harlowe!" Whipping my head around, I saw the most wonderful sight in all the realm. Emmerson, my sassy best friend who had been traveling throughout the kingdoms for the last three months at her father's behest, stood in our dining hall, arms outstretched, beckoning me to her.

I wasted no time jumping out of my seat and rushing straight into her waiting arms. Jumping up and down, we gripped each other tightly, squealing with delight. I heard the scrape of metal on metal and turned to see the men sheathing their swords.

I mean, they weren't wrong to identify her as a threat.

As the daughter of the Commanding General of our kingdom's forces, Emmerson was well-versed with a blade. She could easily out-spar most of my father's best infantry soldiers. And unlike me, none of the soldiers complained about her heavy training schedule. It's not that they thought she should train, but more like they were too afraid to voice that opinion for fear it might get back to her.

She was a sight to behold with her wild brown hair hanging loosely in slight waves halfway down her back. Her blue eyes were sizing up the competition behind me, and her delicate, soft lips and perfectly manicured eyebrows could fool most into underestimating her. Good luck to them, I thought with a snort.

Gods, I had missed her.

Linking my arm with hers, I led her to the table and made swift introductions. Teller and Fionn were already shamelessly flirting, blissfully unaware that she would devour them whole given half the chance.

With lunch winding down, we said our goodbyes, and I headed towards the exit, my arm still locked with Emmerson's. The sound of a throat clearing had me halting mid-stride.

"Princess, where do you think you're going?" Silas asked in a challenge, one eyebrow raised.

"To help Emmerson unpack," I responded in confusion.

"Not if you want me to keep training you, you're not. Like I said, I train... hard." He let the last word simmer, and I could almost grasp the sexual tension as it contorted and solidified between us.

Emmerson raised her eyebrows in surprise, glancing at Silas and then at me.

Groaning, I said to Emmerson, "I'll catch you up at dinner," and her wicked smirk told me she was definitely here for it.

Striding out of the dining hall, I could already envision Silas's shit-eating grin that he undoubtedly wore plastered across his handsome face as he followed behind me.

Chapter Six

The next few days followed a similar pattern; I trained with Silas, ate lunch with the Cathal, and spent my evenings with Emmerson. Zeke had departed on some errand for my father, and he hadn't returned yet.

When the end of the week came around, I was more than ready for a day of respite. Heading to the stables early, I saddled my gelding, Raja, and headed out into the woods for some much-needed solitude.

I had become so accustomed to seeing the dragons flying about that when the telltale humming of wings sounded overhead, it barely registered. As I tilted my head to the sky, I saw the vibrant red underbelly of a dragon. Since my encounter with them earlier in the week, I hadn't been near the dragons again. Their behavior had been strange that day and it seemed not even Silas understood it. They were beautiful, regal creatures, to be sure. But they were also lethal, and I had escaped death once already where they were concerned, and I wasn't tempted to push my luck any further.

Deep in the forest, there was a beautiful lake where the water cascading over a waterfall pooled and glistened at its base. It was a diamond in the rough, nestled deep within the forest, and had long been my sanctuary. Few people knew of its location, which made it the perfect retreat.

I could hear the sounds of rushing water not far up ahead. I inhaled deeply, and the smell of pine and moss, earth, and soil, engulfed me. It smelled like home.

Breaking through the tree line, I caught my first glimpse of the waterfall. It was serene yet imposing. Dismounting, I shrugged out of my tunic and untied my leather pants. Kicking off my boots and clothed only in my undergarments, I dove headfirst into the body of water before me.

The water was rejuvenating. It washed away all the aches and pains I had accumulated throughout training this last week and breathed new life into my body in its wake.

I spent hours swimming and lounging in the water before finally retreating to the bank for the midday meal. I had stopped by the kitchens on my way out this morning and snatched some supplies before the cook had the chance to catch me in the act. Raja was already devouring the apples I had swiped for him.

Stretching out on the bank, I closed my eyes and relished in the sun's warmth. I must have fallen asleep because I awoke with a start sometime later, to the unnerving feeling of being watched. Getting to my feet, I grabbed up my tunic and threw it over my head. Retrieving my dagger, I surveyed the trees surrounding me.

Nothing.

I took a few steps into the tree line to make sure nothing was lurking just out of sight. I was startled when a branch snapped to my left and a small huff sounded seconds later. Whipping my head around, I locked eyes with a magnificent black bear. Its fur was shiny and thick and looked as though it would be soft to the touch. The size of the creature was incredible, easily standing a head taller than I did. Its brown eyes bore into my green ones, and I didn't dare blink while I stared the creature down, waiting for it to decide if I was a threat. Opening its mouth, the creature's tongue lolled out, and it ambled towards me. As the bear approached me, it nudged my hand, and I raised my palm for it to sniff. Mouthing my hand, the bear gave my palm a wet lick before disappearing into the forest without a backward glance.

While the encounter with the bear was certainly bizarre, I couldn't say it was the strangest thing I'd encountered in the animal kingdom this week.

I strode back towards the lake and washed my hands. Deciding I had time for one more swim, I shrugged out of my tunic once more and dove in.

Relaxing on my back, I let the current move me about when I heard a beautiful song sound below the water. Despite being muffled by the water, I could make out the notes perfectly. It was calling to me, beckoning me. Diving under the water, I searched for the source of the melody. Finding nothing, I returned to the surface, inhaling deeply.

The sweet tones of the song were like a gentle caress on my skin. I felt compelled to find the source. Diving below the surface once again, I searched desperately. A shadow flickered out of the corner of my eye, and I spun towards it. Mere feet before me was the most beautiful male. His light hair drifted lazily to the tune, his bare torso displayed well-defined muscles, and a glittering blue tail made up the entirety of his lower body. He crooked a finger at me, signaling for me to come to him.

I began swimming towards him, but with every stroke I made in his direction; he moved deeper into the water's depths. The deeper I swam, the sweeter the music became. It filled my head and made me feel as though I was floating on a cloud.

Somehow, somewhere deep in my subconscious, I could tell something was wrong. But the more I tried to think about it, the hazier my mind became. There was something I needed; something I needed to do. The thought was almost tangible, like a piece of string that I could reach out and grab if I could just stretch far enough. But every time I felt myself clasping that thought, the music played louder in my mind and my thoughts evaporated.

Darkness crept into my vision, peeking up at the edges and slowly engulfing me. It was getting so dark now, and I couldn't remember what I was supposed to be doing. Just as I was about to give into the darkness, to the song still playing around me, powerful hands gripped me below my arms and tugged me to the surface.

There was a sudden ache in my lungs that rapidly turned into white-hot pain as I struggled to take a breath. I coughed up the water I didn't realize I had inhaled, as someone tugged me toward the shore. Back on dry land, I continued heaving until there was nothing left to bring up. Collapsing on the ground, I heard the murmur of voices from all around me. Someone was rubbing soothing circles on my back as I caught my breath. A short distance away, I could hear Raja whinnying in distress.

Someone was trying to talk to me, as they tapped my cheeks lightly to rouse me.

"Princess. Princess," the voice called. "Come on Little Menace, open your eyes." Groaning, I rolled onto my back and cracked one eye open and then the other. Leaning over me, the sun framing his brown hair like a halo, water droplets making their way down the bridge of his nose, was Silas.

"You," I groaned again and tried to sit up. I regretted the idea when a wave of nausea washed over me, and I lay back down.

A light chuckle filled my ears, and I closed my eyes once more.

"Come now, Little Menace, is that any way to greet your savior? I did just spare you from a watery grave at the bottom of the lake, after all." I tried to scoff, but it came out as more of a gurgle.

"What happened?" I asked, trying to sit up once again, and this time, succeeding.

"You were caught in a Siren's call," he said, all teasing disappearing from his voice.

I had learned about the water-dwelling creatures and how they could lure a person to their death as they followed the sweet lure of the Siren's song. Someone caught in the Siren's call forgot about everything else, even the need to breathe, as they followed the enticing melodies into the deepest depths, never returning.

I just hadn't heard about them being anywhere near Valoren.

I knew they frequented the Seas of Bás, accurately named for the death they harbored, but I had not heard of them occupying waters anywhere else within Aetherian.

Turning my stunned gaze to Silas, I said, "But they don't come this far inland."

"It appears they do," Silas murmured. "Things are...," he paused, "things are strange at present. The creatures of the realm aren't behaving how they should be. Even the forest feels... off."

I shuddered, despite not catching his entire meaning. There was more he wasn't telling me.

I returned my gaze to Silas and said, "Thank you." I had been so close to death, and he had been the only thing standing between us.

I looked him over again, still dripping wet from his unexpected swim to the bottom of the lake. A droplet of water slid off his chin and I tracked it as it made its way down his throat and over his tattoos. Heat banked in my core, and I tore my gaze away before I could get caught staring, only to find Silas staring at my chest. Peering down, I realized I was still dressed in my undergarments, all but transparent now that they were wet. My nipples had pebbled from the cold and were now poking through the material across my breasts. I wrapped my arms around them and looked about for my tunic. With a predatory grin, Silas met my eyes, tunic in hand, and offered it to me. I snatched it back and quickly pulled it over my head.

I made to stand, only for my legs to wobble and collapse beneath me. Before I could hit the ground, Silas caught me, lifted me into his arms, and pulled me against his chest.

"I can walk," I protested and then cringed. Even I could hear the lie in my voice. Silas growled low in his throat and said, "I'm not feeling particularly patient today, Little Menace." He continued in a saccharine tone, "So try to be a good girl and don't make things more difficult than they need to be."

I wanted to hit him, but I was also exhausted. So, I let him carry me to my horse. Only he walked straight passed Raja, and for the first time, I noticed he wasn't alone. Cillian, Cian, Fionn, and Teller were with him. Passing me to Cillian, he mounted his horse. Cillian, the strong and silent one of the group, said nothing as he clutched me to his very solid and very muscular chest. It was at this moment I realized I had also failed to retrieve my pants. Gesturing for Cillian to pass me up, I was pulled onto Silas's horse and positioned in front of him, his rigid body flush against my back.

Reaching around me to grab the reins, he flicked his head back in the lake's direction and said, "Fionn, grab her things and lead her horse back." Fionn acknowledged the order with a nod and headed in the direction we had just left. Telling the others he would meet them back at the palace, Silas nudged his horse forward, and we were off, trotting through the forest.

I was shifting in the saddle trying to get comfortable when Silas's warm breath flushed against my neck as he leaned in to whisper, "If you keep moving like that, I'll be forced to divert so I can spank that ass you keep rubbing against me." He pushed his hips against my backside to press his rock-hard erection into my ass. I gasped, and he chuckled wickedly.

"What were you doing out here, anyway?" I asked, trying to distract myself from the feel of him against me.

He paused before responding, "Taking stock of our surroundings."

"Taking stock of your surroundings," I repeated, skeptical. I felt him shrug against my back.

"Were you following me?" He barked out a laugh in response, and my cheeks heated.

"Believe it or not, Princess, I have other things to occupy myself with, other than you," he purred the last part.

Of course, he did. He was the Commanding General of the Cathal. Why had I even said that?

Clearing my throat in embarrassment, I redirected the conversation. "Find anything interesting while you were out?"

"A few things," he answered cryptically. It was clear this conversation was over.

We rode in comfortable silence for a time, the sounds of the forest our only companions. As we approached the clearing that led to the palace, I recalled my current state of dress, or undress rather.

"Umm, I'm kind of, you know, naked from the waist down," I said, wincing. "I noticed," Silas said huskily. I reached over and slapped him on the arm, and he chuckled.

"This is serious. I can't very well walk into the palace dressed like this." He was silent for a beat before responding, "I think I saw some blankets in the stables before we left. We'll grab one and I'll sneak you in through the servant's entrance." Well, damn. That was very considerate of him.

"Umm... thanks." It sounded like a question, and he just laughed again. I could get lost in that sound. Just like I got lost in that Siren's call, I thought bitterly. Given the day's events, I should probably heed the warning. Instead, I let my head rest against his shoulder as weariness set in.

Reaching the stables, Silas dismounted and found a blanket, as promised. I moved to follow, but he growled at me and pulled me down into his arms, wrapping the blanket around me as he did so.

"This really isn't necessary," I began, but one glare from Silas and my protests died on my tongue.

Feeling the flex of his biceps as he carried me into the palace was playing havoc on my lady parts. "Which way?" he asked, startling me out of my reverie. I directed the way to my chambers, trying very hard not to think about the way his body felt wrapped around mine... and failing miserably.

When we made it to my chambers, he nudged the door open with one foot and carried me passed the antechamber into my bedroom. He didn't put me down until he placed me on my bed.

He turned towards my drawers, rifling through them. "What are you doing?" I asked with a voice that was a touch too high as he retrieved fresh nightclothes.

Turning back to me, he said, "Unless you want to freeze to death sleeping in wet clothes, I suggest you change out of them."

"Oh," was all I could manage in response.

Silas gestured for me to lift my arms and my cheeks flushed in embarrassment, but I complied, nonetheless. He placed a dry nightgown over my head and told me to remove my undergarments. After I had removed them, he gathered up my wet clothes and carried them to my bathing chamber before returning. Pulling back the covers of my bed, he nodded for me to get in.

Once I was dry and warm under the covers, he made to leave, but I gripped his wrist to stop him.

"Harlowe," he growled in warning. It was the first time I had heard him use my name, and on his tongue, it sounded sexy and erotic. I wanted to hear it again.

I pulled him down onto the bed and settled on my knees before him. I studied his face, but he gave nothing away. Tentatively, I leaned in, placing my lips gently on his. The kiss was soft and gentle one minute, then hungry and demanding the next. Silas pulled me onto his lap and threaded his fingers through my hair, securing me to him. His tongue darted across the seam of my lips, and I parted for him. His tongue battled with my own, dominating and devouring.

And all too soon, it was over.

He rested his head against mine, our breaths coming out in ragged pants.

"Please," I begged.

"Not tonight Little Menace. You nearly died today. You need to rest." It looked as though it pained him to deny me. That look was all the confidence I needed.

Locking eyes with him, I said, "Exactly, I just want to feel... alive." When he didn't immediately respond, I swallowed nervously. Maybe I'd misread the situation.

But then he was crashing his lips against mine, and all thought escaped me. He pushed me onto my back, running his hands up the length of my body. Traveling back down, he tugged the hem of my nightgown up. He hadn't given me underwear when he changed my clothes, leaving me bare to his touch. Peering down, he cursed harshly under his breath at the sight before him.

Silas traced his fingers up the inside of my thighs, and my legs quivered in anticipation. Trailing one finger up my slit, he breathed, "Is this what you want?" I nodded mutely.

"Say it, Harlowe," he rumbled.

"Yes," I whispered.

"You want me to fuck you with my fingers? Make you come while you're riding my hand?" I moaned at the mere thought of it. Somewhere in the back of my mind, a part of me screamed that I didn't trust Silas and that putting myself at his mercy was a terrible idea. But when he growled low in his chest, all thoughts of resistance left me.

"Tell me, Harlowe," he demanded.

"I need your fingers inside me. I need you to make me come." Not wasting a second, he plunged a finger inside me, and then another. I rode his fingers with abandon, not caring how desperate I appeared. I had been unable to stop thinking of his hands on my body, his lips on my skin, and the feel of his muscles under my palms. And now that I had the opportunity to feel him, I wasn't going to waste it.

He plunged a third finger inside me and stroked small circles around my clit with his thumb. I could feel the orgasm building, that sweet promise of release just beyond my reach. He watched me with a rapacious intensity. Savoring every buck of my hips, every moan that escaped me as I chased my release. I was on the edge, about to tumble over into that promised bliss, when Silas growled into my ear, "Come for me Harlowe, show me what a good girl you can be."

And then I fell.

The orgasm flooded me, reverberating through me, lifting me high. Silas continued to pump into me, drawing out my release. Breathing hard, I slumped against my pillows, lost in the feeling. When I came back down, I opened my eyes to see Silas peering down at me, a satisfied smirk on his face.

I reached forward towards the ties on his pants but halted when he barked out sharply, "No." Confused, I peered up at him. Anger flashed across his face, but it was gone as quickly as it had come. "No," he repeated, calmer this time. Clearing his throat, he said, "Rest Harlowe." I just stared at him, unsure of how to take his sudden outburst.

Sighing, Silas ran a hand through his hair. "I'll see you for training tomorrow," he said as he stood to leave. He didn't glance back once as he strode out the door and left me stewing in my tangled emotions.

Chapter Seven

I did not meet Silas for training the next day.

I analyzed every moment in my bedchamber from the night prior, trying to figure out if I had misread his signals. It didn't matter, though. It had been a mistake. A huge mistake. The guy was hot, sure, but I didn't trust him and that was a complication I just didn't need.

No, riding that dick would be a horrendous mistake. Absolutely horrendous. I just needed to convince my traitorous body of that.

So, instead of showing up to training, I had hidden in the palace, clinging to my mother's side like the coward I am. It worked for a time, but she got so sick of my 'help' she ejected me from her study. So, I retreated to Emmerson's room and stayed hidden for the rest of the day. I avoided having my meals in the dining hall by raiding the kitchen early in the morning, and I waited long enough that most of the palace had retired to bed before skulking back to my chambers like a creeper.

Not my proudest moment.

I have no idea why I did any of it. It's not like Silas would be out looking for me. I was work for him. If I didn't show, he had plenty of other things to get on with. I just couldn't convince my ego of that.

So, I repeated the same routine the next day. And the next.

I figured Silas had got the message by the fourth day. So, finding him lounging in the sitting chair next to my bed when I woke that morning caught me off guard.

"There she is," he drawled as soon as I'd opened my eyes. There was no hint of amusement, anger, or any other emotion.

A mere observation.

It was unnerving. I sat up in bed and watched him warily, but he remained quiet.

"Can I help you?" I snapped when I couldn't take the silence any longer.

"So glad you asked," he said cheerfully. Too cheerfully. "You can get your sullen ass out of bed, get dressed, and meet me for training."

Trying for civility, I said, "Look, I appreciate the time you have spent training with me so far, but I think it's best if I go back to my lessons with Zeke. He should be back any day now." Silas's gaze hardened, and he pinned me in place with his stare.

"Is that so?" he snarled.

"Yes," I said, turning away from him.

Silas's muscular arms wrapped around me, pinning my arms at my sides. That same jolt of lightning I felt the first time he touched me seared my flesh, and my pulse quickened. He ran his nose along the curve of my neck and inhaled deeply.

"So, what's this all about, Princess? You embarrassed my fingers fucked you so hard you had the best orgasm of your life? Or are you pissed it wasn't my dick?"

I snorted. "It was one orgasm. Don't let it go to your head. Besides, it's nothing I can't do myself."

"Good. Then we don't have a problem. Get dressed."

Silas released me and gently shoved me towards my dresser before heading to the door. Pausing, he said, "If you're not out in ten minutes, I'm coming in and dragging you out in whatever you're wearing." Then he slammed the door and left.

Who the fuck did he think he was?

I was the gods-damn heir to this kingdom, and he was our guest! He had no authority to command me. No right.

Yet, I knew he would make good on his promise.

Grumbling, I got up and got dressed.

Silas handed me my ass for the rest of the day. He was either eager to prove a point or making up for lost time.

"I'm done for today," I said, hitting the ground once again.

My ribs hurt, my shoulders hurt, my hips and thighs hurt. Hell, it would be quicker to list the parts of me that didn't ache.

Zero. Zero parts of me didn't ache. My body felt like one giant bruise.

"I say when we're done Harlowe, not you. Now get up and take your stance." I got the feeling he was no longer talking about our training session.

"You've made your fucking point," I spat.

He cocked a brow. "Have I?" Crossing his arms over his chest, he drawled, "Please, tell me what point that is, Princess."

I gritted my teeth. "What's your fucking problem, Silas?"

"My problem," he snarled, "is that you still haven't taken your fucking stance. You asked me to train you, Harlowe. I warned you I train hard. I left you alone for three days while you sulked because I hurt your precious feelings, and now I expect you to obey me and learn. Take. Your. Fucking. Stance."

Oh, fuck this, and fuck him.

Taking my stance, I faced him with renewed determination, and when he curled his fingers forward to signal I should attack, I unleashed on him. I got in some good hits, too, but Silas outclassed me in every way that mattered. He took me to the ground and pinned me there.

"Good," he panted from above me. I tried to ignore the hard panes of his body flush against my own. "Next time, do as I instruct without the whining." He stood and extended his hand to me. I swatted it away, and he shrugged nonchalantly.

"Now we're done."

I marched away from him without a single glance in his direction.

As I approached the front steps leading into the palace, I noticed the sole female Cathal, Sienna, lounging on the balustrade and sharpening a blade. I stomped passed her, not in the mood for her or whatever bullshit issue she had with me.

"Did you know Princess," she crooned, "that Silas asked me to come on this mission with him... personally." The innuendo was clear in her tone. I stopped short but did not face her.

"You see, he and I have a long history together. And while you may be a princess in this kingdom, that means nothing in ours." My shoulders tensed at the reminder he wasn't one of my subjects and would eventually leave Valoren, and me, behind.

Noticing the shift in my mood, she continued, "Yes, ours. Because no matter what sweet words he might whisper in your ear at night, or how many times you spread your legs for him, he will be coming home with me. Home to Pyrithia."

I winced.

"You have the wrong idea about us." My voice didn't waiver as I expected it would.

She chuckled. "Oh, I know exactly how things are. Do you think you're the first woman he has bedded to pass the time? You're not. You're not special in that regard, even if he tells you otherwise."

I forced myself to move, stalking into the palace and ignoring Emmerson as she called after me.

Irrational hatred towards Sienna simmered in my veins, and it took me a moment to realize I was jealous. I was jealous because I had developed feelings for Silas, the Commanding General of the fucking Cathal of Pyrithia.

I was such a fool.

How had I fallen for someone I didn't even trust? Someone I suspected was in my kingdom for reasons other than what he purported?

Entering my chambers, I locked the door behind me, grabbed a pillow from my chaise, and buried my face in it, screaming. I screamed until my voice was hoarse from the effort. I screamed until I could no longer make a single sound. And when I couldn't scream anymore, I straightened my shoulders and vowed to never be so foolish again.

Chapter Eight

I spent the rest of the week trying to limit my interactions with Silas as much as possible, while still training with him daily. He didn't press me on why I was so withdrawn, and I didn't volunteer any information that would enlighten him.

I didn't trust myself around Silas. He captivated me like no other man had ever done, and I found myself wanting... more. It was a constant struggle to remind myself that he could very well be my enemy. I was certain he was keeping things from me, but that didn't stop my blood from rushing straight to my lady parts any time he was near. I wanted him. And I couldn't afford to give him that kind of power over me.

Not only did I want him, but Silas brought out the worst parts of me; jealousy, immaturity, arrogance. Yet, he also challenged me. He didn't coddle me, didn't treat me like the heir who needed to be protected. No, he was teaching me how to protect myself, so I didn't have to rely on others to do it for me.

Ignoring him was becoming difficult, however, because the soldiers the Cathal were instructing had started to work with the dragons as part of their training, and I desperately wanted to know what it was like. The dragons still terrified me, especially because they seemed to be particularly interested in me whenever I was around. If I was ever in their vicinity, they would stop what they were doing and watch me, as if some unseen force compelled them to do so. Their serpentine eyes followed me, tracking my every movement. The way they looked at me was unsettling, yet not threatening. They weren't protective of me exactly, but it was like they were curious, and they were beckoning me closer so they could explore that curiosity.

And I wanted to know why.

Starting the conversation, I asked, "So, how does it all work? How do you get a dragon to accept you?"

Silas studied me for a moment before saying, "You can't get them to do anything. Being accepted by a dragon, and bonding with them, it's intuitive. Either the connection is there, or it isn't. Despite what people believe, dragons don't just go around killing those who try but ultimately cannot bond with them. Most of the time, it's the person trying to force the connection, the bond, that oversteps some boundary and pays dearly."

I just stared at Silas before shaking my head in confusion. I had always been taught how temperamental dragons were, how unstable. This was what our kingdom had been taught ever since my grandfather had abandoned the practice centuries ago.

"So the soldiers you're training, what are you teaching them?"

"Working with dragons requires skill. We are teaching them how to interact with them. To recognize signals that warn against approaching them or those that encourage you closer. While a dragon will only bond with one person at a time, you can get a sense of whether a person can bond with a dragon by observing if the dragons respond to them or not. By having your soldiers interact with our dragons, we can eliminate, or advance individuals based on how receptive our dragons are to that person. Then we can teach those left the best ways to seek those bonds and enhance their chances of succeeding."

I contemplated his words. They differed greatly from the idea that I had created in my mind. Thinking of dragons as ruthless and merciless, I had assumed they would value cunning and brutality, with the dragons only choosing those who exemplified those traits.

"Once a bond is established, how does it work? How do you communicate what you need from them?"

Silas shrugged, "The same way we are communicating now."

My mouth fell open in a very undignified way, and I just gaped at him. Then I asked, "Dragons can talk?"

Something halfway between a snort and a chortle escaped Silas. Regaining his composure, he said, "They can't talk, but they can communicate telepathically with the person they are bonded to. But only that one person. They can't talk to other humans. It's the bond that facilitates communication."

My mind was reeling. How much were we in the dark about these creatures? Had we not known this was possible in the past, or did we lose the knowledge when we stopped bonding with them?

"Wait, does your dragon have a name?"

Silas scoffed, "Of course he does."

"And?" I prodded.

"It's Caolán."

"That's beautiful," I murmured. "And he is the large grayish-green one with red-tipped horns and tail?"

Silas laughed. "He would be offended if he heard you describe him as grayish green. He would say he has chrome coloring with green undertones. Dragons can be very sensitive, you see." He winked at that. "But yes, that's him."

"He seems like he is in charge. As far as the dragons are concerned, I mean."

Shrugging, Silas said, "He is."

"Does your bond impact your ability to manifest fórsa?"

"No, we are just the same as everyone else in that regard. We can all feel it within us, but not all the Cathal can manifest it."

"Can you?" I blurted.

He hesitated before answering. "I can."

"I can't. I can't even feel a connection to it. My parents are worried I'm going to die before I can take up my birthright and become queen."

For the love of all things holy, where in the realm had that come from? I had just word-vomited out a deadly secret to someone from a rival kingdom. If other kingdoms knew that the line of succession in Valoren wasn't secure, they would have little to stop them from trying to conquer us.

Yep, Silas definitely wasn't good for me.

He studied me for a minute before indicating I should resume my stance.

At the end of our session, Silas informed me I would take part in weekly sparring matches with the rest of the Cathal going forward. He said he needed to determine how I was progressing by testing my abilities against others. I was keen to see other fighting styles and to see how I would hold up against the rest of the group.

Excited anticipation filled me as I went to bed that night. I wasn't foolish enough to think I could take any of the Cathal, but I was hopeful my technique had improved under Silas's guidance.

There was also a part of me that wanted to prove myself. Worthy, if not victorious.

So the next morning, I had a spring in my step as I made my way to our usual sparring spot. All ten of the Cathal were there, standing around in a circle formation. Emmerson was there too. I mentioned the match to her during dinner and she promised to come and watch. I noted a few soldiers lingering around the fringes, curiosity getting the better of them.

As I approached, Silas broke away from the group and met me halfway.

"I want you to treat this match as if you were facing a genuine threat," he started. "You Cathal are a genuine threat, practice or not," I interrupted. He chuckled, and the sound tugged at my heart. It was beautiful.

Do not get carried away, I chastised myself.

"That's true. But I want you to give it your all. Don't pull your punches. Don't worry about hurting anyone. I need to assess how you're progressing and what you can do." I nodded. A slight nervous energy settled over me.

Silas pushed me into the center of the circle and instructed me to warm up. There was muffled chatter around me, but I blocked it out while I stretched. I could see Sienna whispering something to Cian. She had a small smile on her lips, but his stony expression remained unchanged.

When I finished stretching, I indicated to Silas that I was ready.

"Sienna, you're up." Sienna smiled sweetly at me, the threat in it only evident to me. We squared off against one another and Silas gave the signal to start.

Sienna came straight at me, her punches connecting while I defended. When there was a break in her attack, I took a step back and shook off the assault.

We started circling each other, and when she came at me again, I was ready. I ducked low just as her fist was about to connect with my head and darted behind her. Before she could recover, I kicked out with one leg and sent her tumbling forward.

Enraged, she spun rapidly and came at me again. This time she connected with my rib cage and the force of her hit left me breathless. I jogged back out of her reach as she came at my other side.

Breathing through clenched teeth, I straightened, ignoring the searing pain racing up my side. I really hoped that my ribs were not broken.

I raised my hands again, and she didn't hesitate. She lunged, grabbing my shoulders, and taking me to the ground. I wrapped my legs around her and rolled onto my shoulder as I fell, coming out of her grasp and straddling her waist. It was a move Zeke had taught me, knowing that I would often face opponents larger than me and would need to prevent myself from being trapped under their heavier frame.

I hit out at Sienna, connecting with her face again and again before she brought her knees up to my chest, and pushing forward, freed herself.

Both staggering to our feet, we once again circled each other. Blood was flowing from Sienna's nose, and I hoped I'd broken it. The bitch had it coming. She had been nothing short of hostile towards me from the moment she met me, and I was all too eager to pay her back for that.

Emmerson whooped in support. Sienna snarled, animalistic, barely recognizable as human.

She pounced, and at that moment, I remembered just who she was; Cathal. The most deadly warriors who were second to none. I had been kidding myself to think that I could hold my own against one after a few weeks of training. She shot a fist out towards my ribs and connected with the tender flesh already smarting from her earlier assault. She continuously pummeled me, targeting the same spot. I tried to pull back, but she gripped my hair so I couldn't retreat. I couldn't do anything except try to shift my body sideways to protect my already injured side.

I heard yelling but couldn't discern the words amidst the pain.

I heard it a moment before I felt it. A crack. And then pain, like I had never felt before, ripped through me. I collapsed to the ground, struggling to take a breath. All I could manage were shallow pants. Still, Sienna refused to release me, following me to the ground and landing on top of me.

One moment, the crushing weight of Sienna's body on top of my bruised and battered one was all I could focus on, before it was... gone... ripped away, allowing me to get a minuscule amount of much-needed oxygen into my struggling lungs.

Strong arms encircled me, and I cried out in pain as I was lifted from the ground. We were running, and the pain that radiated through my body with each jolting step had darkness swimming at the edge of my consciousness.

Silas's panicked voice yelled, "Get a healer," and it was then I knew I was in trouble.

Still, he ran, and when I recognized the soft yellow hues of my chambers, I felt myself calm. Silas placed me on my bed with care and yelled out for the healer again.

"Don't close your eyes, Little Menace. Just look at me, okay?" Was I closing my eyes? All I could focus on was the searing pain and the crippling need to make it stop. The surrounding darkness offered me sweet, sweet relief.

I heard a muffled commotion somewhere in my chambers as if I was hearing it from underwater. Warm hands touched me, but I couldn't stop the darkness as it swallowed me whole.

Chapter Nine

Light fluttered across my eyelids as I heard the curtains being pulled open. Blinking, I opened my eyes to see bright, golden sunshine filling my room. I tried to sit up and an intense stab of pain sparked up my side.

Gentle hands pushed on my shoulders as Zeke came into view. "Easy," he said, as he lowered me back down onto the bed.

"What happened?" I rasped. My throat was dry; my voice hoarse. Zeke, noticing the issue, held up a glass of water to my lips, gesturing for me to drink. I greedily obliged.

Licking my lips, I tried again. "What happened?"

"You cracked several ribs, and one punctured your lung. The healers think your lung collapsed, and that was why you were struggling so hard to breathe." Instinctively, I ran my hand down my side, feeling the thick bandages wrapped around my rib cage.

"How?" I prodded.

"You don't remember?" I shook my head.

"You were fighting in some makeshift ring with that Cathal woman. Things got out of control, and she went ballistic. They tried to get her to stop, but she had to be pried off you before the General could get to you. The King and Queen were furious. The King, in particular, was not impressed that his orders were disobeyed."

I winced. I knew I would hear more about this from the source directly.

Sienna.

I remembered then. I had been sparring with Sienna and she had targeted my injured ribs, repeatedly, ending our match.

"What did my father say about it?"

"He tried to forbid you from any training but, your mother insisted that you continue your training with me." He flashed me a crooked grin.

"But," — he took a deep breath before continuing — "you have to split your time with your tutors."

I groaned and instantly regretted it when the throbbing in my side intensified. I had been avoiding my tutors at all costs over these last few weeks. Their lessons had become downright oppressive. I'm not sure what their brief was, but it felt like they were trying to mold me into something obedient and meek.

Good luck to them.

"I don't know why he is so insistent I study court protocols to this extent. I have been studying and implementing them all my life."

Zeke just shrugged.

Changing the subject, I asked, "So what's the damage? How long will I be out for?"

"Not long. The healers got to you quickly and were able to work their magic. You'll be sore for a few more days, maybe a week. You have a wicked bruise up your side, but the strapping will help."

Breathing a sigh of relief, and then immediately wincing, I replied, "Okay, not too bad. I can work with that."

Zeke chuckled. He knew how much I hated being prone. After all, he was the one who had caused most of my injuries during our training sessions.

"Now that you're awake, I have some things to do this morning, but I will come by later if I get a chance," Zeke said, standing from his position next to my bed.

"And Harlowe?"

"Yes?"

"Don't be a pain in the ass to the staff. They want you out of their hair just as much as you want to be out of it." He winked before darting out the door.

"Smart ass," I muttered under my breath.

"Who's a smart ass?"

I glanced towards the door and saw Emmerson strolling in.

"Thank the gods. Help me get up, will you?"

"Harlowe," Emmerson whined. "Why do you always rope me into the things that you're not supposed to be doing? My father has already threatened to skin my hide for letting you spar!" she huffed.

I snorted. "Like you could have stopped me!"

Emmerson threw her hands up in the air. "Thank you! That's what I told him."

"But to answer your question, it's because you're my best friend. And best friends help each other do stupid shit they know they really shouldn't. And as my best friend, you are to be that constant source of endorsement for my bad ideas. It's practically a requirement."

She nodded her head as if it was obvious.

"Now get over here and help me." Emmerson did as I bid her and helped me get out of bed. After some pained expletives on my behalf, I dressed and pulled on my boots.

"Where are we going?" Emmerson had obviously chosen to abandon any pretense she was going to enforce my bed rest.

"I just need to move around. It will help with the healing."

Entering the hall outside my chambers, Emmerson didn't waste any time berating Sienna. "I can't believe that psycho bitch went rabid on you! Everyone was calling out to her, telling her to stop and she just wouldn't! Three of those Cathal had to pull her off you before Silas could get you out of there. And I know she did it on purpose. She was intent on causing damage, which is why she targeted your injured side and wouldn't yield." I had already surmised as much.

"She's lucky your father didn't have her put down like the rabid animal she is! If she was still skulking around, I would have stuck a dagger in her." She thrust out her hand to emphasize her point. And I knew she meant it too. Gods above, I loved my bloodthirsty little hellcat of a best friend.

"What happened to her?" I asked.

"She left. Sent back to Pyrithia," she shrugged.

I wondered if Silas was upset by that. And then I chastised myself for caring.

We wandered the halls for a bit before I grew tired and had to retreat to my chambers for rest. Emmerson stayed until lunch, explaining in explicit detail her plans to seduce Cillian, Silas's second-in-command. Cillian had shown himself to be the strong and silent type. He was the only Cathal, apart from Silas, who had not shown interest in Emmerson's flirtations, and she was determined to change that.

That girl loved a challenge.

Zeke had returned in the early afternoon, as he said he would. He promised to let me train once I felt up to it, but left before I could pin him down on the specifics.

My parents soon followed, both climbing over themselves to get to me. I had to admit; it was nice to see how much they cared, even if my father threatened to end me himself should I do anything so reckless again.

I had spent the rest of the afternoon reading in my chambers. A particularly scandalous book had me enraptured, and it was late into the evening before I put it aside to ready myself for bed.

There was a knock at my door, and I called out for the person to enter. A few moments later, Silas emerged at the open door to my bedchamber. He folded his arms across his chest and leaned against the door frame.

"It's good to see you awake," he said.

I nodded, unsure of what to say.

He pushed off the door frame and made his way towards me.

Gods damn, the man was lust incarnate. His every move accentuated his muscled physique, and his cocky smirk was downright sinful. His tattoos only made him sexier, edgier. Every time I saw them, I wanted to run my tongue over them and beg him to do bad, bad things to me. I had to drive my nails into my palms to stop myself from licking my lips at the sight.

Clearing my throat as though that would banish the depraved direction my thoughts had careened down, I asked, "So, Sienna was sent home?" I watched him closely to gauge his reaction, but his face remained neutral, impassive.

He stood over me now, arms folded, imposing.

"Can you please sit down? You're all broody and intimidating when you're looming over me like that." He smirked but obliged.

"Yes, Sienna is gone. I sent her home to Pyrithia with Fiadh after the incident."

"That's her dragon?"

He nodded in confirmation.

I continued to scrutinize his reactions, to see how he felt about Sienna's departure, but still, he revealed nothing of their relationship or how he felt now that she was gone.

Leaning forward, Silas reached a hand out and tugged up the hem of my tunic.

"What are you doing?" I demanded a panicked tone in my voice.

Smirking, he replied, "No need to panic, Princess. I'm just assessing the damage."

"You could have asked first," I grumbled.

"May I?" he asked in an exaggerated tone. Relenting, I nodded.

He unwound the binding until my side was uncovered for his inspection.

I placed an arm over my breasts so I wouldn't expose myself to him. He clenched his teeth when he took in what I had to assume was some nasty bruising.

He rebound my ribs before saying, "You should be right in a few days."

That's it. No apology on Sienna's behalf or well wishes for a speedy recovery. Just give it a few days, I thought incredulously.

I snorted, and he smirked, likely guessing my thoughts.

He leaned in close again, his lips now inches from my own.

"Does my observation not satisfy you, Princess?" His breath fanned across my lips, mingling with my own.

"I mean, it wouldn't kill you to inquire after my well-being, see how I am fairing and all that," I said breathlessly. Gods above. It was like all my brain cells fled and left me floundering whenever he was around, dissolving the strong, capable woman I knew I was.

He lowered his voice to just above a whisper and said, "Why ask when there are better ways, more... enjoyable ways to make that assessment?"

My breath hitched, and that was all the invitation he needed. He slammed his lips against mine, my mouth parting and permitting him entrance. I ran my hands up his muscled forearms and his hand snaked into my hair. Our tongues danced together, seeking and caressing. The kiss became a struggle, each of us vying for dominance; hungry and powerful.

When we could no longer deny our need for oxygen, we pulled apart and Silas whispered, "I think you're doing just fine, Princess."

Panting, I said, "I'm not so sure. Maybe you should check again." He chuckled before returning his lips to mine. This time when we broke apart, Silas rose from the bed.

"When you're ready to train again, send word and I'll come find you," he said before heading to the door.

"My father has prohibited me from training with the Cathal. I mean, he was serious this time," I said.

"I know," Silas responded.

Throwing me a grin over his shoulder, he walked out the door.

Chapter Ten

I had recovered enough after three days that I resumed my training with Zeke and had sent word to Silas as he had instructed. A week had passed since Silas's late-night visit to my bedchambers, and yet he hadn't returned or come to get me for training as he had promised he would.

Zeke had attempted to initiate our usual romp between the sheets that first night after training, but I rebuffed him. It hadn't felt right to continue sharing my body with him when I had spent our last encounter imaging it was Silas. He hadn't so much as pressed me for a reason, which left me feeling surprisingly irritated. It wasn't that I wanted him, or that I wanted him to want me, but it would have been nice to know he was at least a little disappointed.

But that was just my ego talking.

Trying to shake myself out of my musings, I exited the main hall of the east wing and approached the balcony that wrapped around the exterior of the palace, seeking some fresh air to clear my mind. My senses were instantly on alert, feeling a shift in the air.

It was quiet. Too quiet.

A warning sounded in my head. A warning that danger lurked close by.

I narrowed my eyes and surveyed my surroundings carefully but found nothing amiss. Cautiously, I reached down and unsheathed my dagger from my thigh holster. Dagger in hand, I made my way forward, scanning every shadow for a sign that the source of my unease hid within the darkness.

When no attacker jumped out at me, and no trap was triggered, I sighed in relief and re-sheathed my weapon. I was on edge, and I was blaming Silas for the current state of my nerves. Brushing it off, I continued on my way.

Just as I was about to round the corner, I spotted a mane of dark hair in my peripheral vision. I swung towards the threat but was too slow. Strong hands grabbed mine as I tried to reach for my dagger once again. My arms were yanked behind my back, and I was propelled towards the handrail of the balcony. My upper body was launched over it, separating me from the safety of the palace and the abyss that now stretched out below me.

I tried to rear back, hoping to connect my head with the nose of my attacker, but they only tightened their hold; dodging my attack with ease. My boots tipped up off the stone floor beneath me as I was pushed further over the railing. Standing on the tips of my boots, I struggled to maintain my footing, desperately trying to regain the ground I had surrendered.

A hard, muscled body pressed against my back, and a deep, masculine voice sounded next to my ear, "You forgot my first lesson, Harlowe. Always be prepared for an attack, as foes often disguise themselves as friends."

I could not mask the relief in my exhale as I released a shaky breath. "For the love of the gods, Zeke, I am going to kill you. You scared me half to death."

His deep laughter reverberated against my ear as he slowly lowered me back onto solid ground. He released my hands and took a step back, as he folded his arms across his broad chest. All amusement was gone, he furrowed his dark brows, and the set of his angular jaw told me I was about to be graced with one of his lectures.

"It was far too easy to disarm you, Harlowe. You felt my presence and yet you re-sheathed your weapon and failed to maintain a proper watch on your surroundings. If I truly was an enemy, you would be dead right now, lying in a crumpled heap after your pretty face collided with the ground."

And there it was. It was an effort not to roll my eyes.

"Zeke, I am tired. I'm still not fully recovered from the last attack on my life. Can we take a breather with the sneak attacks?" I pleaded.

Zeke snorted. "Tired, my ass. Your body is present, but your mind has been absent for days," he said sternly. Then, softening his tone, he continued, "Is this about the incident with Sienna?"

My cheeks flushed with heat, not wanting to divulge the real reason behind my wandering thoughts.

Zeke noticed my reaction, and mistaking it for confirmation, he said, "It's okay to be rattled, Harlowe. Coming so close to death," he shuddered before recovering himself. "But you can't let it stop you from getting back up. Use it to fuel your training. Allow it to motivate you to be the best."

I just nodded my head, not wanting to alert Zeke that he was completely off-target. He studied me for a moment longer before a wicked grin spread across his handsome face. He pulled me into a tight hug and said, "And about going easy." I groaned, knowing exactly what was coming next. "I would miss your company too much. You're the only one who really tolerates me anyway," he finished with a wink.

I scoffed. "I'm forced to tolerate your company. It was basically a royal decree, remember?"

His grin only widened. "All the better," he said, and I pushed him away roughly, failing to hide my grin.

Laughing, he turned to leave but paused before saying, "Oh, and Harlowe," — he peered at me over his shoulder as he continued — "you can bet your sweet ass we will address your little slip up here today in our next session." He threw me a sly smirk and left me standing there, gaping after him.

I pushed off the railing and groaned, knowing all too well that Zeke would have me praying for the swift death that eluded me today by the time our training session finished tomorrow.

I continued toward my mother's study, intent on making a direct plea to her about ending my lessons with my tutors. As I approached, I noticed the door was ajar. Muffled voices sounded from within the room, and I moved closer, realizing it was my parents.

"You can't just spring something like this on her, Atticus," my mother argued. "I have been patient. I haven't defied your wishes, but you need to be truthful with her. She can't go into this blind."

My father huffed. "And what of her constant training with Zeke? Is that your idea of not working against me?"

"She has to be prepared. You forced my hand in this, but I'll be damned if I won't give my only child a fighting chance," my mother hissed venomously.

I cracked the door open wider and cautiously stepped inside the room. My parents whirled on me, obviously not expecting to be disturbed.

"What's going on?" I asked cautiously.

"Harlowe, you're here, good," my father said. My mother just crossed her arms over her chest and looked pointedly at my father.

"We were discussing the upcoming ball to celebrate your birthday." By the look on my mother's face, that was not all they had been discussing.

"We have invited several important dignitaries to attend, which is why I have instructed your tutors to intensify your studies surrounding the court protocols of our allied kingdoms." My mother shot my father another withering look, and he cleared his throat nervously.

"Specifically, the King of Netheran will be in attendance."

I didn't get what all the flustering was about, but I just nodded, hoping my father would continue.

"He has expressed his interest in courting you," my father finally managed.

My jaw slackened.

"No," I said.

"No?" my father repeated.

"Everyone has heard the stories about the King of Netheran. He's cruel and mistreats his people. I have heard he is especially vile towards the women in his court. So no, I will not allow him to court me."

"Those are just rumors, Harlowe. We can't know what goes on behind the walls of someone else's home."

If looks could kill, my father would be dead where he stood, considering the look my mother was shooting in his direction.

"If enough people are telling the same tale, chances are it's a fairly accurate account of things," I countered.

My father sighed, "Just... give him a chance. Please Harlowe, it would be very... helpful... if you could just give him this opportunity to get to know you and you him. At least just grant him that. Please?" he begged.

I don't know why I cared, especially with how much my father had been keeping from me lately, but seeing him before me now, defeated and begging, something in me slackened my resolve. My shoulders dipped in resignation, and I said, "Fine. I'll give him a chance."

My father brightened before I continued, "But if he's the bastard everyone portrays him as I'm done."

My father's lips tightened into a thin line. I flicked my gaze towards my mother and saw the concern reflected in her eyes.

"I actually came to let you know I am done with my tutors. Their lessons are no longer useful, and if I am to meet with the King of Netheran in a few weeks, then I should prepare for that." Of course, I had no intention of doing any such thing, but my parents needn't know that.

My father opened his mouth to argue, but it was my mother who said, "Of course, Harlowe." I smiled at her in gratitude.

"Great. Well, I'm sure you're both busy, so I will leave you to it." Not wanting to chance my father overruling my mother, I turned on my heels and hightailed it out of there.

Chapter Eleven

Zeke did, in fact, make me regret ever being born in the next day's training session. I was half walking, half hobbling towards the palace after we had finished when I saw Emmerson heading in my direction.

When she was within shouting distance, she hollered, "Are you fucking kidding me? The King of Netheran wants to bed you, and your parents agreed to let that psycho —"

I rushed forward, placing my hand over her mouth before she could finish.

"Just announce it to the whole fucking kingdom why don't you? And he asked to court me, not bed me."

When I pulled my hand away, she responded, "It's the same thing, Harlowe. And if shouting it to the entire kingdom will highlight the idiocy of this idea, I think I might just go ahead."

I growled at her, but she just crossed her arms and lifted her chin.

Motioning for her to follow, I said, "I agreed to let him get to know me and for me to get to know him." I put my hand up to silence her as she opened her mouth to interrupt. "That is all. I don't have any intention of seeing it through."

"Good," she huffed, "because he is a brute and I'll be damned if I send my best friend off to be brutalized in the Kingdom of Snakes. I mean, I'd obviously have to come to rescue you and all that, but it would be a serious inconvenience."

I snorted.

"Besides, it would be just abhorrent to deny Zeke all that glorious pussy," she teased, wiggling her eyebrows. I didn't bother telling her that was already done.

"You're a real treat, Emmerson, you know that."

"Thank you," she said brightly. I rolled my eyes.

"What's got you walking like you have a stick up your ass, anyway?"

"Zeke," I said simply. I hadn't realized how bad that would sound until Emmerson roared in laughter, hunching over her knees, and wheezing in between spluttered breaths.

"Not like that, you harlot," I hissed at her. "We were training, and he was working me hard." This only made her howl louder. I threw my hands up in exasperation and stalked away from her as she struggled to control her rolling fits of laughter.

I had set about drawing a bath when I returned to my chambers, not bothering to call Louise. Lowering myself into the piping hot water, I laid my head on the rim, closing my eyes and allowing the heat to soak my aching muscles. I could feel the tension seeping out of my body as I lay there.

I must have fallen asleep as I jolted awake when a deep, male voice said, "That's new," pointing to my recently waxed lady parts courtesy of Emmerson the day before. She insisted it was popular in other kingdoms and recommended I try it. Personally, I thought it was very little gain for a whole world of pain.

"Oh my gods, Silas, get out," I yelped as I tried to find something to cover my nakedness.

There was nothing, absolutely nothing.

So I settled for placing one hand over my breasts and one hand over the juncture between my thighs.

Silas just stood there, watching me squirm with a wry grin on his face.

I glowered at him. "What are you doing in here?" I gritted out.

"Oh me," he said nonchalantly, "I'm just checking in, seeing as you missed dinner this evening."

"I haven't seen you in over a week, Silas. Why would you need to check on me now?" The irritation was clear in my voice.

"Are you trying to tell me you missed me, Little Menace?" he asked, amused.

"Just... get out... would you?" I pointed towards the door, realizing too late that I had exposed my breasts to him once again in doing so. He wiggled his eyebrows at me.

I chucked the small bar of soap I had been using right at his head, but of course, he dodged it. He walked out of my bathing chamber with a chuckle.

When I emerged from my bath, I saw a tray had been placed carefully on my small breakfast table. I tied my robe around me and walked over to it, lifting the lid. The enticing smell of steaming vegetables and roasted beef with gravy met me. There was a slice of chocolate cake waiting for me, too.

Louise really knew how to pamper a girl.

I didn't realize how hungry I was as I gulped down my dinner before getting ready for bed. I was exhausted. Not just from the rigorous training I had been doing, but also from the mental drain of recent events. I had nearly been killed while visiting my lake, and then Sienna had tried to beat me to death. And to top it all off, the wicked King of the West wanted to court me, because, why not?

I climbed into bed and sighed. As soon as my head hit my pillows, I was asleep.

The pressure of a hand covering my mouth drew me from sleep as someone shook me gently. I thrashed about, trying to claw the hand away.

"Shh Harlowe, it's me," Silas said in the darkness. He removed his hand but motioned for me to stay quiet.

"What's going on?" I whispered.

"The grounds are under attack. They haven't infiltrated the palace yet, but I'm here to make sure you're secure."

"Under attack, by who?" I demanded.

"We're not sure. They flew in on dozens of roc."

The roc were enormous eagle-like birds that could rival dragons in size and wingspan. They possessed razor-sharp beaks that could rip a person to shreds, and talons so large they could carry objects as big as a horse over many miles. Even their feathers were weapons, as they sported small bone-like fragments across the tips that were as effective as any dagger.

They were a flying armory.

Silas pulled me out of bed, fastened a cloak I didn't realize he was holding around my shoulders, and retrieved my boots. He motioned for me to put them on, and I did. Once I was dressed, Silas gripped my hand in his and started leading me towards the door.

He passed me one of his daggers and unsheathed the sword from his back. As we exited my chambers, Silas swept his gaze over the surrounding area before we crept along the passageway, away from my rooms.

"We need to see if my parents are alright," I whispered in the quiet of the night.

"They're fine. Your father is leading the soldiers securing the palace, and I took your mother to safety before I came for you."

"What about Emmerson?"

"With her father."

Of course, she was.

"Zeke?"

Silas paused briefly, and I could see his jaw clenching as I studied his profile. I was about to push him to answer when he finally said, "He's leading another contingent around the exterior of the palace grounds."

"That's where we need to be," I said, determined.

"Wait Harlowe," Silas said, gripping my hand as I tried to walk passed him.

"We have no idea how many of them are out there or why they are here. Your father's instructions were explicit. I am to take you to your mother."

"Fuck that!" I said, anger rising. "If Zeke and others are out there risking their lives, I am going to aid them."

"You're the fucking heir Harlowe. It's not your job to risk your life."

I narrowed my eyes at him, and he growled, running a hand through his hair in frustration.

"Fine," he finally said. "But you do as I fucking say."

I nodded.

"I mean it, Harlowe. If I tell you to run, you fucking run. Got it?"

I nodded again.

Still muttering under his breath, Silas led us towards the servant's entrance while slipping me another one of his daggers.

The clash of metal echoed into the night as he pried the door open. Silas leaped into the fray and immediately we were set upon. Two figures loomed before us, advancing. Silas swung his sword at the closest figure, and I threw my dagger at the head of the second, who went down with a loud thump. Silas had dispatched the first by the time I had retrieved my dagger.

Grinning slightly, he said to me, "A Little Menace indeed."

We darted forward into the melee, and I spotted Zeke up ahead engaged with an enemy fighter. He swung his sword high; the clashing of steel surrounded us as the two faced each other. Zeke parried, sidestepping his opponent's blow with ease. He was a skilled swordsman, deflecting and countering each strike. Zeke feigned right, and the warrior leaned into it. Swiftly thrusting his blade forward, Zeke impaled the warrior, ending his opponent's advances.

Another warrior came at Zeke from the side, and before I could shout a warning, he had sent an orb of fórsa sailing at his would-be assailant, colliding with their chest. They went down hard, and Zeke easily dispatched them with a swift blow of his sword.

Zeke's eyes locked with mine, and fear flashed across his face. "Harlowe!" he bellowed, and I whirled around in time to see another warrior advancing on me. He was huge, and given I only wielded daggers, I would need to get in close in order to end him. My hand shot out swiftly, and I raked my dagger across the exposed flesh of his forearm. He hissed out a curse and danced backward. I went on the attack and lunged at him before he could recover. Feigning high, I dropped into a low crouch at the last second, sweeping his feet out from underneath him. I straddled his waist, and with a quick flourish of my dagger, I plunged it straight down into his heart. I rose to my feet, panting heavily, and engaged my next enemy.

They were coming thick and fast, and I was growing tired. The flashing of light in my periphery caught my attention, and I turned to see Silas hammering the incoming assailants with blast after blast of fórsa. One after another, they fell. Silas was unrelenting, seemingly unaffected by the strain of the battle, as he continued to pull fórsa from the realm to vanquish the enemy.

I turned back to the skirmish in front of me, and danced between my enemies, slicing my dagger across the throat of one, and thrusting the other under the ribs of another. I cut, stabbed, and sliced my way toward Zeke, and by the time I reached him, bodies scattered the ground all around us. The remaining warriors were retreating, and the roc were taking to the skies.

As quickly as it had started, it was over.

I hunched over my knees, catching my breath. Blood covered me, and I had gained a few wounds of my own. Zeke grabbed my arms, pulling me upright.

"What the hell Harlowe? I thought you were secure inside the palace. What are you doing out here?"

"It is my kingdom to defend Zeke," I wheezed out.

He just stared at me, mouth hanging open before he burst out laughing. It was a chuckle at first but quickly escalated into raucous laughter. When he finally gained control of himself, he shook his head and said, "You did good

Harlowe. You did good."

Emmerson rounded the corner at that moment, twin blades drawn, blood spattering her face, her torso, her... everywhere. The huge grin on her face told me little to none of it belonged to her.

"That was exhilarating. I haven't seen action like that in ages," she beamed. I just shook my head at her. She lived for this shit.

"Harlowe!" my father barked from behind me. I spun on my heels and saw him stalking toward me.

Trying to head him off at the pass, I said, "I'm fine. I didn't die, and this is why I train."

Lucky for me, his General, Emmerson's father, approached him and redirected his attention. They bowed their heads together and a whispered conversation was passed between them.

Silas approached me from the other side.

"Where were the dragons?" I asked, noticing I hadn't sighted them during the battle.

"Too far away to make it in time," he replied.

Loud wing beats sounded overhead, signaling they had just arrived. Silas excused himself and headed in their direction. Zeke herded me inside and called for a healer.

"I'm fine, just a few cuts, nothing deep. Let them tend to someone else more injured. I can clean these up." Zeke begrudgingly agreed.

I could tell the debrief was going to take a while, so I excused myself and headed to my chambers. The weariness was setting in, and I needed sleep.

Chapter Twelve

I entered my bathing chambers and cleaned my wounds, washing the blood off as well as I could. I then wrapped the deeper cuts before changing out of my ruined nightclothes and cloak. Pulling on a fresh nightgown, I was ready to collapse into bed.

When I emerged from my bathing chamber, it was to find Silas leaning against the wall next to my bed. He pushed off the wall and prowled towards me, power radiating from his body. He settled in front of me; his hungry gaze working its way up my body. As he took in the sight of my bare legs, he looked as though he was a starved man, and I his last meal.

Before I could lose my nerve, I stepped into his arms and placed my hands on his chest. His hands went to my hips and grasped me tight. I peered up at him from under my lashes and held my breath, waiting for him to say something.

"This is a bad idea, Little Menace."

"It seems I am full of bad ideas tonight," I purred. This elicited a low growl from the back of his throat.

"You can't handle me, Princess, I will wreck you."

"Are you trying to warn me or tempt me?"

He narrowed his eyes into slits and said, "If I cross this line with you, Princess, then you become mine. There's no going back. If I claim you, you'll belong to me."

His words sent a jolt of apprehension through me. I could tell he was serious, and that he had uttered them in warning. But Silas wouldn't be here forever, and no matter what he said to the contrary, I was one woman who couldn't be owned.

And I was done fighting my intense attraction to this man. I knew he was dangerous and maybe even the enemy, but at this moment I just didn't care. So I tipped my head up, angling my face towards him, and said, "Then what are you waiting for?"

"Let's get one thing straight," he snarled, gripping my chin with his hand. "You may be heir to this kingdom Princess, but inside this bedroom, I am King," he growled in a low, seductive tone that had liquid heat pooling at the apex of my thighs.

Silas leaned in, his mouth pressed against the shell of my ear, and whispered, "Now be a good girl and get on your knees. Bow before your King."

His words sent a sharp thrill through my body, making my nipples harden beneath the sheer fabric of my nightgown. My instinct was to refuse him, and he growled low in his throat as if sensing my hesitation. He gripped my chin harder, and locked his eyes with mine as he said, "Don't disobey me, Harlowe." The threat lingering unspoken between us.

Oh, how I desperately wanted to.

I wanted to know exactly what he would do to me if I disobeyed him. Heat pooled low in my stomach and my core throbbed at the thoughts swirling in my mind. His knowing smirk only intensified my arousal.

I gulped, and a wicked chuckle escaped him as his tongue swiped out and licked at my bottom lip. Without breaking eye contact, I gripped the hem of my nightgown, pulled it over my head, and lowered myself to my knees before him. Silas curled his upper lip, snarling his approval.

"Good girl," he purred. Silas reached down and untied the laces of his leather pants, pulling himself free. His cock was enormous, thick, and intimidating. Yet, the sight of it still had me salivating at the thought of it buried in my throat.

He pumped his length twice before tangling his free hand in my hair, guiding my lips towards the tip. I opened my mouth and swiped out my tongue to lick the salty bead of pre-come glistening there. Silas hissed and then groaned when I took more of him into my warm mouth, swirling my tongue around the head and licking up and down the sides.

"Yes, Princess," he half moaned, "show your King just how talented that tongue of yours can be."

I moaned around him, arousal slickening the inside of my thighs as I worked him deeper into my throat. I couldn't take all of him. He was too big. I used my hand to pleasure the rest of his length; moving in time to the swirls of my tongue. Silas groaned again; louder and more guttural.

"That's it, Harlowe," he strained out. I cupped his balls with my free hand, massaging them to the rhythm I had set. My head bobbed up and down and he continued to moan above me.

"I'm going to come in your mouth and you're going to take it. You're going to take my seed and swallow it down like a good girl, aren't you?"

When I didn't respond, he pulled on my hair, forcing me to meet his gaze.

"Aren't you?" he snarled. I nodded, his large cock preventing me from saying anything.

"That's my good girl," Silas growled. "And you are mine now, Harlowe. Make no mistake about that."

His balls tightened, and he pulled my face flush with his stomach; seating himself all the way to the back of my throat. My eyes burned and began to water. Silas threw his head back and groaned as he emptied himself inside my mouth. I swallowed, his salty taste sliding across my taste buds as he released me.

As I stood, I caught the small trickle of come that escaped my mouth and pushed it back inside with my thumb; sucking hard.

Silas's feral eyes zeroed in on the movement.

His lips crashed against mine so hard we were a clash of lips and teeth. His tongue invaded my mouth, dominating, conquering my own as he sought to savage me. He wrapped one muscular arm around my back, and the other gripped my ass as he lifted me. My legs wrapped around his waist, and Silas moved with a predator's grace as he walked me back towards my bed.

He threw me down and pulled his tunic over his head. Kicking off his pants and boots, he crawled his way up my body. He nibbled on my earlobe before whispering, "Are you ready to scream my name over and over and over again, until it is the only word you can fucking remember?" I shuddered and red-hot need scorched my body.

Silas nestled himself between my thighs as he started kissing his way down my body; across my jaw, down my throat, until he reached the juncture between my neck and my shoulder, where he nipped and sucked at my skin. I shivered beneath him, lost in the sensations.

He trailed his tongue down my chest, between the valley of my breasts as he made his way to the swell of one breast, and then the other. My nipples were rigid beneath his warm breath, and he took each swollen tip into his mouth, sucking and tugging before repeating the actions on the other. I moaned in delight. The heat pooling low in my stomach, coiled tight with every touch.

I needed more.

"Please," I croaked out.

"Please what Harlowe?" Silas growled. "Use your words."

But I couldn't. Not with the sensations he was creating with his hot mouth as he explored my body.

"Please," I tried again, delirious, completely lost in the feel of him. Silas chuckled darkly against my breast, but he continued his slow descent down my body, his tongue licking every sensitive spot on his way.

I worked my hands up his corded arms, stroking his tattoos, and across his muscled back, feeling them flex under my palms.

It was heaven. His body, his mouth... his tongue. He was heaven.

Silas reached the juncture of my thighs and paused, inhaling deeply. He growled his approval against my opening, which sent small vibrations straight to my core. His tongue darted forward as he licked the length of my entrance, savoring me as though I were some decadent dessert.

Silas drove his tongue deep inside me, lapping at the arousal he had created. I moaned unabashedly. He retracted his tongue from my center and instead sucked my sensitive, throbbing clit into his mouth. One finger entered me roughly, and I gasped at the fullness it created. A second followed and his thumb replaced his mouth, rubbing circles around my clit.

He crashed his lips onto mine, capturing my bottom lip between his teeth. I moaned into his mouth as I rode his hand, his fingers working in and out of my center.

"That's it, Harlowe. Fuck my fingers. Show me just how wild and demanding you can be."

I climbed higher, reaching for the orgasm I knew was just beyond my grasp. Panting, I increased my rhythm and reached down to pinch one nipple between my fingers. Silas followed my lead and bit down on its twin, tugging and sucking until I couldn't take it anymore. I peaked that glorious mountain and plunged right over without stopping to catch my breath. My orgasm was hard and intense. I closed my eyes, letting the waves of pleasure roll over me until my breathing slowed, and eventually evened out.

Once I had come back down, Silas withdrew his fingers, and placing them into his mouth, he sucked them clean, groaning as he did so, never breaking eye contact with me.

The action was so arousing, that heat began pooling in my core once again. I peered down at his length, seeing it hard and standing to attention, ready for more.

Silas followed my gaze and gave me a wicked grin. He lowered himself down, pressed his weight against my body, and positioned himself at my entrance.

"Did you think I was done with you, Harlowe?" Silas purred. "I promised to have you screaming my name until it was the only word you could remember."

Silas didn't hesitate before thrusting his full length inside me, seating himself to the hilt.

"Oh gods," I gasped, as the fullness created a delicious burn that quickly turned to pleasure.

"There is nothing holy about what I intend to do to you, Little Menace. Now say my name," he demanded.

"Silas," I moaned.

"Good girl," he praised. "Now scream it."

He pulled out all the way to the tip and thrust back inside me. Hard. He set a brutal rhythm, and it was all I could do to hold on, as I screamed his name over and over and over, just as he had promised.

"Louder." Silas challenged, no... commanded. And I obliged. Just as I thought I could take no more, my voice hoarse from screaming his name as he brought me to the edge of oblivion, he hit that glorious spot nestled inside me, sending me crashing over the edge, pleasure searing my every nerve-ending. He continued to pump into me until he, too, tipped over the edge, spilling himself inside me.

The only sound was our ragged breathing as he slowed and then stilled above me. Our gazes met and for a moment, there was nothing outside this room. No duty, no battles, no death. Just the two of us, basking in the glow of shared release.

He withdrew from my body as he collapsed on the bed beside me. He wrapped a large, muscled arm around my shoulders and pulled me into his chest.

"You are mine now, Harlowe. Only mine. Now that I've been inside you, I'll never let anyone else have you," he whispered against my hair.

I couldn't speak, couldn't articulate that wasn't his choice to make. I was so spent from the intensity of the orgasms he'd given me, I could only murmur something incoherent as I drifted off to sleep, nestled in his tight embrace.

Chapter Thirteen

I woke to the feeling of a calloused hand trailing small circles over my hip. Rolling onto my back, I stretched out my limbs, moaning as my muscles tensed and then released.

"Careful Little Menace, making sounds that delicious will see you pinned beneath me so quickly your head will spin." Silas thrust his hard erection into my side for emphasis.

I turned towards him and scanned his face for any hint of his usual aloofness following one of our sexually charged encounters. But I only found a sly smirk pulling up the corner of his lips. My gaze followed the pattern of his tattoos as they made their way across his shoulder and down the length of his arm. I bit my lip. They truly were a sight to behold and sent all the blood in my brain rushing straight to my core.

I shook off the mental image my thoughts created and looked up to meet Silas's gaze. His smirk had only grown throughout my perusal of his naked flesh. Flushing, I changed tactics and said, "Did you get any information on the attack last night?"

His smirk widened. "I was somewhat occupied last night if you recall," he purred.

"Before you came to my chambers," I said, rolling my eyes.

He chuckled softly and then sobered. "They were soldiers from the Kingdom of Vidyaa."

"What?" I sat bolt upright, the sheet dropping to my waist as I did so. Silas's eyes darkened as he took in the sight of my exposed breasts. I pulled the sheet up to cover myself and barked, "Focus!" His lazy grin returned to his face as he looked up at me.

"Why would they attack? We haven't been in conflict with them since the Skirmish of Power."

Silas shrugged. "We're not sure yet. Your father is sending an emissary to the King of Vidyaa today, but we won't hear back for a while."

"What the fuck is going on here, Silas? This attack, the Siren, not to mention how strangely the animals have been behaving. I saw a bear in the forest that day with the Siren and it just, well, I don't know exactly, but it came over to me and licked my hand. No hint of aggression, nothing. I've never seen a wild animal, let alone a bear, behave that way before, and I've been hunting in that forest all my life. And then there are the dragons and whatever is going on with them." I was rambling, and I wasn't sure if I was making any sense. "Wait, can you ask Caolán what's going on with the dragons?"

"I already did." He paused briefly before continuing, "He only said that the dragons were drawn to you."

I furrowed my brows. "What the hell does that mean?"

Silas just raised a shoulder in a half-shrug.

"Something is wrong. I can feel it." I chewed on my bottom lip, contemplating. "My father is keeping things from me. He didn't even tell me you were coming to our kingdom or of the services trade your kingdom and mine had agreed to. Then he wouldn't let me train with you, insisting I needed to study royal protocols. Which I know is rubbish because I've studied them my whole life as the heir. And then last night, I was the last one to be alerted of the attack. Everyone was in full battle mode before I had even been roused from sleep."

I focused back on Silas and asked, "Why was that?"

"Your father said you were in the safest position, given where your chambers are and where the battle was playing out, so he wanted to organize the soldiers first to prevent a breach of the palace. As soon as that was done, he sent me to you. In practical terms, it was only a slight delay."

"Then why did you cover my mouth when you woke me?"

"Because I couldn't be sure the enemy hadn't made their way inside undetected, and I didn't want to alert them to our presence if that was the case."

Okay, that made sense.

"I don't know about the other things. That's something you will need to talk to your father about."

I nodded my head in agreement.

I threw off the cover and went to get out of bed. Silas grabbed my wrist and pulled me back down.

"And where do you think you're going?" he growled.

"To speak with my father."

"After I've feasted," he said as a wicked grin spread across his face.

"What do you..." I was cut off as Silas settled between my legs and lowered his mouth to my core.

"Oh," I breathed, already lost in the haze of lust as the sensual creature between my thighs devoured me.

When I finally emerged from my chambers sometime later, I was feeling entirely satiated, if not a little sore. A small blush crept up my cheeks, thinking about all the things Silas did to my body this morning. The man certainly knew what he was doing. It made me wonder just how old he was. I hadn't thought to ask, and I made a mental note to rectify this.

I started towards my father's study, my head swimming with the questions I needed answered. I was reluctant to get into a sparring match with him, but if he didn't give me the information I needed, I was all too prepared to take him to task over it.

When I arrived at his study, I found my father deep in conversation with Samuel, Emmerson's father, and the General of our armies. Several military advisers were also present, but they hadn't noticed my entrance.

I cleared my throat and said, "I would like a word with you, Father. It is a rather pressing matter if you don't mind."

Their heads all swung towards me, registering my presence for the first time.

"We are rather busy now, Harlowe."

"It will only take a moment."

My father studied me for a minute; the hardened expression on my face, the stiffness of my posture, the battle leathers I wore, before inclining his head towards the door. Immediately, the men surrounding him departed.

"What is this about Harlowe?"

"You tell me. You've been keeping things from me. I have been trained as a warrior all my life and suddenly you forbid me from training with the Cathal. Why?"

My father sighed, the weariness from the night's events clear on his face. "First, I didn't want you training with the Cathal because dragon bonding is dangerous. As the kingdom's heir, risking your life in this endeavor would be foolish."

"Why all the theatrics? You specifically instructed the staff to keep quiet about it in my presence. When the Cathal arrived, I was caught completely unaware. It made me look foolish. And as you have already pointed out, I am heir to this kingdom. Looking foolish to visiting delegations from other kingdoms does not send the right message about the strength of our own."

"I may have misjudged my approach in that regard," my father admitted reluctantly. "However, I knew that once you had learned of the Cathal, you would disobey my direction not to train with them." The accusation was clear in his tone.

Resisting the urge to lower my head like a chastised child, I continued, "You said first. What is the second reason?"

"And second," — my father paused, casting a glance to the side as though he was lost in his thoughts — "I want you to have an intimate understanding of all court protocols. They are just as important as the ability to wield a sword. Often more so."

"Father," I said, frustration creeping into my tone. "I have been trained in court protocols from the moment I could speak!"

"Perhaps," my father countered, "but you have not mastered them. Surviving on the political front requires just as much training as surviving on the battlefield. You are fierce and capable Harlowe. I saw that for myself last night. However, I worry the other rulers will eat you alive when it comes to the games they play and the maneuvers they make. You need more weapons in your arsenal, and your tutors inform me you haven't been taking your lessons seriously."

I scoffed. "What? Am I not meek or obedient enough for their liking?"

"Never underestimate the power and strength that comes with playing a part, Harlowe. Those skills might just save your life one day."

Snorting, I responded, "And you play meek and obedient so often, Father."

He sighed heavily, before continuing, "Whether you like it or not, your experience on the throne will not be the same as mine, Harlowe. I just want you to... survive." He said the last word so softly I almost didn't catch it.

There was a long pause. I held my breath and waited. But he said nothing.

"What else aren't you telling me?" The slight edge to my voice didn't escape him.

"That is all for now, Harlowe," he replied firmly. "As I am sure you can appreciate, I have many tasks to get on with after last night. Now, if you'll excuse me, I need to return to those tasks."

I deflated slightly. I knew my father well enough to know he wouldn't be pushed any further for today.

I went to leave when he called after me again.

"Harlowe, I love you. Please always remember that. The things I do, and the decisions I make, are for the benefit of our people, but also you. It is a difficult balance to strike, but I try my best to achieve it. Please try to remember that. Even when I fail."

A sudden heaviness settled in my heart. Unsure what to make of it, I only said, "I love you too, Father," and strode out of his study.

Chapter Fourteen

Days after the attack, things were beginning to settle back to normal. The emissary my father had sent to Vidyaa had not yet returned, so we were no closer to learning the intent behind the attack.

Thankfully, the villages surrounding the palace had been spared, so we at least knew that whatever they came for, it lay within the palace walls.

Zeke had resumed our training sessions, and he had upped the ante in response to the attack. I was training harder, longer, and developing more skills than I ever had before. It was exhilarating, and I found myself understanding Emmerson's enthusiasm for warfare.

And then there was Silas.

Silas had become a constant fixture in my bed each night since the attack, and I eagerly anticipated the end of each day, just knowing he would be waiting to ravish my body. The man was addictive and occupied my mind far too often. I couldn't let him have that kind of power over me. And yet, I found myself wanting more of him.

Needing more of him.

I was finding it challenging to keep him out of my mind this morning, however, as I recalled how I had spent the night running my tongue over his tattoos as I had so often fantasized. Or my hands exploring the carved panes of his stomach, and how the power of his body demanded I yield to it, to him. It was intoxicating. I lost all sense of myself when I was with him. And that both excited and terrified me.

Silas had also resumed our training sessions since the attack. And like Zeke, he had increased the intensity. Unlike Zeke, however, he found interesting and creative ways to soothe the aches he created in my muscles each night.

Today, the Cathal and the soldiers they were training were spending the day away from the palace grounds. They were finally going to fly with the dragons. Unfortunately for me, Zeke was among the soldiers who were away. With Silas and Zeke both absent, I was left to the mercy of my mother and the party preparations.

Lost to my musings, I had not realized my mother was trying to get my attention. "Which one, Harlowe?" she asked, referring to two table runners draped over her desk.

I looked at them and sighed. One was white with gold embroidery, and the other was ivory with mauve embroidery. I honestly did not know which I preferred, or why it mattered so much.

To conceal my ignorance, I asked, "Which do you prefer?" Emmerson snorted from across the room, very much aware I wasn't the least bit interested.

"Harlowe, I'm not oblivious to the fact that you haven't been paying attention these last few hours," my mother chided.

"If you already know, why do I have to be here? You've just been selecting the ones you prefer anyway, so why can't you continue to do that without my input?" I whined.

My mother narrowed her eyes at me. "I expect you to give every task you undertake your full attention. Whether it be with a sword or a table runner, every duty you perform reflects on you and your kingdom."

I groaned, and Emmerson flat-out laughed this time. That was until my mother directed her to sort through the centerpieces. Now it was my turn to grin. Emmerson had no domestic bones in her body. None. She would rather go to war than be assigned the task of choosing tableware.

Emmerson and I scrambled to get out the door once my mother had dismissed us hours later.

Emmerson moaned, "I would rather poke my eye out with a dagger than endure another lesson on how to pair your utensils with the chandeliers." I rolled my eyes at her dramatics but somewhat agreed.

"I don't even want a ball, so I don't know why I have to be dragged into all the preparations," I said bitterly. "If anyone had bothered to ask me my opinion, I would have said a bonfire and ale would suffice."

Emmerson grinned. I was speaking her language. "With some very sexy, very deadly men who just so happen to be experts at mounting and riding untamed beasts," she winked.

Subtle. Very subtle.

"Emmerson," I said dryly, "not every conversation has to lead back to the Cathal and how many you plan to bed."

Emmerson scoffed, before replying, "Why stop at one when there are so many to sample?"

"There's something wrong with you," I teased.

"Or something very right," she said, wiggling her eyebrows.

As we exited the palace and approached the training square beyond the entryway, Emmerson stilled abruptly, mid-stride.

"Hot damn," she muttered.

"What?"

She just pointed. I followed her outstretched finger and saw what she was gaping at. The training party had returned. Cillian, who had removed his tunic, was leaning over a bucket of water, washing his muscled arms and torso. He straightened, and lifting the bucket, he tipped the contents over his head and chest, shaking out his hair as he did so. Water trickled down his chiseled stomach and his body looked as though the gods themselves had crafted it.

I gulped.

"Yeah," was all Emmerson said.

A throat clearing behind me had me spinning around, guilt no doubt evident on my face.

Leaning against the wall, arms crossed over his chest and one foot braced on the wooden door of the palace, was Silas.

He quirked a brow at me, and I snapped my mouth shut, only now realizing it had been hanging open. Emmerson, not bothered at all by being caught ogling Cillian, remained fixed on the male in question, who was now reaching down to retrieve his tunic.

Silas pushed off the wall and approached us. "Ladies," he said, a faint hint of humor in his tone.

"Hey," was all Emmerson managed, eyes still locked on Cillian as he made his way towards us. "I'm going to..." she paused. "I'll see you later," she finished as she made to intercept Cillian.

I wanted to see how she would play this, but Silas's mouth pressed against my ear diverted my attention.

"It looks like I haven't done a good enough job of reminding you who you belong to, Little Menace," he growled low in my ear. "Something I will remedy tonight."

The threat in his words had me trembling in anticipation. Silas, having noted the movement, smirked in approval.

"Until later then," he purred as he sauntered off beyond the threshold of the palace entryway.

I returned my gaze to Emmerson, who had indeed intercepted Cillian. I watched with rapt fascination as she flirted with the Cathal, a light touch here, and a flick of her hair there. He might act indifferent to her advances, but I didn't miss the way he tracked her fingers as she played with the ties of her tunic that sat just above her breasts. There was hunger in his stony stare as he took Emmerson in.

"What are you doing?" a familiar male voice asked from next to me, a hint of mischief in his tone.

"Watching Emmerson hunt," I informed Zeke.

"Ah," was all he said as he followed my gaze, which was locked on the pair.

Emmerson said something that had Cillian crack the faintest of smiles. Oh, she was wearing him down all right. How did she do that?

"How did it go out there today?" I asked, returning my focus to Zeke, and pointing to the dragons lounging nearby.

"It was more difficult than they make it out to be," Zeke said, huffing out a breath. "It was also amazing, exhilarating, and I was shit scared the entire time."

I noticed the grin he used to mask the truth of his words. "Well, well, well, don't tell me the big bad warrior is afraid of something?" I teased.

"There are many things that I'm afraid of. I'm just good at pretending I'm not," he winked, and I nudged him with my shoulder playfully.

"They will be a tremendous asset in warfare, though. I can see why Pyrithia continued pursuing dragons when the other kingdoms abandoned the practice." Zeke cocked his head to the side as he took in Emmerson, who now had Cillian's arm linked in her own, as they made their way towards the palace.

"Huh," was all he said. Huh, indeed.

The broody, silent second-in-command who didn't have any other moods except deathly serious, was now being led cheerfully up the front steps, arm in arm with Emmerson. And Cillian looked just as puzzled as we were when he registered the situation.

"We'll see you both in there for dinner," was all Emmerson said as she led

Cillian inside.

"I have to see this. I have never seen Cillian unsure about anything. And knowing Emmerson shits about to get a whole lot weirder for Cillian. I might just be witnessing history," Zeke said as he moved to follow them.

I couldn't fault him. Emmerson always came up with weird and wonderful ways to push people beyond their comfort zones. And something told me Cillian didn't leave his often.

Hesitating, I turned back towards the dragons. As if sensing my eyes on them, they turned and looked me over in equal measure. For reasons I didn't understand, I dipped my chin toward them in silent acknowledgment. As I turned back to make my way inside, I could have sworn they returned the gesture.

Chapter Fifteen

Silas wasn't at dinner with the rest of the Cathal that night. He had been meeting with my father to give him a progress report on the training.

As I neared my chambers, I felt his powerful presence behind me as he slinked from the shadows in my wake. I always knew when Silas was nearby. My body zinged with an awareness only he elicited, and his presence overwhelmed my senses.

I made to turn around, but Silas's firm hold, one hand gripping my hip and the other curled gently around my throat, kept me in place.

"Eyes forward, Princess," he murmured against my neck. Anticipation swirled in my veins, and I was sure he could hear the uptake in my heartbeat it was pounding so loudly.

"Move," he commanded, and I took the remaining steps toward my door. "Open it."

I turned the doorknob and stepped into the antechamber adjoining my bedroom. Once inside, Silas released me and closed the door, locking it behind him. My pulse quickened in response.

When Silas turned back to face me, it was with a predator's gleam shining from the dark depths of his brown eyes. He stalked towards me, and I took several steps back. A malicious grin spread across his face as I did so.

"You can try to run from me Harlowe, but when I catch you, and I will catch you, I'll punish you for denying me what's mine."

Arousal filled my core at his words, and a giddy sort of excitement crept up my spine.

Seconds, I had seconds to decide what I wanted to do.

I lurched sideways, pivoting out of his grasp as he lunged forward to capture me. A high-pitched squeal escaped me as I darted into my bedchamber. As I scanned the room, I looked for any place to hide from him, or at least hold him back. I quickly came to the realization that no such thing existed where Silas was concerned.

He seemed to realize it too because he stalked towards me again, victory sparkling in his eyes. Not ready to relinquish control to him just yet, I jumped up on my bed, surveying him as he prowled around me.

He moved left, and I moved right. Keeping him in my sights, I observed every move he made, anticipating him, and countered.

He growled in frustration, and a small smile played on my lips.

My cockiness cost me as he charged forward and grasped my wrist. I hadn't even seen him move from his spot in front of me. He wasted no time climbing onto the bed and pushing my face into the mattress, pinning me beneath him.

"I have you now, Little Menace. Tell me, what should your punishment be for disobeying me?" I shivered and heat ignited low in my belly.

Through ragged pants, I said, "What did you have in mind?"

He chuckled darkly and lifted off me slightly.

He pulled my hips up so my ass was pointed in the air and purred, "Maybe I should spank this pretty ass until you beg me to fill it."

I clenched my thighs together to relieve the pressure building between them.

"Get up," he commanded as he removed himself from behind me. I rose onto my knees and peered at him. He stood and strode over to the armchair next to my bed.

Silas sank into the chair, reclining, as he removed his tunic, revealing the taut muscles of his stomach and the tattoos that drove me wild.

"Take off your clothes," he said, eyes darkening as they locked onto me.

I kicked off my boots and pulled up the hem of my tunic when he said, "Slowly."

So he wanted a little show, did he?

I let my tunic fall and placed my hands on my breasts. Ever so slowly, I ran them down my body. When I reached the hem of my tunic, I gripped it and twisted it in my fingers for a moment before dragging it higher to just above my navel.

I flicked my gaze to his as I ran my tongue over my bottom lip, sucking it into my mouth. I continued to raise the material up my body, exposing the binding of my breasts. Silas shifted in his chair, his erection straining against the fabric of his pants.

I resumed removing my tunic and pulled it over my head, letting it drop to the floor. Then I reached down, keeping my eyes trained on his, and with deliberate slowness, untied the leather ties of my pants. I pushed them down over my hips and let them fall to the ground before stepping out of them.

I moved onto the binding at my breasts, pulling it down my arms to reveal the pebbled nipples waiting there. My fingers trailed over my breastbone before I reached down and pinched my nipple between my fingers. This elicited a growl from Silas, and I peeked at him from under my lashes, the picture of innocence.

My hands traveled down my stomach, and I reached between my thighs, cupping my sex above my panties. As I rubbed myself through the material, I let out a quiet moan and tipped my head back, relishing in the sensations I created.

Silas growled again and toed off his boots. He untied his leather pants and reached his hand inside, pulling out his massive length, and stroking leisurely.

My hands moved to my hips, and I once again glided over them, taking my panties with me. I let them fall to the ground and stepped out of them.

"Now that you've unwrapped me, what is it you intend to do with me, Silas?" I asked, voice husky.

His eyes raked over my naked flesh while he continued to stroke his impressive cock.

"Get on the bed," he jutted his chin towards it, and I obeyed, taking my time, allowing him to take in the view.

"Get on your hands and knees, Harlowe."

Again, I did as he commanded.

I heard Silas stand and remove his pants. He prowled behind me, anticipation flooding me with every step.

The mattress dipped as he settled himself behind me. A calloused hand ran the length of my spine from my nape to the small of my back. He placed his large palm over my right ass cheek and gripped it.

A sharp stinging erupted from the spot he had touched, and it took me a moment to realize he had spanked me. His hand slapped down on my cheek again, once, twice, three times. A small whimper escaped me, and he soothed the reddened flesh with his hand. He repeated the pattern with the left cheek.

I was moaning and writhing as he delivered his punishing blows. The pain mixing with pleasure had my pussy weeping with my arousal by the time he finished.

"The next time I tell you to do something inside this bedroom, Harlowe, I expect you to obey," he snarled next to my ear. He knotted his fingers in my hair and pulled me up to face him.

"Do I make myself clear?" he hissed.

"Yes," I said breathlessly. He claimed my lips with his own in a punishing kiss that left me panting.

"You lusted after another male today, Little Menace. After I claimed you and told you, you are mine." His chest heaved as his ragged breaths escaped his lungs.

"You need to learn who you belong to, Princess," he let his other hand drift to my opening and stroked my entrance.

Hand still in my hair, he angled my head forward and plunged his thick length into me, sheathing himself to the hilt. I gasped at the intrusion, surprised by the abrupt fullness that caused my core to throb.

Silas withdrew to the tip and then drove himself inside me again.

Forcing my head to the mattress, Silas caged me in with his body. He thrust savagely as he bit down on the side of my neck, breaking the skin. I cried out as the pain overtook my pleasure, but then Silas reached around me and started stroking my clit.

Silas released my neck and licked at the wound, whispering, "Now every single man who dares to look at you will see that I have marked you. That you are mine. And every time you glimpse your reflection, you'll remember who you belong to."

The violence of his actions and the deathly seriousness of his tone momentarily shocked me. It should have felt demeaning, humiliating even, to have this man put an ownership tag on me. But... it was erotic.

"Who do you belong to Harlowe?" he demanded, as he withdrew and plunged himself back inside me once again. The slow, languid movements had me pushing myself up and wiggling my hips, trying to entice him to move faster.

"Answer me," he growled as he thrust himself into me once more.

"You," I moaned as he repeated the movement.

"Good girl," he purred.

"Please, Silas."

"Please what, Harlowe?" he taunted.

"Please, make me come."

He brought his lips back to my ear and whispered, "Do you think you deserve to come, Harlowe?"

"Please," I repeated, lust coloring my vision.

Silas thrust inside me again, hard and fast this time. I flattened my ass against him, meeting him thrust for thrust.

"Hmm..." he growled. "You're a lascivious little thing, aren't you? You offer yourself up to me so I can fuck this sweet flesh." He gripped my hips hard and set a punishing pace. The orgasm that had been building inside me exploded. My forearms gave out as I collapsed onto the bed. Silas continued to pound into me. One thrust, two, three, until he too was snarling his release.

Silas collapsed on top of me, trapping me beneath the weight of his body.

We stayed like that, panting, while our breathing evened out. Silas rolled off me, curling his arm around my shoulder and bringing me with him.

Satiated, I curled into his side, watching the rise and fall of his chest with each intake of breath. I traced the tattoos adorning his shoulder, drawing lazy circles over them. Silas placed his arm behind his head and closed his eyes.

"I need to talk to you about something," I said, still idly tracing his tattoos.

"Hmm..." he murmured, and it was the only sign he heard me.

"A delegation from the Kingdom of Netheran will arrive in two days for my birthday celebrations. The King will be in attendance."

Silas stiffened at this.

I continued, "The King has asked my father's permission to court me."

His eyes flew wide and narrowed into slits as he peered down at me.

"I told my father no, but he was rather insistent that I meet with him, so I agreed to spend some time with the King and get to know him."

Silas growled threateningly.

"I only agreed to spend some time with the King, but I have no intention of taking things further with him. I've heard the stories about him, and how he treats women in particular. I'm only doing this to pacify my father."

Silas was still beneath my hands, and I looked up at him. His glare was murderous as he peered down at me.

"No other man is going to lay his hands on you, Harlowe. I won't share you with anyone," he sneered.

Anger simmered in the pit of my stomach, flowing through my veins at his overt possessiveness. It was one thing in the bedroom, but outside these four walls, he had no real claim to me, despite his belief to the contrary.

"Don't think for one second this," — I pointed at the mark on my neck — "gives you any right to dictate my life, Silas. I choose how I spend my time and with whom."

Silas only cocked a brow, the intensity of his gaze making me shift uncomfortably.

Leaning over to extinguish the lantern, Silas wrapped an arm around me and pulled me in close to his chest.

I lay there, waiting for him to respond, but he said nothing.

As I was just about to drift off to sleep, he murmured, "If you let another male touch what's mine, I'll fucking end him."

For the love of the gods, this man was incorrigible.

Deciding it was tomorrow's trouble, I surrendered to the darkness.

Chapter Sixteen

I stood atop the stairs leading into the palace, flanked by my mother on one side and my father on the other. I tried not to adjust the skirt of the navy blue dress I wore as I waited for the delegation to arrive.

Louise had taken particular care in dressing me this morning. The dress she chose was modest but elegant, with a high neckline and sleeves that met my wrists. A layer of fine lace, embroidered with intricate, swirling patterns, covered the bodice and tapered off at the cinched waist of the gown. The flowing silk that made up the skirt cascaded in layers toward my feet, which were covered in midnight-colored slippers.

My copper hair had been braided into a crown atop my head, and small diamond pins had been placed throughout to enhance the comparison. Kohl had been used to line my eyes, which highlighted the iridescent green of my irises, while my lips had been painted in a dusty rose.

Rings and bracelets adorned my hands, and two small studs of black tourmaline were nestled in my earlobes.

I felt completely out of sorts.

In contrast, my mother, dressed in a deep violet gown identical to mine, stood tall and regal, her pale skin glowing in the soft morning light.

My father also bore the finery of his station, and if the confidence with which he held himself didn't identify him as king, the large obsidian crown atop his head left little doubt.

The retinue behind us was dressed similarly, and when I glanced towards Emmerson in her ruby red gown, I noticed her scowl, which told me her current attire also displeased her. Unlike me, however, she had somehow slipped through any inspection of her footwear, as I could make out the curve of her combat boots peeking out from under her hem.

I couldn't help but smirk at her defiance.

My gaze turned to Silas, and I took in the black leather pants, black polished boots, and black tunic that fit him like a second skin. A dark gray waistcoat, embroidered with the symbol of the Cathal, was placed atop his tunic, and secured at his hip with a scabbard. Our eyes met, and I saw the lust simmering in my veins reflected in his eyes as he took me in.

I pulled my gaze away from Silas and glanced over at Zeke, who stood behind my father and off to the right. Dressed similarly to Silas, Zeke had also donned his emerald green coat that denoted my father's house.

The sound of horse hooves meeting gravel signaled the arrival of the incoming party, and I returned my attention ahead as I tracked their approach. At the head of the party was a magnificent, large warhorse. Its sleek black coat glimmered in the sunlight.

Atop the magnificent beast was the King of Netheran, identifiable by the snow-colored hair that hung loosely to his shoulders. The tattoos that snaked up the left side of his throat became more visible the closer he came. His stunning blue eyes met and held mine, and I felt the shrewdness that now assessed me. He dismounted gracefully, which was surprising given his broad, towering frame.

There was no denying that he was beautiful, but the coldness of his eyes provided a glimpse of that much-rumored cruelty.

My father moved to greet him, extending his hand as he said, "Welcome to Valoren, Kieran." Kieran clasped my father's hand in his own, gripping his forearm with the other.

"Thank you for inviting me," he said, glancing towards me as he spoke.

Having noted where Kieran's interest settled, my father turned towards me and my mother.

"You will remember my wife and Queen of Valoren, Clementine."

My mother, tight-lipped, inclined her head only a fraction in his direction.

"Lovely to see you again, Clementine," Kieran said, a wolfish grin spreading across his face.

It was unmistakable to those gathered that my mother did not like the King of Netheran and that he knew it. Reveled in it.

"And this is my daughter Harlowe," my father said, sweeping his outstretched hand towards me.

Kieran climbed the steps until he stood in front of me and bowed, holding his hand out to me. I hesitated only a moment before placing my hand in his. When our hands touched, a strange sensation tugged at my chest. He kissed the back of my hand and said in a seductive tone, "I look forward to getting to know you, my dear Harlowe... intimately."

A low growl sounded behind me at his tone, and the innuendo explicit in it. I had expected it to be Silas, however, it was Emmerson who I saw vibrating with anger when I cast a glance over my shoulder.

"My Lord," Emmerson said as she donned a feigned mask of demure shock. "Ladies are present, please remember to behave yourself," she gasped, her saccharine smile only enhancing the malice sparkling behind her eyes. Only Emmerson would be so brazened as to challenge the cruel — and if reports could be believed — unhinged King of Netheran.

I tensed, waiting for the King's reaction. He just tsked and laughed as though Emmerson was a misbehaving child, a mere annoyance.

My father cleared his throat and ushered Kieran into the palace, announcing his retinue should join us in the hall for refreshments.

Emmerson made her way towards me and hissed low so only I could hear, "I'll cut off his hands if he even thinks about touching you." She glowered after Kieran, who had now disappeared inside the palace. Emmerson gave my hand a small squeeze, letting me know she was in my corner should I need her. She fluttered off ahead, following Cillian, who had proceeded inside.

Zeke joined me on my other side and whispered, "Do you think he knows what he's gotten himself into?" referring to Cillian as he took in Emmerson's retreating form.

"Absolutely not," I laughed, and Zeke flashed me a wicked grin before sauntering in after them.

As I started towards the hall, not feeling enthusiastic about playing the doting daughter or the demure princess, someone shoved me roughly into an alcove along the wall. Silas's intoxicating scent filled my nostrils as he pressed his hard body against mine, flattening my back against the wall. Concealed somewhat by the pot plants decorating the alcove, Silas shamelessly ran his hands all over me.

He palmed one breast in his hand and placed soft kisses along my jaw, as he murmured, "Did you enjoy being the object of the King's attention, Harlowe?" He pinched my nipple through the silk of my dress, and my body trembled in response.

"No," I rasped.

"No?" he mused.

"You covered up my mark," he accused as he ran his hand across my ribs, over my hip, and gripped the back of my thigh as he wrapped my leg around his waist.

"I didn't pick the dress," I muttered, breathless.

His hips jutted forward, and I could feel the hard outline of his erection as he pushed against me.

"Are you wet for me, Harlowe?" Silas purred as he continued, placing small kisses behind my ear and along the underside of my jaw.

"Yes," I panted. Silas growled his approval.

"Remember how good I feel against you, Harlowe, when you walk into that hall." He thrust his hips against my core again to emphasize his words.

"Silas," I moaned. He chuckled darkly and lowered my leg, taking a step back as he adjusted the front of his pants.

I braced my hand on the wall, catching myself as I came back down from the high Silas had induced in me.

I scowled at him, realizing he had every intention of leaving me unfulfilled.

Silas smirked wickedly and purred, "Be a good girl and I'll show you every way you are mine later tonight." His sinful words did nothing to cool the raging inferno coursing through my body. The knowing glint in his eyes told me he was all too aware of what he had done.

I pushed passed him as I exited the secluded alcove, and he followed behind me, chuckling.

As I entered the hall, I scanned the room, finding Emmerson deep in conversation with Cillian. Well, Emmerson was deep in conversation. It was hard to tell whether the stony-faced Cathal was an active participant or not.

I caught Zeke's eye as he surveyed them across the hall, and he smirked over the edge of his cup.

My father stood in a semicircle with my mother, Kieran, Samuel, and another male I did not recognize. When my father saw me, he gestured for me to join him. I headed in his direction, begrudgingly.

"Harlowe, I was just telling Kieran how lovely our gardens are this time of year. Perhaps you could show them to him," my father suggested not-so-subtly. I almost rolled my eyes.

My mother passed me a goblet, and I accepted it eagerly, before replying, "Of course." I guzzled my wine and when I lowered my goblet, it was to find Kieran smirking at me as he took my measure.

"A little early to be drinking wine with such haste, is it not Harlowe?" he teased, but the humor behind his words showed his disapproval.

"Is that not wine in your goblet, my Lord?" I arched a brow in challenge.

"Indeed it is," he paused before continuing, "and please, call me Kieran."

Gesturing towards the unknown male, Kieran said, "This is Kaleb. He is one of my court advisers."

The male in question appeared to be less approachable than Cillian. His lip seemed to be pulled up in a permanent scowl and his dirty blond hair was unkempt. He barely acknowledged my presence with the briefest of nods in my direction. So I returned the favor.

"He hails from the Kingdom of Vidyaa," Kieran said, a predatory smile spreading across his face. "I hear you've had some troubles with your neighbors of late."

"That remains to be seen," my father supplied. "We were attacked, yes, but we have yet to establish whether those ruling the kingdom or dissidents within directed the assault," my father explained.

Kieran lifted his shoulder in a half-shrug, unperturbed by the prospect of conflict.

"Did you know Harlowe, the Kingdom of Vidyaa, is home to the visionaries?" Kieran purred.

"You mean truth-tellers? Prophets?"

"Yes," Kieran replied, mirth twinkling in his eyes. Although, on him, it was far from joyful. It was as though he was taunting me. Teasing me with the knowledge only he possessed. Trying to get a rise out of me. About what, I did not know.

My parents, who were watching our exchange, studied Kieran, as though they too were trying to decipher some hidden message in his antics. Although, like me, they must have come up blank as they looked as confused as I felt.

"So," Kieran started, changing direction, "how about that tour?" He crooked his elbow and offered it to me. With a quick glance in my father's direction, who gave a small nod of his head, I reluctantly accepted.

"Shall we?" Kieran stretched out his arm, indicating I should lead the way.

I stifled a sigh as we headed out the door.

Chapter Seventeen

We walked down the path that meandered throughout the garden, and I pointed out various plants and their uses. The healers tended to the plants that were used for medicinal purposes, others had more sinister origins, and some were purely for enjoyment.

Kieran took it all in his stride. No evidence of the calculating predator from inside the hall. In fact, Kieran was the picture of a gentleman as we continued to stroll the gardens.

"Tell me about yourself, Harlowe. What interests you?"

"I enjoy training. I am quite adept at swordsmanship and hand-to-hand combat."

He grimaced at this but concealed it quickly.

"I actually took part in the battle against the Vidyaa warriors when they attacked," I continued, pushing to see if he would reveal his true feelings on the subject.

He nodded his head; A grave expression on his face.

"Tell me about your connection to the realm. Do you possess the ability to manifest the powers of Aetherian? As a daughter of Valoren, I'm sure we can expect many great things from you." His voice was playful, yet the hunger in his eyes suggested otherwise.

Did he know of my inability to manifest the power of the realm and sought to taunt me?

My cheeks flushed as I said, "No, not yet."

"Ah," was his only reply.

We continued in silence for a time before the discussion turned to my upcoming birthday celebrations.

"You must be excited to be celebrated at such a grand event," he smiled broadly, and I tried to match it.

No, I was not excited. I hated being the center of attention and all the pomp and ceremony grated on my nerves.

I didn't say any of that. I simply inclined my head in answer.

"And dare I ask if you have an escort for the occasion?" I grimaced but shook my head.

He interpreted my grimace as disappointment at not being asked yet, saying, "Well, please allow me the honor of rectifying the situation."

I wanted to say no. I wanted to tell him I never attended any event with an escort, besides Emmerson, of course. It was hard enough to endure those suffocating events without the added pressure of entertaining someone else.

But again, I smiled and gritted out, "Of course." If he sensed my displeasure, he did not acknowledge it.

The conversation tapered off again as we approached the center of the garden. A small bench sat nestled within the overhanging vines, which created a natural walkway that led towards the southern end of the gardens.

I relished the cool reprieve the shade provided as I sat and studied Kieran's profile while he looked out over the landscape. I wondered what kind of mask he wore when terrorizing the subjects of his court or his unfortunate bedmates.

Kieran had appeared nothing short of gracious during our time in the garden, but I could sense the cruelty within him. He could put on a pleasant smile and whisper sweet nothings, but he couldn't hide that cruelty that glowed from the depths of his crisp, blue eyes. I had promised my father I would allow Kieran the opportunity to get to know me, but I was taking his measure, too.

As if sensing the direction of my thoughts, he said, "I do hope you'll allow me the chance to get to know you better, Harlowe. You have long been the apple of your father's eye, and I would very much like to see that side of you for myself."

I almost snorted. My father loved me, true, but I was far from perfect to him. He criticized many of my decisions and often fought with my mother about my priorities.

Apple of his eye indeed.

"And what about you?" I asked, changing the subject.

"What about me?" he said, giving me a radiant smile. "I'm an open book."

"Can you tell me about life in the Kingdom of Netheran?"

"Very similar to Valoren, I would imagine."

I very much doubted that.

"You might have heard stories about my court, but I assure you, they are only rumors."

"So you don't mistreat your bedmates then?" I blurted.

"Only in ways they enjoy," he winked. He was trying to be seductive, and it likely worked on most occasions. Being king probably didn't hinder his advances, either.

"And what about you? Anyone special in your life?"

"No," I lied.

"Good," he grunted.

I snapped my head up at his tone and caught a possessive gleam in his eyes that unsettled me. He had made me all but his in his mind's eye.

"And your magic?" I continued trying to move past the discomfort I was feeling.

"That, my dear Harlowe, is a closely guarded secret."

"You fought in the Skirmish of Power, and if rumors are to be believed, you played a crucial role in pushing back the attack, allowing for peace talks to be considered. So, you must be a strong wielder," I mused.

"Ah, I enjoy an inquisitive mind," he teased. He made a flourish with his hand, indicating I should continue my pondering.

"I have heard rumors it surpasses the abilities possessed by the rest of Aetherian. Is that true?"

"My magic is unlike any other in the realm," he said. He wasn't bragging, just stating a fact.

"Is it channeled from the realm?"

He smiled impishly before saying, "Clever little fox."

His answer was neither a confirmation nor a denial. He liked to play games, and he was playing them with me.

"What things can you do with it?"

"Far more impressive things than summon little balls of light, I assure you."

Those 'little balls of light' could burn right through a human body. The best wielders could destroy entire homes or wipe out large contingents of soldiers. All at the hands of one individual. The thought of Kieran's capabilities, if he regarded that power as insignificant, sent shivers down my spine.

Kieran's mouth pulled up in a half-smirk as he took in the trepidation that I'm sure I was unable to keep off my face.

I suddenly felt vulnerable, so far from the palace, and all alone with this man. I suggested we make our way back, feigning concern for his well-being given the long journey he had just undertaken.

The knowing grin he gave me told me he saw right through me. And not only that, but he also enjoyed the discomfort he was causing me.

Crooking his elbow once more, Kieran offered me his arm. I ignored the tautness that had been steadily building in my chest as we made our way back towards the palace, and the safety of numbers.

Chapter Eighteen

"So he's dangerous, we knew this," Emmerson mused as we walked towards the training fields.

"It's more than the rumors suggest. I don't know what exactly, but there is something inside him. Something dark. He's not just deadly, he's..." I trailed off, not sure how to describe what I felt in Kieran's presence. People had portrayed him as cruel, calculating, and a little unhinged. But when I asked him about his powers, and he made light of what the realm offered, I'd sensed it then; A lurking danger.

"That doesn't really help," Emmerson muttered.

More terrifying than any of that, though, was the pull I felt towards him. There was something inside Kieran that called to me. Something that recognized me. I was too much of a coward to give voice to my fear, however.

We were silent as we made our way towards the rest of the soldiers readying themselves to depart. The Cathal were leading the soldiers they had been training into the mountains bordering the Kingdom of Vidyaa. Those mountains housed the few dragons that called the Kingdom of Valoren home. Today, our soldiers would put their training to the test. I tried not to focus on the fact that some of them might not come home.

Zeke was amongst the soldiers preparing to leave, and Emmerson and I had come to bid him good luck. Sensing our approach, he whirled to greet us.

"We have come to say our last goodbyes," Emmerson teased and lowered herself into a dramatic bow. I dug my elbow into her ribs and rolled my eyes.

"If I get eaten, you will forever regret not appreciating me more, dear Emmerson," Zeke replied, but Emmerson only snorted.

"Cut it out, you two," I interjected.

Zeke stood the best chance of succeeding, I reminded myself, as my eyes searched him over. He was strong, had good intentions, integrity, loyalty; all the things that the dragons apparently valued in a bond mate.

"I'm surprised you're not sneaking along," Zeke said, mischief plain on his features. While I would have begged to join the party, I knew my father would never allow it.

"I mean, it never actually occurred to me to want to go," Emmerson mused. She pivoted on her heel and abruptly departed in the direction Cillian now stood, discussing something with Cian.

I moved to stand next to Zeke. Both of us with our arms crossed over our chests as we tracked Emmerson's determined stride right to Cillian.

"What do you think her chances are?" Zeke questioned.

I scoffed. "Have you ever known Emmerson to not get her way?"

Zeke contemplated that for a moment before shaking his head. Emmerson dove right in, and Cian patted his friend on the shoulder as he left them to it. Cillian ran a hand through his hair in what I could only imagine was frustration.

"Have they slept together yet?" Zeke asked casually, still observing them.

"You know, I haven't asked. I just assumed she would tell me if they had." I felt a sudden pang of guilt towards my best friend. Silas had me so engrossed that I didn't think to ask about Cillian.

"What about you and Silas?" Zeke asked.

My breath caught as I turned to look at him. I expected to see anger on his beautiful face, but he merely grinned, all too knowing.

"How long have you known?" I asked quietly.

Zeke just shrugged before saying, "I didn't know for sure, but I had my suspicions."

"Zeke, I'm —," but Zeke just held up a hand to silence me.

"Harlowe, you don't need to apologize. We were well aware of what we had from the start. It was fun while it lasted. I don't begrudge you or hold any ill will towards you for moving on. I'm happy for you. Besides," he continued with a wink, "I made up for it with Louise."

I gasped, and he laughed outright. Unable to hide my smile, I said, "You scoundrel. Louise is much too good for you. Just so you're aware."

"Oh I know," he said, face serious but his tone was mocking. We both turned back to Emmerson, checking on her progress.

Cillian was now waving his hands about as the argument picked up a notch. Emmerson went deathly still, and I waited with bated breath to see if she had finally met her match or was about to explode. Cillian seemed to notice too, as he took a step back.

But Emmerson didn't explode. She didn't even raise her voice. She simply stepped into Cillian's space and placed her hands on his chest. There was a brief pause, and then Cillian's shoulders slumped as he lowered his head, pinching the bridge of his nose. He turned his face skyward before locking his gaze with Emmerson's once more.

"They are a unique coupling," Zeke muttered, half to himself.

"Very," I had to concur.

Emmerson turned back towards us, a broad smile on her face.

"They're totally fucking," Zeke said.

"Definitely," I agreed.

Emmerson reached us, victory radiating from her as she said, "Saddle up bitches, we're going dragon hunting."

"What did you say to him?" I asked incredulously. Cillian did not strike me as the soft type. I'd had every expectation that he would politely, but firmly, deny her.

Emmerson only winked as she tossed her hair over her shoulder.

I laughed at her antics and said, "Have fun, you two," before turning to leave.

Emmerson grabbed my arm and asked sweetly, "And where do you think you're going?"

I caught the glint in her eye, and I knew trouble was headed my way. Realization dawned on me, and I said, "I'm not going with you, Emmerson."

She placed her hand on her hip and jutted it out. "And why not?" she asked, her tone sassy.

"One, my father strictly forbade it when he told me, and half the kingdom, I was not permitted to train with the Cathal."

Rolling her eyes, Emmerson countered, "And that really stopped you, didn't it?" Zeke chuckled beside her, and I narrowed my gaze at him. He put his hands up in surrender and backed away, leaving me to face Emmerson by myself.

Coward.

"And two," I continued, ignoring her comment entirely, "my father has already scheduled events on my behalf for today. I am going to have lunch with Kieran." As hard as I tried, I couldn't keep the grimace off my face.

A twisted smirk formed on Emmerson's face. "All the more reason to disobey him," she purred.

I groaned. She wasn't playing fair. Emmerson knew I wanted to go more than anything. She also knew I had no desire to spend more time with Kieran.

As if sensing victory, Emmerson continued, "What was it you said to me the other day when forcing me into doing something I knew would get me in trouble?" She tapped a finger on her chin before saying, "Oh yes, best friends help each other do stupid shit they know deep down they really shouldn't do. And as my best friend, you are to be that constant source of endorsement for my particularly bad ideas. Consider this my particularly bad idea," she concluded, wiggling her brows.

Her grin was so smug I may as well have handed her the reigns to the kingdom and declared her queen.

Sighing and instantly regretting my decision, I said to her, "Lead on."

Chapter Nineteen

An hour later, the palace had disappeared from view. Emmerson and I had only taken twenty minutes to dress and pack after sneaking back into the palace. The early hour of our departure aided us in returning undetected.

The trip would take a few days, with everyone traveling on horseback. The Cathal could not transport this many soldiers on their dragons, so the dragons were flying ahead, and we would meet them at the pass leading into the mountains.

I knew that when I returned, there would be hell to pay. So, I intended to enjoy every moment of my freedom.

Saddled on Raja's back, sharing an apple with him, I listened to Emmerson and Zeke bicker about battle strategies. Zeke hated to admit it, but being the daughter of my father's General had led to Emmerson being one kick-ass warrior in her own right, but it was the equally shrewd mind she possessed for strategy that set her apart.

"They can't be used in that way because the landscape would make it difficult, if not impossible, for them to be effective," Emmerson was arguing.

"Yes, but they could be used on the outskirts as a fall-back plan should the battle shift with a retreating army," Zeke countered.

I zoned out, leaving them to it, and enjoyed the tranquility of the forest. Fionn rode up next to me, a mischievous smile on his face. I had seen little of him lately, being too preoccupied with my training to have a spare moment outside of meals.

"Are those two always like that?" He inclined his head towards Emmerson and Zeke.

"Always," I confirmed. Fionn chuckled. Companionable silence settled over us as we continued on our path.

With some hesitation, I asked the question that had been lingering in my thoughts.

I cleared my throat and ventured, "I have never asked you guys how you felt about Sienna being sent away from Valoren." I glanced in his direction to gauge his reaction, but his face remained blank. "If it caused any problems for you, as a group, I mean."

Fionn considered my words before he eventually said, "It didn't cause problems exactly. We all saw what happened." An apologetic smile flashed across his face. "Your father was justified in wanting her removed. However, some believed we should have left with her. To stand with her as a fellow subject of Pyrithia, despite her being wrong."

I thought about that for a moment. I could definitely see that perspective. If Emmerson had done something similar, I would stand with her no matter what. And given Emmerson's temperament, there was a high possibility I could find myself in the same predicament.

"It was mostly Cian and a few friends," Fionn continued. "The rest of us were satisfied with the outcome."

It surprised me that Cian would have been among those calling for a revolt. As Silas's third-in-command, I expected him to be more pragmatic. And yet, I had seen the way Sienna leaned into Cian, sharing secrets and plans. I pondered if there was something else going on between them.

As if guessing my thoughts, Fionn said, "Sienna is the daughter of the King's cousin. In Pyrithia, she holds some influence. Some are drawn to, or at least are wary of, that influence."

Ah, that made more sense. Cian may be concerned about the political situation back home.

"So, which dragon is yours?" I asked, changing the topic.

Fionn smiled broadly. "The blue one. Her name is Niamh."

"They are so majestic," I mused. Fionn nodded along beside me.

"So, Your Majesty," Fionn drawled, amusement sparkling in his eyes. "How are you getting along with a certain, tall, tattooed, broody, and handsome General of the Cathal?" Fionn wiggled his eyebrows at me and my face heated.

Did everyone know?

"What do you mean?" I tried for nonchalance but missed the mark, which was confirmed by Fionn's raucous laughter.

"Oh, I don't know. You almost landed a blade in his throat on our first day in Valoren —"

"That was a misunderstanding," I interrupted.

"To doing the nasty in the alcove outside the dining hall," he finished as if I had said nothing.

I turned towards him, mouth agape, and stared. Whatever he saw in my expression had him grinning widely, like a fool.

"So you did do the nasty. I didn't take you for an exhibitionist, Princess. How very naughty of you," he crooned.

"We...didn't, gah!" I tried again. "We didn't do the nasty, as you so eloquently put it. We simply..."

"Did the nasty," Fionn finished for me, chuckling.

"Does everyone know?" I asked, echoing my earlier thought.

"You don't get to be this close as a unit by keeping your nose out of everyone's business," Fionn quipped, and I groaned.

"Frankly, you're not even the most exciting news around here, Princess. That firecracker of a friend of yours and Cillian have taken over that mantle."

Thankful for the change of subject, I grinned.

"She cracked the uncrackable warlord. He is one scary dude. Don't get me wrong, I would die for the guy, but he terrifies me. Most of us wouldn't dare to glance sideways at him. And then, in walks, this tiny, petite brunette, all five-foot-nothing of her, and starts cursing him out for deigning to suggest training with the Cathal may not be in her best interests. But it doesn't end there," he said conspiratorially. "Then she goes ahead and bloody challenges him."

"Challenges him?" I asked, confused. I hadn't heard this story, which surprised me because Emmerson was many things, but humble certainly wasn't one of them.

"Yeah," Fionn continued. "She throws down the gauntlet and tells him they will settle it in the ring. And I don't mean, she asked him to spar with her. I mean, she literally dragged him outside and forced him into it."

I couldn't help the laughter that bubbled up at the mental image of Emmerson dragging the stoic warrior outside like a misbehaving child.

"They fight, and I see Cillian go down for the first time in my life. And who took him down? A teeny, tiny girl. Honestly, I think Cillian is still trying to figure out how it happened. He was broody and sulky for days and I'm pretty sure that's why he rebuffed her for so long. And I was grateful for it, because let me tell you something Princess, I wanted my shot at her. But alas," he sighed, "the war brute changed his tune and now here we are." He gestured to where Emmerson now rode side by side with Cillian up ahead.

By the time Fionn had finished speaking, my ribs were aching from laughing so hard. That story could only belong to Emmerson.

"She's something else," he grinned.

"That she is," I agreed.

We chatted until Fionn took his turn on point. Teller joined me in his absence and kept me company with stories about his life in Pyrithia, his younger sister Kingsley, and what it was like bonding with dragons. Teller was easy to talk to, and I enjoyed his company.

When we finally stopped for lunch, I was hot, and my muscles ached from sitting in my saddle for hours. I went to dismount, and large hands wrapped around my waist. I peered over my shoulder and my eyes locked with piercing brown ones.

Silas guided me down Raja's side and gave his reigns to Teller with instructions to water him.

Titling his head toward the water I could hear rushing nearby, he silently asked me to follow him. Clearing the tree line, I took in the glistening river and moved passed Silas towards the inviting coolness. Leaning down, I washed my hands and arms in the water. Cupping water in my palms, I splashed it across the back of my neck and repeated the process with my face.

When I turned, Silas greeted me with a wry smile as he leaned against a tree.

"Little Menace, what have you done?" he crooned when I reached him. I flushed slightly, feeling like a chastised child.

Silas just chuckled mirthfully and placed his hands on my hips, drawing me near.

"I like a woman who misbehaves," he whispered in my ear, sending a shudder through me.

Pushing me back so I was standing at arm's length, he continued, "As much as I relish stealing you away from that psychotic prick, I believe your father will have a thing or two to say about you gallivanting around the kingdom when he specifically forbade it."

I gave a slight shrug. "Kieran is not my problem. As for my father, well, that's a problem for another day."

Silas gave another small chuckle. "I didn't have time to ask you last night," he said, dark brown eyes flicking to me. "What did you two discuss when you were alone?"

There was a serious edge to his tone, but none of the jealous possessiveness he usually used when talking about other men in my orbit.

I thought over my answer. I had not done an outstanding job describing what I felt from Kieran in the garden when sharing my concerns with Emmerson. I guess I didn't really know myself.

"He wanted to get to know me," I grimaced, and Silas stiffened. Any reprieve I thought I had from Silas's possessiveness was short-lived.

I hastily continued, "He asked about mundane things at first, like my hobbies. Then he asked about what power I possessed. Truthfully, the way he built it up, saying great things could be expected from me, I kind of got the impression he knew I hadn't yet manifested any and was taunting me, without coming straight out and saying it." I thought back to that conversation. I was almost certain that's what he was up to. "Anyway, then we circled back around to the mundane, birthday celebrations and the like," I winced, remembering I had agreed to let him escort me.

"Harlowe," Silas growled, having obviously picked up on it.

"He asked to escort me to my birthday ball, and I couldn't come up with any excuse to refuse, so I kind of agreed."

Silas growled again and looked down at me.

"No other man will touch what belongs to me, Little Menace, least of all him," Silas scowled.

I snorted, while my hand absently cupped my throat where Silas had marked me. I had hidden the mark under my clothing, so I wouldn't be asked to explain it. But it was still there, and a small part of me was comforted by that. Not that I would tell any of this to the egotistical manic standing in front of me.

"What?" he raised an eyebrow in challenge.

"You think you own me?"

"I don't think, I know I do," he growled, and I rolled my eyes.

"I allow you to think that because it suits my purposes and I quite enjoy your possessiveness, behind closed doors that is. But you don't own me, Silas."

"Little Menace, do I have to spank you again? You might not appreciate it given how many people are loitering nearby, but I'm game," he said, wiggling his eyebrows at me.

I scoffed in answer. Silas swatted my ass to demonstrate his point, and I yelped. That sly smirk returned to his lips.

"Anyway," I drawled.

"Anyway," Silas repeated.

"There's something about him, Silas, something that's not... good."

"There's plenty about him that's not good."

"I'm serious. I don't know how to explain it exactly, but I think it's tied up with how he wields his power. I think he's strong, stronger than anyone else in Aetherian. With his reputation, that could be lethal."

Silas was quiet for a time, contemplating. Then he merely jutted his chin towards the water and said, "Are you done with the river?" I nodded.

"Then let's go back." Silas took my hand and led the way back to the group.

When we arrived back, Teller was in the middle of trying to hoard the more palatable dried meats and fruit. Silas promptly withdrew them from his grasp and started redistributing them. Ignoring Teller's protests, he settled down to eat, motioning for me to take the seat next to him.

Across from me, Emmerson was sprawled out, her hair pulled away from her neck as she attempted to cool herself.

"The river is blissfully cool," I said, pointing back towards the water as I took a bite of my apple.

"Excellent idea," she said enthusiastically and hurtled into a standing position from flat on her back. The soldiers nearest us gaped in awe. Emmerson didn't even register it. Many of the men, the Cathal included, watched her retreating form with something between admiration and lust, as she disappeared among the trees.

A moment later, Cillian followed.

I met Zeke's gaze, and we both grinned. We were no better than children, but we did not let that deter us.

Silas was quiet during lunch as he pored over the maps he had brought with him. This was the first time I had seen him in full general mode, I realized. As the others joked and played, he strategized, planning the best route, and countering our obstacles.

It was fascinating to watch.

All too soon, it was time to get moving again and my ass protested when I retook my seat in my saddle.

Cillian and Emmerson were the last to return. When she resumed her place beside me, I grinned conspiratorially and asked, "Where have you two been?"

She just winked.

We didn't stop until nightfall was almost upon us. We barely had enough light to set up camp. There would be no tents tonight, just bedrolls, and dinner was whatever we could catch. The soldiers followed Zeke and the Cathal's lead in how they treated me, so I felt like part of the group. I was not a princess here.

It was liberating. I felt like I could breathe for the first time in a while.

After dinner, many of us gathered around the campfire, drinking wine, and telling tales. I was certain that many of Teller's stories were grossly elaborated or made up entirely.

The heat from the fire was warm, but not oppressive. The flames glowed between us and sent small, red embers floating away in the breeze. It was nice and peaceful.

As nice as it was, I was growing tired, the day's travel catching up to me. Yawning, I caught Silas's eye from across the camp. He tipped his head toward the makeshift sleeping quarters and I nodded.

After saying goodnight, I rose from my spot on the ground and made to follow Silas, who was waiting for me.

"You can share my bedroll."

"How very gallant of you," I teased.

He pinched my hip. "Don't make me regret it, Little Menace." I just laughed, enjoying this carefree, relaxed side of him.

Both snugly tucked away in his bedroll, I curled on my side and placed my head on his bicep. He tightened his arm around me in response.

"I could get used to this," I said sleepily.

"You should already be used to it, Harlowe. I've been in your bed every night for weeks," he chuckled.

"Hmm..." was all I could manage. Sleep already dragging me under.

"Sleep Harlowe," I heard Silas say. And then he placed a tender kiss atop my head as I drifted off into nothingness.

Chapter Twenty

We were on the road again early the following morning. Silas had informed me that we should arrive at the base of the mountain pass before noon. From there, the Cathal would go on ahead with the Valoren soldiers to seek out the dragon's mountain lair.

I was excited to see dragons in their natural habitats, albeit from a distance. Silas had also mentioned that the mountain lairs were used as hatching grounds, which made the dragons more territorial and aggressive. Emmerson and I would be staying behind to limit the stress on the dragons.

By the time the sun had reached its highest point in the sky, signaling noon was upon us, the mood in the group had become subdued. The excitement overflowing around the camp this morning had morphed into quiet anticipation mixed with tendrils of fear as the reality of the situation dawned on the soldiers. What they were about to undertake was dangerous, and some of them might not make it home in the end.

I could see the enormous shadows cast by the dragons of the Cathal up ahead, and as we rounded the corner, the beasts came into view.

Every time I gazed upon them, they stole my breath away. They were majestic, beautiful, and radiated power. I spotted Caolán and Niamh among the group.

A large red dragon stood, extended its wings, and shook them out, making the surrounding air vibrate.

I leaned in close to Emmerson and asked, "Which one is Cillian's?"

"The blue one with the red underbelly. His name is Oisín, I think."

He had been the second dragon to approach me after Caolán that first day in Valoren. It seemed the dragons followed a similar chain of command as their Cathal counterparts.

The Cathal dismounted and made their way to their waiting dragons. I scrambled off Raja's back, following suit, and stood around awkwardly, not knowing what to do.

Cian approached a black dragon while Teller approached an amber one. Fionn made his way towards Niamh, very much eager to be reunited with his dragon.

Silas cut a path toward me, and the serpentine eyes of the assembled dragons followed him. I found it challenging to not fidget under the weight of their intense gazes.

Silas grabbed Raja's reins and said, "Wait here for our return, Harlowe. The men will take a few hours to scale the mountain while we monitor their progress from the skies around the pass. Do not wander far from this spot. I don't want you in harm's way today." I nodded in agreement.

"You have provisions in your packs which will see you through until we return. West of here, there's a lake that runs along the side of the mountain. Take the horses there for watering but return here afterwards. We'll return before dark and camp by the lake in the woods."

He reached out and cupped my face. It was so out of character for the broody, bossy General that I just blinked up at him. He turned, nodded once to Emmerson, and stalked towards Caolán. Cillian followed on his heels, nodding first to Emmerson and then to me as he made his way towards Oisín.

Zeke came up behind us and stood between Raja, and Emmerson's horse, Rogue, and said, "Wish me luck!" His perpetual grin plastered on his face.

"You don't need luck," Emmerson said, surprising both Zeke and me with the sincerity of her tone.

"She's right. If anyone will succeed today, it is you. You are strong, you have integrity, and you are loyal to those deserving of it. The dragons will see the good in you." I choked out the last few words as emotion clogged my throat.

"I wouldn't go that far, but you get the idea," Emmerson said, cutting the tension.

Zeke cleared his throat and said, "I will see you both for dinner." He turned on his heels and marched towards the soldiers, awaiting further instructions from Silas.

Silas swung one leg up and over Caolán's shoulder. He mounted the gigantic beast with such precision he made it look effortless.

From Caolán's back he hollered, "You all know what to do," and with a last glance in my direction, Caolán shot into the sky, the rest of the Cathal following suit.

"Direct and to the point," Emmerson muttered.

We watched as the Valoren soldiers, led by Zeke, made their way into the mountain, disappearing from view.

"So," Emmerson hummed, "What shall we do to pass the time?"

"Whatever you're thinking, the answer is no." I led Raja toward the lake Silas had pointed out, while Emmerson dismounted Rogue and followed suit.

"All I'm suggesting is a mild stroll to explore our surroundings."

I turned to look at her, my eyes narrowing. "Nothing about you is mild, Emmerson, and I don't believe for one second that is all you're suggesting."

Dropping the charade, she said, "Well, I, for one, do not plan to let the men have all the fun."

She put up a hand to stop me when I opened my mouth to argue.

"I am not saying we need to go into the lair of the beast, but it will not hurt to take a peek."

"And how would we go about taking this peek?" I asked cautiously.

Of course, I wanted to go. I just didn't want to die in the process, or risk Silas's wrath when he found out we had disobeyed him. If we were going to do this, we had to be stealthy.

Emmerson launched into her plan as we led the horses to the lake and watered them. Emmerson reasoned that dragons were more likely to be found at the top of the pass, so sticking to the bottom and midsections would be safer. The elevated height of the midsection, however, should provide us with the opportunity to observe the bonding process from relative safety.

"But what about the Cathal? Silas said they would monitor the soldiers from the sky, and the whole point of this exercise is to make sure we don't get caught."

"We'll hide. There are plenty of natural alcoves along the pass."

I agreed, secretly thrilled by the idea of seeing the dragons in action.

We spent some time securing the horses and checking the provisions in our packs before heading off.

After a time I asked, "So, why didn't you tell me how far you'd taken things with Cillian?"

"Why didn't you tell me about Silas?" she countered.

Guilt flushed my cheeks at the accusatory tone in her voice.

"It was intense at the beginning, so I needed time to adjust. To be honest,

I'm not sure I have adjusted. He... casts a large shadow." I finished.

"He's not forcing you, is he?" she said sharply.

"No, no, nothing like that. He just, he's an alpha male and I'm not used to that. I guess I'm used to things being on my terms, that's all."

"Ha," Emmerson barked. "Then it sounds like he's good for you."

"Is he though? He'll return to Pyrithia when this is over. And I'll still be in Valoren. I mean, it's fun, but there's no longevity." It surprised me how much it pained me to admit that. "And then there's Kieran."

"There is no Kieran," she said, taking on that sharp tone once more.

"No, I know. But my father asked me to allow him to court me so it's not like I can rub Silas in his face. I have to be cautious while Kieran is at the palace. My father practically begged me to give him a shot, so I think there must be something else at stake, like a trade agreement or something. I just need to play nice until he's gone."

"Fuck that," Emmerson growled. "You're not some deal sweetener."

I couldn't argue with her. However, my father's desperate tone that day in his study made me concede. He had asked nothing from me before.

"Anyway, none of that is an excuse. I should have told you and I didn't. I'm sorry."

She just inclined her head in my direction, apology accepted, and she was ready to move on.

"So Cillian?" I pressed.

"I just wanted to fuck Cillian. And now that I have, I want to keep doing it."

I blinked, her bluntness throwing me for a beat before grinning. "That good, huh?"

"That good," she smirked.

We continued up the pass until we had made it about halfway up. It had taken us a couple of hours and I was thankful for the long summer nights, as we would need the extended daylight to make it back down before the rest of them.

Perched high on an opening in front of a cave, we settled in to observe the others. We had seen no one, not even the Cathal in the sky. We had heard them, however, so we knew we couldn't be too far away from the action.

"Over there," Emmerson pointed, and I could just make out a soldier approaching a cave entrance from below us. We couldn't see who it was, but we felt the mountain rumble as something big emerged from the cave. We had felt that same rumbling as we climbed and had assumed it was a dragon.

Now we knew for sure as a brilliant green dragon emerged from the depths of the cave.

I gasped. It was a deep green, like the grass and leaves in springtime. In a show of respect for its majesty, the soldier knelt before the beast. The dragon approached slowly, sniffing at the air around the soldier. The soldier raised his head and stood. He reached out a tentative hand and placed it on the dragon's chest. The pair remained like that, frozen, until the dragon lowered its head, meeting the soldier's as he did the same; forehead to forehead.

The soldier moved around the dragon and tried to swing up on its back. It took him a few tries, but he positioned himself between the dragon's wings. Holding tight to the dragon's neck, the immense beast launched skyward, the soldier seated on its back.

"Holy shit," I whispered. "That was it, wasn't it? The forming of the bond."

"I think it was."

When I looked towards Emmerson, both of our eyes shone with unshed tears. The beauty of the moment captivated us. Wiping at our eyes, we glanced around, seeking others just so we had the chance to witness that again.

We watched in awe as soldier after soldier found their bond mates before taking to the skies in celebration.

I spotted a familiar dragon with a red underbelly approaching and sprang to my feet. I darted inside the mouth of the cave, pulling Emmerson along with me, as I waited for the dragon to pass.

"Who was it?" Emmerson asked.

"Cillian."

Too afraid to re-emerge, we remained concealed inside the cave, backs pushed flush against the wall.

A low growl sounded from the darkness surrounding us, and we both whipped our heads towards the sound, searching.

"Can you see anything?" Emmerson whispered.

"Nothing."

The growling intensified, and two serpentine eyes appeared from within the darkness.

"Oh gods," Emmerson breathed.

The eyes grew larger, and the whites of pointed teeth became visible as the dragon moved closer.

I took a small step back, pushing Emmerson behind me.

The dragon snarled at the movement.

"Okay. Okay. So we're staying put. Got it."

The dragon continued to move towards us, and I could make out its black scales as it came closer to the light peering in from the mouth of the cave. It sniffed the air around me, the rumbling of its chest ricocheting around the walls of the cave.

I felt a wave of calm wash over me all of a sudden, and I loosened my grip on Emmerson.

"Step back into the light, Emmerson," I commanded, tone sure.

"What?" she hissed. "Are you crazy? I will not leave you."

The dragon snarled a warning, this time at Emmerson, the first acknowledgment of her presence it had made since we entered the cave.

"Please," I begged. "Just trust me." I couldn't explain it, but I knew this dragon would not hurt me. Just like I knew it perceived Emmerson as a threat.

Slowly, reluctantly, Emmerson took a step back. And then another, and another, until she was once again standing in the sun's afternoon glow.

"Who are you, Daughter of Fire and Flame?"

Chapter Twenty-One

The low masculine voice filled my head and somehow, I knew I was the only one who could hear it.

"I'm... Harlowe," I breathed.

"What?" Emmerson said behind me. I ignored her.

"Where do you hail from?" the dragon asked.

"Umm... Valoren."

"What is going on?" Emmerson pleaded.

"Daughter of War then."

It had been a while since Valoren was known as the Kingdom of War. Hearing it again stirred a feeling of foreboding within me.

"What rank do you hold?"

"Umm, I'm the heir, actually," I offered.

I could tell Emmerson was losing her mind outside the cave, only able to hear my side of the conversation.

"My friend," I started, "may I check on her?"

The dragon stayed quiet, offering no resistance as I made my way back to her.

"What the actual fuck is happening, Harlowe?" she hissed low in my ear.

"I can communicate with the dragon. In my head. I can hear him." At least I presumed it was him, given the low gravelly tone. As I had no experience with dragons, I couldn't be sure.

"Of course, I am a male," the dragon retorted in my mind.

"Like the Cathal?" Emmerson asked, not having heard the snide comment from the dragon.

"It appears so."

"And why have you come to my mountain seeking a bond?" the dragon asked.

"I, umm, didn't. I came with a contingent of others who are here seeking bonds, but I was not myself, you know, seeking a bond." I cringed. I was no wordsmith.

"Yet here you are," the dragon replied.

"I wanted to watch," I said, but it sounded like a question. "Wait, how are you communicating with me without a bond?"

"There is something different about you," the dragon mused. **"I can feel a connection to you, even without the bond. It's not just the bond of a bond mate... it's something more. Something in you calls to me."**

I had no idea what to say to that, so I said nothing.

The dragon moved closer and closer until it joined us in the small opening before the cave.

He was not black as I had thought inside the darkness of the cave. Rather, he was a dark gray color with indigo hues.

He was extraordinary. Power incarnate. Beautiful.

Emmerson gasped behind me in an echo of my thoughts.

He was huge too, perhaps even bigger than Caolán, when standing at his full height.

"Whatever you are, whatever you will become, I know one thing for certain: you were always meant to find me. To be my Cathal, Harlowe, Daughter of War and Ashes."

"What... what exactly does that mean?" I asked, overwhelmed by what was happening.

"Do you accept my bond?" the dragon asked, dipping his head towards me.

"What is he doing?" Emmerson asked from behind me.

"He is asking if I accept his bond," I supplied.

"Oh. Okay. Well, go ahead," she made a shooing gesture, pushing me forward.

"What?" I hissed back at her.

"You're obviously worthy, just... accept it or whatever." Emmerson gave me another gentle push towards the dragon.

I took a step closer to the dragon, followed by another. When I was within reach of his bowed head, I lowered my own to his.

A tingling sensation washed over me, and then it was like being struck by lightning. A burning power raced through me, scouring every inch of my body, delving, and searching. Something pulled taut in my mind and then settled around me.

And just as quickly as it had started, it was over.

The bond, I realized. It had been the bond settling into place.

"My name is Misneach," he said, dipping his shoulder towards me.

"What am I supposed to do now?" I asked, unsure.

"You must climb on. The others return and are gathering."

"What?" was all I could manage. Nothing was making any sense to me right now.

"Climb on," he repeated. **"We must join my brethren."**

"Who?" My head was spinning, and annoyance flickered across Misneach's face as he gave me the dragon equivalent of a snort.

"A darkness gathers," he tried again. **"We all feel it. The dragon folk. It is why so many of us have taken bond mates. We will join you when the time comes. Now, climb on."**

"How?"

"Did they not train you before bringing you all to our mountain?" Misneach scoffed.

"I wasn't meant to be taking part, remember? So I haven't undertaken the training the others have."

Misneach huffed out a breath before saying, **"Use the jagged edges of my scales to climb up."**

I glanced towards Emmerson. Another huff.

"Your friend too."

Emmerson was not at all keen to attempt flying on Misneach's back. It took some convincing before she agreed to it. I think the threat of being left behind convinced her to cooperate.

Both nestled between Misneach's shoulders, the giant dragon stalked towards the edge of the mountain and launched himself into the sky.

Emmerson screamed behind me, and the only thing preventing me from doing the same was the fear I would vomit all over Misneach and he would throw us both off.

"Do not do that," he warned, having followed my train of thought. At least, I think that's what he did.

"It's what I did," he confirmed.

We flew down the mountain and over the forest of sprawling trees. I clung to Misneach's neck, so fearful that if I released my grip, I would tumble to my death.

What had taken us hours to ascend earlier took Misneach only moments to descend, and as we circled the base of the mountain, the river we had taken the horses to earlier in the day came into view.

We landed along the riverbank with a thud that sent me lurching forward and across Misneach's neck, the sharp angles of his scales biting into my cheek as we collided.

"Gods above," Misneach muttered. The absurdity of the situation caught up with me and I burst out laughing, hysterics taking over.

Emmerson launched herself to the ground, clinging to it as though she had been fearful she would never set foot on it again. She straightened, taking stock of the situation we now found ourselves in.

Emmerson's newfound resolve straightened something in my spine, and I sobered.

Around twenty dragons lined the river. Some standing alone, others in groups of two or three. Scattered amongst them were soldiers, Cathal now, who looked around awkwardly, not really sure what to do now that they had done what we previously thought of as unachievable. I scanned the gathered soldiers, searching for Zeke.

"Incoming," Emmerson hissed as she peered around Misneach's flank.

I swiveled in my position on Misneach's back and peered over my shoulder. As I did so, I took in the furious expression on Silas's face as he stalked towards me.

Chapter Twenty-Two

I slid off Misneach's back and landed on the ground. Wobbling slightly, I corrected myself and straightened.

Misneach curled his body around me, his colossal head appearing next to my shoulder. He bared his teeth and snarled as Silas continued to make his way towards me. The fury radiating from him was palpable.

Emmerson had joined my other side, and I was vaguely aware that other dragons had moved in too, flanking us.

"Did you call for reinforcements or something?" I muttered to Misneach.

"I told you. Something in you calls to me. They feel it too," he tipped his head slightly toward the other dragons. **"You are connected to all of us. They protect you, as I do."**

I couldn't ask what any of that meant as Silas stopped in front of me, fists clenched.

Misneach growled low in warning.

"He won't hurt me, he's just upset," I soothed.

"Upset," Silas spat. His voice was low and menacing as he continued, "You put your life in danger by going up that mountain after I specifically told you not to." His chest was heaving, and his restraint slipped as Silas shouted, "Why can't you ever do as you're fucking told?"

Another growl rumbled from Misneach's chest and others sounded to the left and right of us.

What in the realm was up with the dragons? I mused, echoing my thoughts from earlier.

"You are ours, and we don't take kindly to threats against us." This is exactly what I imagined having an older brother would be like; protective and overbearing. The thought had a grin tugging at the corner of my mouth, but I suppressed it given that would only inflame things further.

Silas ground his teeth together.

"Caolán is telling me you are," — he paused, as though trying to find the right word — "connected to them somehow." He waved his hand towards the dragons assembled around me. "How?"

"Not just us," Misneach interrupted.

"What do you mean?" I asked. I put up a finger to tell Silas to hold on, as he clearly thought my question was for him.

"Not just us," Misneach repeated. **"Every dragon along this bank can feel you. Can feel the tug towards you."**

"How do you know that?" Misneach rolled his eyes.

"We are discussing it right now. No dragon has ever felt a connection to another Cathal who is not their bond mate. Now we can all feel this pull to you. It is very strange."

"What did he say?" Silas demanded.

"He said all the dragons are connected to me, not just the ones standing beside me."

Silas tilted his head as though he were listening for something. He was talking with Caolán, I realized. Silas nodded once.

He shifted his attention to me and said, "All the men have returned. We should set up camp. You and I," — he gestured between us — "are not done here."

Misneach snarled again at Silas's tone, but he ignored him and stalked off in Cillian's direction, barking orders as he went.

Emmerson released a breath from beside me and I jumped, having forgotten she was there.

"As far as things go, that wasn't too bad."

I whirled on her. "Not too bad. He is fuming. He looked about ready to throttle me."

"Well yeah," she shrugged, as if that explained everything.

"Just wait until Cillian gets a hold of you," I said, pointing my finger in her general direction, needing to share my unease.

"Please," she drawled. "I've kicked Cillian's ass once already. I doubt his ego is ready for me to do it again." She buffed her nails on her tunic. "You shouldn't let Silas go all... Silas on you. You're the gods-damned heir to a kingdom, Harlowe. Act like it."

Misneach made a noise that sounded like a chortle.

"He gets it," Emmerson said, hoisting her thumb over her shoulder in Misneach's direction.

I was getting a headache, and I rubbed at my temples, trying to relieve it.

"Look who's a big, bad Cathal."

I snapped my head up, taking in Zeke as he grinned. I lurched forward, flinging myself into his arms. I hadn't realized until this moment just how worried I had been about him. Zeke rubbed his hand up and down my spine, soothing me.

"The General is watching you and he does not look impressed," Misneach chuckled.

I glanced over Zeke's shoulder and saw Silas glaring at me from across the clearing. Let him. I was just glad that my friend was alright.

"Alright, alright," Emmerson said, pushing me out of the way and moving to hug Zeke. "Bring it in Z," she said as he wrapped her arms around him. "I'm glad you lived."

Zeke chuckled and said, "Don't get all sentimental on me now Em, it would throw me off kilter."

"So, did you bond, Zeke?" Emmerson asked impatiently.

"I did," he said, grinning.

"And?" Emmerson pressed.

"See that blue one with the bronze stripe down his front," he said, pointing out a dragon standing in a group of three others about twenty yards away. "I bonded with him. His name is Rónán."

I peered over at the dragon. It was clear he was on the larger side. His powerful legs were on full display, and he held himself in a manner that hinted at the strength within.

"He is very strong," Misneach confirmed in my mind. **"He will make a good bond mate for your friend."**

"I knew you could do it." I grinned at Zeke.

Turning his attention to me, Zeke said, "Tell me everything."

And so I did.

After I finished relaying the day's events, Zeke said, "I knew something was going on with those dragons. They kept watching you and every time you were around, they couldn't pull their focus away from you. Not to mention they didn't eat you that first day."

I snorted, recalling that first interaction.

"But what does it all mean?" he asked.

"I don't know. I don't think the dragons understand it entirely, either."

"Okay, so we'll figure it out."

Misneach dipped his head in agreement at Zeke's sentiment.

"So what happens now?" I asked Misneach.

"Caolán says we are to rest here overnight before returning to your palace home."

"What about tonight?" I asked.

"Some dragons will return to the mountains for rest. I will be wherever you are. I do not trust that General."

"He's just upset," I repeated.

"Be that as it may, I think I will spend my first night close to my bond mate."

I lifted my shoulders in a half-shrug, signaling it did not bother me either way.

I watched as Silas guided his men in assembling a tent. We hadn't used a tent the last time we camped. Perhaps he needed some privacy to discuss plans with his men. Another thought quickly entered my mind. Maybe he wanted privacy for whatever discussion he had planned for me the moment he could get me alone.

Dread filled me, but then I remembered Emmerson's earlier words. I was heir to Valoren. He might be a General in Pyrithia, but while he was in my kingdom, I outranked him.

Misneach growled in approval.

I straightened my shoulders and headed towards the main fireplace where dinner was being prepared.

I was thankful to realize Misneach didn't mean he was literally going to stick to my side. He remained with the other dragons by the lake.

"Close enough to intervene should it be necessary, Fire Heart," he replied to my thoughts.

"That's going to take some getting used to," I muttered.

"It would be less awkward if you stopped vocalizing half our conversation out loud."

"What do you mean?" I asked... out loud.

"I speak to you in your mind. You can do the same in mine. You don't need to say what you are thinking out loud. I can already hear it when the thoughts first take shape in your mind."

"Oh," I said and then cringed when I realized I said it out loud again.

Misneach just huffed a breath in amusement.

As we ate our meal around the fire, we were regaled with stories of how the soldiers found their dragons. Some were straightforward, others felt like they were from an adventure epic. Plenty of missteps abounded and death-defying feats ensued. On and on the adventure went until the epic conclusion where the Cathal found their bond mates.

"Some did not bond dragons?" I whispered to Zeke as I noticed they skipped some soldiers in the retelling.

"No. Some soldiers said they could sense their bond mate was somewhere else. The Cathal are already planning a journey to the Mountains of Dragonia upon our return for those who still wish to bond."

"Does that mean some soldiers no longer wish to bond a dragon?"

Zeke nodded and said, "They have decided that the life of a Cathal is not for them."

Emmerson snorted and added, "I can't imagine why." She had not been fond of the brief time she had spent on the back of Misneach.

Zeke nudged her with his shoulder. "I don't know Em, I can picture you on the back of a dragon. You would be one badass Cathal."

"Please," Emmerson said, rolling her eyes. "I'm a badass, period."

Zeke and I both laughed. She wasn't wrong.

Silas caught my eye from where he sat across from me. He inclined his head towards the erected tent and beckoned me to follow.

Our showdown resulted in the need for privacy, after all.

At least it sat back a bit from the camp. Hopefully, those gathered would not hear the dressing down I was about to receive. Or the princess-sized one I intended to return if necessary.

"I'll see you both in the morning," I said to Emmerson and Zeke as I made my way towards the tent.

"Kick his ass!" Emmerson called behind me.

I locked eyes with Silas. He had a single eyebrow raised, which told me he had heard Emmerson's inspired words.

Perfect.

Head held high, I prepared for battle.

Chapter Twenty-Three

Silas held the flap of the tent open for me as I made my way inside. Two bed rolls were already laid out, and I assumed this was where we would spend the night.

I took a seat on one of the bedrolls, and crossed my legs beneath me, bracing my elbows on my thighs, as I waited for him to start.

Silas studied me briefly before exhaling. "I should spank your ass for the shit you pulled today."

I didn't respond, no longer buying into his bullshit.

My non-response seemed to agitate him as he hissed, "Do you know what would have happened to me and my men if I had returned to Valoren without the heir apparent?"

Actually, no. I hadn't thought about that.

If I had died, my father would have blamed the Cathal thinking it to be an attack on Valoren instead of my own stupidity. I didn't plan on conceding that, however. Instead, I said, "You had witnesses. Everyone saw you tell me to remain behind. Zeke would have vouched for you."

Silas scoffed. "You think your little fuck boy would save us, woman?" he said, his voice dangerously calm.

Again, I didn't take the bait. Silas wanted a screaming match because he knew how to dominate. He knew overwhelming intensity that made people cower in his presence. But I was done playing his game. Emmerson, Zeke, my father, they were all right. It was time I wielded the power of my station.

"Silas," I began. "You should reconsider the way you speak to me. As you just pointed out, I am the heir apparent, and I outrank you while you remain in Valoren."

Silas's eyes narrowed into slits, and I had to resist the urge to swallow. Instead, I straightened, lifting my chin.

Silas darted forward, and gripping my throat in his large hand, he lifted me from the floor to stand before him.

"Do I have to remind you I am King inside these walls, Princess?" he spat.

Yes, please!

I shook my head to disperse the lust clouding my determination. I refused to submit.

"Silas, I don't want to spar with you. It happened. I'm alive, and there is no undoing this."

His eyes darted between my own; searching. He seemed to consider my words and I could see the fight leaving him as he worked to calm his anger, recognizing the significance of what had transpired today.

"Tell me what happened out there today, Harlowe," he said, as he removed his hand from my throat.

I repeated the story, just as I had when I'd told Zeke earlier.

Silas blew out a breath, mulling it all over in his mind.

"What does any of this mean? How can you be connected to every dragon here?" he asked.

"I don't know," I answered, honestly.

"Are all dragons affected, or just the ones from Valoren?"

"Well, didn't Caolán say he felt connected to me? He hails from the mountains of Pyrithia, not Valoren. I don't know if that means I'm connected to every single dragon in the realm, but it seems it's not contained to Valoren, at least."

"Maybe it's because he is in Valoren. Perhaps when dragons are in your territory, you can somehow... feel them," he pondered.

Silas studied me for a long while before saying, "We need to contain this. I asked Caolán to caution the other dragons against informing their Cathal about what occurred today."

"Why?" I asked, suddenly concerned.

"Until we know more, it is best to keep this between us and those who already know. This is big, Harlowe. Who knows where this could lead? Whenever power is up for grabs, you can't underestimate what some people might do to obtain it."

A sobering thought.

"Everyone will know I have bonded a dragon when we return home."

"Being bonded to one dragon is different from being connected to many," Silas said.

I nodded my head in understanding.

"Okay. So, we're good then?" I asked, waving a finger between us.

A familiar, wicked smirk pulled up the corner of Silas's mouth.

"Are you asking if I intend to punish you for your disobedience, Little Menace?" he purred.

Silas moved towards me. Very much the predator cornering his prey.

My core turned molten, and I swallowed.

"I mean, that wasn't what I was asking, but I can't complain about the direction this discussion is taking."

Silas laughed huskily. "I think I might enjoy your punishment as much as you do."

Without warning, Silas pulled me down to the ground, gripping my ass as he sat me in his lap.

"Untie my pants, Harlowe," he said as he nipped at my earlobe. Silas trailed soft kisses down my neck as I reached for his pants, trying to untie them as he'd ordered. The hard length of him pressing into my core, causing that delicious friction, made it difficult to concentrate, however.

"Need some help there Harlowe," he crooned, as he thrust his hips into my center. I gasped and then moaned as he rubbed himself against me.

I untied his laces and reached into his pants, freeing his glorious cock. I licked my lips. Silas's gaze dipped to my mouth as I did so.

"Take me in your mouth, Little Menace," he instructed.

I shifted backward off his lap, giving myself space, as I leaned down and ran my tongue over the head. Silas hissed in pleasure.

Wrapping my lips around his cock, I took him into my mouth, letting him slide down my throat before gagging at the intrusion.

"Fire Heart?" Misneach asked, concerned.

Caught by surprise, I spluttered in shock and almost ended up choking on Silas's dick.

Death by dick, how mortifying.

"Are you okay, Harlowe?" Silas asked once I had recovered.

"Misneach," I supplied by way of answer.

Realization dawned on Silas's face, and a small smirk lifted the side of his lips.

"Fire Heart?" Misneach tried again. **"What's wrong? What are you..."** he trailed off with a growl.

"A warning would have been appreciated," Misneach grumbled. **"I'll give you some privacy."**

I winced at the awkwardness of the situation. Never had I envisioned a moment like this playing out. Ever. Silas did not share in my embarrassment, as masculine pride emanated from him in waves.

"Tell the General not to take long. I dislike being cut off from you when in unfamiliar company."

"Uh-huh," I squeaked.

It would be a cold day in hell before I repeated Misneach's instructions not to dally.

"Is he gone?" Silas asked.

"I think so."

Silas grinned, before looking back at his cock, standing proudly at full mast. My core throbbed in excitement.

I resumed my ministrations, using my mouth to pleasure Silas while squeezing his balls in my hand. When he came, he groaned his release, fisting his hands in my hair as he did so.

Silas pushed me onto my back, making quick work of removing my clothes, and then plunged two fingers inside me. When I climaxed, he muffled the sound with a hungry kiss, maintaining his rhythm as I rode out my release.

By the time we had finished reaching oblivion for a second time, his body atop mine, I was exhausted. Not only from sex but also from the feelings threatening to overwhelm me.

Tomorrow, we would be returning home. To my father's fury. To Kieran.

That last thought had me shivering, and Silas wrapped his arms around me. I didn't want to play his games anymore, no matter what I had promised my father. I had to figure out a way to extricate myself from Kieran's orbit without injuring the relationship with one of our closest allies.

No pressure, I thought, as I allowed myself to drift off to sleep.

Chapter Twenty-Four

"No," Emmerson said, her mouth pressed into a tight line.

"It's me or Cillian, Emmerson. Pick."

"I don't see why I can't just ride Rogue back with the others. I can handle myself and it would only be a few days' delay," she huffed.

I sighed, pinching the bridge of my nose to ward off the growing headache. When we packed up camp this morning, I had told Emmerson she could fly home with me on Misneach, and she had flat-out refused. Cillian had tried to coax her into flying on Oisín with him, and she had told him that while she trusted him to bring her to orgasm, that did not mean she trusted him with her life. Failure to climax, she argued, could easily be rectified with her own skillful fingers, while failure to remain on a dragon... not so much. The raucous laughter that followed had Cillian glaring murder, but true to form, Emmerson was unfazed.

"Please Emmerson," I begged. "I can't face the wrath of my father without backup. Besties support each other's poor decisions, remember? This is part of the gig."

Emmerson tipped her head back, groaning. I knew if anything would convince her, it would be duty.

"I could just carry her in my jaws," Misneach offered, amused by her fear of flying.

"Not necessary," I told him. I had finally stopped communicating with Misneach aloud every time he spoke to me. Once I had the hang of it, it quickly became instinct.

Emmerson returned her gaze to me and said, "Fine. But only so you don't take credit for my fabulous idea of tagging along in my absence."

I grinned and reached down to grab her hand as I pulled her up onto Misneach's back behind me.

"I'm not sure we are at risk of anyone thinking this particular idea was fabulous," I told her.

"Why not? We now have a badass Cathal as the heir apparent. Valoren just got a whole lot deadlier."

Perhaps she had a point.

"Wrap your arms around me, okay? I'm secure on Misneach, so as long as you are secure to me, you'll be fine."

Emmerson held my chest so tightly, I had to force her to loosen her grip, otherwise I might just asphyxiate before we made it home.

"Okay, now that everyone is settled," Silas shouted from the back of Caolán. "It is about a six-hour flight back to Valoren and we'll only be stopping for the dragons to rest. Caolán and I will lead the formation with the Pyrithia Cathal flanking. Everyone else is to follow behind us."

Misneach snorted, displeased with taking orders from Silas.

"He threatened you, Fire Heart. That's not something I'll easily forgive."

"I told you already, he was just upset," I said, rolling my eyes. We had already been over this... repeatedly.

"That is beside the point," Misneach muttered.

"You're sounding an awful lot like a bratty teenager right now," I teased.

"I'll have you know I am a quarter of a century old," he huffed.

"Seriously? Isn't that young for a dragon?"

"I may be young Fire Heart, but you shouldn't underestimate what I'm capable of!"

I grinned to myself as I realized I now had a best friend and a dragon with matching personalities. I was so fucked!

At that moment, Caolán launched into the sky, with the rest of the dragons following.

"Hold on," I told Emmerson as Misneach prepared to launch.

And then we were flying.

It was exhilarating now that I wasn't only focused on surviving the journey. I still feared falling, but I trusted Misneach not to let me.

"You will need to train when we return to your home. Remaining on my back alone is inadequate. To become a battle queen, you must master aerial warfare," he advised.

Things were going to get a lot more interesting, I thought as excitement coursed through me.

We took a break three hours into the journey for the dragons to rest and hydrate. Emmerson didn't waste any time getting clear of Misneach and headed towards the lake to freshen up. When it was time to remount, she made it abundantly clear what she thought of the situation… again.

Since we were nearing Valoren, I deemed it wise to warn Misneach of a possible unwelcoming reception due to how we joined the party. I didn't want him to eat my father when he lost his shit at me upon sight.

"My father did not want me to go along with the Cathal when they left to seek out the dragons," I said. **"He will be furious at me for disobeying him."**

"He should be proud you were successful. No one from Valoren has bonded in centuries," Misneach countered.

"I get that. But my father won't see it that way. He didn't want me to risk my life by going along. He had also made other plans for me, but I left without explaining." Misneach only chuckled.

"You are worthy of your name, Daughter of War and Ashes."

"I don't even know what that means, but it's beside the point right now. I just need you to promise you won't eat my father when he starts lecturing me. He will not harm me. No matter what it might look like. Okay?" I finished.

Misneach ignored me and said endearingly, **"It means you are trouble and mayhem, Fire Heart."**

"I don't know if that was supposed to be a compliment or a criticism, and if it's a compliment, that's… problematic. And besides, you're evading. Promise me Misneach."

When Misneach remained silent, I pushed, **"Misneach."**

"I give you my word," Misneach said in a tone that sounded an awful lot like a whine.

"I do not whine," he snapped, and I chuckled.

The palace came into sight up ahead, and my anxiety spiked thinking about what I would say. I didn't want to get into an argument in front of everyone, but I wasn't sure that my father would afford me that opportunity.

The dragons leading the formation started to descend as I said to

Emmerson, "Well, this should be fun." I thought I heard her speak, but it quickly turned into a yelp when Misneach dove toward the ground.

He landed a little less gracefully than I was used to, and I suspected that the jarring descent was for Emmerson's benefit.

The chuckle that sounded in my mind was all the confirmation I needed.

"Bad dragon," I scolded. Misneach peered at me over his shoulder and gave me an exaggerated roll of his eyes.

"Where is she?" my father bellowed from up ahead. I couldn't see him beyond all the dragons in front of me, but his tone left no confusion regarding how he felt about my little expedition.

The crowd ahead parted down the center, creating a path directly to me. My father was standing on the palace steps, his face a mask of blazing fury, flanked by my mother on one side and Kieran on the other.

I made my way towards my father, Emmerson, on my left, looking as though she didn't have a care in the world. I realized Misneach had followed me when my mother's eyes widened in shock.

"Hello, Father. Would you like to accompany me inside so that we can catch up?"

"Cathal," my mother breathed, her voice barely above a whisper. Every head swiveled in her direction as she looked at Misneach, and then me.

"He is yours, isn't he Harlowe? You bonded a dragon." The shock was still there, but something else shone from the depths of her eyes as she took me in. Pride.

"Or she," my mother added.

I nodded my head and said, "His name is Misneach." My mother beamed at me, and I grinned right back.

"What is the meaning of this little stunt, Princess?" Kieran asked, drawing my attention to him. There was an iciness to his tone that made me uncomfortable. Misneach obviously detected the same thing I did because he bared his teeth and snarled at Kieran.

Those assembled on the palace steps recoiled at the obvious threat in Misneach's warning. All but my mother, who wore a small smirk, mirth twinkling in her eyes.

"Easy," I told Misneach as I placed a hand on his neck to calm him.

"He is dangerous Fire Heart. I can feel it radiating from him. If he moves to harm you, I will not hesitate to kill him." So the dragons could sense it, too.

Kieran held my gaze for a moment, eyes narrowed in displeasure, before he donned his mask of civility, and dipping his chin he said, "My apologies Harlowe. We were all very concerned about your welfare, as I am sure you can imagine."

Unlikely. I didn't know what game Kieran was playing, but my best interests were certainly not at the heart of it.

My father's fury seemed to abate somewhat, after Misneach's warning to Kieran.

As he took me in he said, "Come daughter, I am sure you are tired from your journey." He held out his hand to me, although some twenty steps separated us.

Turning my full attention to Misneach, I said, **"I am safe here, so you can take this time to rest. The other dragons often return to the mountains that surround the villages, but you are welcome to remain anywhere that suits you."**

"I will remain close, Fire Heart. This may be your home, but there are vipers slithering." He flicked his gaze towards Kieran, and I nodded in understanding.

Turning to Emmerson, I said, "Do. Not. Leave. Me."

"Never," was her only reply. Like Misneach, she had yet to peel her gaze from Kieran.

We started our ascent towards my father when I noticed Zeke had joined me on my other side. I glanced at him, and he nodded once. A silent message that he, too, would stand beside me.

When we reached my father, he thrust his hand toward the entryway of the palace and said, "We have many things to discuss."

Chapter Twenty-Five

My father led us into his study, where we remained for hours. First, he chastised me for my recklessness and failing to meet the expectations of my station when I abandoned my responsibilities on a 'whim'. He was referring to his expectation that I entertain Kieran during his visit.

My mother had insisted this discussion was a family affair, despite Emmerson and Zeke remaining by my side, and refused to allow Kieran to join us. Kieran had sulked off, irritated at being left out.

After my father had unburdened himself, the discussion turned to what had happened and how I bonded with a dragon. I relayed the story, leaving out the part about all the dragons feeling some sort of connection to me. I did not trust that my father would not share this information with Kieran, not understanding the danger he posed. For their part, Emmerson and Zeke gave no indication that the tale was incomplete.

My mother gushed over me and Zeke for a time, telling me how proud she was of what I had accomplished, and eventually, my father had to concede he, too, was impressed, albeit begrudgingly. I could almost hear Emmerson thinking, "Told you. Fabulous idea!" but she contained herself.

After we were released from my father's study, he gave us instructions to meet the following morning to review some of the final preparations for my birthday ball in two days, which had been delayed because of my absence.

Outside, Emmerson, Zeke, and I all exchanged a look before exhaling in relief.

"Thank you both for coming with me."

Zeke gave a slight nod, and Emmerson squeezed my hand. I choked up for a moment, feeling grateful knowing the two of them had my back.

"Do you want me to return the favor when you see your father?" I asked Emmerson.

She rolled her eyes. "He might look big and scary, but with me, he's a kitten."

"One that'll claw you to death," I caught Zeke muttering under his breath.

Emmerson just laughed and lifted a shoulder in a shrug.

"Harlowe," a voice sounded from behind us. "A word."

We froze and turned towards Kieran, who had emerged from the shadow of the alcove.

"We're heading to the dining hall," I said, searching for an excuse to avoid being alone with him.

"Excellent. I will walk you." The gleam shining in his eyes was unsettling.

I hesitated, turning to look at Emmerson and Zeke.

"I promise I will not keep you from your friends for long. Just a moment of your time is all I need."

I knew they would both refuse to leave my side if I so much as gave them a hint of how uneasy I felt around Kieran. But that would cause more trouble than a simple conversation was worth. I was probably making something out of nothing.

"Sure," I managed. I nodded to Emmerson and Zeke to go on ahead.

Kieran approached me, taking my arm in his as he led us towards the dining hall.

"I must say, Princess, I was disappointed to have my engagements with you left... unfulfilled. I do hope that you intend to make it up to me."

I glanced at him out of the corner of my eye but said nothing. Kieran slid his arm down my own until he clasped my hand in his. His grip was tight. Uncomfortable.

As he tightened his hold on my hand, he continued, "You and I need to get to know one another, Harlowe. We have a long future ahead of us."

"And what is that supposed to mean?" I said, my voice hardening along with his grip.

His wicked grin had my stomach doing back flips, and not in a good way.

"Our kingdoms are allied, are they not? I hope they remain that way, dear Harlowe," he purred.

Was that a threat I detected under his calm veneer? What would he do if I didn't comply? Withdraw from the alliance?

Almost at the dining hall now, he pulled me up short, taking my other hand in his. He moved his fingers around my wrists and gripped me so tightly, I had to fight a wince.

"Let me go, Kieran," I demanded.

A menacing growl sounded inside my head.

"What is happening Fire Heart? Why are you in distress?"

"Tell Rónán to send Zeke back outside. He will understand the message," I pleaded.

Misneach growled again.

"Harlowe, Harlowe, Harlowe. What am I to do with you?" Kieran mused.

"You don't need to do anything with me," I snapped.

He raised a brow and smirked venomously.

His grip tightened around my wrists again and I didn't think I could take the pain much longer. I could feel the bones rubbing against one another. They would eventually snap under the pressure.

"Let me go," I said. This seemed to please Kieran as his smirk grew into a grin.

"I believe the Princess asked you to release her," Zeke said from behind me.

I almost sagged in relief.

Startled, Kieran released his grip but did not let me go.

Zeke stared pointedly at my wrists before returning his gaze to Kieran's.

"This does not concern you, boy," Kieran spat.

"I think you'll find it does," Zeke replied.

Kieran studied Zeke, taking his measure before returning his cold, blue eyes to me. Anger blazed within them, but there was possessiveness, too. And it was the latter that had me swallowing.

Kieran released me and said, "Until tomorrow, Harlowe."

He gave a slight bow and strode off down the hall.

Zeke was at my side a moment later.

"Are you okay?" he asked, placing his hand on the small of my back and leading me into the dining hall.

I swallowed before answering, "Yes. Thank you for coming."

Zeke's jaw flexed before he said, "That guy is a piece of shit. He's well known for hurting women, and your father agreed to let him court you."

Quiet fury was simmering below the surface of Zeke's composure and at that moment, I realized how unfair my father had been to ask this of me. He knew of Kieran's reputation, everyone did. And yet, he had tried to play it off as mere rumor.

I rubbed at my wrists, which would surely bruise, and sent a mental thank you to Misneach down the bond.

Zeke caught the movement, and a low growl left his throat.

"I'm okay," I said, trying to placate him.

"It's not right, Harlowe. He has no right to treat you so," he hissed low so only I could hear.

As we neared our usual table, already full of the Cathal and Emmerson, I quietly added, "He'll be gone soon."

Emmerson looked at me, concern etching her features as she picked up on the tension surrounding us.

I shook my head and mouthed, "Later."

She dipped her chin to acknowledge she understood.

Tuning in to the excited chatter around us as the newest Cathal discussed flight and battle lessons, I allowed myself to get excited for the days ahead.

Chapter Twenty-Six

Preparations for the ball and flight lessons consumed the next couple of days. The flight lessons were exhilarating and Misneach was impressed by the progress I was making. The exhilaration did not fend off the exhaustion, however, and when the night of the ball arrived, all I wanted to do was crawl under my bed covers and sleep for days.

I was not so fortunate, however, I thought to myself, as I sat at my vanity while Louise readied me for the evening.

Tonight I was wearing a beautiful silver gown with a tight bodice that flared into a flowing skirt at my waist. The sleeves of the gown were long, reaching my wrists, and the sweetheart neckline showed a modest amount of cleavage. Sewn throughout the dress were small white diamonds that sparkled when they caught the light. Pinned within the intricate braid atop my head was a matching tiara, small but regal.

I wore more makeup than I was used to, with powder covering my smattering of freckles across my nose. Blush adorned my cheeks, and my eyes were lined in kohl. A light brush of powder the same shade as my dress topped my eyelids. My lips were painted in a delicate rose hue and my fingernails had been painted to match.

I looked beautiful. I looked like a queen.

Louise had taken her leave, and I sat in my chambers procrastinating as much as I could, trying in vain to delay the inevitable. Kieran waited for me downstairs to escort me to the ball. I had tried to explain to my father why I no longer wanted to have him escort me, but he had insisted that Kieran must not have realized he was hurting me during our discussion two days prior.

I doubted that very much.

I had opted not to tell Silas about the incident after Emmerson had been frothing at the mouth when I informed her. I had partly agreed to Kieran remaining as my escort to settle Emmerson down. If I was combative towards him, Emmerson would have been ready to wage a one-woman war. As much as I loved her for it, I did not want to risk her neck if she attacked the ruler of Netheran while in our home. So here I was, delaying the inevitable at an event that was supposed to celebrate my birthday.

I gathered my strength and stepped out of my chambers, plastering a smile on my face. I acknowledged the soldiers bowing to me as I made my way to the staircase that would lead me into the ballroom.

Standing at the foot of the staircase, dressed in black dress slacks, black boots, a cream-colored tunic, and a tailored navy coat, was Kieran. His snow-colored hair was tied at the nape of his neck, exposing the tattoos on the side of his throat. When he heard my approach, he turned to look at me, a small grin playing on his supple lips.

He was beautiful. But even as I took him in, a chill ran up my spine as his cunning blue eyes assessed me.

Kieran's gaze followed me as I made my way down the staircase. Every inhale of breath, every swish of my skirts, the flutter of my eyelashes, he took it all in; calculating. When he was done, he smiled roguishly, as if preparing to consume me whole.

He held out his hand to me, and I reluctantly placed my hand in his. He brought his lips to my knuckles and placed a chaste kiss on them.

"You look ravishing tonight Harlowe," he said huskily.

"Thank you," I replied rigidly.

He crooked his elbow, and I placed my arm through his. As we approached the entryway to the ballroom, our arrival was announced to the awaiting guests. Loud cheers erupted as we stepped over the threshold, and I forced myself to smile at those who had come together to celebrate my birthday.

I spotted Emmerson right away, glaring at Kieran over the lip of her glass. Cillian, to my surprise, was standing with her. Dressed in his finery, he was a sight to behold.

Next, I spotted Zeke who stood with my parents and Samuel, Emmerson's father, along with a congregation I recognized from the Kingdom of Elysarah, my mother's birth kingdom. I nodded in their direction, and they returned the gesture.

I scanned the crowd, looking for the soulful brown eyes with the perfectly arched brows. The hint of dark stubble adorning his chiseled jawline, and the sinful smirk that enhanced his full lips. But Silas was nowhere I could see.

"Looking for someone, my dear Harlowe?" Kieran purred against my ear, which sent shivers racing down my spine. Unlike the shivers I experienced when Silas whispered sweet nothings to me, these shivers filled me with apprehension.

"Just taking in my guests," I lied. Kieran chuckled darkly, aware it was a lie.

"We should greet my parents," I said as I directed us towards them.

"Harlowe, you look amazing," my mother said as she pulled me into a tight hug.

Kieran did not release my arm as she did so, which became awkward as I attempted to return the gesture.

My mother narrowed her eyes on him, and he smirked at her.

My father gripped me next, pulling me against him as he whispered, "You look stunning, daughter," and he kissed the top of my head.

I pulled my arm out of Kieran's hold this time and embraced my father.

Zeke leaned in to kiss my cheek, followed by Samuel. Samuel had always had a soft spot for me, having watched me growing up alongside Emmerson. He was like a stern uncle who only melted for his girls. My mother made quick introductions to the visiting contingent from Elysarah, and I felt myself relaxing.

Emmerson made her way over to me and introduced Cillian to her father. I was not certain that Samuel understood just how acquainted the Cathal was with his daughter, but Cillian was the picture of proprietary and respect.

I peered over at the dance floor where couples were swaying and twirling with the music as it filled the air. The light overhead cast a soft glow over the dancers, making them appear ethereal as they moved in perfect synchronicity, gliding across the polished floor. Emmerson and Cillian soon joined them, and I found myself enthralled by the gracefulness of their forms.

Kieran approached me, extending his hand, and I felt my heart race in my chest.

"May I have this dance?"

I could feel the weight of my father's gaze as he waited expectantly, noting the slight hesitation before I took Kieran's hand. Swallowing my disgust, I smiled and let him lead me into the center of the dance floor.

Kieran pulled me flush against his muscled chest, and I wrapped my arms around his neck.

"Are you enjoying yourself, Harlowe?" Kieran asked in a low, throaty whisper.

"I am, thank you," I said, although it was a lie. He chuckled as he spun us.

Kieran ran his hand down my back as he leaned in, his lips against my ear, and whispered, "I thought about you incessantly while you were off on your little adventure with the Cathal."

My spine stiffened, and he chuckled at my response.

"Come now Harlowe, you have to know you are a beautiful woman. I would very much like to take you home with me when I depart in a few days."

The thought of going anywhere with Kieran had bile rising in my throat.

I tried for diplomacy and said, "As lovely as I am sure your kingdom is, I am needed here."

He leaned back so he could look me in the eye and asked, "Is that so? And pray tell sweet Harlowe, what does your father have to say on the subject?"

"My father wants me to focus my energies on learning about my kingdom, and what it means to rule it."

Kieran narrowed his eyes, and something akin to malice flashed within their icy depths.

"Is that right?" he asked darkly. "What has he told you of your duty?"

I opened my mouth to answer but cut myself off when my eyes collided with chocolate brown ones as they peered at me over Kieran's shoulder.

Dipping his head in a slight bow, Silas asked, "May I cut in?"

He didn't allow Kieran to respond as he twirled me out of his grasp and across the room. His eyes glistened with mischief as he smiled at me. His grip was firm as he pulled me against him and everything fell away as we moved to the music, controlled by the rhythm as it wrapped around us.

Silas, I noted, was an excellent dancer.

"You dance as well as you fight," I said breathlessly.

He beamed at me, and I knew I would do just about anything to keep that smile on his face. Silas was gorgeous at the best of times, but when he smiled, he was exquisite.

"You look beautiful, Harlowe," he praised, and I saw the awe in his expression as he took me in.

I blushed as I thanked him.

Silas continued to dance us around the room, surprising me with his knowledge of the different dances unique to Valoren.

"You are just full of surprises, aren't you?" I teased.

He leaned in, his cheek resting on mine as he said, "Oh Harlowe, you don't know the half of it."

His tongue darted out to brush the shell of my ear and I shivered in the way only Silas could make me.

"Tonight, in your chambers," he purred, "I'll show you a few of the other surprises I have in store for you."

I blushed, and he chuckled darkly.

Someone caught his attention over my shoulder, and he excused himself as I made my way to the edge of the dance floor. I grabbed a glass of champagne from a passing waiter and watched as the couples got lost in the music and each other.

I was smiling to myself, thinking of all the wicked things Silas would do to me later tonight when I felt a presence approach me from behind. I knew it was Kieran without turning around. His power filled any room he entered; suffocating and oppressive.

"Will you accompany me for a stroll in the gardens, my dear Harlowe?" Kieran said as he gripped my elbow.

"I think I should stay. It is my birthday celebration after all, and I haven't had the chance to thank everyone for coming."

"Nonsense," he said as he pulled me away from the safety of the crowd. "We will only be a moment."

I was outside before I could put up any resistance as Kieran led me deeper into the darkness of the night.

Panic engulfed me and I said, "I think we should get back."

Out of sight of any revelers and hidden in the shadows, Kieran turned, pinning me to the stone wall. His body caged me in.

"I will tell you this once and once only Harlowe, you belong to me. I own you. Any thoughts you have of the General warming your bed, ends here. You. Are. Mine."

I gasped both in shock and pain as he pushed me further into the wall, the open back of my dress allowing the stone to scrape against my flesh.

"I am not yours," I spat.

A cruel smile curved his lips as he said, "Oh, but you are sweet Harlowe. You have been my betrothed since infancy. Your father sold you to me in exchange for my allegiance and soldiers in the Skirmish of Power."

My breath faltered as I forgot how to breathe.

"What's wrong darling?" he crooned. "Did Daddy forget to mention the purpose of my visit? You are to become my wife. You will leave this kingdom behind and join me in Netheran after we are married in two days."

"No," I whispered in disbelief.

"No," I repeated, sounding stronger than I felt. "I will not marry you and I will not be leaving my kingdom."

Kieran's face contorted with fury as his hand snaked out and wrapped around my throat. The force of his grip had pain exploding where his fingers met my flesh. I tugged at his hand with both of mine, desperately trying to rip his hand away. My lungs burned as they screamed out for air, and dark spots danced in my vision.

"You will marry me, and you will come home with me, Princess. You best acclimatize quickly, or your new life will be off to a difficult start," he snarled in my face. "I like my women obedient, and those who disobey me find out why that isn't a good idea."

Frantic now, I clawed at his hand as I tried to pry it away. Kieran gnashed his teeth at me as he snarled again.

A deafening roar sounded behind us, and Kieran froze before peering over his shoulder. His grip loosened, and I sucked air into my starving lungs. Kieran released me and I took a single step away before falling to the ground, coughing, and wheezing as I reeled from Kieran's attack.

"Come to me, Fire Heart," Misneach said, coaxing me out of the fog that had captured my mind.

I lifted my head and saw Misneach standing mere feet away, eyes trained on Kieran, teeth bared and snarling viciously. And he wasn't alone. Flanking him on one side stood Rónán, his tall frame imposing, a menacing growl sounding from deep within him. On Misneach's other side stood Niamh, her head lowered, her body tense as she poised to attack.

I continued coughing as I crawled towards them until I was within the safety of Misneach's forelegs. The dragons continued to growl and snarl at Kieran as he watched them, readying his defenses.

"I will kill him for harming you," Misneach growled in my mind.

"Leave him. He has dangerous magic. I fear what he is capable of."

"He is not more dangerous than I am, Fire Heart."

"Please, Misneach, take me away from here," I pleaded as I clumsily climbed onto his back.

One last vicious snarl escaped the dragon before he crouched low and launched skyward.

Chapter Twenty-Seven

I returned to my chambers, locking the doors from the inside, ensuring no one could enter. Misneach remained perched on the battlement that adjoined the balcony outside my rooms, and I could sense Rónán and Niamh close by.

Silas came to my chambers later in the night, just as he had promised, but I refused to open the door or even acknowledge his presence. I wasn't ready to see anyone just yet. My world was shattered, and I needed time to digest the fact that my parents had sold me to a psychopath.

Everything I thought I had been preparing for was a lie. I would not be the next ruler of Valoren if I was locked into a marriage contract with the King of Netheran. Would I be his Queen or his Consort? What was to become of Valoren? Was this all because I couldn't manifest the realm's power? Had my parents decided to try for another heir? But Kieran had said my betrothal had been established as part of an alliance when I was an infant. This wasn't a recent development borne out of my parent's disappointment in the heir I was turning out to be. No, this betrayal had been a long time coming.

Why had I spent years training to become queen one day if they had already sold me off to the highest bidder?

Whoever said your training was for Valoren, an insidious voice inside of me jeered.

My father had been the one to insist I master the court protocols not just of Valoren, but also those of our allies. Netheran, it turns out. It had been my father who had insisted that I learn how to wield meekness and obedience as a weapon. Did he know I would need these skills to survive in Kieran's court? Is this why he kept the training arrangement with the Cathal a secret and prevented me from taking part? Was he aware that Kieran would not approve? He had never supported my combat training. It had been my mother who had insisted I knew how to defend myself. I thought I was training to one day lead my people as their battle queen. Perhaps my mother had also recognized I would require certain skills to survive Kieran and his debauchery.

No matter the reasons, they had both betrayed me.

Sleep eluded me as my thoughts raced rampant through my mind.

When dawn finally broke through the bleakness of the night, I rose from my bed and dressed for battle. I would confront my parents and demand an end to this madness.

I peered into the mirror and winced at the deep purple bruising that wrapped around my throat. The angry red welts had receded somewhat, but they were still visible amongst the bruising. It hurt to swallow, and I was certain that when I spoke, my voice would be rough and gravelly.

I chose a collared tunic to conceal the markings. Although not a complete mask, the collar hid most of my injuries. I did not dare apply makeup to those that remained visible, as I could not bring myself to brush against the bruising, knowing it would feel like my skin was on fire.

Not caring that the rest of the palace was slumbering, I marched towards my parent's chambers on the other side of the palace. Misneach circled the exterior walls, letting me know he was close by should I need him.

As I approached the doors to the King and Queen's rooms, the soldiers stationed outside moved to prevent my entry.

"I apologize, Your Highness, the King and Queen have not yet risen and are not to be disturbed," a young man, no older than twenty, advised me.

"Harlowe has always been an exception," a voice said from behind me.

Samuel, fully dressed in his general's uniform and sipping coffee from his mug, stopped beside me, kissing the top of my head. He nodded to the soldiers as he passed by them. The soldiers obeyed the silent order, stepping back and opening the doors wide.

I strode into my parent's antechamber and marched towards the doors leading to their bedchamber. Banging loudly, I waited for my father's grunt of acknowledgment before swinging the doors wide and storming in.

My mother's eyes widened, and panic filled her expression.

"Harlowe, what is it? What is wrong?" she started frantically. Pulling the covers away, she sat up and reached for her silk dressing gown before approaching me. She gasped when she took in the bruising on my neck and a delicate hand fluttered to her mouth.

Tears filled her deep blue eyes as she asked, "Who did this to you?"

My eyes narrowed. "My fiancé." The croaked sound my voice made had my father rushing to join her at my side. He took my shoulders and turned me towards him, taking stock of my injuries. Fury lit his gaze, and he took a step back, running his hand through his copper hair.

"Were you ever going to tell me?" I asked quietly. I observed their reactions carefully, which told me everything I needed to know. My mother closed her eyes and silent tears fell down her cheeks. My father could not meet my gaze, the guilt crippling.

I snickered. "Kieran tells me I am to marry him in two days' time and then I am to leave Valoren for Netheran."

Again, my parents remained silent.

"All those lessons you insisted on, your little pep talk about wielding meekness and obedience as a weapon. It was all to prepare me for a life at Kieran's mercy!"

My father lifted his head to meet my gaze, but still, he said nothing.

"You didn't want me to train in combat because you knew it would displease my soon-to-be master. You knew he has certain expectations of his women, and you have been trying to mold me into what he desires for years."

"Harlowe," my father said. The single word a warning. A warning I refused to heed. They were gambling with my life, and I intended to have a say.

"I will not yield to this, and if you had any love for me as a father should, you would not sell me off like a piece of cattle."

"It is not that simple, Harlowe. This is not something I wanted to do, but it was the only way to secure Kieran's allegiance during the Skirmish of Power. We needed his allegiance and his men to fend off the attack. I had to save my people, and Kieran was the only option. Without him, Valoren would have fallen, leaving no kingdom for you to inherit."

"I won't inherit it now," I screeched, or at least I tried to. The damage to my windpipe prevented me from raising my voice. "I cannot rule Valoren from Netheran."

"Once you wed, you will become Queen of Netheran. And once you have served Kieran for a time, I will recall you to Valoren and have you crowned as queen of our kingdom. As the sole ruler of Valoren, we will need you here and you will have to spend most of your time in our kingdom," my father explained.

A deranged sort of laugh escaped me in response to my father's declaration. "You are fooling yourself, father. Kieran will never allow me to leave, no matter what you try to convince yourself of to the contrary. He made his intentions clear last night when he told me he owned me."

My father tensed, and his face darkened with rage. My own fury bubbled within me. He knowingly chose me as his sacrifice, despite knowing what kind of man Kieran was.

"Don't act so surprised, Father. You knew what he was like. Everyone knows what he is like. You tried to pretend it was otherwise so you could delude yourself into believing your plans would all work out in the end, and that everything would be alright. It won't. Kieran is cruel, and he is powerful. You knew this when you sold me to him as an infant, and nothing has changed."

"Please try to understand Harlowe. Our kingdom was suffering," my father pleaded. "Kieran was the only ally willing to aid us against those who planned to conquer us. I had to do whatever I could to save our kingdom, no matter the cost."

I snorted. "Except, you're not the one who will have to pay that cost, now are you, Father," I said, the derision clear in my tone.

My father's spine straightened. "I will speak with Kieran. He will know my displeasure at his treatment of you —"

"Call off the engagement," I begged. "There must be another way."

My father ignored me. "I will make my expectations crystal clear to Kieran."

"You and I both know that any commitment you receive from Kieran will only be lip service. Once I am away from Valoren, he will no longer answer to you."

"Atticus," my mother began, but my father raised his hand, silencing her.

"I will not risk a war with Kieran," he seethed.

"You will marry him, Harlowe. I have given my word. He will, however, understand the consequences of what will follow should he harm you again."

"Oh, and what consequences would those be, Father?" I crossed my arms and raised a brow, waiting expectantly. If he was unwilling to risk a war with Kieran, then my father had already conceded his power to the King of Netheran. He had just failed to realize this.

My father narrowed his eyes on me but remained silent.

"That's what I thought," I snickered.

"Return to your chambers, Harlowe. I will send for you when I am ready to meet with Kieran."

I glowered at my father, and he returned my stare, unflinching. He was stubborn, but he was being unrealistic. There was no way in all the realm that Kieran would ever agree to let me leave him or his kingdom. His need for me extended far beyond his simple desire to possess me. I saw it in his eyes when he proclaimed me as his.

I realized that if I were going to escape Kieran, I would need to do it myself.

My father would not save me. It was time for me to stand on my own and defend my worth.

Chapter Twenty-Eight

The palace was still quiet as I made my way back to my chambers. A few servants had risen and were preparing for the day. Left to my own musings, I tried to work through the problem at hand.

Again, failing to heed Zeke's lessons, I was caught off guard when a calloused hand gripped my arm and pulled me into the shadows. Fear flooded my system as I fought off the hands that held me.

"It's only me, Little Menace," Silas whispered against my ear. "You're a skittish little thing today, aren't you?" he chuckled. My body instantly relaxed as I leaned into him.

Silas brushed his lips against my neck, and I winced when they pressed against my tender flesh. The action did not go unnoticed. Silas spun me around to face him, and pulled my collar away from my throat, taking in my injuries. His eyes darkened and a feral snarl escaped his lips.

"Who touched you, Harlowe?" Silas growled.

"Silas don't," I said but stopped when he let out another low growl, dripping with menace.

Apprehension prickled across my skin, and I realized at that moment just how deadly Silas was.

"I won't ask you again. WHO FUCKING TOUCHED YOU?" he roared.

I flinched before whispering, "Kieran."

"Fire Heart?" Misneach questioned, having sensed my discomfort.

"I'm alright. It's Silas. He is none too pleased by what Kieran did

last night," I told him.

"The General and I agree once," Misneach snarled in response.

"I'll fucking kill that bastard," he seethed, turning from me. Silas's voice was a low whisper, but the threat in his tone was deadly.

"Silas, for the love of the gods," I said, exasperated. "What do you intend to do? He is the King of Netheran for gods' sake."

He spun on me then, voice controlled as he said, "Nobody, not even the fucking King of Netheran, touches what is mine."

There it was again. Ownership. As if one could simply possess a human fucking being. The thought enraged me and had my hands balling into fists.

"You're just as bad as him! I am a person, Silas. I can't be fucking owned. What's more, I'm heir to this fucking kingdom. If anyone owns me, it's my subjects. You think you have some claim on me because we fuck? Newsflash dickhead, you don't."

Silas prowled towards me, pushing me flush against the stone wall, caging me in with his arms on either side of my head. I didn't back down from his intense gaze. I met his stare and raised my chin, daring him to challenge me.

"I don't think I have a claim to you because we fucked. I fucked you because I claimed you," he retorted. "I warned you, Princess, once we crossed that line, you would belong to me. And what did you do?" he purred huskily. "You begged for my cock. So yes Harlowe, you are mine, make no mistake about that. There is no going back for us. I won't allow it." His voice was rough, full of gravel.

I scoffed, unsure of how to even untangle what he had just declared.

"Your body knows who owns it," he continued, voice low and seductive. "It's evident every time your cunt drips with arousal when I command you to open for me." I tried not to tremble, knowing he would see the truth of his words.

"Every time your body trembles, just like that," he purred, running his fingertip over the curve of my breast. Silas moved his hand lower, yanking the laces of my pants open, and dipped his hand below the waist. I gasped and glanced around, ensuring no one was nearby.

Silas ran his finger up the entrance of my slit and then withdrew it. He placed his finger in his mouth and sucked, cleaning my arousal from the digit. "Mmm..." he growled. "Yes Harlowe, your body knows exactly who owns it, even if your mind hasn't caught on."

Silas pushed off the wall and turned on his heels, storming away.

Panting, I adjusted my pants and called after him, "What are you going to do, Silas?"

Without looking back, he just said, "To remind that prick of what happens when someone touches what belongs to me."

I blew out a breath. This whole situation was getting away from me.

"Men," I snorted as I started towards my chambers again. I was surrounded by a bunch of assholes all peacocking about, trying to lay claim to me. I'd let those fuckers walk all over me and bend me to their will.

But not anymore.

There was no denying the fact that I enjoyed it when Silas did it in the bedroom, but he was taking it too far. Trying to control me outside of the bedroom, asserting he had some claim on me simply because he decreed it. He had no claim on me. Kieran had no claim on me, and my father was delusional if he thought I would tolerate this. I was a woman, not an object to be owned or traded. There was no way this was going down how any of them thought it would.

"About time, Fire Heart," Misneach grunted inside my head. **"The power that lives within you is more potent than anything I have ever felt before. It cannot be suppressed. Let it out and show everyone who you truly are."**

"What the hell are you talking about, Misneach?" I questioned, flustered by everything coming at me all at once.

"There is a fire inside you. We all feel it, the dragons. You call us to you with that power. You just need to release it."

"I can't even sense fórsa, let alone wield it, Misneach. You have the wrong girl," I retorted.

"What you house is stronger than the power offered by the realm. It is fire and flame. It is war and ashes," he said with a certainty I did not understand.

I paused. **"Are you trying to tell me I have magic within me?"** I asked cautiously, not wanting to get my hopes up.

"What you have is more than magic. It is something else entirely," he replied. I threw my hands up in the air, frustration overtaking me once again.

"That doesn't help me, Misneach. You say the dragons sense something within me, what is it?"

"I do not know Fire Heart. All I know is that it is powerful and that it is linked to the energy of dragon folk. That is why all the dragons are drawn to you. It is up to you to discover what it is and how to

wield it.”

“So it is magic?” I mused.

“It is a weapon,” he countered.

“Insightful,” I muttered.

At least the dragons believed in me. Now I just had to figure my way out of this rapidly deteriorating shit show that was my life.

Chapter Twenty-Nine

Silas

The need for retribution coursed through my veins as I headed towards the guest chambers that fucker had been occupying. I knew Kieran had an interest in my girl, but I had no idea how unhinged he was when it came to her. The marks around her throat were a testament to that.

And now I was on a fucking warpath.

As I rounded the corner of the hallway, I almost crashed into Cillian and only managed to avoid a collision at the last second.

Cillian recovered quickly and then looked up at me, confused. He studied my expression, seeing something there that concerned him.

"Gods, Silas, what the fuck has you turned inside out?" he asked, worry etching his tone.

"Stay out of this, Cill," I warned, but he had already fallen into step beside me. He didn't ask me any more questions, already knowing there was no deterring me from my current path.

Cillian had been my best friend since childhood and my right-hand man for almost as long. We could communicate with just a glance. And the look on my face right now told him I was about to riot.

As we approached Kieran's chambers, a large contingent of guards moved into our path to stop us from reaching their King.

"Move out my fucking way or I swear to the gods above that I will end your miserable lives by ripping your entrails out through your throat."

"Vivid," a familiar voice chuckled from behind the guards, who remained unmoving.

I was pacing like a caged animal, waiting for any sign of weakness that would allow me to break free. I'm sure I looked half-crazed.

"Tell your guards to stand down and face me, you fucking bastard," I growled.

"Well look at this, the young pup has some bite after all," Kieran taunted as he appeared between his guards.

"Why are you surprised? Shouldn't you understand your own, seeing as you're a fucking animal," I spat.

Kieran threw his head back and laughed maniacally. The bastard really was unhinged.

When he stopped laughing, Kieran leveled me with a pointed glare and said, "Is there a reason you have come calling, General?"

"You touched what belongs to me," I snarled, pointing a finger at him. My whole body was vibrating with fury over what he had done to Harlowe.

Kieran's eyes darkened as he narrowed his gaze on me. "I'll tell you what I told the Princess last night, whatever you two had going on is done. She is MY bride!" he yelled while slapping his palm to his chest.

Power pulsed around me as I called fórsa to my fingertips. I wanted to end this mother fucker right where he stood.

"She has been mine since the moment she took her first breath," he continued. "Harlowe was a deal sweetener between myself and her father when we first entered an alliance during the Skirmish of Power, so you are wrong General, she belongs to me. Perhaps I should thank you since it was Pyrithia entering the war that forced the King's hand," he smirked.

A red haze descended across my vision, and I leaped forward, striking Kieran hard in the face. Blood gushed from his forehead as I hit him again and again, pulverizing his flesh with each blow. Kieran's guards tried to pull me off him, but I was lost to my own blood lust, unable to stop.

Boots connected with my ribs, my shoulders, and my head, but I felt none of it.

Over the sound of the blood pounding in my ears, I could make out Cillian shouting something as he engaged his own attackers. Beneath me, Kieran's hysterical laughter sent an icy chill running up my spine, but it was not enough to halt my attack. His hair was matted with blood and his teeth glistened with the metallic substance as he grinned up at me.

"Is that all you've got, boy?" Kieran asked as Cillian finally pulled me back.

Kieran stood, and as he did so, dark shadows swirled around him. They covered his feet before they slowly climbed up his body until he was concealed beneath the darkness.

"What the fuck?" I heard Cillian breathe from behind me.

As quickly as they had come, the shadows withdrew until they disappeared entirely.

Kieran raised an eyebrow. No evidence of the beating I had just unleashed on him moments ago, before sliding his gaze up and down my frame.

"Pity," he said, sounding almost disappointed.

My palms itched as small orbs of energy took shape in each hand. I could end the King of Netheran's reign right here, right now.

"Stop and think, Silas," Cillian hissed against my ear.

"You should heed your guard dog's advice," Kieran smirked.

"This doesn't help Harlowe," Cillian tried again.

"The fuck it doesn't," I snarled, not dropping my focus from Kieran's dead eyes. "I'll end the threat against her here and now."

"This isn't smart, Silas. Too many unknowns. Let's step the fuck back and regroup," Cillian said low so only I would hear.

Cillian tugged on my arm, dragging me backward as my eyes remained locked on the crazed fucker in front of me. As he turned me around, Cillian continued pushing me away from Kieran before I could change my mind.

"Oh and Silas," Kieran called after me.

"Keep walking," Cillian hissed.

"I'll be sure to show Harlowe just how much of an animal I truly am when I have her in my bed, beneath me."

I spun on my heels and launched an orb at the King of Netheran, missing his head by a hair's breadth.

"THAT WAS A FUCKING WARNING!" I roared. "Come near my girl again and I won't fucking miss."

Kieran's laughter followed me down the hall as Cillian used every ounce of strength he had left to keep me moving forward and away from the man behind me.

Once we were a reasonable distance away, Cillian released me as he ran a hand through his hair.

"What the fuck was that back there?" he asked. This had my footsteps halting mid-stride as I had never heard Cillian sound nervous or apprehensive before in his life.

Turning to face my best friend, I could see that he was very much unsettled by what he had witnessed Kieran do.

"I don't know," I said, continuing down the hallway leading to the dining hall. "That's a problem for another time. Right now, we need to step up our timeline."

"Is that a good idea?" Cillian said as he cast a glance my way from the corner of his eye. "We haven't laid the groundwork yet."

"Then we move with force," I snapped irritability.

Cillian knew better than to question my command, but I could sense his unease as it rolled off him in waves.

Upon entering the dining hall, I noticed Harlowe had not yet made an appearance.

"Where's the Princess?" I asked Emmerson, who had become a regular at our table during meals.

"She had a big night," she replied, shrugging. "Harlowe hates being the center of attention. She needs a breather before she can people again." Turning in her chair so that she was facing me, Emmerson continued, "And you'll leave her be Silas," she warned as she waved a spoon in my direction. "You can't know the pressure she's under and if she wants to take a break, you'll let her. Am I clear?"

I nodded my agreement, having no intention of letting things be, but the spitfire in front of me didn't need to know that. Emmerson was unwaveringly loyal to the Princess, something I was thankful for.

A plan began to take shape in my mind as I mulled everything over while I ate.

There was one thing that I knew with absolute certainty; my Little Menace belonged to me, and I'd tear the head off anyone who tried to take her from me.

Chapter Thirty

I had spent the better part of the morning plotting how I would get out of this situation without causing an all-out war. So far, my plans had been complete and utter failures. Emmerson was the strategist in our dynamic duo, and I wasn't ready to drag her into this mess for fear of her reaction.

All I knew was this; I wouldn't be marrying Kieran. There had to be another way. There had to be.

A loud knocking on my door interrupted my musings. My heart leaped into my throat at the sound, and a second knock quickly followed after I failed to answer the first. I took a deep breath to calm my racing heart and headed towards the door.

Four soldiers were waiting outside when I opened my door. I looked them over, unease settling within the pit of my stomach.

"We have been asked to come and collect you, Princess," one soldier said, signaling I should step into the hallway.

"For what purpose?" I questioned.

"The King said he needs to meet with you. He said you were aware of the meeting and were expecting his summons." I swallowed my nerves and stepped into the hallway, gesturing for the soldiers to lead on.

Two soldiers walked in front of me, while two walked behind me. I felt caged in, trapped, like a prisoner on my final death march. My thoughts did nothing to help relieve my growing panic.

Upon entering the throne room, I saw my father and my mother seated on their thrones atop the dais. Kieran stood to the side in front of them. I glanced at him, and he flashed me a roguish grin in reply.

"You summoned me," I said to my father as I reached the spot in front of him.

My father cleared his throat and began, "Kieran explained the events of last night and assured us that his conduct was out of the ordinary for him and would not happen again."

I scoffed, dropping my mouth open in astonishment. That was it. That was all it took to quell the fire that had been raging in my father's emerald depths this morning. So much for the consequences he had promised to deliver.

My father narrowed his eyes at me before directing his gaze towards Kieran and inclining his head.

Kieran turned to face me and said, "I must apologize for my behavior last night, my dear Harlowe. It was very much out of character for me and was in response to the knowledge that another man had been," — he paused and flicked his gaze in my father's direction before continuing — "intimate with my intended bride. I was caught in jealousy's wrath and acted poorly." He dipped his head in what I presumed was supposed to pass as contrition.

My face heated knowing that he had appraised my father of my relationship, or whatever it was, with Silas.

When Kieran raised his eyes to meet mine again, mirth twinkled in them, finding my discomfort humorous.

"First, I am not your anything," I said, regaining my composure. "Second, you had no right to lay a hand on me. And third, it is none of your business what I do, or with whom I do it. Despite what you and my father may have discussed, I am my person and cannot be bartered and sold."

"Harlowe," my father growled.

I spun on him, letting him see the condemnation burning in my eyes.

"No Father. I will not be married off to Kieran, or anyone else. You require my consent for the marriage to be binding, and I will not give it."

My father stood as he approached me, and I crossed my arms, standing firm. Kieran watched with amusement while my mother glanced between us, unsure who she should worry about.

"You will do this for your kingdom daughter," my father gritted out.

I narrowed my gaze at him and said, "No, I will not."

My father held my gaze, waiting to see if I would buckle under the intensity of his stare. I refused to do so.

My father returned to his throne and retook his seat. He motioned the soldiers who had escorted me from my chambers forward.

"Return my daughter to her room. Ensure that her balcony doors and windows are locked and that no one is given permission to enter her quarters."

"Atticus," my mother's high-pitched voice sounded against the blood pounding in my ears.

Locking his eyes with my own, my father said, "You will do your duty to your kingdom Harlowe. You will marry Kieran, and you will consent to the union. Until then, you will be confined to your rooms." He nodded, and the soldiers took hold of my arms.

"Atticus," my mother repeated. I couldn't hear my father's response as they escorted me out of the room. Servants stopped to stare as they took in my captors, their hands gripping me. They were not rough, but their hold was firm.

Upon reaching my chambers, one soldier entered while I waited outside with the remaining men. I presumed he was securing my windows and doors, as instructed. Once he returned, he escorted me inside and promptly locked the doors behind me.

I was reeling, unsure of what to do next. I had not expected my father to be so callous towards me. Now, I found myself locked inside my rooms with no way to escape.

"What happened, Fire Heart?" Misneach asked, his tone reflecting my distress. I recounted the events in the throne room and Misneach snarled his displeasure.

"I will burn down the entire palace to get you out of there."

"Thanks, but that's not the approach I'm aiming for," I said despondently. **"Violence only ever ends up harming the innocent people who get caught in the crosshairs, and I vowed to protect my subjects. I won't risk even one life needlessly."**

A low growl echoed inside my head, his anger clear.

"Promise me you won't do anything without my agreement, Misneach," I commanded. A moment passed before he responded.

"I promise, Fire Heart," he paused before continuing. **"But I also promise you this; I will not let any harm come to you. And that includes at the hands of your father."** Another snarl sounded, this time on the battlement outside my now prison.

I lay on my bed, trying to process all that had happened since last night. What could have been minutes or hours later, I heard shouting coming from behind my locked doors.

"Open this door right fucking now, before I run you through with my blade." A pause sounded and then, "I don't give two fucks what your orders are. LET ME THROUGH!" Emmerson bellowed.

I jumped up from my bed and raced to the door.

"Emmerson," I shouted as I tried the handle. Still locked.

"Harlowe. Thank the gods. Are you okay?"

"I'm not sure how to answer that right now," I said.

"What is going on?" she pressed.

Unsure of how much I should be screaming through the locked door, I said, "My father wants me to do something that I can't do. He has sequestered me to my rooms in the hopes I will change my mind. I can't say too much at the moment, Emmerson. See if you can visit me and I'll tell you everything."

"Okay, Harlowe. Hang tight, okay."

"I can't exactly go anywhere, Em," I laughed bitterly.

"Right," she said, guilt plain in her tone.

"Don't worry about me, Emmerson. I'm alright. I am going to be alright," I said, half trying to convince myself of that. "Emmerson," I hesitated, wanting to get a message to Silas but not wanting to alert Kieran or anyone else to that fact. Deciding it was too risky, I said, "Don't do anything reckless, okay?" worried she would do exactly that.

Emmerson sighed heavily on the other side of the door. "I'll be back Harlowe," she promised.

I heard her retreating steps, and I suddenly felt a loneliness I had never quite experienced before. Even when Emmerson had been away the last few months, acting as a representative for her father, I still had people around me. Zeke, for one, had kept me occupied and even though I missed her, it hadn't felt like this. I felt so... cut off. Isolated from everyone around me. From those who cared about me.

"You are never alone, Fire Heart," Misneach said gently in my mind. **"Even when it feels that way, know that I am always with you."**

His quiet encouragement eased the mounting dread building inside of me. I needed to remind myself that while I was alone in my chambers, I was not alone in this fight. I had people who loved me and cared about what happened to me.

As angry as I was, I could see why my father had made the choices he had. He believed he had no alternative and was striving for the best outcome for his people. My father was genuine in his belief that he could make this work out in the long term and that his plan to recall me from Kieran's kingdom would succeed. Despite being misguided, he had also tried to prepare me for this moment by insisting on my tutelage. Of course, he had been wrong, but I couldn't bring myself to hate him for his decisions as much as I wanted to at this moment.

I couldn't hate my mother, either. Even though she had kept her knowledge of my fate from me, she struggled with it almost as much as I did. Despite her obligation to our people, she would call off this engagement without a second thought if she could. She wanted to spare me. It was plain in her eyes every time she had looked at me in that throne room, and in the undiluted hatred she showed towards Kieran. She had been the one to insist on my combat training from before I was old enough to hold a sword. She had never underestimated Kieran's cruelty, and she wanted me to be able to defeat him when he eventually came for me.

Yes, my mother loved me. And I wasn't certain she would forgive my father for what he had done to set this day in motion. That, however, was not my worry.

I climbed onto my bed, needing to rest after the night I had spent tossing and turning while sleep eluded me.

"Stay close, won't you, Misneach?"

"Always," he answered. Secure in that knowledge, I drifted off to sleep.

Chapter Thirty-One

A disturbance in my chambers pulled me from sleep. It was late afternoon, judging by the sun's position in the sky. I sat up and rubbed my eyes, peering around my room.

My room appeared undisturbed, and yet, I could feel that someone had been in here with me while I slept.

Movement in my periphery caught my attention, and I turned, peering into the shadows lining the wall of my chambers. Gooseflesh erupted over my arms and the hair on the nape of my neck stood to attention. I couldn't distinguish anything or anyone lurking there.

I moved to get out of bed but paused when Kieran emerged from the shadows. As he strolled over to my bed, I sat frozen, watching him. The mattress dipped under his weight as he lowered himself onto it.

"You are a sight to behold when you sleep, Harlowe," he smirked at me. Unease rushed through me at the thought of this monster lurking in the shadows, watching me sleep; unaware and vulnerable.

"No snarky comments or sneers of disdain," he crooned. "Just a beautiful, radiant... silent woman." His smile grew vicious. "What else could a man ask for in a bride?"

"How did you get in here?" I demanded. "Did the guards let you in?"

That vicious grin grew even wider. "My dear Harlowe, if I want to get to you, nothing in this world will keep me from reaching you."

I didn't know what he meant, but his words sent fear spiking through me as the truth of them settled over me.

Kieran crawled towards me on the bed, moving like a predator stalking his prey, and my stupid fear kept me paralyzed and rooted in place. He knelt before me, locking my eyes in the turbulent blue depths of his own as they sparked with danger. Kieran placed his hand on my chest and pushed me onto the bed. My breathing hitched, and I remained still as he looked down at me, studying me.

I trained with the best warriors in Aetherian. I knew how to fight back and disarm men twice my size. But something in the way Kieran looked at me in that moment had me too afraid to make a move against him. I could sense the power within him, and his desire to hurt me if given cause.

Kieran straddled my hips before lowering his body onto mine; caging me in under his larger frame. Still, I said nothing. I winced as he nuzzled his nose against the damaged skin on my neck. Kieran kissed the bruising he had inflicted the previous night, and I felt the smile tugging at his lips as he did so. "You sent your little pet dog to warn me away from you, didn't you, Harlowe?" he said sardonically.

It took me a moment to realize he was talking about Silas.

I swallowed before answering, "No."

Kieran chuckled darkly. "He thinks he has some sort of claim on you," he said in bemusement before running his nose up to the shell of my ear and inhaling deeply. "I thought I'd made myself clear last night. You belong to me, and only me."

"I don't belong to anyone!" I stated, more strongly than I felt.

"That's where you're wrong, Harlowe," Kieran purred against my ear before his tongue darted out and he tasted me. He lifted himself off my chest, bracing his weight with his hands as he placed them on either side of my head. His powerful thighs continued to trap me beneath him, holding me in place.

"Let me tell you a little tale, Bride," he said in a saccharine tone. "Twenty-five years ago, when the Skirmish of Power first broke out, I offered your father some of my troops to reinforce his own. He compensated me, of course, and with the fighting contained to the Kingdoms of Vidyaa and Zarinia initially, our combined troops were sufficient to hold them at bay."

Kieran moved his hips against my own and I could feel the outline of his erection against my core. Heat pooled low in my belly and my uneasiness grew as I registered the desire I felt from his movements.

"However," he said as he continued with his tale, "having seen the aid I offered your father, the Kingdom of Pyrithia joined the fighting, growing fearful of what an alliance between Valoren and Netheran would mean for them given their proximity to your border."

"So, once again, your father requested my aid. And again I gave it to him. Providing him with the reinforcements he required to hold off the attacks. This wouldn't work forever, of course, which was exactly what I was counting on."

I met his striking blue eyes, trying to discern his meaning. Mirth sparkled there, but it was the slyness and cunning that shone brighter. His cruel smirk grew wider as he watched me trying to piece it all together.

"When your father realized he could not maintain the defense of his borders indefinitely, now under attack on three fronts, he again requested further aid," Kieran said, relishing in the telling of his story. "But this time, when he offered me more gold and riches for my help, I refused."

Surprise flickered within me, and I knew it was mirrored on my face. I had not heard this version of our history. I was aware of my father's alliance with Netheran, but not the details.

"I knew of something far more valuable that I desired," he looked pointedly at me.

"I was only an infant when that war broke out," I said, confusion marring my features.

"Indeed," Kieran agreed. "But I was acquainted with a truth-teller of sorts, who told me a little tale many years before about the birth of a wee babe who would one day hold the key to me fulfilling my vision for my kingdom. I knew you were the one that I had been waiting for," he stated, with a conspiratorial smirk gracing his sensual lips.

I contemplated his words and then something else clicked into place.

"Is that why you kept bringing up the Visionary Kingdom when we first met? You wanted to know if we had heard the same story as you?"

"Clever fox," Kieran smiled. "You have a very special role to play in my future, and I won't let you go, no matter the cost. I have already done far too much to secure you." I had no idea what the hell he was talking about, and I told him as much.

"I know," he purred, his broad smile lighting up his entire face. He was handsome, in an evil, I-intend-to-ruin-your-life kind of way.

"Do you want to hear a secret, Harlowe?"

I said nothing as he leaned in to whisper in my ear. "I set it all in motion. I had my witches spell the Kings of Vidyaa and Zarinia to attack Valoren, convincing them untold powers awaited them in victory."

Of course, Kieran had witches within his kingdom.

Centuries ago, people revered the witches and gave them positions of influence as advisers to the kings and queens throughout the kingdoms. They used their magic for good, which led to many advances in the art of healing and diplomacy. Their compassionate nature allowed them to serve as negotiators between the kingdoms and the realm prospered under their influence.

All that changed when a group of witches reached for their own power and used dark, tainted magic to achieve it. They spelled monarchs to start wars with their rivals, intending to seize control in the chaos. The realm suffered years of bloodshed before they could restore peace. It cost kingdoms their lands and rulers their thrones. The witches' fall from grace was harsh and unforgiving. They executed most for their role in the conflict and monarchs exiled any still serving as advisers, whether they commanded darkness or not. I had not known that Kieran still had witches in his arsenal, but it certainly matched his character.

I reared back from him as far as I could manage. Which wasn't that far, considering his body was draped over mine.

"Why?" was all I could manage.

"I told you," Kieran said. "Valoren had something I needed, and I had to make sure your father was desperate enough to give it to me," his grin was one of triumphant victory.

"Why are you telling me this? You know I will go straight to my father."

Kieran threw his head back and roared in laughter. When he returned his gaze to mine, the mirth still twinkling in his eyes, he said, "And who will believe you, Harlowe? You have made it abundantly clear that you do not want to marry me, and your father will see it as a futile attempt to avoid our arrangement." He lowered his voice huskily and said, "Your little performance this morning only aids in that conclusion."

I swallowed. He was right.

Kieran had deceived all of us. He smirked as he saw realization dawn on me.

"Why me?" I asked, barely above a whisper.

"I won't ruin all the fun, but I will tell you this Harlowe, you're special. You and I are going to do great things together." He paused for a moment before continuing, "It also doesn't hurt that you come in a very enticing package." His eyes dipped to my mouth and then back up again. He rocked his hips against me once more, and his erection pulsed against my core.

Panic gripped me, and I tried to wiggle out from under him. I only succeeded in pressing his erection further into my core, and he growled in response.

"Careful Harlowe, I might just take that as an invitation," he said gruffly. When I met his gaze, I could see the lust pooling within them as he took me in.

"Get off me," I hissed.

"Not yet. There is one more matter we need to discuss before I take my leave."

He studied my features, and I squirmed, uncomfortable under his assessing gaze.

"You are to be my bride, and therefore, you are done fucking that boy, or anyone else," Kieran said, his voice too calm to be genuine. "You are mine, Harlowe. In two days, you will become my wife, and I will not allow another to touch you. I don't need to remind you what happens when you disobey me. Do you understand me?"

He waited for me to respond and when I didn't, he gripped my chin in his hand as he leaned down, crushing his lips against mine. The kiss was brutal, dominating. He was exercising his ownership, punishing me with his tongue as it warred against my own. My lungs were starved of oxygen, and yet, he still didn't end the kiss. When he pulled away, he rested his forehead against my own, both of us panting hard.

Kieran regained his composure and whispered, "The only cock that will enter your tight sheath from this day forward will be mine, Harlowe." He ran a hand down my stomach and cupped my sex to emphasize his point. He massaged my clit through the material of my pants, and a moan escaped me without permission.

Kieran chuckled darkly. "That's my good girl," he purred. Kieran brushed his lips against mine once more and then moved away from me. I felt his weight lift off the bed, and then he was gone.

I hesitated a moment before I rose from my position and peered around the room. Once I was certain he was gone, I lowered myself back down against my pillows. My heart was beating erratically, and my mind was whirling.

What the fuck had just happened?

When Kieran kissed me, my body had come alive instead of being repulsed, like my mind was. I had responded to him. I had kissed him back, and I had enjoyed it. And then he touched me, and I could no longer contain the desire building within me.

Now that the haze of lust had abated, I felt dirty and repulsed, hating that I had reacted to him at all.

I realized Misneach had been silent throughout my encounter with Kieran, which was unlike him considering he didn't refrain from butting into my thoughts at any other time.

"I am here, Fire Heart," he responded to my unspoken thoughts. **"Something numbed my connection to you. I could sense you were alive, but nothing more than that."**

"That's troubling, considering Kieran was in my chambers."

Misneach snarled, his hatred for the male in question abundantly clear. **"He told me I am connected to him and that he knew I would be before I was even born."**

I tried to recall everything he had said to me, attempting to piece it all together in the hope it would make some sense.

"He said that I hold the key to him achieving his vision for his kingdom and that he had set up the Skirmish of Power to back my father into a corner so he would offer me in exchange for his support."

Misneach's growl promised death.

"We need to get you away from him, Fire Heart."

"I know. I've been working on a plan. I just need to get out of the palace."

He repeated his earlier offer. **"I can burn it down for you."** I sent him a mental image of me rolling my eyes, and he chuckled.

Misneach was right though, I had to figure out how to get away from Kieran before I found myself giving in to him.

Chapter Thirty-Two

I had spent the last two days mapping out my escape route, planning every step I would make if I could only get out of my chambers. Emmerson had been unable to visit me. The guards stationed outside my chambers never faltered from their direction to keep me contained within, while they kept everyone else out.

I was growing desperate now. Apparently, the entire palace had been abuzz with preparations for my upcoming nuptials, which would take place tomorrow morning.

Kieran had not returned to my rooms, apparently content that I would play along. The thought made me furious.

Without risking the lives of my people living and working within the palace and the grounds, I couldn't have Misneach assist me in breaking free of my room. I had attempted to break the glass in the window leading to my balcony where Misneach would be waiting. However, the glass was reinforced somehow, and I hadn't been able to make so much as a crack.

My only other plan was for Misneach to intercept me on the way to my wedding. I assumed the wedding would take place in the chapel on the hill, as was customary. I was almost certain that a full retinue of soldiers would escort me. Once I was out in the open, however, Misneach could grab me and fly my ass out of dodge.

A single knock on my door sounded, signaling my evening meal was ready. I waited for Louise to enter, only it wasn't Louise who walked into my bedchamber. My mother stood before me, looking disheveled compared to her usual perfection. Her blond hair appeared tousled, with wisps standing out in every direction. Dark circles stood out prominently beneath her eyes and her lids were swollen, as if she had been crying. In her petite hands, she held a pack with a bedroll strapped to the top.

My mother rushed to me, dropping the pack at my feet as she cupped my cheeks.

"Harlowe," she breathed, tears swimming in her eyes as she took me in. "I am so sorry, daughter. How will you ever forgive me?" The tears spilled down her cheeks as she closed her eyes. I gripped her shoulders and placed my forehead against hers, needing to provide her comfort from her despair. Sobs wracked her body as sorrow overtook her. I didn't speak, sensing she needed to unburden herself.

When my mother pulled herself together, I asked her the one question that had been burning inside me for days.

"Why?"

Her blue eyes met mine, and she studied me for a moment before taking a steadying breath.

"I was not a party to this decision, Harlowe. You need to understand that. I am not trying to excuse my actions, but I need you to know that I love you, and I would never trade you for anything. I have been trying to undo this betrothal since I first learned of it." As I searched her gaze, I found the truth of her words reflected back at me.

"How did this all come about?" I asked.

"It was during the Skirmish of Power. I knew your father had entered an alliance with Netheran during that period, but I never knew of the cost associated with that alliance. I stumbled upon them discussing your betrothal," her voice broke as she said the words. Her expression revealed the pain and betrayal she felt as if she was reliving it.

"When I confronted your father," she continued after a moment, "he told me there was nothing to be done. I fought him for years to have it revoked, but he feared what Kieran would do." My mother moved to sit on the edge of my bed, and I followed her, gripping her hand in mine, and encouraging her to continue.

"I knew I had to protect you, so I insisted on you training with the soldiers. I wanted you to be prepared in case that monster got his hands on you." I didn't bother to tell her I was no match for Kieran, and that her efforts had been futile.

"Over the years, I continued to push your father to seek an alternative to your betrothal. I refused to bear more children, hoping he wouldn't hand you over without another heir."

Her confession floored me. I knew my mother had wanted to give me siblings, just as she'd had when she was a child. She often apologized for failing me, and I always found this strange, assuming it was her inability to conceive more children that prevented her from fulfilling her wish.

"Your father has convinced himself that his plan to recall you to Valoren will work." She looked up at me. The sad smile that graced her lips told me she knew Kieran would never let me go once he had me.

"When your father informed me that Kieran was to attend your birthday celebration, intending to get to know you, I knew there was more to it. I tried to find out their plans, but I didn't know they would use the opportunity to force your marriage with Kieran. I should have told you long ago what I knew Harlowe, and for that, I am sorry." My mother cupped my cheek as fresh tears slid free. I pulled her to me, gripping her tightly as I hugged her to my chest.

After a moment, she pulled back, seeming to have regained control over her emotions.

"Do you know why Kieran is so insistent on marrying me?" I pried, wanting to know if my mother or my father were aware of Kieran's motives.

"He is a vicious creature," my mother spat. "He doubtlessly enjoys knowing we are desperate to keep you, so he is unwilling to let you go." Fresh tears spilled down my mother's cheeks as she tried to stifle a sob. It was heartbreaking to watch, and I knew if I let my churning emotions overtake me, she would fall apart.

"We're out of time, Harlowe," my mother said, regaining her composure. Her voice lowered as she whispered, "You must leave. Tonight. If you stay, you will be forced to marry that monster in the morning and he will take you away from me, where I cannot protect you." Her eyes flicked to my neck and the bruising that was still evident there, and she flinched.

"It was not your fault," I said gently, and she smiled tightly at me.

"I have the key to your balcony door."

My mother reached into the pocket of her dress and produced the key.

"I have packed a bag for you. There is food, weapons, and clothing. Zeke helped me gather your weaponry, assuring me you were most familiar with the ones he selected."

I smiled. Zeke knew me so well when it came to combat. I could almost guess which daggers and short swords he had selected, considering that I had previously defeated him while using them.

"Zeke wanted to come with you, but I couldn't let him Harlowe. Samuel knows him too well. He could anticipate what moves he would make and where he would take you. I can't risk them tracking you through him. I hope you understand." I nodded, knowing that would not have been an easy decision for her to make.

"You have a little over an hour before the soldiers guarding your door wake up." My eyes widened at her admission, and she smiled sheepishly. "Zeke too."

"What did you do?" I asked, intrigue taking over.

"I may have brought them refreshments that contained a sleeping draught," she said, wincing. "I already gave it to Zeke because he wouldn't hear me about the risk he posed if he went with you."

I opened and closed my mouth a few times, not knowing what to say. My mother was a badass. A broad grin crept across my face and my mother made a small, strangled noise in the back of her throat.

"Of course that impresses you, Harlowe," she said while rolling her eyes. I only grinned wider.

My mother started pushing me towards the doors leading out to my balcony. "Hurry, you need to put as much distance between you and the palace before the alarm is raised."

I hesitated before saying, "They will know it was you, Mother."

A fierceness swept over her as she straightened her spine. "I will not apologize for saving my daughter. I will not see you harmed. Not again."

I hugged her tight once more before whispering, "I love you."

"I love you too, Harlowe. Please be safe."

I could hear the tears in her voice as she struggled to contain her renewed sorrow. She took a step back, wiped her eyes, and nodded. Taking a deep breath, I unlocked the doors and stepped out onto my balcony. I was leaving my home, and I didn't know when I would be back.

"Fire Heart," Misneach breathed as I emerged from my chambers. Someone moved in the shadows and before I could register the threat, Emmerson stepped into view.

She smirked at me and said, "Didn't think I'd let you go without me, did you?" I grinned and rushed towards her, sweeping her up into a tight hug.

"Gods damn, it's good to see you Harlowe," she said as she exhaled a shaky breath.

"So how come you got a pass, but Zeke didn't?" I asked as I released her.

"Please, I am many things, but predictable is not one of them." She grinned, throwing my own words back at me.

"So, where to?" she asked as she shouldered her pack. I noticed she had an identical one to mine, ready to go.

"You're not going to like it," I told her.

"Where?" she asked as she scrunched her nose up.

"The Forest of Nightmares," I replied, shrugging one shoulder.

"Harlowe," Emmerson gasped.

"Shh, keep your voice down, woman. Do you want us to get caught before we have even taken a single step outside the palace?" I hissed.

"Sorry," she murmured. "That is suicide, though. You know that, right?"

"Exactly," I smiled. "No one will think to follow us there."

Emmerson sized me up, as though encountering me for the first time. "You know, you're either brilliant or idiotic," she grumbled.

"I'll take the former," I replied.

"Fairly sure it's the latter," she muttered, and I laughed.

"How are we getting there?" she asked. By the color leaching from her face, she knew exactly how we were traveling and was just hoping I wouldn't confirm it for her.

I looked at Misneach and Emmerson paled further.

"Great," she groaned. "Perfect. The Forest of Nightmares, flying on a dragon, what could go wrong?"

I opened my mouth to respond, but Emmerson cut me off, narrowing her eyes at me.

"That was a rhetorical question, Harlowe," she grumbled before taking a steadying breath.

"Let's do this." Emmerson looked at me then, embarrassment coloring her cheeks. "How do we do this again?"

Misneach huffed, but it sounded suspiciously like a chuckle.

"I'll climb on and pull you up behind me," I encouraged. I took Emmerson's pack, so she had one less thing to worry about and climbed into place. Once I was settled, I extended my hand towards Emmerson, who regarded it with suspicion as if it might harm her in some way.

"We need to go, Emmerson," I growled in frustration.

"I know," she snapped back at me. Emmerson was stalling; her fear of flying was paralyzing her. The thunderous beat of Emmerson's heart was loud enough that even I could hear it trying to jump free of her chest. Inhaling a deep, steadying breath, Emmerson held it for a moment before exhaling. Before she could talk herself out of it, Emmerson took my hand, and I pulled her onto Misneach's back.

Rotating in my seat, I turned and passed Emmerson's pack to her so she could secure it over her shoulders. She made a small keening noise in the back of her throat at having to release her iron grip on me to accept the slight burden. Taking one last look at the home I was leaving behind, I sighed and then straightened.

Misneach bent low before launching himself off the battlement, allowing himself to free fall for a moment, before beating his wings and climbing skyward. I relished the thrill of flying and admired Misneach's powerful wings. The indigo hues that adorned his body were indiscernible, as his scales appeared black against the darkness of the night.

We were free.

Now all we had to do was live long enough to get some answers.

Chapter Thirty-Three

The Forest of Nightmares was located northeast of the border of Valoren. It backed up against the border of Pyrithia before cascading over a sheer cliff face to the ocean below. The forest was aptly named as it housed the monsters from legends, and no sane person willingly trespassed against the death it promised.

"What's the plan, Harlowe?" Emmerson screeched against my ear over the whipping sound created by Misneach's wings.

"It will take a few days to reach the border between Valoren and the Forest of Nightmares. We need to fly in a direct path, as we can't risk diverting. Everyone in the kingdom will probably be alerted to our disappearance by morning."

"What's our plan once we reach the forest?"

"You know the story about the witch who lives in the outermost edge of the forest before the cliff face?" I asked, and Emmerson groaned.

"Are you fucking kidding me? Do you mean to tell me your entire plan hinges on a fucking fairy tale?" she hissed.

"What if it's not a fairy tale?" I quipped.

"So let me get this straight; your brilliant plan is to trek into the Forest of Nightmares, where the beasts of legend roam just waiting for wayward travelers to rip them apart?"

I could all but hear the eye roll in her tone.

"And if by some miracle we survive the forest, we are to seek out the Lost

Witch, who may or may not have survived The War of Witches?" she finished.

"Yes," I replied.

"And for what purpose are we seeking her?" Emmerson questioned.

"To get answers."

"Answers to what?" she asked.

"Kieran told me he started the Skirmish of Power by having his witches influence the Kings of Vidyaa and Zarinia, in order to back my father into a corner so that he would trade me for Kieran's aid in the war," I rushed out in one long breath.

"What the fuck are you talking about, Harlowe?"

"I'm not sure exactly," I sighed, exhaling my frustration. "I only know what Kieran said. He confessed to having sparked the conflict so that he could come in and save our kingdom, ensuring my father would accept him as my betrothed. Kieran seems to believe that I can help him realize his vision for his kingdom. I'm not sure how, but that's what he said."

"What does any of that mean?" Emmerson whined.

"Honestly, I don't know. That's why I must find the Lost Witch. She is rumored to be a truth-sayer so if I can get to her, she will be able to give me the answers I need." Emmerson groaned as she lowered her forehead to my back.

"Your friend has little confidence in your plan, Fire Heart."

"To be fair, it is kind of a shitty plan. But it's the only one I have right now." Misneach snickered, and I glowered despite him not being able to see me.

"I know two things, Misneach; first, we need a place to hide where no one will find us and drag me back to my father. No one is foolish enough to hide in the Forest of Nightmares."

"Except you," Misneach snorted.

"Yes, except me," I conceded.

"And second, Kieran dropped a bunch of shit on me in our last conversation and I need to figure out what he wants me for."

"You are quite crude for royalty. You are nothing like how I envisioned a queen would behave," Misneach chortled, and it was my turn to snort.

"Do you even know anything about truth-sayers?" Emmerson piped up, halting my retort to Misneach.

"I know their particular type of magic is rare, and that they cannot lie when called upon to speak truths. They can answer any question you have about yourself by peering into your destiny," I supplied.

Emmerson scoffed. "They're deceivers," she stated. "They played a crucial role in swaying the monarchs during the War of Witches. They manipulate their answers and twist your mind, making it impossible to understand what they reveal. Even after going through all of this, we may still be no better off."

"I have no better plan, Em," I confessed.

"What if we were to seek refuge in the Kingdom of Elysara?" she pleaded.

"That wouldn't work," I said.

"Why not? After all, they are your mother's people."

"Even if my mother pleaded, the Kingdom of Peace won't fight against Valoren. The kingdom provides a safe haven for all citizens of the realm, and anyone who threatens that is removed to preserve the sanctuary. They wouldn't help me, even if they could."

Emmerson muttered, "Back to the crazy witch and the monsters that will surely devour us."

My lips twitched, but I remained silent, deciding I had pushed her far enough for one night.

We flew through the night, only stopping for brief periods so Misneach could rest. By the time the sun broke over the horizon, we were all exhausted and sought shelter in the thick vegetation of the woods surrounding a nearby village.

Having decided it was safest to travel by night, shrouded in darkness and protected from prying eyes, we spent most of the day sleeping. It was early afternoon when I was jerked awake by Misneach shouting in my head.

"Wake up Fire Heart."

"What is it?" I asked, panic lacing my tone.

"Cathal."

Shaking Emmerson awake, I placed my finger against her lips, a silent warning to keep quiet. We both reached for our weapons; Emmerson unsheathed her dual short swords, which she had somehow slept with, strapped to her back, while I grabbed daggers in both hands.

"Do you know which dragon it is?" I asked Misneach as I heard a screeching sound above us.

"No. But if I can sense them, they can sense me too."

"Shit."

"What's going on?" Emmerson asked, barely above a whisper.

"Misneach says the Cathal are coming. He can't identify the dragon, but he says if he can sense them, they can sense him, too."

"Shit," Emmerson said, reiterating my sentiment.

"We need to move so that they can't pinpoint our location," Emmerson instructed, taking the lead, every inch the general's daughter. "It's too early to fly without the cover of darkness to conceal us. Stick to the denser areas of the woods and head northeast until nightfall."

I nodded, packing up my bedroll and shouldering my pack.

"That one is worth keeping around," Misneach said as he inclined his head towards Emmerson.

I couldn't help the grin that spread across my face at his praise for my best friend.

"Is this funny to you?" Emmerson hissed. "If we get caught, we're done. Why the hell are you smiling like a fool?"

Her words sobered me. "Misneach thinks you're brilliant," I muttered under my breath, properly chastised.

"Of course I am," she huffed. Emmerson wasn't gloating. She knew her strengths, and this was one of them.

"I take it back," Misneach grumbled.

I peered over my shoulder to see him hunched low on the ground, slinking along the forest floor behind us. Had it not been for the seriousness of the situation, I might have laughed at the ridiculousness of this massive beast trying to conceal himself in the vegetation.

We spent hours navigating the thick shrubbery of the woods, the screeching of our pursuer lessening with each passing hour. Misneach was on high alert the entire time, tracking the dragon as it followed us overhead, unable to locate us despite its best efforts. The Cathal was alone, as no other dragons joined the beast hunting us. They must have sent them all in different directions to canvass as much of the kingdom as possible. Given our kingdom had only recently re-established the Cathal, they were likely spread thin. And thank the gods for that because we needed every advantage, we could garner.

When night finally descended, covering the kingdom in darkness, I exhaled a breath of relief. Without hesitation, we took flight, intent on putting a significant distance between us and our pursuers.

The distant sound of screeching and roaring dragons occasionally broke the silence of the night as the Cathal searched for us. None came close enough for us to see them or them us. Even if they did, Misneach's coloring was a perfect camouflage against the backdrop of the starless night sky.

As much as it pained me to do so, however, we had to divert from our path and seek shelter in the caves bordering the ocean pass. We couldn't risk being caught out in the open again as we rested, and with daylight peeking over the mountain range, we were out of options.

Chapter Thirty-Four

The next few days passed us by without incident. The tension was slowly leaving our little rebel group, and we made good progress towards our destination. That changed, however, as we edged closer and closer to the border of the forest. None of us knew what lay ahead in the Forest of Nightmares. We only knew it wouldn't be good.

"How are we going to find the witch once we enter the forest?" Emmerson asked as she skinned an apple with her dagger.

"The stories place her home on the forest's outer border, right before the cliff face."

"That's not much to go on," Emmerson pointed out as she popped a slice of apple into her mouth.

"I know, but it's all I have. I figure we head east towards the cliff face and search the surrounding area."

"What's so special about this witch that she gets her own spooky legend, anyway? She wasn't the only witch to survive the war," Emmerson mused.

"I'm not certain, but from what I could read into the stories, she was a powerful truth-sayer, and the kingdoms wanted her captured given how instrumental her particular type of magic was in the war. If I had to guess, I would say fear of her reappearance drove the stories."

It was quite genius of her to hole up in the Forest of Nightmares. It was the one place her pursuers would not dare to follow, despite how much they may have wanted to reclaim her.

Now that we were on the last leg of our journey, we took the risk of traveling in daylight, figuring we must have lost the Cathal since we hadn't heard or seen them in days.

"Misneach, if the dragons get close enough to me, will they be able to identify me through the bond, or whatever it is I share with them?" I asked as I retook my seat on his back. I reached down to grip Emmerson's hand and pulled her into position behind me.

"It will depend on whether the dragon has met you or not. If we are located by one of the dragons from Valoren or Pyrithia, they will likely realize it is you. If we run into another dragon, they may acknowledge the pull to you but won't necessarily understand what it means," he said as he launched heavenward.

We remained silent for some time, everyone lost to their own thoughts about what was lying ahead of us.

"I will give my life to protect yours, Fire Heart," Misneach promised, interrupting my musings.

"That's what I'm afraid of. You and Emmerson both wouldn't think twice about putting yourselves in harm's way if you thought it would spare me."

"You are special Fire Heart. We all feel it. You are needed for whatever is coming our way."

"You don't know that," I argued. **"You're just giving voice to the feelings inside you, but even you don't understand this connection. What it means."**

"I can feel you to the very center of my soul, Fire Heart. I may not have all the answers, but I know this: it is my destiny to stand beside you and protect you with my life. To what end remains unclear, but I know my duty."

I had to fight back the swell of emotion his words invoked in me. I didn't have long to compose myself, however, as a deafening roar sounded behind us.

"Oisín," Misneach confirmed before I could ask the question.

"Fuck, it's Cillian," I breathed. Emmerson swore under her breath and gripped me tighter.

"Just him?" I asked hopefully.

"Two others are with him, but I don't recognize them."

"There are two others with Cillian, but we don't know who they are," I repeated out loud for Emmerson's benefit.

"We need a diversion. If Cillian has been sent to retrieve you, which I would wager he was, there will be no outrunning him. He's relentless," Emmerson declared.

"And what, pray tell, kind of diversion would distract them long enough, we could conceal a freaking dragon?" I asked incredulously.

I peered over my shoulder to look at Emmerson, and a wicked smirk curved her lips. I already knew I hated this plan.

"We don't need to conceal the dragon," she said, grinning. "The dragon is the diversion."

Misneach snarled, having picked up on the plan quicker than I was able.

"She wants me to leave you and lead them away, Fire Heart."

"That's actually a pretty sound plan," I replied. Misneach's answering growl suggested he was not on board with Emmerson's brilliance.

"I'm not leaving you," Misneach snarled in warning.

"How else will we lose, Cillian?" I reasoned. **"You can lead him away. Without me and Emmerson, you can fly much faster and execute all sorts of evasive maneuvers with no limitations. You'll be able to lose them if you're on your own. Then you can double back and use the bond to locate me."**

"You forget Oisín will sense that you're not with me," Misneach countered.

"Not at first. If you stick to the same general area, they will think I'm still with you. By the time they figure out we separated, we'll be concealed by the forest. We just need you to buy us enough time to lose them in the forest."

"You're not entering that place without me to guard you," he argued.

As I glanced behind us, I could make out Oisín clearly now, but the other two dragons were not within sight. Not surprising given Cillian's skill, he likely broke away to close the distance.

A loud rushing sound above me drew my attention skyward. The yellow scales of a dragon's underbelly emerged through the thick cloud cover as it descended towards us.

"Misneach," I shouted, but he was already moving.

"HOLD TIGHT," he roared as he shot forward at speed, only to tilt upward, following a vertical path straight up into the skyline.

Emmerson screamed behind me, and I felt my body lifting away from Misneach's back, tethered only by the grip I maintained on his neck. The pounding in my ears intensified and everything slowed around us as

Misneach pitched back towards Cillian, flying inverted.

Misneach evaded the dragon attempting to box us in from above, while Emmerson and I hung precariously, suspended in the open air, only finding purchase in the rivets along his spine. Time snapped back with a terrifying lurch as Misneach righted himself and gravity slammed us back into place. My breath left me in a rush as I collided with the hard muscles of his body.

I had no time to recover myself though as Misneach came up behind the unknown dragon and then dove into a free fall without warning. Cillian and his companion were left behind as they attempted to correct their path.

My stomach dropped and my heart tried to leave through my mouth as my mind raced to catch up with what was happening around me. We were falling too quickly, and the large mountainside coming into view below us would surely seal our fates. Before I could warn Misneach, he was banking right, as his talons ripped into the side of the mountain. Rocks scattered down the sharp incline while dust plumes filled the air in our wake. I spotted something green in my peripheral vision and realized the third dragon was heading straight for us from the other side of the mountain.

"It seems we are going with the hellcat's plan after all, Fire Heart," Misneach grumbled. **"I am going to fly as close to the mountain as possible before rolling left, and you're going to jump from my back while I conceal you,"** Misneach instructed.

"What?" I screamed. **"We'll break our necks from this height."**

"Trust me Fire Heart," Misneach growled. **"I will not endanger you."**

"You and I have very different ideas of what constitutes danger," I responded somewhat hysterically.

I repeated the plan to Emmerson, who looked about ready to vomit.

"Hold my hand, Em, and when I say jump, you jump, okay?" Emmerson just nodded, gulping air.

"Get ready, Fire Heart," Misneach growled as he flew in close to the mountainside. I tightened my grip on Emmerson's hand as I felt the tipping of Misneach's wings as he glided parallel with the mountain.

"NOW!" Misneach roared, and I screamed for Emmerson to jump.

The sensation of weightlessness lasted only a moment before I collided with the mountainside. Gravity had me tumbling downward as I scrambled to find a foothold. I tried to grab onto anything in my path to slow my descent. Snagging an upturned root, I felt my body jerk as I fought gravity's attempt to drag me down. Emmerson's outstretched hand caught my free one and my body jerked again as the momentum threatened to displace us both.

I was panting hard as I hoisted Emmerson into a sitting position before releasing my hold on the root. I scanned the surrounding sky, but I couldn't see Misneach or any of the other dragons that had been pursuing us.

"They are with me Fire Heart. Move before they realize you are not. I will circle back to you when I can."

I blew out a breath I did not realize I was holding when I heard Misneach's voice in my head. The maneuvers he had executed were lethal, and I feared him injuring himself in the process.

Misneach snorted, unimpressed by my assessment of his abilities.

"We," Emmerson panted, "are never doing that again," she finished.

"Agreed."

I took stock of my injuries, logging my bloody palms and my knees that were grazed through the fabric of my pants. My ankle was sore and swollen from the impact of our landing and my shoulder muscles were burning from being jerked with the force required to slow our descent. I turned to Emmerson and noted she had fared little better. I let myself catch my breath for a moment before pushing up off the ground to continue our decline.

"Come on," I said as I hauled Emmerson after me. "We can't lose the advantage that Misneach just gave us."

We descended the steep mountainside, taking care to avoid falling. When we reached the bottom, we allowed ourselves a moment to take in what we had just survived, as we braced our arms on our knees and inhaled greedily.

"That was by far the stupidest thing I have ever done," Emmerson confessed. "And I have done plenty of stupid things in my lifetime."

"Let's not dwell on it because it is unlikely to be the stupidest thing we will do before we finish here," I countered.

"Great pep talk," Emmerson grumbled in displeasure at my prediction.

I straightened and took a step towards the imposing forest that lay about a mile ahead of us. As we reached the border, I took stock of the eerie silence that permeated the air from within the forest.

"Are you sure about this?" Emmerson whispered.

"Not at all," I replied before stepping across the threshold into a land of untold horrors.

Chapter Thirty-Five

Frustration and anger were my dominant feelings as I contemplated Cillian's words. Harlowe and Emmerson had been in his direct line of sight, and they had still managed to lose him somehow. Cillian, and the two Cathal he had taken with him, had implemented a tried and tested maneuver that should have yielded their submission, and yet, my Little Menace had slipped away.

"That dragon of hers," Cillian started, "he is something else. I have never seen such precision and discipline. Any number of Cathal and their dragons would have been eviscerated attempting those maneuvers, and he made it seem easy. Not to mention our runaways are both untrained, but he compensated for their lack of experience flawlessly. And what's more, Oisín tells me he's only twenty-five years old. He shouldn't be that capable at his age. I doubt he's even seen battle."

The astonishment and awe were apparent in Cillian's tone, and he was a hard man to impress. He was my second because he was a skilled fighter and flier, and he accepted nothing less from those he trained. He was not one to coddle the men, either. If he thought Harlowe's dragon was impressive, then he was likely exceptional.

"Misneach," I said.

"What?"

"The name of her dragon," I supplied. "It's Misneach."

Cillian inclined his head in acknowledgment. "Fitting name," he mused.

"He is certainly strong of spirit and fortitude."

I dragged a hand through my hair as I tried to map out our next steps. Exhaustion was seeping into the very marrow of my bones. Ever since Harlowe had been detained inside her chambers, I hadn't been able to sleep more than a few hours at a time. I had gotten so used to the feel of her supple body pressed against mine that the absence of it had been startling.

It had been days, maybe even a week since I had last seen her. This only made me want to kill Kieran all the more. He and Harlowe's father foolishly thought locking her away would be enough to break her resolve. I had been a veritable bastard when I'd been denied access to my Little Menace. It was more than pure possessiveness, though. I had felt compelled to protect her, to defend her, on a level so profound that I was unwilling to look too closely at why those needs had arisen within me.

"What's the plan, brother?" Cillian said, pulling me from my ruminating. I knew he was just as eager to get his Little Viper back as I was to feel my Little Menace beneath me.

"Show me the map again," I sighed. Cian pulled the map from his pack and rolled it out on the ground between us. I squatted low to get a closer look at the path my girl had traveled.

"They were first spotted here," Cian said, using a stick to point out a small village that didn't seem to be far from the palace. "It's about nine hours away since they were flying," he clarified. Okay, so it was further than it looked on the map. Exhaustion really was getting to me.

"They must have flown through what remained of the night," Teller added as he joined us. "The Queen visited around dinner time, and we assume they left shortly thereafter."

A small smirk played on my lips at the thought of the dainty, well-mannered Queen drugging her own soldiers to allow her daughter to escape. I hadn't seen that coming, and I am rarely surprised. And then that pompous asshole Kieran had threatened her. All the while, she remained composed, regal, refusing to acknowledge him. She had a spine of steel, that one.

"And where did you catch up with them, Cill?" I asked, returning my attention to the task at hand.

"Here," he pointed to a section of Valoren near the northeastern border.

They were traveling in a direct path, heading to the furthest edge of the border. There was nothing out there that could shield her from her father or Kieran. As far as escape plans went, this one seemed to be lacking. I had expected them to head to a neighboring kingdom to seek refuge or perhaps hide throughout the Mountains of Dragonia. Misneach would have the home-field advantage and with Harlowe being... connected... to the dragons, seeking refuge among them made some sense.

The only two kingdoms close enough for them to cross into following their current trajectory were Pyrithia and Elysara. Considering the kingdom's stance on any form of trouble, it was unlikely that they were headed to Elysara, as they were undoubtedly aware that Kieran would pursue them. They could go to Pyrithia, but there were other entry points that would have shortened their journey. Plus, it's unlikely they would conceal themselves in our homeland without seeking our aid in doing so.

The only other option was the Forest of Nightmares, and I was not willing to accept that as a possibility.

"How likely do you think it is that they crossed into Pyrithia?" I asked no one in particular. The men around me furrowed their brows as if they had reached the same conclusion.

Not fucking likely.

I groaned, rubbing a hand down my face.

"The Forest of Nightmares," Fionn suggested tentatively. I looked at Cillian and the set of his jaw told me he was none-too-pleased by the thought of his Little Viper strolling through the domain of monsters. When I caught up to my Little Menace, I would punish her for her recklessness.

"We need to find her before Kieran does. If he gets his hands on her, he will take her straight to his kingdom, and our chances of extricating her from him at that point would be next to none," I said, daring the men to argue.

That could not fucking happen.

I wouldn't give up my Little Menace to anyone, especially not that prick. I had wanted to rip his throat out when I confronted him about the bruises he had left on Harlowe's neck. Her voice had been raspy, and I could tell it had pained her to speak. The sound had sent white hot fury pulsing through me and in that moment I didn't care if Kieran was a king. I wanted him dead. And when I had attacked him, he had laughed coldly, telling me my Little Menace was his to torment as he pleased. Had Cillian not been with me, I would have probably started a fucking war by removing the pretentious prick's head.

"What do you plan to do with her once you've retrieved her?" Cian asked, his expression guarded.

I knew what my orders were, and I didn't appreciate my loyalty being questioned.

"The plan remains the same," I snapped.

"And you have no issue following through with that?" Cian pressed. I pierced him with a murderous glare.

"As I said, the plan remains the same," I repeated, menace dripping from my voice. "Make no mistake, though," I continued. "That girl is mine." I'd claimed her, and I would keep her. "You best remember that when we catch up to her because if any of you steps out of line where she is concerned, I'll make you fucking regret it," I promised.

I rose from my crouched position and headed towards Caolán. Pausing, I turned to peer at Cian over my shoulder.

"Never question my loyalty again, Cian. I won't forgive it a second time."

Cillian jogged up beside me, falling into step with me as I started issuing orders to the men.

"We aren't taking them with us?" he questioned when I directed the others I had brought with me to return to Pyrithia.

"No. We will have a better chance of going unnoticed if we keep it tight," I answered. Cillian murmured his agreement.

"The Forest of Nightmares is no playground," Cillian said after a moment.

I dropped the pack I had been filling and turned towards him.

"I'm aware, and my girl is likely wandering through it right now, unprotected. You want me to leave her there, alone? What about Emmerson? Are you telling me you're okay with her making her merry way into the monster's den without you?" I challenged, my frustration getting the better of me.

Cillian snorted. "I'm more concerned about the inhabitants of that forest and what that girl might do to them than the other way around," he joked, but I could see the truth as his eyes pinched in the corners.

There was no doubt that the girl was lethal. But they called it the Forest of Nightmares for a reason.

Cillian sighed. "I'm not questioning if we should go after them. That's a given." He waved his hand as if dismissing any suggestion to the contrary. "What I am saying is, maybe you should sit this one out. These are high stakes and in no way did this factor into our plans."

This time I scoffed. "I'm the fucking Commanding General of the Cathal, Cillian. I am the best warrior here. It's why he sent me."

"No one is questioning your abilities, brother."

"Then what exactly are you questioning, Cillian?" My patience was running thin.

"All I'm saying is you're not someone easily replaced. You're needed back home. Our kingdom can't afford for you to become collateral damage because you're caught up chasing tail," he said knowingly.

"I'm going," I said, ending the discussion.

Cillian put his hands up in surrender as he backed away towards his pack.

"Cill," I called after him, and he paused to look back at me.

"It's exceptional tail," I said, grinning.

"Tail worth dying for, apparently," he laughed, and I winked.

Indeed, it was. And when I survived the trial of monsters, I would reclaim my girl, making sure she felt me for days after I'd left her body. A wicked grin curved up my lips as I thought about all the ways I would ruin her.

Chapter Thirty-Six

From the moment I had crossed the threshold into the Forest of Nightmares, an eerie sense of dread had settled over me; clamping around my chest as though I were locked in a vice. The feeling had cascaded down me like an oily substance, the taint a tangible thing that I could almost grasp in the surrounding air.

Emmerson had fared no better. The color had drained from her body, leaving her pale, and stricken.

As I peered towards the sky, I saw the high treetops that crowded one another, blocking out the sun and casting the forest in bleak darkness. The temperature had dropped with the loss of the sun, and gooseflesh had erupted under my tunic. Dead, decaying leaves crunched under my boots, serving as a reminder that very few escaped this place alive.

More troubling was the fact that I had not heard Misneach speak to me since crossing the threshold. My connection to him felt muted somehow, like he was too far away for me to reach him. It reminded me of what had occurred when Kieran had accosted me in my chambers.

We had been traipsing through the thick growth surrounding us for hours. The winding path seemed to lead nowhere as we struggled to part the low-hanging branches. We couldn't tell which direction we were headed in anymore, as we had already been turned around more than once.

I had the ominous feeling that something watched us through the dense cover of the foliage. My eyesight failed to detect the source of my unease, but as I peered around me, the prickling sensation spreading over my skin whispered that the forest was ever watchful.

"This place is all kinds of creepy," Emmerson murmured as she struggled through a thick crop of shrubbery.

"It is that," I agreed. We had barely spoken since we stepped into the forest, fearful of alerting the creatures within of our presence here.

"We will need to find some shelter before we lose any more light," Emmerson said as she examined the dark clouds that had moved across the sky above us. The first sprinkle of rain had fallen, seeping into my exposed flesh, making the bitter chill in the air intensify.

"I haven't spotted any caves or other forms of shelter, Em. Not sure what we are looking for, exactly."

Emmerson pondered my words for a moment, rubbing her forefinger and her thumb across her chin as she assessed our options. The rain had started pelting down now; furious and chaotic.

"I think the best option is to go up," Emmerson shouted over the thundering downpour.

"Up?" I questioned.

"Up," she repeated, pointing towards the trees. I groaned, knowing exactly what she had in mind.

When we were children, we often played in the forest surrounding the palace. We would climb the trees, pretending to be watching over the kingdom from the turrets. Sometimes we hid within the branches, refusing to surrender our vantage point, intending to remain overnight. Of course, eventually, one of the soldiers was forced to climb up and retrieve us. It had been a grand adventure when we were children, but the thought of spending the night nestled amongst the treetop with the rain pouring down on us was far less appealing in reality.

Emmerson didn't hesitate, and I followed behind her, watching her test each limb before pulling herself onto it. I had to hand it to her; she adapted quickly.

The first branch I reached for was sturdy and rough beneath my palm. I swung my leg over it and pulled myself up to stand. I continued to follow the path Emmerson was carving out ahead of me. Halfway up the tree, I paused to peer down at the forest floor below me. I hadn't realized just how high I had climbed. My pulse began to jackhammer, and I struggled to control the tremble overtaking my hands. I swallowed and refocused on Emmerson, climbing her way expertly through the tree's limbs above me.

Don't look down. Don't look down. Don't look down.

I reached for the branch extended above me and launched myself up and onto it. It wobbled beneath my weight and made a harsh groaning noise. The fear of falling clamped around me, and I threw myself forward, grasping for any available offshoot within reaching distance. I wrapped my arms around the scaly exterior of the branch I was clinging to and swung my legs up to stabilize my hold. My hands scraped against the rough bark; the sweat coating my palms making it difficult to get a solid grip. As I heaved my body over the outstretched limb, I paused for a moment, panting while I caught my breath. My palms were bleeding, having reopened the wounds I sustained coming down the mountain, and a sharp sting erupted as my sweat mingled with the open cuts.

"Harlowe," Emmerson's panicked voice sounded from above me.

"I'm alright," I called back, still calming my breathing. Once settled, I continued my climb upwards until I reached Emmerson, who had perched on a thick limb and was nestled against the wide trunk.

"You okay?" she asked as soon as I reached her.

"Fine. Just got spooked, is all."

"Let me see your hands." I laid my palms flat for her inspection. She collected rainwater as the clouds continued to thrash us from above. Emmerson poured the water over my fresh wounds and cleaned the cuts of the dirt and debris that had become lodged within them.

"It's not too bad," she said as she wrapped my palms; first the left, followed by the right.

The adrenaline was wearing off and the bone-chilling cold was setting in as I sat in my drenched clothing. My teeth began chattering uncontrollably.

"Here," Emmerson said as she pulled my cloak out of my pack and wrapped it around my shoulders. She then reached for her own pack and pulled her cloak out, huddling under the warmth it offered. It wouldn't take long for the rain to seep through the material, but it was a slight comfort for the time being.

"We'll use our ropes to secure ourselves to the tree. They should stop us from falling if we move too much in our sleep."

"Should?" I arched a brow in question. Emmerson lifted one shoulder in a slight shrug and then tipped her hand from side to side, indicating we had an even chance of remaining secure or falling.

I had to laugh, or I would break down and cry at the ridiculous situation we found ourselves in.

"We'll take turns keeping watch as well," Emmerson continued. "If either of us slips, the other will know," I nodded my head in agreement.

The rain finally eased as we ate a dinner of dried meat, bread, and cheese that my mother had packed for us. None of our food had become water-logged with the downpour, thanks to the extra covering my mother had wrapped our rations in. As I leaned back against the trunk, I closed my eyes, allowing myself to register the exhaustion created by the last few days.

"Maybe I should have just cooperated and gone with Kieran," I mumbled, my eyes stinging from the lack of rest.

Something hard connected with my stomach and my eyes flew open as my breath was forced from my lungs. Emmerson was glaring at me, and I released she had backhanded me.

"Gods, Em, what was that for?" I wheezed.

"Don't you ever speak like that again," she gritted out. "You are not property that can be bartered or sold. You are the heir apparent to Valoren, and your kingdom needs you."

A small pang of guilt sparked to life within me at the mention of the kingdom I had abandoned. "If marrying Kieran prevents a war, am I being selfish by not agreeing to it?"

"No," Emmerson replied fiercely. "From what you have told me, Kieran wants you for more than a wife. Who is to say that by giving in, you aren't condemning Valoren to a fate worse than war?"

I turned her words over in my mind. Kieran was certainly up to something, and whatever it was, it couldn't be good considering the steps he had already taken to secure me. I felt a slight burden lift from my heart as I accepted her words of reassurance.

"You need to sleep Harlowe," Emmerson advised. "You're injured and you need to rest so that your body can recover."

"What about you?"

"I'm good for a while longer. Sleep for a few hours and then I'll rest."

I settled deeper beneath my damp cloak as Emmerson secured the ropes around us.

As night descended, the activity within the forest grew louder; sharper. Animals scurried by, rustling in the undergrowth beneath us. At least I hoped they were animals and not the more sinister inhabitants of this forest. The hum of insects assaulted my senses, and the branches of the trees creaked in the breeze.

The cacophony of sounds had me on edge, which made sleep difficult to find.

Just as I thought I might drift off, the forest suddenly went silent, raising the hairs on the back of my neck as a sense of foreboding washed over me.

"Do you feel that?" I whispered.

"Yes," Emmerson replied, voice strained.

A low keening noise sounded a short distance away and steadily grew into a loud, shrill shriek.

As I locked gazes with Emmerson, I could see my fear reflected in her features as the moonlight illuminated her face.

We both remained perfectly still, too afraid to even breathe as the sharp wailing moved closer.

Chapter Thirty-Seven

The screaming was a constant feature throughout the night, making sleep elusive. Whatever was making the sound moved throughout the forest; the screeching growing louder as it moved closer to our position and then becoming faint as it moved away again. It never left the area entirely, though. Instead, it appeared to be circling us, with the sounds reaching a crescendo before falling away and starting again.

By the time the sky lightened, I was exhausted. My nerves were frayed and the dampness still clinging to my clothes made for a miserable start to the day.

Emmerson and I shared a meal of dried fruit and bread that had again remained dry overnight, much to my delight.

"We need to reorient ourselves and make sure we haven't veered off course," Emmerson muttered as she canvassed the surrounding forest.

I could tell that getting lost had bruised her ego, and no amount of encouragement from me had soothed that sting. Frankly, if she hadn't come with me when I left the palace, I'm certain I would be dead already.

"We need to find a break in the canopy so I can use the sun's location to get us back on track. And we need to do it soon before the sun rises too high to be useful," she said.

Emmerson trudged off down the path, chasing the minuscule rays of daylight seeping in through the canopy. The shadows cast by the overhanging branches made it difficult to make out the path, and more than once, I snagged my foot on an overgrown root.

"I'm going to climb back up to get a good view," Emmerson grumbled. "I can't make out shit. It's so fucking dark in here."

Emmerson passed me her pack and then swung herself onto the first limb of the tree. By the time she had made her third leap, she had disappeared from view; the density of the branches swallowing her retreating frame.

I lowered our packs and slid down the tree trunk until I felt the sodden earth beneath me. I closed my eyes and inhaled the pungent aroma of decay mingling with the crisp morning air, still heavy with the scent of rain. The forest was primordial; commanding and unbroken. The groaning of the ancient trees whispered to me, enticing me to share my secrets. It was a living entity; one that watched me with cold indifference, wondering if I would make it out alive or if I'd join the countless others who had been ensnared before me.

A light breeze tugged at my hair, and small wisps played across my face. A small moaning noise sounded around me, and my eyes flew open, fearful the creature from last night had found us. I blinked, struggling to rid myself of the bleariness obscuring my vision. The gentle breeze turned biting as it whipped around me, stinging my cheeks and battering my exposed flesh. It howled its displeasure at my intrusion until its deafening roar drowned out all other sounds.

And then, just as quickly as it had started, everything stopped, and the forest was silent once more.

A chill slivered up my spine, caressing me as it settled at the base of my neck. I gave an involuntary shudder as I sensed the eyes boring into the back of my head. Turning, I gripped the hilt of my dagger that I had left strapped to my leg.

Sitting perched atop a fallen log was a woman with swirling silver eyes and long raven-colored hair that was a stark contrast against the pallor of her skin. She was bare from her neck to her waist, and her legs were covered in a mass of mahogany and ash feathers. Where her feet should be, sharp, black-tipped talons sat while tail feathers fanned out behind her. Plumes of feathers adorned her arms, which she spread wide, showcasing the impressive span of her wings. She smiled cruelly at me, revealing rows of razor-sharp teeth.

I swallowed, uttering a single word, "Harpy."

Her vicious smile grew, and violence sparkled in her eyes.

"Come closer, little one, I won't bite," she purred. "I have something for you," she said as she produced a rosy, red apple from behind her back. I took an involuntary step back, and she laughed wickedly.

At that moment, Emmerson landed on the ground next to me with a thud. She wiped her hands on her pants and said, "From what I could tell, it looks like we veered off course and started tracking south."

"Em," I whispered, never taking my eyes off the Harpy, who continued to grin.

"But we didn't make it too far with the rain and the dense vegetation slowing us down," she continued.

"Em," I repeated, louder this time.

"So it's not as bad as I first thought," she finished.

"Emmerson," I hissed.

Emmerson followed my gaze, finally taking stock of the situation. My focus remained fixed on the creature weighing us greedily.

"Fuck," Emmerson breathed.

"Are you lost, my darlings?" the Harpy crooned. "Here, take a bite," she said, offering the apple once again. "You must be famished."

The apple blackened in her hand, shriveling, and decomposing until only the rotted core remained.

She threw her head back and howled in laughter; the sound turning manic and unhinged.

I passed Emmerson her pack, which she slid onto her back. Reaching down, I took hold of her hand and whispered, "Run."

Without hesitation, we pivoted and sprinted away from the crazed monster, her laughter echoing around us as we fled.

"Aww, what's the matter my pretties?" she taunted. "We haven't even had our fun yet."

My feet pounded the forest floor; my breathing was harsh and uneven.

"If you run, I'll only chase you," she cackled.

"Don't stop," I hissed as adrenaline spiked in my veins.

"Wasn't planning on it," Emmerson panted as she pumped her fists in the air, forcing herself to move faster.

Sweat trickled from my brow and the pulse at the base of my throat was hammering as I sucked in ragged breaths.

The stillness of the day was swept away by thundering wind. It tugged at our bodies with a force that had me gritting my teeth to keep my legs moving.

I caught movement out of the corner of my eye before something pierced my side and a sharp stinging pain erupted. I cried out, and the air rushed from my lungs as I went careening to the ground. The impact jarred my bones, sending another burst of pain radiating up my hip as it connected with the hardened earth. I touched my hand to my side and then pulled it away as my wounded flesh protested the contact. Wetness coated my palm, and I peered down to see the crimson color of my blood staining my hand.

Emmerson grabbed my shoulders and pulled me to my feet as I cried out once more from the pain searing my side.

"We have to keep moving," she said over the howling wind that continued to slam into us. She caught sight of the blood on my hand and frantically started searching for injuries.

"Where are you injured?"

"My side," I panted as I lifted my tunic. Emmerson swore under her breath before running a hand through her chocolate-colored hair.

"That bad?" I groaned.

"It's not too bad," she winced, convincing neither of us.

Cruel laughter sounded as the wind died down and the Harpy emerged from behind a tree, appearing in front of us.

"You taste delicious," she said huskily, as she took in the blood seeping through my tunic with hungry eyes.

Metal clanged beside me as Emmerson unsheathed her short swords.

"Back the fuck up, bitch," she growled, taking a defensive position in front of me.

"Aww, that hurt my feelings," the Harpy crooned.

"Good. That was the fucking point," Emmerson spat.

I reached down to the twin daggers strapped to my thighs and pulled them free. With one in each hand, I flanked Emmerson as we prepared to fight for our lives.

"Let's play," the Harpy said as she cackled sinisterly.

Moving together, Emmerson and I stepped forward, just as the Harpy disappeared.

Chapter Thirty-Eight

The wind died down, but I wasn't stupid enough to think the Harpy had abandoned us. Emmerson and I moved back-to-back, scanning our surroundings, as we tried to pinpoint where the next attack would come from.

I heard a rustling sound to my left, and I whipped my head around in time to see a flicker of movement as a slight breeze fanned across my face.

"Damn, she's fast," Emmerson breathed.

Something scraped against my thigh, and I hissed as pain blossomed from the site. I looked down, seeing a single cut that exposed the flesh beneath my trousers. Crimson specs bubbled to the surface, coating the wound in my blood.

"What is it?" Emmerson asked without diverting her gaze.

"She got me with one of her talons," I answered, and Emmerson growled in frustration.

Wild, cackling laughter sounded once again, and it seemed to come from all directions, surrounding us, cocooning us in its wicked embrace.

The wind howled and filled the surrounding space, stirring up debris that littered the ground. It was like we were trapped in our own storm, held captive by the force of it, unable to break through as it smothered us.

Emmerson cried out behind me, moments before a sharp pain exploded from my shoulder. This cut was deeper, and I could feel my blood flowing freely down my arm. My hand flew to the site, and I cried out as an intense throbbing erupted from my touch. I felt lightheaded as nausea rolled over me, and I gripped my daggers tighter, distracting myself from the pain that stole my breath.

Emmerson called out to me, but I couldn't hear her over the screeching wind. My strength was waning as I succumbed to the pain and blood loss of the injuries I had already sustained.

Another talon found purchase in my flesh, this time scraping across the exposed skin of my forearm. Behind me, Emmerson howled in pain, alerting me to the fact that the Harpy had also got to her.

Desperation ensnared me as frustration roiled and churned inside me. I let my frustration escape me as I tipped my head back and screamed my fury to the heavens.

Time seemed to slow, and I could make out each individual spec of dirt and shriveled leaf as they whirled, suspended in the surrounding wind. I wanted to reach out and grasp them in my palm but feared disturbing the beautiful chaos they represented.

All of a sudden, they dropped to the ground while the last remnants of the wind hissed and dissipated. Fiery red flames erupted all around me and I waited for my body to register the pain as the heat seared my skin. I could smell the acrid scent of burning flesh, but the pain I expected to accompany it never surfaced.

The flames glowed brightly for a moment and a calmness settled over me. As the flames receded, I tracked the embers as they floated in the surrounding air before falling to the ground. At that moment, I glimpsed Misneach, soaring in the clear blue sky, somewhere not too far from us.

"Fire Heart," he breathed, relief clear in his tone. Before I could respond, the connection wavered and faded away once more.

Fear tightened my chest, and I whirled around, seeking Emmerson. I prayed to any gods that might be listening that the burning flesh still violating my nostrils did not belong to her.

Relief flooded through me as I took in the picture of my best friend; she was standing rigid, her mouth agape, and her eyes locked on mine. I swayed on my feet and sagged a little as Emmerson threw her arms out to catch me. We fell to the forest floor, and just stayed there a moment, breathing in a lungful of air, and marveling at the fact that we were alive.

"What the fuck just happened?" Emmerson whispered, breaking the silence.

I peered up at her. Her face reflected a combination of awe, confusion, and also concern as she continued to stare down at me, cradling me in her arms.

I furrowed my brow in confusion. "What do you mean?" I said, straightening myself and moving to sit beside her.

"Harlowe," she whispered, almost reverently. "You just exploded into fucking flames." My eyebrows shot into my hair as I gaped at her.

"What do you mean, I exploded into flames?" I asked, the high pitch of my voice revealing my mounting panic.

"I mean, one minute we were enveloped by that relentless fucking wind, getting chunks taken out of us by that crazy bitch who somehow hid herself in the fucking storm she held us captive in. And the next minute, the wind became flames and when I looked back at you, I saw the flames were coming from you."

"From me?" I repeated, unable to process what she was telling me.

"Yeah," she shrugged. "It started in your hands and then moved, well, everywhere. They were covering your whole body."

"Flames," I repeated, still not comprehending what she was telling me.

"Yeah. I thought we were toast, but the flames didn't burn me, or you, apparently." Emmerson just lifted her shoulder in another shrug, as if what had just happened was not completely insane.

Remembering the source of our predicament, I spun, searching for the Harpy. Just a short distance from us, I spotted a crumpled heap of mottled flesh and ashen feathers. Smoke tendrils were still rising from the unmoving figure.

A small gasp escaped my lips as I raised my hand, covering my mouth.

"Is she..." I couldn't finish that sentence.

"Only one way to find out," Emmerson said, brandishing her swords and moving closer to the figure. The smell was overwhelming, causing Emmerson to cover her nose with her forearm. She reached down and placed two fingers against the creature's throat.

I watched, holding my breath, before Emmerson turned towards me, shaking her head. I exhaled before standing to join her.

As I looked down at the Harpy, I was confronted by the sight before me. It looked as though her skin had melted away, exposing the soft tissue below the surface. What remained of her flesh was covered in red, angry blisters, and her body had charred bones protruding from it where the flames had been concentrated.

I turned away, heaving, as I dispelled the little food I had consumed that morning. I kept vomiting until I expelled nothing but bile from my body, and even then, my body continued convulsing. Emmerson rubbed my back until the shuddering subsided. I wiped my mouth on the back of my arm and accepted the canteen of water Emmerson offered me. I drank greedily, wanting to rid myself of the vile taste of vomit still clinging to my tongue. Returning the canteen, I straightened, thanking my best friend for her silent support.

I glanced back at the mess left of the Harpy and whispered, "I did that?" Disbelief colored my tone.

"She took chunks out of your body and mine. Don't waste your sympathy on her. She had none to offer either of us," Emmerson declared with derision.

"Which reminds me," — she said, as she pointed towards my shoulder — "let me see." I removed my tunic, wincing as I raised my arms above my head to pull the fabric free.

"By the gods," Emmerson breathed.

"How bad?" I asked, repeating my question from earlier.

"I won't lie this time," she grimaced. "It's not good." Blood was still running down my arm, dripping from my fingertips, before colliding with the forest floor.

"We need to wrap this one on your shoulder to stem the bleeding," Emmerson muttered. "She just about tore your muscle from the bone." The imagery made me want to heave all over again.

I glanced at my shoulder, taking in the rows of tiny puncture wounds that formed an 'O' shape, with a deep angry gash that ran through the center. It looked as though the Harpy had bitten down before dragging her top teeth across the bone of my shoulder in an attempt to remove my flesh.

It was nasty and hurt like a bitch.

Emmerson cleaned the wound for me and began suturing the bloody flesh back in place. Removing a length of fabric from her pack, she wrapped it over the wound, and the throbbing lessened.

"That'll have to suffice for the time being. Now show me the other one." I obliged, moving so she could get a closer look at a similar wound on my side. Emmerson tended to it in the same fashion, before moving on to the cut on my thigh. Thankfully, the cut on my forearm was barely more than a scratch. When she was done, I took over and did the same for her. Emmerson had fared much better than I had and only had a shallow bite and a cut from one of the Harpy's talons.

Now that the threat had vanished, we took a moment to catch our breath.

"I don't think we should tell anyone about what happened here,

Harlowe," Emerson said, concern lacing her features.

"About the Harpy?"

She made an exaggerated eye roll, telling me without words that she wasn't in the mood for joking.

"I've seen nothing like it before and while it was impressive as shit, you can't trust what others might do if they find out you have that kind of power."

I considered her words before asking, "Do you think that's why I haven't ever felt fórsa? Because I have this… fire magic… or whatever it is."

"No idea," Emmerson shrugged. "But that would make sense, I suppose."

"You suppose," I laughed.

"Well, you wouldn't need fórsa if you can just incinerate your enemies, right?"

She had a point.

"I guess we just add this to the shit we ask the Lost Witch when we find her."

I nodded my head in agreement.

"Right at the end, when the flames were receding, I heard Misneach, but before I could say anything, he just… faded away again."

"That's… troubling." Emerson glanced around before asking, "Why can't you hear him in here? You had no problem with the bond before we crossed over into the forest, right?"

"No, not at all. This has only happened once before when Kieran entered my room while I was being detained."

"Maybe it's something to do with assholes?" she offered. "That Harpy was an asshole, and there's no denying Kieran is a major one." I laughed, but it fell flat. I was worried about Misneach and his presence in my mind had become a constant comfort.

"We should get moving," Emmerson declared as she hoisted me up alongside her.

I was already feeling fatigued after a restless night with limited sleep, and now I was utterly drained. The muscles in my legs burned with each step I took, and my injuries protested each time I jostled them. It made the journey even more miserable than the day before.

Despite our slow pace, we managed a full day of travel, only stopping to rest for brief periods. When we finally stopped for the night, my body sagged in relief.

Emmerson was inspecting a tree up ahead, and I internally groaned at the idea of having to climb it. I doubted my shoulder was up to the challenge if I was being honest with myself.

"Over here," Emmerson called to me, and I forced my legs to stand as I made my way to where she stood.

Emmerson pulled aside a curtain of low-hanging vines, revealing the hollowed-out trunk, which was large enough for the both of us to fit.

I grinned, overjoyed by the fact I would not be required to raise my arms above my head, at least for tonight.

We settled into the base of the tree and used what remained of the daylight to rifle through our packs for dinner. I relaxed against my pack and thanked the gods for our small respite while studiously ignoring the insects crawling around me.

"I have to be honest, I am surprised we survived the day," I mused.

"Don't tempt the fates, Harlowe," Emmerson warned.

I stifled a yawn and closed my eyes before settling in for sleep. I was so exhausted that even the screeching and wailing of the creature that had stalked us the previous night could not fend off the growing blackness.

Chapter Thirty-Nine

The next morning was already off to a better start when we emerged from our hiding place, and nothing was waiting to kill us.

I took a moment to stretch and test my injuries. My shoulder was still humming along to a rhythm of its own, but at least it had stopped bleeding. The pain from the injury to my side had receded overnight, so it only hurt when I moved it. The cut on my leg was the least of my worries that I barely registered it. My muscles were tight and aching from the fight and being cramped all night. I hadn't moved an inch; exhaustion kept me cocooned in sleep the entire night.

As I peered over at Emmerson, I noted that she too was testing her injuries; tensing and flexing her muscles, hoping to release the strain from the events of the day prior.

I prayed to whatever gods were feeling merciful that today would be uneventful.

"Ready?" I asked Emmerson as I slung my pack over my shoulders. I winced when the weight of my pack bore down on my injured shoulder. Soon enough, though, the sharp burst of pain settled back into the rhythmic throbbing I was getting used to.

"Ready."

We walked silently, too exhausted to do anything else but observe our surroundings.

"So what's the plan for when we find the witch?" Emmerson said, pulling me from my thoughts.

"I guess it depends on what she tells us."

"Okay, but we aren't going to keep kicking back in this forest trying to end us, right?"

I chuckled. It was good to know that there were some things that even disturbed Emmerson.

"No," I reassured her. "I don't know where we will go after this, but hiding out in some village in a neighboring kingdom has to be safer than taking our chances in here." I gestured to the surrounding forest.

"Good, because I didn't much enjoy having literal bites taken out of me."

I snorted in agreement.

We lapsed back into a comfortable silence as we continued to make our way northeast. It was past midday when I heard the sound of rushing water nearby. Eager to clean myself up after accumulating days of dirt and filth, I veered left in the water's direction.

Once we broke through the thicket of trees, a beautiful, glistening lake appeared before us. The sun reflected off the surface, making it appear as though tiny gems were floating and glittering atop the water. I shrugged out of my pack and rolled up the sleeves of my tunic. Getting down on my knees, I leaned over the bank and cupped the cool water in my hands. I splashed my face and reveled in the refreshing iciness the water left in its wake. I cupped more handfuls of water, rubbing it over the back of my neck, my throat, and up my arms. With each splash, it felt as though I was washing away the fatigue and weariness of the past few days. I wanted to dive right in and submerge myself in the healing depths.

"Don't get too close," Emmerson said as if sensing my thoughts. "We do not know what is lurking within that lake."

I looked over my shoulder and took in her raised eyebrow and pointed stare, which told me she knew where my thoughts had wandered. I smiled sheepishly before returning my attention to the water to continue with my task.

Emmerson joined me, and I could tell she was also enjoying the refreshing coolness. I was feeling much better, and cleaner, as I returned to my pack and pulled out some rations for lunch.

"The bread is going stale," I informed Emmerson, as I chewed. "We still have plenty of dried meat, fruit, and cheese, but we should start hunting some smaller game, so we don't run too low on supplies."

"It will have to wait until we leave this forest," Emmerson replied, moving from the bank to join me. "I don't want to risk a fire when we don't know what might be around to see it."

"Good point," I muttered, hoping we completed our task soon. I would be dead by now if she hadn't insisted on joining me. I had never thought of myself as a pampered princess, especially with my father's constant criticism of the activities I spent my time perfecting. But out here, surrounded by enemies, it was clear I was outmatched. If I wanted to survive whatever the fates had planned for me, I had to up my game. I could no longer play pretend at being a warrior. I needed to hone my skills, and truth be told, I had to be smarter with the decisions I made. I'd let too many people determine the course of my future by being willfully ignorant, and now I was paying for it.

We rested longer than we usually would have but given our injuries and general fatigue from our fight with the Harpy, we figured our bodies had earned a slight reprieve. All too soon, though, it was time to move. I forced my legs to hold me upright as we continued trekking northeast.

The dirt crunched under my boots as we made our way down the path. The deeper we came into the forest, the more manageable the foliage became. It was as if the outer depths were left to grow wild and untamed, as though they stood in warning to everyone who entered that the forest was lethal and unforgiving.

Not that we had heeded the warning.

Well-worn trails had emerged the deeper we trekked, and that was both a comfort and a cause for unease. Navigating the forest became more efficient without the need to hack through dense vegetation. However, it was also a stark reminder that we weren't alone in this place, with countless monsters having walked the same paths.

As if summoned by my errant thoughts, a growl sounded beside me. I whipped my head toward the sound, seeking the source of the noise that was sending ripples of unease cascading over me. The sound of growling intensified, coming from all around me.

I swung my head back and forth, trying to see what my ears had already alerted me to, but the dark canopy of the trees overhead provided too many shadows for creatures to lurk within.

Emmerson and I stepped closer together, instinct taking over. If we ran, whatever waited for us in the shadows would give chase, and I somehow knew that would be a fatal mistake.

"Don't move," I whispered to Emmerson.

"They are surrounding us," she replied through gritted teeth.

"If we run, they will give chase. And something tells me that is not a race we will win."

"We won't survive if we just stand here either Harlowe," Emmerson's tone was pleading, but my gut told me we were safer remaining where we were.

"Get your weapons, but don't move," I commanded. I heard metal against metal, the telltale sign Emmerson had withdrawn her short swords. The growling intensified further.

"Okay, maybe that wasn't the best idea."

"They can growl all they want. I'm not lowering my weapons," Emmerson scowled.

A pair of glowing yellow eyes emerged from the shadows before more joined them. Five sets of predatory eyes scrutinized us, seeking any hint of vulnerability.

A large, black mass of fur stepped forward, and I swallowed a gasp at the sheer size of the beast before me. A massive wolf emerged from the shadows. At its full height, it would stand just below my chin. I trembled, unable to stop my body's response as I took in the threat before me.

"That's a monstrous wolf," I breathed, not daring to move an inch, fearful I might provoke it into attacking.

The wolf curled its upper lip in a snarl, revealing pointed canines nestled amongst sharpened teeth. Saliva dripped from its mouth as the wolf snapped its lethal jaws, making me flinch at the power behind them. If this wolf wanted to, it could shred us to pieces.

"That's not any wolf," Emmerson muttered. "That's a dire wolf."

Its black fur bristled, and it continued to growl low in its throat as it took another step toward us. Its massive paws shuddered with the movement, and its broad shoulders showcased the muscled physique of the animal.

This creature was the embodiment of deadly.

More wolves stepped forward, following the first one, until they surrounded us.

"What now?" Emmerson hissed. Honestly, I had no idea. I was pretty sure we were about to die, but I didn't vocalize that thought.

"Just stand your ground," I said, straightening to my full height.

"Oh yes, of course. That's a brilliant plan. Why didn't I think of that?" she snapped back at me.

"They're animals Em, they respond to dominance or some shit. We need to show we are stronger than they are and that we're not afraid of them."

Emmerson made a strangled noise in the back of her throat, not believing the bullshit coming out of my mouth. I didn't blame her. I didn't believe it either.

But then the first wolf stopped growling, taking a tentative step towards me, and sniffed the surrounding air.

"See," I hissed, noticing the other wolves doing the same.

"Even you can't believe the shit you just spouted actually worked," Emmerson said, giving me a sidelong glance. I gave the wolves a meaningful look and then returned my gaze to her. I was rewarded with an incredulous snort.

The first wolf crept closer. When it was within reach, it extended its tongue, running it up the side of my face. I scrunched up my nose, forcing myself to stay put rather than leaping away from the wet, slobbering creature as I wanted to. A nudge at my back made me turn and see the other wolves crowding around. They had moved in close, pushing Emmerson out of the way while they sniffed, licked, and pawed at me. It was eerily similar to the day I first encountered the dragons.

I reached down and patted one on the head and it panted in approval, its tongue lolling to the side as I continued. The wolves, all vying for my attention, pushed me to the ground, where they continued to fight over who was within arm's reach. I patted them all in turn and laughed as they playfully nipped at each other. They settled around me, one with its head in my lap while the others enclosed me in a mass of black fur.

I peered over my shoulder to where Emmerson stood, gaping at me. I lifted a shoulder in a shrug, not understanding what was happening, but pleased that we no longer seemed to be on the menu. We stayed like this for some time, me on the ground petting the wolves and them forming a protective circle around me. Emmerson sat off to the side, incredulous, and rubbing her eyes in disbelief.

Something caught the wolves' attention, and they each lifted their heads, ears twitching as they listened to something my human ears could not detect. One by one, they rose, giving me a last nudge or flick of their tongue, before sauntering off into the forest.

"That was fucking insane," Emmerson said as she scrambled to her feet.

I wiped my hands over my pants before returning them to my face and wiping away the saliva left by the wolves.

"I mean, I thought we were dead for sure. And I know you did too, despite that bullshit you came up with to keep me calm." Emmerson gave me a knowing look at her last comment.

"But then, what?" she said, throwing her hands up in the air. "They just decide they like you and want to pet you?" When I didn't answer, she just rolled her eyes and mumbled, "This place is making me crazy."

Something shimmered through the trees up ahead and then settled. A small cottage took form before my eyes.

"Emmerson," I said in astonishment, "look!" I pointed in the cottage's direction that had just emerged from thin air, and her eyes widened as her gaze settled over it.

"What is that?" she breathed.

I sucked in a deep breath and said, "Only one way to find out," as I stepped forward.

Chapter Forty

The brownstone cottage was larger than it had first appeared. Up close, I could see that it extended farther back, hidden amongst the forest, making it grander than I expected. Age had dulled the worn wooden door, and I observed that the roof had tiles instead of thatch, which were common in our kingdom.

I looked at Emmerson, who nodded. I exhaled a measured breath before reaching up and knocking.

"I hope whoever is inside doesn't intend to eat us," I mumbled.

The words had barely left my mouth when the door opened to a dark, lifeless entryway.

"Creepy," Emmerson muttered under her breath.

I glanced inside but couldn't make out any inhabitants lurking in the shadows.

"Do we go in?" I asked Emmerson. A shiver ran up my spine and a cold sweat erupted on the back of my neck. "This place is not giving me a very welcoming vibe," I admitted.

"This was your plan, Harlowe. The sooner we get what we came for, the sooner we can leave. So put on your big girl boots and step inside."

I stepped inside and stood in the middle of what seemed to be a sitting area. In front of us sat a large blue velvet settee with a matching armchair to its side. A plush cream rug adorned the floor and bookshelves lined the walls, displaying the many tomes packed neatly within.

Emmerson closed the door behind us, and it groaned loudly.

Beyond the living space, a small kitchen was nestled in the corner, partly obscured by a wall, but I could make out a round dining table and chairs. On the left, a long corridor was shrouded in darkness, but doors along the walls hinted at more rooms.

The eerie sense of being watched slithered over me and unease wrapped around my middle. I swallowed my nerves and called out in greeting. The sound echoed around us, but still, the witch did not appear. At least I hoped it was the witch's home.

Candles flashed to life, and I jumped, startled by the movement. My heart started hammering inside my chest and I willed my body to calm down. My gaze swept the area again, and I spotted someone observing us from the shadows.

I swear they had not been standing there moments before.

A woman stepped forward, a coy smirk on her pouty lips as she watched us. She was stunning and appeared younger than I had imagined her. Of course, she was immortal, so she looked no older than twenty-one, but I knew she was at least four centuries old if she survived the War of Witches.

"Bold," she purred, flicking her waist-length, brown hair over the shoulder of her red dress. "To enter the home of someone you do not know, living in the Forest of Nightmares no less," she chuckled. Amusement sparkled in her deep brown eyes, and she quirked a single brow in challenge.

"We are looking for the Lost Witch," I stated, sounding calmer than my racing heartbeat would suggest I was.

"Indeed," she grinned. "It is why I revealed my home to you." So it had been magic concealing the cottage from our view.

Clever.

The witch smirked as if she had just heard my thoughts.

"You pleased the dire wolves, and this intrigued me," she continued.

"They belong to you?" I asked. "The dire wolves, I mean."

"They protect my home from the beasts that live within this forest," she confirmed. "You are the first to survive an encounter with them." She looked me over, as though trying to figure out why that was so. Next, she directed her eyes toward Emmerson and repeated the action. She huffed out a breath as she seemed to come up short.

"Tell me, what is it you have come seeking, Queen of Fire?"

I swallowed hard.

Was she aware of what had occurred with the Harpy?

"Why do you call me that?"

The witch gave me a knowing smirk but said no more.

"I have come seeking answers," I said, my voice wavering, having lost all my false bravado with her proclamation.

The witch laughed, throwing her head back as she cackled.

"Everyone wants answers, girl, but they don't always like the answers I give."

"That's because you give half-truths," Emmerson muttered under her breath. The witch swung her gaze towards her and narrowed her eyes.

"People seek knowledge they have no business knowing," the witch hissed, her upper lip curling into a snarl. "And then they blame my kind for the consequences of their stupidity."

"So, there were no dark witches, then?" Emmerson said, crossing her arms over her chest. "During the War of Witches," she continued, not backing down from the rage clear in the witch's glare. The witch only snarled in answer.

She turned away from us and headed in the kitchen's direction. The witch peered back at us over her shoulder and said, "Come then, I want you out of my home as soon as possible."

"She is downright hospitable," Emmerson grumbled.

I stalked after her, wicked anticipation bubbling to the surface within me. I needed to know what Kieran had planned for me.

"Sit," she said, pointing to the wooded chairs surrounding her table. I pulled one out and sat down, Emmerson doing the same at my side.

The witch bustled about her kitchen, pulling open cupboards, and removing various items, before she started grinding herbs with a pestle and mortar. She worked diligently, adding this and that before she moved towards the wood fire stove and boiled some water.

I watched with fascination, enraptured by the steady twist of her wrist as she ground the herbs into a fine powder. I could feel the buzz of magic in the air, which only intensified as a tingling sensation spread over my skin.

With the kettle boiled, the witch poured the water into the mortar before combining the contents. Satisfied with her work, she opened another cupboard, retrieved a chipped porcelain mug, and poured the concoction into it.

The witch returned to the table and placed the mug in front of me. "Drink it. It will help me see your path."

I eyed the mug with suspicion, and the witch sniffed.

"What will it do?" I asked as I picked it up.

"It will help you open up to me. Allow me to see into your soul," she said, a grin spreading across her sensual lips.

"It won't kill you, or even harm you," she added when I still had not consumed the concoction.

I lifted the mug to my mouth and took a tentative sip. The liquid scalded my tongue as it slid over the tissue. Saliva pooled in my mouth to ease the burn and I almost dropped the mug on the tabletop in my haste to rid myself of it.

"I thought you would have the good sense to blow on the damned thing before throwing it down your gullet," she berated me.

I didn't respond, the burning sensation still swelling my tongue. Emmerson looked on, concern etching her features. I wasn't sure if she was worried about my injured tongue or whether she was worried about the situation generally.

Probably the latter if I had to guess. A burnt tongue would not register high on the list of things that scared Emmerson.

We sat in tense silence as I continued to drink the hot liquid, cooling it down with my breath before each sip. When I was nearing the end, the witch leaned over the table and tipped the mug up high.

"Every drop," she instructed.

Finished with the drink, I sat the mug back on the table and asked, "What now?"

"The brew needs a few minutes to take effect," the witch responded. "Place your hands on the table, palms up, and extend your arms towards me."

Doing as she said, I slid my palms onto the table and leaned forward so she could reach my hands. The witch grasped my hands in her own and studied the lines of my palms. Her hands were softer than I expected them to be, especially compared to the calloused hands I offered from all my training with Zeke.

The witch looked up at me; her stare penetrating the very center of my being. I fought the urge to fidget under her scrutiny.

"What do you feel?" she asked, her voice low and whimsical.

"Feel?" I asked, confused.

"Has the brew taken effect?"

"Oh," I said, as I considered her words.

I felt calmer than I did when we first arrived. No, not calm. It was more like the tension had left my muscles and my body was no longer wound tight. A slight buzzing noise sounded next to my ear, and I peered around me to see where it was coming from.

"Do you hear that?" I whispered.

Looking at Emmerson, I could see that she did not know what I was talking about. I turned back to the witch and her broad smile told me that this was what she had been waiting for.

Prickling erupted over my skin, and I felt lightheaded, like a fog had moved in across my thoughts and I was struggling to clear it.

"What did you do to me?" I slurred, becoming panicked now.

"Shh," the witch said. "The brew is just shedding your inhibitions or any other resistance to my magic. You are safe, and your friend is here keeping watch over you."

I did feel safe, but I wasn't sure if that was the magic's influence, or if the witch genuinely harbored no ill-will towards me.

She leaned down and licked my left palm before repeating the process with my right. I suppressed the urge to cringe, mindful of what had been on my hands. Specifically, the saliva of five dire wolves.

In my periphery, I saw Emmerson shudder, remembering what I just had.

The witch lifted her head, her eyes meeting mine, as candle flames flickered around us. The air grew tense, and my muscles tightened in anticipation.

"It is time," the witch crooned, and all the flames were extinguished at once, leaving us in an unnatural darkness.

Chapter Forty-One

I tried to pull my hands back, but the witch's grip was strong. As I peered around the darkness, I struggled to make anything out.

"Harlowe," Emmerson breathed.

"I'm here," I panted, unable to hide the fear leeching into my voice.

"Ask your questions, Queen of Fire," a deep masculine voice said across from me.

Before my panic could set in, the candles flicked back to life, illuminating us in the soft glow of their flames. I sighed with relief when I realized it was the witch, not another creature, holding my hands.

"Ask," she repeated in the same deep baritone.

"What does the King of Netheran want from me?" I asked, licking my lips.

"The King of Serpents," the witch hummed.

"He said," — I paused and collected myself, unsettled by whatever was happening with the witch — "he said that he received a vision. That I was instrumental in fulfilling his dreams for his kingdom."

"You are the Daughter of War and Peace," the witch said. "The Daughter of War and Peace is the other half of the Serpent King."

"What does that mean?"

"It means, Queen of Fire, you are both two sides of the same coin. The power you house is the twin to that which the Serpent King possesses. Your power and his power are interconnected. With the blessing of the fates, yours will strengthen his."

"How can that be? Kieran... he is not a good man. I'm unsure of his intentions, but they won't be good. Why would the fates allow for anything to amplify his power?"

"The fates are fickle," the witch mused. "They enjoy sowing discord and upheaval. But they are not stupid. Your power was made to strengthen his, true, but it is also the balance."

"I don't understand."

"Everything requires balance. When someone holds power like that of the Serpent King, another must rise with power to equal it. The Serpent King will seek to use your power for his own nefarious purposes, and if you let him, the two of you would set the realm on a collision course of catastrophic proportions."

"I don't even know what's within me," I said, aware of the desperation leaking into my tone. "Until recently, I couldn't even feel, let alone wield, fórsa."

"You do not wield the realm's power," the witch stated.

"Then where does it come from?"

"The only place fire can be contained," she said simply. "The dragons."

"The dragons?" I repeated, not even trying to conceal my confusion.

"You call to them, do you not?"

"I... I mean, yes, I guess so. At least they seem to think I do," I stuttered.

"You are the conduit of their flames."

"Okay," I said, although it sounded like a question. "Where does this leave me? What am I supposed to do?"

"You can either be our salvation, or our damnation."

"I'm still not sure I understand?" I tried again.

"I know," she said, a sympathetic smile crossing her lips. "You must choose your own path, and only that choice will determine your fate."

I contemplated her words, trying to piece it all together. My time was limited, and I couldn't waste this opportunity to learn everything I needed to know.

"I must warn you Queen of Fire, not everyone will sit by idly and allow you to choose your path," she continued. "Some will seek to destroy you before you get the chance to choose ruination."

I shuddered at her warning.

"Vidyaa," I said quietly, everything clicking into place. The witch nodded in confirmation.

"What?" Emmerson asked, interrupting for the first time.

"The attack on our kingdom came from Vidyaa," I mused. "They didn't attack the kingdom itself but concentrated their attack on the palace. We all thought they were looking for something." I swallowed when I realized that something was me.

"What if they know about this... this... prophecy, or whatever it is? And came to kill me before I could choose Kieran," I finished.

"It would make sense considering they are literally the Kingdom of Visionaries," Emmerson offered.

"I thought they were just being pretentious. You know, their way of saying that their people were the most forward-thinking or something like that," I shrugged. I considered myself open-minded and was receptive to being convinced of almost anything. Prophets, however, were not one of them. I detested the idea of fate or anything that sought to undermine my free will.

"Apparently not," Emmerson muttered.

"They are not the only ones, and they will not be the last," the witch warned. Emmerson tensed beside me as if she was preparing to defend me against an unseen threat lurking nearby. Meanwhile, the memory of the Siren rose unbidden to my mind.

"You must leave this place, Queen of Fire. Only death awaits you here," the witch said, more urgently now.

All of a sudden, the feelings the magic had induced within me receded, and the brightness of the day returned, cradling us in the glow of the soft afternoon sunlight.

The witch pushed back from the table and slid her chair out as she stood. "You must leave at once," she said, her voice returning to her normal feminine tone.

"What?" I asked, confused, my mind trying to catch up to the sudden change in her demeanor.

"Talk about a split personality," Emmerson grumbled.

"You are not safe to be around," she hissed. I glanced towards Emmerson, who wore a similar look of confusion, as she reached towards her dagger, gripping the handle.

"I have one more question," I implored.

"I have given you all the answers you are getting."

"Please," I tried again. "The animals," I started, "why are they drawn to me?"

The witch rolled her eyes as if my stupidity offended her. "Nature seeks balance. In the intricate tapestry of nature, balance is the silent orchestrator, weaving together the threads of life into a harmonious existence. In the wilderness, all life coexists in a symbiotic relationship, each dependent on the other for survival. You were born to be the balance, and that which comes from nature will recognize you," she supplied.

I furrowed my brows, no clearer on the subject than before I asked the question.

"You have your answers, now go." The witch was brooking no arguments this time.

Emmerson and I pushed up from our seats and moved to retrieve our packs, which we had set down near the front door.

"Girl," the witch called after us. I turned to look at her, not knowing if she meant me or Emmerson.

"Be careful out there," she said, directing her comment towards me. "And choose wisely. Not everyone is who they seem. Not all friends are allies, and not all enemies are adversaries. Choose. Wisely."

I dashed out of the cottage, eager to put space between the witch and me. Her parting words had left me with an uneasy feeling.

Emmerson seemed to understand my need for quiet contemplation as we walked in silence, too caught up in my ruminations for chatter.

As the sun slid lower and lower, I sighed, recognizing we would need to stop soon to find somewhere to sleep for the night.

"We should find a safe spot to camp for the night," I said, breaking the silence.

"I wonder if those dire wolves are still around," Emmerson pondered aloud.

"Why?"

"Maybe we could sleep on the ground while they stood guard. I do not relish sleeping tied to a tree or cramped in a small hole with all kinds of creepy crawlies running over my flesh." Emmerson shuddered at the thought.

"I think there are deadlier things in the forest than dire wolves. Even if they were here, I doubt they could protect us from everything that lurks after dark."

"True," Emmerson conceded.

"It was a nice thought though," I said, nudging her with my shoulder.

We kept moving west. With our mission accomplished, there was no reason to stay in the forest. We needed to backtrack until we found our way out of here. I was desperate to connect with Misneach and hear the comforting sound of his gruff voice again.

The sound of feet shuffling drew me out of my thoughts, and Emmerson grabbed me, pulling me to the ground behind a large bush. As the seconds passed, the sound grew louder, yet I couldn't distinguish who was coming. Judging by the rhythmic sound of heavy footfalls over gravel, whatever was headed our way, there were a lot of them.

A huge, horned creature with moss-colored skin broke through the tree line. A mix between a horse's muzzle and a pig's snout made up its face, while long, pointed horns sat atop its head. Smaller horns curved away from the creature's head, reaching in the opposite direction, coming to sharpened tips that looked deadly. The creature had a muscular build, with broad shoulders and strong, corded arms, prominent abdominal muscles lined the creature's torso, and thick muscled thighs tapered off into well-defined calves, which met hooves, making up the creature's powerful legs.

I stifled a gasp as dozens upon dozens of the creatures emerged from the dense forest. They wore a single piece of brown leather that wrapped around their waist and fanned out over their thighs. Similar strips of leather were woven over their forearms into a gauntlet, tipped with a razor-sharp spike at the elbow. Leather greaves encased their lower legs before settling over their hooves. Over their shoulders, they wore a leather pauldron, also sporting an array of lethal spikes that would easily dispense with enemies in battle.

"We have to get out of here," Emmerson whispered, only loud enough for me to hear. She pointed behind her, demonstrating that she wanted me to crawl backward, stomach flat against the ground, moving slow enough not to make a disturbance.

I spared a glance back at the creatures, noting their red irises, which sent fear spiraling within me.

Those creatures were why this place was called the Forest of Nightmares.

I started backing away, just as Emmerson had instructed. Once we were concealed in the coverage offered by the thick forest, I moved to stand.

Turning towards Emmerson, I saw her eyes widen in shock as a large, rough hand covered my mouth, while another gripped my shoulder, pulling me back against a solid wall of muscle.

Chapter Forty-Two

I was dragged backward as I struggled against the hold of my attacker. I had lost sight of Emmerson, unable to move my head sideways in the tight grip of the hand wrapped around my mouth. With the army of monsters still within hearing distance, I was in a precarious position, unable to make any noise in my struggles for fear of alerting an even bigger threat to my presence.

My attacker continued dragging me deeper and deeper into the forest, as I reached out for anything that might stall my attacker's progress. Fear for Emmerson clawed at my chest, but I knew she was more than capable of freeing herself. I just had to make sure I wasn't too far away from her when that happened.

"Stop fighting me, Little Menace," a familiar deep voice hissed against my ear. My fight left me all at once as if evaporating and drifting away on a breeze.

I allowed Silas to continue walking me backward as the density of the forest provided us with cover from the prying eyes of the monstrous inhabitants of this place.

Having judged us to be a safe distance, Silas stopped, spinning me around in his arms. His soulful brown eyes locked with mine, and then his lips were crashing against mine in a scorching kiss. His tongue brushed against the seam of my lips, and I permitted him entrance as he devoured me like I was the oxygen he needed to sustain life.

"Hey assholes," Emmerson hissed. "How about you have your face-sucking session when we're not in the middle of the forest, surrounded by fucking beasts who look like they would rip your head off for fun?"

Embarrassed, I broke the kiss and tried to take a step back. Silas wasn't having it though, and he pulled me in closer, resting his forehead on my own. His actions caused a stir in me that I didn't want to scrutinize right now.

"Are you both okay?" I heard Cillian ask Emmerson from beside me.

As though a reminder of the severity of our situation, Silas broke our embrace and turned towards his second.

"Harlowe's hurt more seriously than it appears," Silas informed Cillian. It surprised me he could take in my injuries in the short time we had been in each other's company, let alone give voice to what I was unwilling to acknowledge out loud.

"What about you, Emmerson? How have you fared?"

"I'll live," she replied, raising her shoulder in a shrug. I caught the start of a small smirk on Cillian's lips as he shook his head at her response.

"Okay, then let's get back to the others before we take a proper look," Silas said. He turned to me and asked, "You okay for a few more miles?" I nodded.

Silas took my hand in his, leading us further into the forest.

"How did you find us?" I asked as we walked. Silas looked back at me, an amused smile playing on his lips as he arched a brow.

"Did you think I would let you escape me, Little Menace?"

The raw possessiveness I saw lurking in Silas's heated gaze had me clenching my thighs together. The man was carnal, and his obsessive need to lay claim to my body was intoxicating.

"And what do you plan to do with me now that you have found me?" I asked, shaking myself free from the lust coloring my thoughts.

"I will not return you to your father if that is what you're worried about."

I hadn't thought that he would, but I was worried about what he was planning. I couldn't bring him into my mess and risk Kieran taking it out on Pyrithia.

We continued in companionable silence for a short while before we came across a camp, complete with a fire and tents.

Panicked, I turned to Silas and said, "You'll attract attention with a fire and tents out in the open like this."

He smirked at me before saying, "Concealment spell."

You could only get a concealment spell if you knew a practitioner of the magical arts; a witch. Unlike the power offered by the realm, the magic wielded by witches was not available nor connected to all citizens of the realm. While the people within Aetherian still had to master the art of wielding fórsa, everyone had the inherent ability to do so. Witches, however, received their power through their lineage. Magic was passed from mother to daughter, but no one knew the origins of the first witch's power. After the War of Witches, many speculated it was derived from a dark entity that allowed the power to morph into something evil over time, leading the witches towards the dark arts and their actions during the war.

Given that no kingdom, outside of Netheran, still retained witches in their advisory council, it was curious that Silas possessed a concealment spell.

"A concealment spell?" I asked in disbelief.

Silas didn't elaborate. He only winked and pulled me towards the largest tent. Once inside, he sat me down on his bedroll and indicated for me to remove my tunic. It still hurt to move my arms above my head, but I complied, trying to hide my wince as I did so.

With a gentleness that surprised me, Silas removed the wrapping from my shoulder and let out a curse before leveling me with a narrowed glare.

"What the hell were you thinking when you fled into the Forest of Nightmares Harlowe?" he scolded.

"I was thinking that I didn't want to be forced into a marriage with the King of Netheran, and this was the only place no one would come looking for me!" I returned, my hackles rising. "Well, no one except you, of course," I amended.

Silas growled low in his throat as he continued his perusal of my injury, and I sucked in a breath as he prodded my damaged flesh. Silas exited the tent before returning moments later with a bottle of whiskey in hand.

"This will hurt," he warned, raising the bottle to my shoulder. I clenched my teeth, but a whimper escaped me as a searing pain made its way across my shoulder.

"We need to kill off any chance of infection," Silas said in apology. After pouring whiskey on my shoulder several more times, Silas grabbed fresh wrappings and covered the wound once more. He then moved on to the bite on my side, followed by the cut on my leg, repeating the process.

"They're going to take time to heal, especially the one on your shoulder, but they're clean, and there is no sign of infection. I'm guessing Emmerson took care of those for you?"

I grunted in agreement as I moved to grab my tunic.

"Here," Silas said, stopping me and handing me a clean one of his. He redressed me, saving me from the pain of having to lift my arms above my head again.

"Where are your dragons?" I asked now that he had finished.

"A bit obvious given their size, don't you think?" he said sardonically. "I would ask where Misneach is, but I already know you used him as a distraction while you evaded Cillian." There was something akin to pride in his voice, as his eyes sparkled with mirth.

"I wouldn't be able to tell you. Our bond, it's... dull, I guess. I can sense he is out there, but I haven't been able to communicate with him since entering the forest," I confessed, choosing to keep our brief contact during my encounter with the Harpy to myself.

"Ah," Silas said. "Your bond is new. Dark magic can suppress other forms of magic, including the bond between dragon and Cathal if they haven't settled yet, or if the magic is not strong. In case you didn't notice, this forest is full of dark magic Little Menace," he said. "Your bond will strengthen in time."

I pondered if this was what Kieran wielded, dark magic, as his presence had the same effect on my bond with Misneach.

Silas crouched before me; eyes locked on mine as he studied me. I wanted to peel back the layers of his mind and see what was going on inside his head, but he just kept staring at me with equal curiosity.

Silas sighed heavily before saying, "I was worried about you, Little Menace," and then added, "Never leave me again." Possessiveness crept into his tone, and I could see the anger brewing in the depths of his dark, turbulent eyes. A tingling sensation raced up my spine, and I resisted the urge to shiver at his words.

Why did his possessiveness both infuriate me and fill me with a longing so profound I failed to understand it?

I ignored his antics for now, as I leaned forward, brushing my lips against his. Silas reached up, cupping the back of my neck as he deepened the kiss. The kiss was urgent and searching, as though he was seeking to reassure himself that I was here. When he broke away, he stood, taking my hand to help me stand before leading me back outside.

Emmerson was sitting by the fire with Cillian, who was fixing the wrappings on her wound. I had to smile to myself, knowing full well she had him wrapped around her finger.

As I looked around the group, I saw that Fionn, Teller, and Cian were also here. Fionn smiled at me and stood, gripping me in a tight hug.

"She's hurt, you idiot," Silas scolded him as I gasped in pain.

"Shit. Sorry Harlowe," Fionn said sheepishly as he released me. I waved him off, telling him not to worry about it.

I sidled up next to Emmerson and reached forward to warm my hands on the fire.

"All good?" she whispered, and I nodded.

"Well, I for one want to know what the hell you two ladies have been up to," Teller said with a mischievous grin. Silas snarled from somewhere behind me, which only made him grin wider.

"Hiding out in a forest full of creatures hell-bent on killing us. You know, the usual. And you?" Emmerson teased.

"You wouldn't have had to if you hadn't evaded me when I first found you on the border of Valoren," Cillian muttered under his breath.

Emmerson smirked, "Did that hurt your ego? Two hapless girls getting the jump on you?" she goaded.

"I'm serious, Emmerson. Why did you run? I would have helped hide you," he said, unable to hide the hurt in his voice.

"I'd like to know that too," Silas said as he took the seat beside me.

"You would have stopped us from entering the forest and doing what we came here to do," she said defensively.

"And what would that be?" Silas asked with an edge to his tone.

"Prevent unnecessary conflict," I said before Emmerson could answer. I took a deep breath and continued, "If you or anyone from another kingdom hid us from my father or Kieran, there would have been repercussions," I elaborated, making sure I didn't glance toward Emmerson.

Not that I didn't trust Silas to keep my secrets, I just wasn't ready to divulge everything I had learned over the last week.

I could feel Silas's gaze burning into the side of my head, but I refused to meet his eyes for fear he would see the lie reflected in my own.

"What's going on back home?" I asked, redirecting the conversation.

"Your father deployed all the newly trained Cathal to look for you, along with some ground troops," Fionn answered.

"You were right to worry about the other kingdoms," Teller added. "Your father sent messengers to all of them requesting your return should you arrive on their doorstep."

"And what about Kieran?" I asked, glancing at Silas out of the corner of my eye. He tensed but provided no answer.

"He is eager to reunite with his bride," Cian stated, joining the conversation. Teller snorted as Cian continued, "He sent his men out to search for you as well."

"She is not his bride," Emmerson spat.

"He had a right tantrum is what he did," Teller clarified. "He and your father had a screaming match in the throne room. Everyone within the palace walls heard it. Kieran threatened war if you were not returned to him. He berated your mother for helping you escape, too."

Guilt squeezed around my chest at the thought of my mother enduring the backlash of my disappearance.

"And my mother?" I asked, afraid to hear the answer.

"She's alright Harlowe," Cillian said. "I'm sure her actions have created a few marital problems, but no harm will come to her."

I did not fear my father harming my mother. He adored her, and while he would be upset, he would never hurt her.

No, it was Kieran's wrath, I feared. I don't know how I would react if he retaliated against my mother.

"She has a spine made of iron, your mother. I see where you get it from," Teller winked. Emmerson glanced towards me, a knowing smirk on her face.

We made idle conversation, enjoying the warmth of the fire as we shared a meal.

"What were those things back there?" I asked Silas, turning to face him.

"Minotaurs. Half beast, half man, and a lot of killing power. I have seen them crush a man's skull in one hand. We would do well to steer clear of them as we make our way out of here."

Glancing over at Emmerson, I found her already looking at me. Without speaking, she asked me what the plan was now. I shrugged, and she nodded. We would need to get away from the group to plan our next steps.

I turned back towards Silas and found him glaring at me, having captured our unspoken conversation.

"Come on," he said, taking the whiskey I was nursing out of my hand. "It's been a long day. You need to rest." He pulled me along after him and we entered his tent. I unstrapped my bedroll from my pack and laid it down next to Silas's.

Silas gripped my hips from behind, and I stiffened in response.

"Little Menace," he growled, his erection pressing into my lower back. "I'm going to remind you who you belong to." His hot breath fanned against my ear as he whispered, "I'm going to fuck you so hard, you'll be ruined for any other man but me."

Chapter Forty-Three

Silas's grip on my hips bordered on painful and I could feel myself getting wet in response. His possessiveness was a turn-on when we were in the bedroom. Getting him to drop it when we were outside the bedroom, however, was the issue.

"Tell me," he said as he nipped my earlobe. "Are you wet for me already, Little Menace?"

My breathing hitched and liquid fire pooled at the junction between my thighs. It felt like forever since I'd had him inside me, and my body was on board for a repeat.

Silas slipped his hand under the waistband of my pants, dipping one calloused finger inside me. He growled against my ear when he found just how wet I was for him.

"This pussy is dripping for me," he snarled. He plunged another finger inside me, and I moaned at the fullness he created. My body squeezed around the digits and the delicious friction had me wanting to come undone at first contact. He withdrew his fingers, and I cried out at the loss, wanting him to continue his ministrations.

"You've been a very bad girl, Little Menace," he purred. "You don't come until I say you can."

"Take off your clothes," he commanded, stepping back from me. I complied, eager to see where he would take things.

Once I was naked, he walked in circles around me, perusing every inch of my skin. I resisted the urge to cover myself, noting the thickness of his erection as it strained against his pants. I was unable to stop the shiver of anticipation that rushed through me.

Silas stopped in front of me and cupped one breast in his hand, testing the weight of it before moving to the other.

"These belong to me," he said as he pinched one nipple and flicked the other with his thumb. I gasped in pleasure as his touch sent shock waves careening straight to my core. I was ridiculously aroused and wanted him to do more than just touch me.

Silas ran his hands down my stomach, and he didn't stop until he cupped me between my legs.

"And this," he growled. "This also belongs to me."

"Silas," I said breathlessly, ready for him to do more than tease me.

He studied me, arching a brow.

"Please."

He chuckled darkly. "I do enjoy the sound of you begging for my cock, Little Menace."

"I need you," I panted.

"I got that from the wetness running down your thighs."

His smugness irritated me, but he wasn't done playing with me yet. He ran his hands over my hips and then down to my ass as he gripped me tightly. I wrapped my arms around his neck and pressed my lips to his, needing more of him. He chuckled against my mouth and forced his tongue passed my lips.

Silas broke the kiss as he moved his lips to my ear and said, "Get down on your hands and knees and show my pussy to me."

I did as he instructed and heard clothing being removed from behind me. I yelped when Silas ran a finger over my slit, startling me. His tongue followed, and I moaned.

"Don't make a sound, Harlowe," he demanded. "If you do, I stop. Nobody else gets to hear the delectable noises you make for me, understood?"

I bit my lip, quieting the sounds of my pleasure.

A sharp stinging erupted on my left cheek as Silas's large hand connected with my flesh.

"Understood?" he growled.

"Yes," I panted. "I understand."

Silas returned his tongue to my core, lapping at the arousal he had created. I bit down harder as another moan tried to force its way out of my lungs. Silas chuckled, and the vibrations sent a fresh wave of pleasure washing over me.

I could feel the orgasm building as I rocked my hips, seeking more of the friction he was creating. When I was just about to topple over the edge, Silas withdrew his tongue, leaving me empty and wanting.

"Silas," I hissed, peering at him over my shoulder to see the self-satisfied smirk he was wearing.

Silas lowered himself over me and ran his tongue over the shell of my ear as he growled, "Not until I give you permission."

Without warning, he thrust inside me, entering me from behind. Silas set a brutal rhythm that left me gasping. His fingers dug into my hips so hard, I was certain I would have bruises come morning.

Silas withdrew, pulling out all the way to the tip before slamming back into me. Stars danced in my vision as he sank himself so deeply he could write his name on my womb.

I had no hope of containing the moan that escaped me.

He withdrew again, but this time he didn't re-enter me.

"Silas p-please," I begged.

"What. Did. I. Tell. You?" he said, punctuating every word with a thrust of his cock. "Your sounds belong to me, just like the rest of you. Now grab something to quiet yourself because I'm taking back what's mine."

I buried my face in my tunic as Silas pounded into me.

"Not yet," he growled as I felt my walls tighten around him, ready to explode.

"I need to come," I whined.

"Not until I say you can." I wanted to cry in frustration. Silas's thrusts became jerky as he moved behind me. One thrust, two, three, and then he groaned. Hot liquid exploded inside me as he found his release.

Silas reached down between my thighs and rubbed my clit as he continued to thrust into me. "Now you can come," he rumbled. As though the words themselves pushed me over the edge into oblivion, my orgasm tore through me, causing me to shudder violently.

"Good girl," Silas praised as I struggled to control my breathing.

I fell forward, panting hard, taking Silas with me as I dropped to my elbows. He withdrew from my body, rolling onto his back beside me. I followed suit, too exhausted to hold myself up any longer.

Our ragged breathing filled the tent, and I felt myself drifting off. Silas clasped my hand in his, stroking his thumb against mine as he did so.

"What's your next move, Harlowe?" Silas asked, interrupting the peaceful silence.

"I need to find Misneach," I said. "I know he's alright, but I need to see him with my own eyes."

"And then?"

"And then I keep moving. I need to speak with my father and convince him this marriage is a terrible idea, but I can't do it with the threat of being forced to the altar looming over me." Silas tightened his grip on my hand.

"You're not marrying the King of Netheran, Harlowe. You're mine. I've made that very clear."

"Forget your male ego for one minute, Silas," I snapped. "There are more pressing matters at hand than your supposed claim on me, which I do not accept, by the way."

Silas growled, and I smacked him, catching him off guard.

"What other matters?" he grumbled once he'd recovered himself.

"Like avoiding an all-out war with Netheran for starters."

"Why is Kieran so obsessed with you?"

"You mean, aside from my dashing personality?" I teased, buying myself time to think of a suitable lie.

Silas pinched my hip, and I squealed.

"Why is strengthening the alliance so important to him?" he pressed.

I pursed my lips, thankful that he couldn't see my face in the tent's darkness. Sighing, I offered what truth I could, "I think he's planning something, and he likely wants to call on my father for support."

"He doesn't need to marry you to do that," he pointed out. "Kieran aided your father during the Skirmish of Power, and they've been allies ever since."

"Yes," I said bitterly, "and if Pyrithia, Zarinia, and Vidyaa had stayed within their borders, my father wouldn't have been pushed into that. Tell me, Silas, were you there?"

Silas tensed, and that was answer enough.

"Figures," I muttered, as I pulled my hand from his to search for my clothes.

"Harlowe," Silas said in warning.

"I'll find somewhere else to sleep. In the morning, Emmerson and I will go our own way. We've been fine on our own and we will continue to be so."

"Stop throwing a tantrum and get back here."

When I didn't comply, Silas sat up and reached for me. I struggled against his grip, but he held me close.

"I just want to feel you pressed against me for one night," he murmured. "I've missed having you in my arms while you sleep. Please, Harlowe," he begged.

My shoulders slumped in defeat. If I was being honest with myself, I'd missed sleeping next to him as well. For whatever reason, I was drawn to him, and I struggled to ignore it.

Curled against his chest, I let the rhythmic beating of his heart lull me to sleep.

Chapter Forty-Four

I woke the next morning, gloriously sore, and couldn't help the smile that spread over my lips. I attempted to stretch my arms above my head when I was met with resistance. Peering down at my hand, I found a shining steel cuff attached to my wrist. As I lifted my hand, I saw the other cuff was attached to one of the tent poles.

"Good morning, Harlowe," Silas's voice sounded from within the tent. I glanced around the space and spotted him standing in the entryway, arms crossed over his chest.

"What the fuck Silas?" I said, jingling the cuff for emphasis.

He just stared at me, and every second he did so, I felt my anger building to a crescendo.

"Unlock this now," I growled.

"Can't do that, I'm afraid."

"And why the fuck not?" I shouted.

"You fucking bastard!" I heard Emmerson scream somewhere outside the tent. "I swear to the gods if you don't release me right now, I will fucking end you."

"What have you done, Silas?" I whispered.

"I can't let you go, Little Menace," he said as he moved from his spot by the entryway and came to crouch down in front of me.

I yanked on the cuff, trying to get free as panic set in.

"Stop," Silas said as he reached for me. "You'll only hurt yourself."

I whirled back towards him and raised my free hand, slapping him across the face. Unfortunately, it was not my dominant hand, which was cuffed to the tent pole, so it didn't pack the punch I was hoping it would.

"You treacherous piece of shit!" I screamed in his face as I pulled on the cuff with renewed fury. Silas wrapped his arms around me, trying to stop me.

"Emmerson!" I screamed.

"Harlowe?" she replied, and I detected the relief in her voice. "These fucking bastards betrayed us," she howled. "Harlowe, they will pay for this, I swear it to you. By the gods, I swear it to you."

I wasn't sure what I had done to deserve Emmerson, but I was forever grateful to have her in my life.

"Em," I cried out, unable to stop my voice from wavering as tears pricked my eyes. I hated showing any weakness, especially in the current circumstances, but my thoughts were running away from me. I had no idea what Silas was planning to do. In fact, I knew next to nothing about the General. I had no idea who he really was, and yet, I had let him in.

I had been a damned fool.

"You're alright Harlowe," Emmerson assured me. "Listen to me, everything will be alright. I promise. I've got you, always."

I nodded my head, even though she couldn't see me, and exhaled a shaky breath.

We had survived the monsters lurking within the Forest of Nightmares, only to be taken out by our supposed allies. That betrayal hurt more than I was willing to admit. The witch had predicted one thing correctly, though; some friends were indeed foes, and I had fallen right into their waiting arms.

"You're safe with me, Little Menace," Silas whispered as if reading my thoughts. "No harm will come to you. I give you my word."

I reared back and spat in his face.

"Fuck you," I gritted out through clenched teeth as tears spilled down my cheeks. "Your word is worthless."

Silas clenched his jaw as he studied me. He rose to his feet and collected my clothes from the ground while wiping my saliva off his face. "I'll remove the cuffs so you can dress. Don't try anything, Little Menace," he warned.

I said nothing as I watched his every movement, hoping for an opportunity to strike. Silas unlocked the cuff just as a commotion sounded outside. Grunting followed, and a moment later, Emmerson let out a scream of pure frustration. I guess she had the same idea.

"It's futile," Silas said, reading my expression.

"I'll never forgive you for this," I vowed, as I pulled on my clothing.

Silas ignored me. "We are going to go outside and wait until the camp is packed up, alright?" he said, searching my face for any objection. "Then we are going to make our way to the border of Pyrithia."

"Why? What are you planning to do with me?" I demanded.

He cupped my cheek with his free hand and said, "Harlowe, I'm trying to protect you."

"Bullshit. If that was the goal, you wouldn't need to cuff me. You would offer to stand by me as I planned my next move. So quit lying and tell me the truth," I hissed.

Silas studied me for a moment, contemplating what to say. He sighed heavily before he lowered his gaze. "We have a long day ahead of us, and the sooner we get out of this forest, the safer we all will be."

My lips thinned into a tight grimace as I struggled to contain my anger. Tugging gently, Silas led me out of the tent to where the rest of the group waited. I looked every single one of the Cathal in their eyes so they couldn't escape my condemnation.

As I locked eyes with Emmerson, I almost cried in relief. She ran towards me, pulling Cillian along behind her. When she reached me, she wrapped her free arm around me and pulled me close.

"They have been planning this from the beginning," she whispered against my ear, low enough so only I would hear. "They were sent to Valoren to capture you and take you back to their King."

Emmerson released me, giving me a reassuring smile before baring her teeth at Silas.

Emmerson and I were directed to sit on a raised log while we waited for the others to pack up the camp. Silas and Cillian tried to get us to eat something, but we both ignored them, choosing instead to watch the others while they worked.

"You're hurt," Silas said, pulling my attention back to him. I followed the direction of his gaze to see dried blood around my wrist with the cuff attached to it. I hadn't even realized I'd injured myself while I struggled to free myself from my bindings.

Dismissing the injury and Silas, I returned my gaze to the others, who were making quick work of tearing down the camp.

"Cillian, pass me the water canister," Silas said, reaching out his hand to receive it. He unscrewed the lid and poured water over my wrist, washing away the blood.

"It's not that bad," he said as I continued to ignore him. Silas moved the cuff higher up my arm as he wrapped a length of cloth around my wrist.

"That too," Emmerson muttered.

"What's that?" Cillian asked.

"Just adding Harlowe's injured wrist to the list of things I'm going to make you suffer for," she replied sweetly.

Cillian sighed, running a hand down his face as he did so.

"I told you cuffing them was a bad idea," he murmured to Silas as though we weren't sitting right here.

"And what did you think was going to happen when you stabbed us in our backs?" Emmerson challenged.

"Believe it or not, Em, we're your safest option right now," Cillian said.

"Don't call me that," Emmerson spat, venom dripping from her tone. "Only those I care about get to call me that, and I fucking hate you." Cillian flinched at her words, likely registering the truth behind her statement.

Once the camp was pulled down and everyone was ready to go, we started moving north toward the Kingdom of Pyrithia. I had no idea how Emmerson had deduced that the Cathal coming to train with us had been a ploy so that they could capture me. But if she said it, I did not doubt that it was true.

I turned over what I knew in my mind, trying to figure out why the King of Pyrithia would be interested in me. However, I kept coming up short. The kingdom had only entered the Skirmish of Power once Zarinia and Vidyaa had already begun the fighting. If what Kieran had told me was true, their involvement was only motivated by the need to defend against a larger threat rising from the battlefield once the fighting was over. So, I didn't think conquering Valoren was the plan.

The King was a widower, but there were easier ways to secure himself a wife than to kidnap one. The marriage would never be recognized if it was coerced, anyway. If that was his plan, he would only succeed in making things more difficult for himself as he would be inviting Kieran's wrath, and he wouldn't gain any lands or alliances from the match.

It was possible that he had heard the same foretelling that Kieran had. But that begged the question; was the King intending to eliminate me before I could become some monster hell-bent on destroying the realm, or did he, like Kieran, intend to use me? Neither option was appealing in the slightest, and I had to hope that my secret remained just that; secret.

Chapter Forty-Five

After walking all day, only pausing briefly to rest, I was eager to stop when Silas made camp. I had maintained my silence with everyone except Emmerson. Not that we had a lot of opportunities to speak with one another. I suspected Silas was keeping us separated on purpose. It was smart because we used every chance we got to work on our escape.

Fionn, Teller, and even Cillian tried all day to draw us out of our solitude but failed. Despite knowing they were all just following Silas's orders, they had befriended us and made us feel as though we were part of their group, and none of that was crucial for their plan to betray us. And that hurt. More than it ought to.

Cian was the only one who had been consistent the whole time I'd known him. He was a surly ass then, and he was a surly ass now. So no, I wouldn't engage in their banter to make them feel less shitty about what they'd done. They could pretend that they were acting in my best interests, but I was done with the men in my orbit, all thinking they knew what I needed.

So, I kept my silence while I tried to plan my next move. If nothing else, my silence was fucking with their heads.

After setting up the camp, Silas led me to one side of the fire, while Cillian directed Emmerson to the other. If they thought keeping us apart would stop us from plotting, they underestimated the resourcefulness of a woman pushed beyond her limits. Plus, we had the added advantage of having grown up together. We were as close as sisters and we didn't need words to communicate.

I observed Emmerson from across the fire as she meticulously took stock of all their weapons, carefully noting their positions and the individuals who had placed them. She was assessing the way each member of the group was behaving now that they felt safe within the confines of their concealment spell. Who had dropped their guard, and who remained vigilant.

Just like I was monitoring where Cillian put the keys to the cuffs he had placed on Emmerson after moving it to the other wrist. And how Cian kept himself somewhat separated from the rest of the group. I also noted how Silas tracked everything we did, assessing us as we assessed his men.

Emmerson glanced at Fionn, then back at me. I made the slightest inclination of my head, letting her know I understood her message. Fionn was the weak link. When it came time to make our move, he would be our best option. Being the youngest of the group, it made sense that he would be the least disciplined. He had yet to suffer the losses that forge warriors into formidable foes. The type of losses that are borne out of your own arrogance and confidence in your abilities. The others had. You could see it in the way they always maintained a watchful eye on their surroundings, despite appearing to be at ease.

Silas and Cian would be the greatest obstacles we had to overcome. Neither dropped their guard, and both watched the others just as intently; identifying any weaknesses and correcting them. It would be near impossible to escape from the Cathal. But I would continue to wait and watch, to see what presented itself to me.

"Here Harlowe," Silas said as he handed me a bowl of stew. The concealment spell meant the Cathal had the luxury of using a fire to prepare their meals, something Emmerson and I had sorely missed. I was glad to be enjoying a proper meal instead of stale bread or dried meat.

I ignored Silas's attempt to be gentle with me and took the stew, eating in silence. Silas grumbled something under his breath beside me. Good. I hoped my silence was pissing him off as much as my current imprisonment was pissing me off.

Once I finished, Silas took the bowl from me and held my hand, pulling me up. As he led me towards his tent, I peered back at Emmerson, who nodded, indicating she would continue with her watch.

Once inside, Silas unlocked the cuff on his wrist and reattached it to the tent pole.

"How long are you going to continue ignoring me, Harlowe?" Silas demanded as he ran a hand through his hair.

"I have nothing to say to you, Silas, and that won't change any time soon."

Silas crouched before me so that he could be at eye level with me. "Please try to understand that I'm doing my best to protect you, Little Menace," he pleaded.

"Protect me?" I scoffed.

"I know you were planning on leaving me again. I can't have you wandering around in the Forest of Nightmares unprotected."

"Oh, so once we're free of the forest, you'll just let us go, then?" I challenged.

Silas clenched his jaw, which was answer enough.

"Thought so," I snorted. "Tell me, Silas, how long have you been planning this?"

Silas remained tight-lipped, unwilling to confirm what we both knew.

"See? I already know that you were sent to my kingdom, to my home, under false pretenses to get close to me. And you did get close to me, didn't you," I purred. "Was that part of the brief too, Silas? Will the King reward you for fucking me?" I spat, my lip curling in disgust.

Silas's hand darted forward, wrapping around my throat. "You can be as angry as you want, Little Menace, but you and I both know that you belong to me, and that wasn't by someone else's design."

"I don't belong to you, Silas. I belong to no man."

Silas's grip tightened around my throat. Leaning in close to me so our lips were almost touching, he whispered, "My obsession with you is so consuming it's almost to the point of insanity."

My body trembled at his admission.

"So you better believe me when I tell you I'll never let you go because I can't fucking breathe when you're not near."

With that, Silas crashed his lips against mine in a bruising kiss.

Once he'd pulled away, I said, "None of that matters, Silas, because you're not keeping me. You're handing me over to your King."

Silas snarled. "I'll let no one else have you."

Silas stood up and crossed to the other side of the tent, grabbing a bottle that I assumed was whiskey. He handed it to me, and I took a swig. When I handed it back to him, he grasped my hand in his, refusing to let go even though I had withdrawn my own. We just stared at each other, neither willing to divert our gaze.

"Stand up so I can roll out your bedroll," Silas said, breaking the silence. I did what he asked, settled on my bedroll, and turned away from him as I laid down.

"I know you're upset with me, Little Menace," he started. "I also know you don't want to be used as a pawn for your father or the King of Netheran. So coming with me is in your best interests."

"Don't pretend you're some hero in all of this, Silas. Stupidity doesn't suit you."

"I will protect you, Little Menace. On our way to Pyrithia, and once we arrive. You are mine to protect, and I will defend you with my life. This I vow to you."

I didn't bother to point out that his vow meant nothing to me since he had broken my trust once already. Nor did I voice my concern that he felt the need to vow to protect me in his homeland. If they had no ill will towards me, why was the vow needed? Silas knew more than he was letting on, and I wasn't about to put my faith in him another time.

The wailing creature that had been following us since we first entered the forest started up with its mournful keening somewhere nearby. I found it almost comforting to know that even though my life seemed to have been turned upside down, this one thing had remained constant.

"This fucking forest," Silas muttered under his breath. He reached around me, wrapping me in his embrace. I wanted to shrug him off, but I needed this moment of comfort. I needed to feel safe just long enough to gather my strength and solidify my resolve. Whatever waited for me within the borders of Pyrithia, I knew I'd have to fight my way out in order to escape.

Chapter Forty-Six

The icy cold water was refreshing on my skin as I washed days' worth of dirt and grime from my face and neck. Reaching Pyrithia would be welcome if it meant that I could bathe. As I could not trust that the bodies of water within the Forest of Nightmares didn't house creatures that would try to kill me, I hadn't been able to bathe since entering the forest over a week ago, and it showed.

It was awkward, trying to wash myself one-handed with Silas still cuffed to my other wrist. He didn't complain though, as I pulled him this way and that, trying to make the best of my limited reach. I may have accidentally, on purpose, pulled him down before he was ready by dropping my entire body weight to the ground, just so he would stumble and fall onto the muddy bank. It turns out I was not above being petty.

"Are you almost done?" Silas asked.

I shook my hands, savoring the peaceful moment as I glanced out at the water.

Too soon, we were tracking back to our camp, where the others waited.

"Where's Emmerson?" I asked when I noticed she was missing.

"Cillian took her to wash up," Silas said, pacifying me.

I took a seat on the ground, dragging Silas with me, as I waited until we were ready to move again.

"We should be beyond the forest's borders within the next two days," he said.

I did not appreciate the reminder that our window for escaping was dwindling. After crossing into Pyrithia, we would soon reach the palace where the King awaited our return. I was losing hope that we would escape. Silas was proving himself to be a more than capable adversary.

Thoughts of Pyrithia had plagued my dreams. I didn't know what to expect when we arrived. Visions of my execution kept filling my mind, and when they abated, thoughts of being chained and confined within the dungeon replaced them. I had to hope that they didn't know about whatever power was locked within me. That was the only way I would be safe.

A violent tremor pulled me from my spiraling despair as the ground trembled beneath us. Silas gripped my hand and yanked me to my feet before pulling me in close to his side. The men reached for weapons as Cillian rushed through the shrubbery with Emmerson.

"What is it?" Silas demanded.

"Lindwyrm," Cillian replied while reaching for his own weapon.

Silas cursed under his breath and started issuing orders for the men to take up a defensive position around us.

Emmerson reached for my free hand, gripping it in her own.

"I've got you," she whispered, tipping her hand up to reveal a glowing orb in her palm.

"Wait, can you use that to break the cuffs?" I asked, cursing myself for not thinking of this earlier. I had forgotten all about the fact that Emmerson could wield. As I was so used to being unable to do so myself, it rarely factored into my thought process.

Emmerson shook her head. "Too risky. At this close range, the blowback could sever your arm."

Right. Probably not the best idea.

The thunderous vibrations intensified just as a massive creature lurched from the thicket. The creature had a head like a dragon and a snake-like body. It was huge, easily twelve feet tall as it reared up at us. I could see more of its body, still hidden behind the shrubbery. Its green scaly body slithered closer as it let out a deafening hiss, revealing razor-sharp teeth with pointed incisors.

The men wasted no time attacking. Cian led the assault, sword drawn, and slashed out at the creature. Teller and Fionn fanned out, enclosing the beast, and allowing them to attack it from multiple sides. Cillian moved in too, Emmerson still bound at his wrist, sword raised.

Fionn thrust his sword upward into the creature's side, drawing its attention. It hissed and bared its teeth menacingly, while Teller repeated the move from the opposite side. Distracted, the creature turned towards Teller, allowing all the men to move in at once, slashing, stabbing, and hacking at the beast. Crimson blood flowed down its scaled body with each connecting blow.

The creature regained its composure as it reared back and lunged towards Fionn, who deftly evaded the attack by weaving under the creature. As I watched the scene unfold, it became apparent that the creature's size was working against it within the confines of the small clearing. The men were attacking within close range and the creature struggled to counter the attacks with the limited room it had to maneuver.

Someone propelled an axe through the air beside me, and it took me a minute to realize that Silas had been the one to throw it. The creature fixed its serpentine eyes on us and moved to lunge towards us. Before it could, Emmerson let out a furious battle cry as she pushed forward. A brilliant white orb flew from her palm and connected with the creature's head.

Everything was still for a moment; the sounds of steel meeting flesh having abated. Every single head had swiveled towards Emmerson, who was panting, sweat beading on her forehead. The beast swayed, and everyone jumped back out of its path as it came crashing to the ground.

Emmerson turned her deadly glare on Silas, and marched forward, dragging Cillian behind her as she stalked towards him. Silas stiffened beside me, and even I had to admit I was slightly terrified by the ire seeping out from Emmerson, pulsing from her pores as if it were a living entity.

She stopped in front of Silas and said in a deadly tone, "If you ever endanger my Queen like that again, I won't hesitate to kill you with my bare hands."

And she meant it. Until now, our desire to not harm any of our captors had limited our escape plans. As pissed as we were, neither one of us was comfortable causing them any serious injuries.

Now though, with the way Emmerson was glaring up at Silas, I could see her reassessing that point. However, her demonstration of power had weakened her. It was one reason our soldiers preferred to utilize swords or other types of weaponry whenever they could. The more fórsa that was used, the quicker the individual wielding it became drained and unable to continue the fight.

And Emmerson had used a lot.

She swayed, and I reached out to grab her elbow. Cillian was there, pulling her against his chest, supporting her weight with his body.

Silas clenched his jaw but nodded once to Emmerson in acknowledgment of her chastisement. I don't know what surprised me more; that Emmerson had ended the fight with a single, concentrated blow of grand magnitude, or that Silas accepted her criticism without challenge.

The clearing was silent; the tension permeating the air as everyone waited for someone to make the next move. Cillian was the one to break the tension as he picked Emmerson up and walked her over to a log where she could recover. The others made themselves busy, fixing their packs while sneaking glances towards the couple, watching as Cillian tendered to Emmerson.

I moved to join her, needing to make sure she was alright, only for Silas to pull me back. As I turned to peer at him, I found his intense gaze locked on me.

"I'm sorry Harlowe," he breathed. "I didn't think. I didn't account for the fact that you were defenseless when I all but thrust you into the fray."

His remorse for his actions was clear in his tone. Silas hadn't thought beyond the need to safeguard his men. And that was something I could not fault him for. I nodded and led him over to where Emmerson was sitting with a canister of water raised to her lips and a hunk of cheese in her hand.

Hugging my best friend, I whispered against her ear, "Thank you." She returned my hold, squeezing me.

A horn blared in the distance, causing everyone to freeze and scan the tree line.

"What was that?" I breathed as fear overwhelmed my senses.

A loud rhythmic clashing of steel on steel sounded in the distance, showing that whoever or whatever was out there, they weren't that far away.

"Minotaurs," Silas hissed, gripping my hand in his. "They must have heard the fight with the Lindwyrm."

Silas returned his attention to Emmerson as he asked, "Are you okay to move?" She nodded before Cillian added, "I'll carry her if I have to," as he stood to do just that.

"Put me down, you oaf," she protested. "I can walk."

"You'll have to do more than that," Silas said. "Grab only the necessities," he commanded. "Leave anything not essential to our survival."

The sound of clanging metal grew louder right before a resounding bellow was unleashed, echoed by the war cries of what had to be dozens and dozens of others. Apprehension prickled my skin, threatening to lock my limbs in place as I fought the urge to vomit.

"RUN!" Silas roared, as he dragged me into the forest behind him.

Chapter Forty-Seven

The trees had become a blur around me as Silas propelled us through the forest. Low-hanging branches whipped at my face, but I barely even felt the sting as they tore through my flesh.

The ground vibrated beneath us as the Minotaur army descended. My heart was pounding in sync with the thud of my feet hitting the earth as I sprinted, blindly following Silas as he navigated our way through the endless forest. My breathing was ragged as I struggled to fill my lungs with air and sweat slicked the nape of my neck as it ran in rivulets down my spine.

Despite the urgency of the situation, there was a gracefulness to Silas's movements as he pounded forward. Silas's footwork was agile, allowing him to transverse the uneven terrain while maintaining his speed and efficiency.

Not everyone within the group was as gifted, however. Emmerson, who could usually count herself on the more gifted side, was struggling to keep upright, still drained from her use of fórsa. Her frenzied steps betrayed her as she fled, causing her to stumble over her own feet. Before she could hit the ground, Cillian's nimble hands flung out and grabbed her, righting her without slowing.

Cian whirled around, never breaking stride, as he unleashed an orb of energy from his palm, hitting something behind us. It was hard not to be impressed by the skill and lethality of the Cathal.

A groaning noise sounded, and something heavy hit the ground. There was no time to pause and see how close they were behind us. I knew they were closing in, and we didn't stand a chance if they caught us.

More orbs of energy flew by me, and as I raised my head, I saw Teller and Fionn had joined the fight. Silas thrust his free hand behind him, not even looking as he unleashed his power. A loud thud sounded mere feet from us, letting me know that Silas's aim had hit true.

A surge of adrenaline hit me, and I forced my legs to push harder, recognizing that the Minotaurs had bridged the gap. Something whizzed past my ear, and I yelped in surprise. A wicked-looking axe dug into the trunk of a tree up ahead, and I couldn't prevent the shudder that wracked my body.

More objects flew towards our group and a mix of arrows, axes, and daggers landed in various trees, while others fell flat on the forest floor. The Cathal moved with precision, dodging, and weaving to avoid the incoming attacks, without once breaking stride or peering over their shoulders. I caught flickers of green skin out of my periphery, followed by sharp flashes of light, before they disappeared from view.

We ran for what felt like hours before the unmistakable sound of cascading water filled my ears. As we broke through the tree line, I peered around me to see a thunderous waterfall dipping over the edge into nothingness. I scanned our surroundings, trying to figure out how we would evade the Minotaurs before they caught us.

"We're going over," Silas said, and I whipped my head around to look at him. He was looking straight ahead towards the waterfall, determination etched on his face.

Visions of the Siren pulling me under the water while blackness crept across my vision filled my mind, and my whole body started shaking as panic clutched me.

"No, no, no, I can't do that!" I cried, gripping my hair in my hands as I began to unravel.

"It's the only way we will lose them," Silas replied calmly, taking my hands in his as he removed my fingers from my hair.

"Let's just cross the river," I pleaded.

"We need to lose them. The river won't slow them down." I could hear thundering hooves getting closer with each second we stood there.

Silas nodded his head at something, and I didn't register what had happened until a loud splash sounded way down below us. I scanned the group, finding Teller missing. My mouth dropped open in shock as Fionn stepped to the edge and followed him over.

Cian was the next to dive over before Cillian stepped up, Emmerson's hand in his. She peered back at me, a nervous smile spread over her lips. She nodded in encouragement before allowing Cillian to drag her over the edge with him, racing the rushing water to the bottom.

I swallowed hard as Silas moved us closer to the edge. Visions of myself drowning as the sweet sound of the Siren's song lulled me to my death, played on repeat in my mind. I couldn't do it; my fear froze me in place, paralyzing me.

Silas cupped my cheeks, forcing me to meet his gaze. He peered into my eyes, his jaw flexing as he studied me.

"Do you trust me, Little Menace?"

I blinked, confusion halting my spiraling panic.

"What?"

"Do you trust me?" Silas repeated.

"No," I answered incredulously, thinking back to everything that had transpired between us in the last few days.

Silas crashed his mouth to mine, forcing my lips to part as he thrust his tongue into my opening. He devoured me with such raw need, I felt my knees buckling. When he broke the kiss, he rested his forehead on my own, both of us panting hard.

"That's unfortunate," he whispered. Then he gripped my hand in his and launched himself over the edge, dragging me behind him.

The air left my lungs in a rush as I screamed, and I flapped my hands in desperation as I tried to slow my descent. My efforts were in vain, as gravity held me in its clutches, pulling me towards the dark waters below.

"Take a deep breath," Silas yelled over the crashing water, and I barely had time to do as he instructed before my feet sliced through the surface. The icy cold water encased my body, and I felt myself sinking deeper into the water's cool embrace. My feet connected with something solid, and I pushed up with all my might, propelling myself towards the surface. Silas tugged on the cuff at my wrist, pulling me the rest of the way upwards until I breached the water. Gasping, I sucked in air as my lungs burned. For a moment I was too stunned to move, but Silas pulled me along beside him as he swam towards the shore where everyone else stood, waiting for us.

Once we reached the shore, I collapsed onto the riverbank. Heaving breaths escaped me as my mind tried to catch up with what my body had just endured.

Strong hands grabbed me and pulled me up. "We can't stay here," Silas said against my ear.

"Won't they just follow our insane asses over the edge?" I asked, still very much in shock.

"They fear deep water, but that won't stop them from finding a way down. We need to move before we lose the head start we just gained."

I could already hear the howling getting closer and as I looked back up to where we just jumped from, a set of glowing red eyes met mine. The Minotaur snarled its displeasure and raised its axe, sending it flying towards us.

"Move!" Silas commanded, and we only just made it out of the axe's range before it thudded into the damp earth beside us.

Silas pushed us hard, not allowing us to rest until we could no longer hear the Minotaurs pursuing us. When we made camp for the night, it was inside a dark cave that offered some protection from the elements and kept us concealed should any more of the forest's inhabitants venture nearby.

With my clothes still damp from my unexpected swim, the cool night air settled into my bones. Silas picked me up and placed me in his lap, encasing me with the warmth of his body as I shivered.

"Don't," I said as I tried to lean out of his grip.

Pulling me back into his broad chest, Silas said, "You need to stop fighting me."

"And you need to let me go."

"Never," he said fiercely, and I wondered if we were still only talking about our journey to Pyrithia.

"What is going to happen to me when we reach Pyrithia?" I asked, giving voice to the one question that had been plaguing me for days.

Silas's arms wrapped even tighter around my body. "Nothing," he said with determination. "Nothing is going to happen to you because you are mine, Harlowe, and I protect what's mine. Right now, the safest place for you is Pyrithia. The other kingdoms would not shelter you from your father or Kieran, but I will."

"You don't know what your King wants with me, do you?" I asked.

His grip tightened again, but he offered no reply.

"Let me go," I repeated, more forcefully this time.

"I will never let you go, Little Menace. Not today, not tomorrow, not even a thousand years from now. You are mine, and I intend to keep you."

"That's not true," I hissed.

"It is, and you know it," he countered. "It's why you fight me so damn hard. Because you are constantly having to remind yourself why you're doing it. You want me, just as much as I want you," he growled. "Don't deny it."

I forced myself to suppress the shiver that wanted to make its way down my spine. Silas chuckled darkly against my neck as he kissed his way to the shell of my ear.

"Even when you're supposed to hate me, you can't help but respond to my touch," he said huskily. "You were created to be mine Harlowe, and only mine."

"A shiver of revulsion does not count," I said, but it sounded breathless.

Silas chuckled again. "You keep telling yourself that, Little Menace. You belong to me, and I'm done letting you think otherwise. Now sleep. We have lots of ground to cover tomorrow."

He kissed the top of my head as he leaned back against the wall of the cave, taking me with him.

I couldn't trust Silas. He'd betrayed me, no matter his intentions. I also couldn't deny the connection I felt to him. The insatiable need I had for him. He set my blood on fire, and I did want him. I had wanted him from the very first moment I had laid my eyes on him.

I just wasn't prepared to surrender my freedom in order to have him.

Chapter Forty-Eight

We spent the next two days trudging through the forest, making our way towards the border of Pyrithia. Thankfully, we had no further encounters with the Minotaurs, or any other creature that calls the Forest of Nightmares home, save for the wailing creature that serenaded us with its mournful keening each night.

As we neared the forest's edge, time was running out for Emmerson and me. Silas had proven himself to be the better strategist, never providing an opportunity for us to break free. We'd have to readjust our plans and hope that evading our captors within Pyrithia would be easier, but I wasn't holding my breath. The King's intentions remained a mystery to me, and my imagination ran wild.

As I crossed the threshold of the forest, a strange sensation washed over me and rippled down my body, leaving me shuddering. The oppressive darkness of the forest vanished, and I could finally breathe.

The thundering sound of beating wings rang out above me, and I instantly sought the source of the disturbance.

"Misneach?"

The massive dragon descended to perch in front of us, and I felt disappointed when I realized it wasn't him. Caolán stood tall and proud before Silas, dipping his colossal head in acknowledgment. The majestic creature eyed me, but I was unable to discern his intentions.

"Misneach," I tried again, hoping he was close enough to hear me.

"FIRE HEART!" Misneach roared in my head, and I closed my eyes as I allowed my relief to rip through me.

"Where are you, Fire Heart?" Misneach asked, wasting no time on sentimentality.

"I'm on the edge of the forest where it meets the border of Pyrithia," I paused, weighing my next words. **"Silas has taken me captive. His King sent him to kidnap me."**

A furious roar echoed in the distance, and I knew the source without question.

"I will burn him to ashes."

"That may be a little difficult, seeing as I am currently cuffed to him."

Misneach snarled in my mind, and I had no doubt about Silas's place on his shit list.

"Mount up. Now!" Silas barked as the other dragons landed beside Caolán.

Without missing a step, Silas hauled me against his chest and swung his leg over his dragon, as if my added weight was no hindrance.

"I am coming for you, Fire Heart."

"Please hurry."

Until that moment, I hadn't admitted how afraid I was of being given to the King of Pyrithia. Now that escape might be within my grasp, I realized I was terrified. The fear of the unknown was suffocating.

Caolán launched into the sky, his green-gray wings beating wildly as he ascended. Peeking over my shoulder, I saw Oisín behind us, Emmerson secured in Cillian's grip.

"Misneach is coming for me," I told Silas, and he squeezed my hip tight in response.

"He can try to take you from me, Little Menace, but I'm not giving you up."

"But you'll hand me over to your King," I spat. "What does he want with me, Silas? Do you even know?"

"He wants to protect his kingdom."

"By kidnapping me?" I scoffed.

"By ensuring your father can't trade you to the King of Netheran," he spat.

"What?" I sputtered, not having expected Silas to reveal anything.

Silas remained silent behind me, and I realized he had not intended to say what he had.

"How did the King discover my betrothal to Kieran? It was not common knowledge. Hell, even I wasn't aware. And I know you were sent to capture me before Kieran ever arrived in Valoren."

My anger had returned full force now that I was no longer fighting for my life with every miserable step.

"So what was the plan, Silas? You seduce me and then lure me back to Pyrithia?"

"Seduce you?" Silas repeated, sounding amused. "If I remember correctly, Little Menace, it was you who begged me to fuck you."

My cheeks flamed in embarrassment as I thought back to our first sexual encounter. It had been me to push the boundaries, to invite Silas into my bed. But he hadn't kept his desire for me concealed, either. That day in the stables, he'd told me he couldn't keep away from me. He laid the groundwork, and I, naively, ate it up.

"I told you what you were getting yourself into Little Menace," he whispered roughly. "I warned you that once we crossed that line, there would be no going back. And you launched yourself into my arms, sealing your fate. You're mine now, and I'm keeping you. I will allow no other man to taste you or listen to the sweet melody of your moans as you come undone."

I could feel myself getting wet, unable to deny the allure of his wicked words. The intensity of my need for this man overpowered even my anger.

"And now I will protect what's mine. It's true that my King sent me to retrieve you. His reasons for being interested in you no longer matter to me; I won't surrender you to him or anyone else. I would rather burn the entire fucking realm to the ground before allowing another to have you."

"What makes you think you can disobey the King and get away with it?" I asked, wanting to believe his promises.

I felt him smirk against the nape of my neck before he said, "You needn't worry about the King, Harlowe."

I huffed. If Silas couldn't be honest, I couldn't rely on him.

"Then burn the fucking realm down Silas because if you take me back to your kingdom, it will be beyond your control," I challenged.

He was silent for a moment, the tightening of his grip around me his only response.

"Harlowe," he growled.

"Save it," I said, cutting him off. "Whatever you're about to say, just save it. Your words mean nothing to me when your promises are empty."

Silas snarled against my ear, "I mean every word I've said, but there are things you don't know, Little Menace."

"Then tell me!" I shouted, losing my patience with all the half-truths.

"Just trust me for now."

I laughed manically, the stress of everything catching up with me. "Trust you?" I snorted out between bouts of laughter. "Why would I do that?"

Finding some composure, I managed, "You have given me no reason to trust you, Silas. By doing this, you'll only prove me right."

We were silent for a long time. I focused on the feel of the wind against my face, and the sound of Caolán's beating wings as I contemplated everything. In the short time I had known him, Silas had managed to get under my skin; to invade every corner of my mind. I had become addicted to him without even realizing it. I had been trying to convince myself that it was only temporary, and during that time he had become the oxygen I breathe to sustain life.

The pain of his betrayal was too deep and crippling for it to have been a temporary indulgence.

And it didn't change a fucking thing.

This wasn't only about me. As the next ruler of Valoren, my people deserved a queen who prioritized them and fought tirelessly on their behalf. It meant refusing to be a pawn for either the King of Pyrithia or the King of Netheran. I needed to fight my way out and ensure my people were free from both kingdoms' interference.

It was right to flee Valoren. My father had made a decision out of fear of Kieran, but Valoren was stronger than he thought. If we allowed others to interfere with our rule, it would become ceaseless.

I couldn't allow that to happen.

"Silas," I mumbled.

"Yes, Little Menace," he hummed.

"The way I see it, you have two choices," I started. "You can prove you're a man worth having at my side by supporting me and helping me return to my kingdom, ready to take it back from the interference of outsiders. That means not dropping me in the lap of your King to be used as his pawn. Help me figure out how to eradicate Kieran's influence over Valoren without sacrificing my kingdom. Join me in this and everything up to now won't matter. We start fresh. We work together and thrive side-by-side," I paused, taking a deep breath.

"Or you can lead me to your kingdom, where I'll be imprisoned and used. But know this: if you do that, I will fight you every single step. I will never stop trying to escape you. I will never be yours, and I will never forgive you. Don't make me into your enemy, Silas, please."

"It's not that simple, Little Menace."

"It is. You're either in or you're out."

He stiffened behind me, and in a low dangerous tone he growled, "You don't seem to understand your position here, Little Menace."

A shiver ran down my spine, but not in a good way.

"I have tried to be patient, to be reasonable, to let you come to terms with what's happening on your own. It didn't benefit either of us. So let me make something very clear," he rumbled.

"You are my prisoner. You may fight me, but you will never escape me. I won't allow it. You can keep trying to appeal to my better nature, but let me set you straight right here, right now... I don't have one. I take what I want, and Little Menace, I want you. If you need to make me your enemy, then so be it. It changes nothing between us."

Heartache washed over me. Silas had made his choice, and it wasn't me. He wanted to own me, to possess me. He did not want to stand beside me.

Strengthened by my resolve, I squared my shoulders.

"So be it," I repeated solemnly.

Chapter Forty-Nine

Silas had been pushing us hard, not allowing us to stop more than necessary in order to keep ahead of Misneach. However, this didn't deter Misneach. In fact, he had been planning many things he would like to unleash on Silas and anyone else working to keep me from him.

"I'm still leaning towards incinerating him. It's a quick death, but one of the most painful," he growled, having intruded on my internal musings once again.

"It's not intruding when you blast every thought you have down the bond." A small smile graced my lips at my indomitable dragon's petulance.

"Not petulant," he scoffs. **"Exasperated."** I smiled, knowing I'd pegged him.

"Tell me again about these flames of yours," he asked, redirecting my thoughts.

"I don't know what else to say. I was fighting the Harpy, and I was losing. Emmerson was also fading, and I felt overwhelmed and angry with my helplessness. It was like a tidal wave of emotions that started low in my stomach and just... burst free from me."

"And you don't know how you accessed it?"

"No," I sighed.

"And flames covered your whole body, but did not burn you?"

"That's what Emmerson said. I had no idea it was happening, so I didn't bother taking inventory or anything like that. The flames

didn't hurt me or Emmerson, so whatever I did to protect myself, I somehow projected that onto her."

Misneach considered my words.

"So, the witch of yours claimed they were dragon flames?"

"Yes. She said I was the conduit for dragon fire, whatever that means," I muttered.

"And this is why you are connected to us all," Misneach mused.

"That's what I gather. She didn't say that specifically, but that's what I read between the lines."

"Interesting," Misneach hummed. **"Now we just need to determine how it all works."**

My attention was drawn back to my surroundings as tiny structures appeared on the horizon. It was a village, which meant we were getting close to the palace.

"How far out are you?" I asked Misneach, fear tightening my throat.

I had isolated the one person who may have been my ally inside Pyrithia. Not that I regretted it. Silas needed to understand my position. That didn't stop me from wondering how our fight might impact my treatment within his kingdom, however.

"Not far. As I am unencumbered, I have been able to close the distance between us. I can feel through the bond that you are near."

As we flew towards the epicenter of Pyrithia, an increasing number of homes appeared in view. When we crested the top of a mountain, something glimmered in the sunlight, drawing my attention. A vast stone palace stood nestled in the center of the valley below. The glass from the windows of its many turrets and towers reflected the rays of the sun, shimmering brilliantly, creating a prism of light. Dark, green ivy snaked its way towards the spires atop the lower levels of the palace, while massive perches surrounded the largest tower, which was in the very center of the structure.

Dragon perches, I realized.

The crest of Pyrithia, an outline of a golden circle, enclosed by thick, straight lines, tipped with triangular points in imitation of the sun, waved proudly from every flag. Rolling, green hills surrounded the palace and village, which then blended into the magnificent mountainous range that I knew led to the Mountains of Dragonia.

The sight was breathtaking.

"I can see the palace," I said to Misneach, not even trying to hide my rising panic.

"Hold on Fire Heart."

"I don't think I have much of a choice at this point, Misneach."

Caolán's massive wingspan closed the distance to the palace, and before I knew it, he was landing with a thud just inside the palace walls.

Silas wasted no time dismounting, hurling me forward as he jumped down. I lost my footing and stumbled towards the ground, but strong, corded arms wrapped around me.

"Easy," he whispered against my ear.

When I righted myself, I saw that the rest of our group had also dismounted. Everyone was moving quickly, desperately seeking the shelter of the palace before one very large, furious dragon made his appearance.

No sooner had I thought it and a massive shadow swept over us. The beating of powerful wings sounded above me as Misneach descended, creating a small windstorm that picked up dirt and debris, whirling them in the air in front of us. His massive frame thudded to the ground, and he lowered his head before curling his lips back in a vicious snarl.

Wings outstretched, he raised himself to his full height before he let out an almighty roar. He was standing in our path, so close that his spittle landed on my cheeks. His serpentine head rotated at an odd angle as he assessed his surroundings before his full attention returned to Silas. More specifically, to the cuff attached to Silas's wrist, chaining me to him.

Silas pulled me closer to him, and Misneach snarled in warning. My heart raced as the man and dragon faced off against one another.

"I mean her no harm," Silas said to Misneach, lifting his free hand in a placating gesture. Misneach growled low in his throat, leaving no uncertainty as to his feelings about Silas's declaration.

I looked around and spotted Emmerson, still cuffed to Cillian, as she stood motionless, watching in horror while the scene played out before her.

I scanned the rest of my surroundings and noticed that villages and soldiers alike had moved back, leaving plenty of room between themselves and the intense standoff occurring mere feet from them. Mothers recalled children hustling them away as soldiers gripped their weapons.

The situation was deteriorating fast.

"Misneach, what do we do now?" I asked, the desperation leaking into my tone.

"I cannot unleash my fire on him while he is attached to you," pausing for a moment he continued, **"I could just snap his neck,"** he growled.

"We can't harm these people, Silas included Misneach, please," I begged.

"You are too good to them, Fire Heart. They have taken you prisoner, they intend to hold you against your will, they have bound you and may harm you further. They do not deserve your kindness."

"That's what sets us apart, Misneach. I value every life here, even though their King is my enemy. I will not mistreat those who don't deserve it."

"THEY DESERVE IT," he roared.

"Maybe. However, the innocent people around us will be caught in the crossfire, Misneach."

"What would you have me do, Fire Heart?"

Before I could respond, Caolán moved towards Misneach. I sucked in a breath as tension tightened every muscle in my body. The two dragons stared at each other, sizing one another up, assessing the threat each posed. Misneach snarled again, and I took a slow, tentative step towards him.

"He says you will be safe here, that the dragons will protect you," Misneach relayed without taking his eyes off Caolán.

"I told him they have failed you so far."

Caolán turned to face us, either taking stock of the situation or speaking with Silas. I couldn't tell which. When Silas stiffened beside me, I figured it was the latter.

"I can't do that," Silas hissed.

"Do what?" I asked, confused.

"He is telling him to uncuff you as a show of good faith," Misneach repeated for my benefit.

The remaining dragons moved to flank Caolán. I couldn't tell if they were lending their support or preparing to defend against Misneach if things deteriorated further.

The silence dragged on; the tension growing so thick, it became hard to breathe.

Silas faced me, staring into my eyes with a hardened expression on his beautiful face. The muscles in his jaw twitched as he clenched his teeth. Without breaking eye contact, he reached into his pocket and retrieved the key to the cuffs. The snap of the lock sounded, and relief washed over me as the steel left my flesh.

Silas leaned in and whispered, "Emmerson's stay on. Unless you intend to leave her and escape, I wouldn't do anything foolish Harlowe."

I glared at him. Hating that he knew I would never leave Emmerson and would use my loyalty against me.

I stepped back, moving closer to Misneach as all eyes remained trained on me. I took another step, and then another. Silas moved to follow me, but Caolán lowered his head between us, growling low in warning.

For a moment I was so stunned, I forgot to keep moving. Mouth hanging open, I watched Silas divert his angry gaze to his dragon, the two glaring at one another.

"What's happening?" I asked Misneach.

"Caolán is warning the General not to intervene. He has promised to protect you, even against his own Cathal, which he just demonstrated."

I let out a shaky breath until I felt my back hit against Misneach's chest.

"What are the other dragons doing?" I asked, unable to pull my gaze away from what was happening in front of me.

"They have all pledged to protect you, Fire Heart, no matter the cost."

"How will they do that?" I questioned. **"Once within the palace walls, I'm beyond your reach, and anything is possible."**

"According to Caolán, the General is determined to keep you safe, making this the safest place in the realm for you."

"Do you believe him?"

"I believe that Caolán trusts his Cathal and his Cathal believes what he says."

I tried to map my way out of this nightmare but realized I had no real options. Silas had Emmerson, so there was no way I would abandon her, even if she begged and pleaded for me to leave. I also did not want to risk harming anyone that might get in the way if I tried to leave, and a fight broke out between the Cathal and Misneach.

Defeated and feeling utterly exhausted, I said, **"Tell Caolán I will stay."** Before adding, **"You'll stay too, right?"**

"I am never leaving you again, Fire Heart," he promised.

Caolán peered back towards where I stood with Misneach and gave a slight bow of his head, having received the message. The other dragons followed suit while moving to create a protective barrier around me.

Guarded against prying eyes, I turned to face Misneach, who lowered his head to mine. I wrapped my arms around him, letting out a small sob as the tension left me, replaced by the sheer relief of having my bond mate back.

Misneach rubbed his head against me affectionately.

"I was so worried for you when I couldn't speak with you inside the forest," I confessed.

"You needn't have, Fire Heart. You were the one putting yourself in danger, not me."

"I know, but still," I said, swiping at the tears that had escaped me.

"Hush now Fire Heart," he said, warmth coloring his tone. **"I am here, and you are safe. Nothing is going to harm you. Let us make use of our time here to strengthen our bond and work through what we have learned along the way."**

I nodded my head, smiling up at him.

I took a deep breath and exhaled, calming my nerves.

"I am ready," I said aloud so the other dragons would hear me. The wall of dragons parted behind me, and I followed the path they had created straight back to Silas. I glanced at Emmerson and nodded, trying to let her know everything would be okay.

My eyes locked onto smoldering, dark brown ones before I stepped to the side, making room for Silas to lead the way. He hesitated for the briefest moment before he marched towards the palace steps.

A young woman in a maid's uniform scurried over to us, curtsying to Silas as she said, "Your Highness, the King awaits you in his throne room."

I spun my head towards Silas so fast I became dizzy and lightheaded.

"Thank you, Marie," he said without breaking stride or sparing a glance my way.

I closed my eyes, nausea churning in my stomach as the lies smothered any faith I might have had left in Silas.

Silas was a member of the royal family of Pyrithia. He wasn't the king, so that meant he was one of the king's two sons.

Silas was the fucking Prince of Pyrithia, and he had lied to me about everything.

We marched through the entryway to the palace as Silas grabbed a soldier from his post by the staircase leading to the upper levels.

"Take the Princess to my chambers and make sure she has a maid to attend to her needs," he instructed.

"The King has requested her presence as well, Your Highness," the maid, Marie, interjected.

The soldier moved to return to his post, but Silas reached out and grabbed his arm.

"Are you disobeying my orders?" Silas seethed, invading the man's personal space.

"No, Your Highness," the soldier answered.

"Good."

Silas flicked his head towards his men, indicating they should follow him. Cillian passed Emmerson to another soldier as I was quickly taken up the staircase. With a glance, she conveyed she was okay, and that we would find a way out of this.

Whatever this was.

Resigning myself to my fate, for now, I followed the soldier leading me away.

I consoled myself with the fact that I could soon have that bath I had been yearning for for weeks.

Chapter Fifty

I swung the doors to the throne room wide, catching my father by surprise with the force of it. Frustration consumed me at how everything had played out with Harlowe, and now Caolán had taken a stand to defend her.

She was never in any danger from me, to begin with.

I knew he was just trying to show her she could trust him. Either way, it still pissed me off. I ran a hand through my hair, the dust I had accumulated from my travels forming a cloud in front of me.

I lowered myself to one knee and placed a fist to my heart, bowing my head to my father.

"Come, come, my son. I am pleased to have you home," my father beamed.

I rose, standing to my full height, and looked at my father. He was a handsome man, tall and well-built. His brown hair was a shade darker than mine, making it appear almost black. He sported a slight shadow of stubble over his square jaw and his brown eyes gleamed with pride as he took me in.

I wished I could revel in the look he was giving me. However, I was too angry about what I had been forced to do to Harlowe at his direction. I had tried to convince myself that I was doing this to protect her, but that was bullshit. My father had sent me to intervene in the impending marriage of our two rival kingdoms, weakening the alliance that would result from such a union. Just as he had done during the Skirmish of Power. Harlowe had been right. I was there, and I rained down hell on her kingdom under my father's orders. I hadn't answered her, but my silence had been answer enough.

I glanced to the throne on my father's right, seeing my brother peering down at me with a smirk gracing his lips. As a first-born son, August had been indulged his entire life. He never had to do any of the hard lifting like I had when I entered the military. Instead, he had learned the art of political games and quiet maneuvering. It meant he was a fucking snake, not to be trusted. The smirk on his lips told me he was playing his little games right now.

August was a carbon copy of my father. Same dark hair, the same dark eyes, same cut to his jaw. In contrast, I inherited my mother's traits. I still looked like my father, but my hair was the same shade as hers, and my features were softer than the sharp angles of my father. I knew my father preferred me over my older brother, but he would always yield to my brother as the heir apparent. And August always took what he wanted.

"Tell me what news you have for me, Silas."

"As you know, Father, I traveled to the Kingdom of Valoren as instructed and assisted their military to revitalize their Cathal ranks."

August snorted in derision. He opposed arming our rivals with any form of power that might one day be used against our kingdom. Unfortunately for him, it was the only way we were going to be invited to step foot inside Valoren. While the Skirmish of Power ended twenty-five years ago in a ceasefire, we weren't on the friendliest of terms with our neighbors. We stayed out of each other's way and traded at arm's length.

I ignored August and continued, "I became close to the Princess, and when she left the kingdom, I followed her."

"Ah yes," my father said. "I have heard about your... close relationship... with the Princess. I had instructed my guards to bring her here. Where is she?" he asked, looking around.

"She is resting," I said. "It's been a long journey for her."

"I suppose it has," my father agreed.

I wanted to ask him what he knew of my relationship with Harlowe, and more importantly, how he knew anything at all, considering I had sent no word home since arriving in Valoren. However, I refused to bring it up in front of all his courtiers.

I glimpsed a woman slipping from behind the pillars in the throne room. She glided towards my father, her long, wavy hair down around her waist. The dress she wore was almost scandalous, leaving little to the imagination, but I expected nothing less from Sienna. She had an exquisite body, and she used it to get what she wanted. She fawned over my father, who ate it up, despite her being his cousin's daughter. Their relationship was disturbing, to say the least. Sienna must have informed him about me and Harlowe when she returned home.

"Please go on Silas," my father instructed, a fresh glass of wine in his hand courtesy of Sienna.

"Your information was correct. Just before we left, they announced the Princess was betrothed to the King of Netheran."

I did not know where my father had gotten his information. They had kept the betrothal secret from everyone, including the bride.

"Was the Princess amenable to the match?" my father asked, curiosity sparkling in his eyes.

"No," I said curtly. August smirked down at me; the condescension clear in his expression. I had to hold myself back from marching up to him and removing that look.

"Interesting," my father said, sipping his wine.

"It was the reason she left her kingdom; to escape the marriage," I elaborated.

"Really?" my father's tone told me his interest was more than a little piqued.

"Yes. They did not inform her about the match, and she was not agreeable. Her father tried to force the issue, so she fled."

"Fled?" my father repeated, and I nodded in confirmation.

"Are you telling me she escaped you, son?" he said, mirth playing on his lips.

"She did," I confirmed. "She bonded a dragon, so it was rather easy for her to flee."

"Now, that is interesting," my father purred. "She is a strong woman. She will make a very fine queen," he mused.

"Indeed," I glanced towards my brother again, who was still smirking.

"So, she would not support an alliance with Netheran?" my father asked.

I hesitated a moment. I had an urge to be cautious with my words, without understanding why.

"I cannot say she would not still seek an alliance," I offered. "Just not through marriage."

My father was contemplative, which only raised my hackles further. He had sent me to retrieve my Little Menace in order to safeguard her here while any strengthening of the alliance between Netheran and Valoren was thwarted. A sickening feeling overcame me as I sensed there had been a shift in the plan during my absence.

"And the King of Netheran?" my father asked.

"He will come for her," I confirmed. "The King of Valoren did not seem pleased with his future son-in-law's antics while he visited, so we are in a strong position to negotiate an alliance with Valoren. Especially if we give his daughter safe harbor."

"Yes," my father drawled. "Your brother and I have been considering that. We are both of the view that the best way to secure that alliance would be to seek a marriage of our own."

I clenched my hands into fists and ground my teeth together. This is what my brother had been working on during my absence. A plan to force Harlowe to marry, and by the shit-eating grin spreading across his face right now, I was betting he was the intended groom.

"We agreed to keep her safe here, not force her into another marriage she did not choose," I ground out.

"Yes," my father said hesitantly, aware that I was a hair's breadth away from losing my shit.

"You assured me your intentions were honorable, father, as far as the Princess was concerned," I hissed.

"Silas," he said gently, as though he were trying to calm a caged animal.

"No," I snapped.

"Son, be reasonable," my father pleaded. This is how I knew I was his favorite son. He would not accept this type of behavior from anyone else in the kingdom, including August. If I were anyone else, he would have put me in my place with the ruthlessness he is known for. I would have ended up in the dungeons to cool off, son or not. It was my resemblance to my mother that spared me his wrath. He loved her too much to come down hard on me. He feared he would somehow harm her through me. It was also the reason my brother loathed me.

"I said no," I growled.

My father straightened on his throne. My thoughts about him not being able to discipline me may have been premature. Looking at up my father now, I could see the hardened eyes that sparked fear in his enemies. The set of his jaw told me he would not be defied on this.

But I wasn't backing down either. I made a promise to Harlowe, and I'd be dead before I broke it.

"Your brother will marry the Crown Princess of Valoren," my father said.

"She will refuse," I countered.

"Once she carries his heir, she will have a vested interest in cooperating."

I narrowed my eyes and turned my attention to my brother. He flinched under the intensity of my hatred, seeing the death promised there.

"You would rape her brother?" I asked, my tone dripping with malice.

My brother scoffed. "Please, little brother. I do not have to force women into my bed."

"She will not come willingly," I said with conviction. I knew my Little Menace. She had fled into the goddamned Forest of Nightmares to escape a man far more terrifying than my brother.

"You will bring down the wrath of both the King of Netheran for stealing away his bride, and the Kingdom of Valoren for forcing their heir into a marriage against her will. This is not wise, Father."

"We have time, son. She will come around. Once your brother and the Princess are married and have produced an heir, that child will stand to inherit both kingdoms. I understand you care for the girl, but it has to be your brother who marries her so that our kingdom may expand. And once she has settled in Pyrithia, her father will no longer be our enemy. He will be family," my father finished.

I threw my head back and laughed. "You're a fool if you think my Little Menace will roll over and give up just like that," I barked out.

"That's enough, Silas," my father warned, but I ignored him, continuing to laugh just so I wouldn't run my brother through with a blade.

Finally, under control, I leveled my glare back toward my father.

"All she needs is time, son," he said more softly. "And I have good news for you as well," he beamed, albeit somewhat forced.

"I have arranged a match for you, too. You are to wed Sienna."

I glanced to the left where she stood and saw her smiling doe-eyed at me.

"She is your cousin's daughter," I said incredulously. "I will not marry her."

"Silas," my father implored. "He is my cousin through marriage. You two share no blood, and she is a beautiful woman."

Sienna beamed under his praise.

"Then you marry her because I won't do it," I repeated, scowling. "And I won't allow anyone to lay a hand on Harlowe," I declared, meaning every fucking word.

My father sighed, weary of this conversation. "We can pick this up another time, my boy. Now that you're back, I'm eager to catch up and hear about all your adventures. Rest, and then meet us for dinner."

I pivoted on my feet without so much as an incline of my head towards my father. I was seething. So, Sienna had run back home with her tail between her legs after I ended things with her for Harlowe and then cooked up this unhinged plan with my brother to get back at me. Of course, my brother, despising me as he does, would be all too happy to take what's mine.

I was going to fucking murder them both. My Little Menace was marrying no one who wasn't me. No other man would touch what lay between her silken thighs, and I sure as shit wasn't about to stand back and let anyone force her.

I turned to Cillian and the others who had followed me out. "I want one of you with Harlowe at all times," I said, meeting each set of eyes and making sure I was crystal fucking clear.

"Anyone who fails me will be out of my contingent and back with the grunts so fast, they won't even realize they've fallen before they're flat on the ground. Do I make myself clear?" Fionn and Teller nodded their agreement. Cian hesitated for the briefest moment before giving a curt nod.

I turned to march up the stairs that led to my chambers, leaving them behind.

"Cillian," I barked. I needn't bother. He was already following me.

"Move closer to my chambers in case they make a move against Emmerson."

"Already thought of that. I'm taking the suite next to yours," he said.

"We might have fucked up bringing them home," I sighed.

"We had a plan, and your father gave his word. You couldn't know that Sienna and August would whisper poison in his ear," he said, having come to the same conclusion as I had.

"Sienna is obsessed, and August has made it his life's mission to ruin mine. I should have foreseen they would pull something."

"Yes, but this..." Cillian said, mirroring my astonishment. "This is extreme, even for them. If this goes ahead, it will be the ruination of Pyrithia. Harlowe's father may not think twice about forcing his daughter into a marriage contract for his own benefit, but I doubt he will be as forgiving if we do it."

I grunted in agreement.

There is no way Kieran would not punish our kingdom for taking Harlowe away either. He is determined to have her, and without an alliance with Valoren to push him back, even worse, with them both joining forces against us, the kingdom wouldn't survive. It is everything my father hoped to avoid all these years.

"I would not hold it against you if you wished to return Emmerson to her kingdom, get her out of here before any harm can come to her," I told my second.

"The thought is tempting, but I know she will never leave Harlowe."

Stopping outside my door, I turned to Cillian. "I want someone guarding this door right away. I don't care which one it is. Rotate between the four of you, and when it's your turn, bring Emmerson with you. Don't leave her unprotected."

Harlowe would never forgive me if anything happened to Emmerson.

I looked away from Cillian, grabbed my door handle, and steadied myself with a breath. I needed to brief Harlowe before setting her loose into the viper's den tonight at dinner.

Fuck. She was going to kill me.

Chapter Fifty-One

Moments after being deposited inside Silas's chambers, a young woman named Amity came in to draw me a bath. I had enjoyed her company, learning that she was twenty years old and had been working in the palace since she was sixteen. Her mother had been the late Queen's chambermaid, and they had formed a close friendship, according to Amity.

Having a bath had been heavenly. I had so much dirt caked into my skin and beneath my fingernails that I had to scrub them raw before I even made a dent in removing it. Amity had washed my hair while I grilled her about anything and everything I could, but the one thing I was desperate to know she could not answer. I needed to know where Emmerson was and if she was alright. I knew Cillian would protect her, but I was still worried.

Once I was thoroughly cleansed and the water had long since turned cold, Amity helped me dress, despite grumbling to herself the whole time about my choice of attire. I had forgone a dress and opted for my usual tunic and pants. Amity reminded me so much of Louise that a small pang of homesickness jostled me.

Now, all alone, I was left to contemplate my new predicament.

"Tell me again about the dragons, Misneach," I asked.

"You know everything there is to know, Fire Heart," he sighed.

"Indulge me," I droned.

"The pull they feel towards you is stronger than it was in Valoren. Whatever happened inside the Forest of Nightmares has strengthened

that connection. It's still not the same as our bond, though," he huffed.

I smiled, aware that Misneach was slightly jealous of any other dragon feeling connected to me. I was his Cathal, and he wouldn't accept anything else.

Misneach growled in warning, telling me he had heard my every thought, which only made me laugh out loud.

"I did not tell them about you wielding fire," he said, changing the subject.

Misneach did not want to take any unnecessary risks until we knew what we were dealing with. Not that he didn't trust the dragons, but he feared this knowledge slipping through their bonds to the other Cathal. As we could not discern friend from foe, we couldn't take that risk.

"And you saw for yourself how they protected you, even against their own Cathal," he said.

Caolán had tried to be the peacemaker. He knew through his bond with Silas that Silas meant me no harm, and he believed it when he said I would be safe here. I had to admit, after seeing all the dragons protect me at the cost of their bond mates, I felt safer in Pyrithia. That didn't mean that I was safe, though. I would escape eventually, but I needed to be smart and make sure I wasn't leaving the relative safety of Pyrithia without having somewhere suitable to go.

I was lost to my internal musings when I heard the door open and close quietly from the antechamber attached to the bedroom. Misneach growled inside my head, telling me who had entered.

"I am going hunting Fire Heart. Send word if you'd like to revise your no-killing-the-general stance. I can always just eat *him*."

"He's probably poisonous," I muttered, and I heard Misneach's chuckle in reply.

I moved off the bed and grabbed the heaviest thing within reaching distance. I turned the amber paperweight over in my hand and waited. It was translucent, and I could see some kind of fang, or maybe it was a claw, suspended in whatever substance the amber mass had been before it solidified.

Silas crossed the threshold into his bedroom, his head bowed as he rubbed his eyes. I hurled the paperweight across the room, narrowly missing his head as he dodged at the last second.

I then reached for the lantern on his bedside table and flung that at him.

"Little Menace," he growled in warning, "Stop!"

I ignored him and turned towards his bookshelf, grabbing the heaviest volumes I could reach and lobbing them right at him. One book connected with the left side of his head as he tried to shield himself from my attack.

When I turned to grasp another book, Silas struck, grabbing first my left wrist, and then my right, securing them behind my back.

Both panting hard, I could feel the defined muscles of his chest as he pulled me back against him.

"That wasn't very nice, Little Menace," Silas said huskily. The prick was getting off on my violence towards him.

"It wasn't supposed to be, you prick," I spat, struggling against his hold on me.

Silas leaned forward and pressed his nose into my hair. Inhaling, he said, "You smell positively delectable Harlowe."

My traitorous body grew wet and pliant in his hold.

Silas chuckled darkly as he pressed his lips against my ear and said, "Will you behave yourself if I release you?"

I didn't answer him, but I stopped struggling.

"Good girl," he purred and let me go.

I spun on my heels and jabbed my finger straight into his chest. "I will only tell you this once, Silas," I seethed. "You ever threaten Emmerson again, and I will end your fucking life." I leaned closer and whispered, "I don't care if I have to go up in flames right beside you. I will do it." And I was serious. He had gone too far by threatening Emmerson.

Silas's hand darted out, wrapping around my throat as he forced me backward until my spine was pressed against the wall. His grip was firm, but not painful. He would not leave his finger marks on my flesh, as Kieran had done.

"You need to calm the fuck down Harlowe," he growled. "Shit has changed. I need you to work with me so I can make sure I keep my promises to you."

"What's changed?"

"People inside this kingdom are playing fucking games and you're their new favorite plaything," he hissed.

"What the fuck does that mean, Silas?"

"It means," he said, anger marring his tone, "my treacherous brother has poisoned my father's thoughts, who is now deviating from the plan."

"Your father, the king," I scoffed.

Silas removed his hand from my throat and took a step back. He ran a hand through his hair, making it look unkempt and disheveled. Looking at him, I could clearly see his exhaustion. There were dark circles under his eyes and his eyelids were drooping.

"I have made some mistakes, Harlowe. That I will concede," he said.

I crossed my arms over my chest but did not interrupt.

"I could have done things differently." He paused and looked at me with regret. "Should have done things differently," he corrected. "But we're here now, and I need you to work with me so I can protect you."

"Protect me from what?"

Silas ground his teeth together, and I wasn't sure if I was exasperating him or if he was angry about this new threat to me.

"My brother," he spat, "has convinced my father that you and he should be married and produce an heir."

My mouth dropped open, and I stared at him in shock.

"What the fuck Silas?" I demanded after he failed to continue.

"I was indeed sent to Valoren to retrieve you," he admitted. "My father somehow heard that you were betrothed to the King of Netheran, and he wanted to disrupt the arrangement. He feared the threat of a stronger alliance between Netheran and Valoren, just like when he intervened in the Skirmish of Power."

I opened and closed my mouth. How did his father even know about my betrothal? I sure as shit didn't get a heads-up.

"My father only asked me to bring you to Pyrithia. He was supposed to offer you shelter from the King of Netheran, and in return, he hoped your father would align our two kingdoms, and push Netheran back," Silas said.

"And now what?" I asked, throwing my hands up in agitation. "I'm some convenient womb for him to breed his next heir?"

I was fucking seething. I had escaped one arranged marriage, only to be thrust into another. If I could outmaneuver Kieran, the King of Netheran, I would not be forced into marriage by some nobody princeling.

"No one is touching you," he snarled.

"You bet your ass they're not. Do you people realize I am a goddamn heir in my own right? I will be Queen of Valoren soon enough."

"Oh, they're aware," Silas seethed.

"And what is that supposed to mean?" I demanded.

"My brother's entire plan counts on you taking your throne. He has deluded himself into thinking he will wed you, breed you, and then his child would inherit two kingdoms, not one. He's practically crowned himself King of Valoren already."

"Huh, so this is about territory," I snorted. "Does your brother realize marrying me does not make him king? My husband will only be a consort, not a king," I advised. "This is why queens should rule instead of kings. Men are never fucking satisfied. Always taking more than they're entitled to, even when they're told no." I looked at him pointedly and he just glared right back at me.

"Do not compare me with my brother, Little Menace," he snarled.

"Why not? From where I'm standing, you two are cut from the same cloth," I said, provoking him.

He was on me before I could even blink.

Silas grabbed me roughly and threw me down on his bed. He pinned me with his muscular body and stared down at me, panting as he tried to regain control of himself.

He was furious. Good. It was about time he got a taste of his own medicine.

"What I have done, I did, in order to protect you. I have only acted against your will when I believed it to be in your best interests. That is very different from what my brother intends for you, Little Menace," he said through gritted teeth. "You want me, for starters. Just as much as I want you. That's a huge fucking difference."

"That's where you're wrong, Silas. I don't want you," I lied. "I might have wanted you once, but you went and fucked that up by taking me prisoner and dragging me to your hellish kingdom. And guess what, I'm no safer here than I was in my kingdom. You did this Silas. You put me in danger. No one else, just you," I growled.

"No matter how much you deny it, Little Menace, I know how much you crave me. How much your body sings for me. You were made for me. And you will be mine. Only mine," he said as he ran his tongue up the side of my neck until he reached the shell of my ear.

"Fuck. You. Silas." I smiled up at him, but it wasn't friendly. "Maybe I will go check out your brother after all," I taunted. "Hell, even Kieran would be preferable to you. At least he's honest about how much of a sadistic prick he is. And imagine all that hate fucking," I cooed.

Silas snarled at me, and I could feel him trembling with fury as he glared down at me.

"You keep talking about fucking other men, Harlowe, and I promise you won't like the consequences."

This only made me smile wider. I leaned up towards him so I could whisper against his ear, "Promises, promises Silas. You say that word a lot, but you're too much of a coward to do what is necessary to keep them. All talk, and no action. I will fuck whoever I please, so long as it isn't you."

His intense glare made me want to look away, but I resisted. His eyes scanned my face before his lips crashed against mine in a hungry kiss. He devoured me and I could feel my lips swelling from the force of it.

When he came up for air, he pushed away from me and said, "Get some rest, Harlowe. We're expected at dinner. And put on a goddamned dress for once in your life. If you want anyone to take you seriously, you need to play the part. You're the Crown Princess of Valoren. Act like it."

With that, he stormed out of the room, not sparing me a second glance. I picked up another book and hurled it with everything I had at his retreating frame. It hit the wall with a satisfying thud. It would have been more satisfying had it been his skull, but I'd take it.

Panting hard from the anger coursing through me, I allowed myself the time I needed to calm down. Straightening my tunic, I pulled the stray pieces of hair that had come loose from my braid back behind my ear.

If Silas wanted me to play, I'd play. He should be careful what he wishes for because he might just get it.

Chapter Fifty-Two

Amity returned sometime later to help me prepare myself for dinner. She nearly stumbled with joy when I agreed to wear a dress, but her excitement faded when she saw the one I had chosen.

It was a slinky, low-cut, black dress that exposed a considerable amount of my cleavage. The sleeves ran from my shoulders to my wrists, however, each sleeve had a split along its entire length, exposing my skin. The back dipped low, revealing my back, and a long slit ran up the side of my skirt, baring my thigh. While the dress technically covered every inch of me, the firm fit along with the slits throughout the material showcased my every curve. It was not something you would find in Valoren. And while it was the fashion in Pyrithia, the upper echelons of nobility tended towards the more conservative dress styles.

I wore my hair in a braid that wrapped around the top of my head like a crown. A silver circlet with interwoven bands clung to my forehead, and emerald green stones were woven throughout the design. A single, larger, tear-shaped stone hung in the center of my forehead, making me look every inch the queen I had told Silas I would be.

Thick kohl lined my eyes, and crimson paint had been applied to my lips. The contrast with my pale skin made my lips look fuller and I could not deny the raw sex appeal my look generated. I wanted the men who sought ownership of me to be dazed upon seeing me. Let them see I wielded far more power than they thought. I didn't even care I was using my body to make my point. I wanted them tripping over their own feet to fall on their knees at mine. The thought made my lips lift in a slight smirk.

When a light knock sounded at the door, I knew Silas had returned to escort me to dinner. I heard him enter the room before I could respond. When his eyes landed on me, his reaction did not disappoint me. His gaze ran the length of my body, and he paused when he saw my ample breasts on display. A small growl sounded deep in his throat as he continued his slow perusal, noting my bare thigh before he made his way back up my body and locked his gaze with mine.

Silas cleared his throat and said, "You look stunning."

I didn't bother acknowledging his compliment. Not letting him see I cared what he thought of me was all part of the game I intended to play with him and his fucked-up family.

"Shall we go?" I asked.

"Are you sure that's what you want to wear?" he inquired, uncomfortable having others see me dressed like this I'm sure. I hid my grin by looking down at my body.

"Of course," I said sweetly. "Is this not the fashion in Pyrithia?" I replied, raising an eyebrow in challenge.

Silas hesitated for a moment before extending his elbow to me. I placed my arm in his and let him lead me out of his chambers. His body was stiff beside me, and I knew my choice of dress was having the desired effect.

Outside the door to Silas's chambers, Cian stood on guard. Having never left his rooms until now, I had no knowledge of what was happening beyond those doors. Cian glanced at us as we emerged, doing a double take when he saw me. He stared at me, mouth agape, before he slammed his jaw shut and diverted his eyes. Cian never displayed any emotion other than mild disdain, so his reaction pleased me.

Silas groaned as he came to the same realization as I did and dragged his hand down his face.

Good. I intended to torment him relentlessly, using any means at my disposal.

When we reached the doors leading into the dining hall, I spotted Emmerson standing outside with Cillian. She was wearing a beautiful navy gown with a fitted bodice that flared out at her waist and cascaded to the ground. The sleeves of her dress sat off her shoulders, leaving the skin of her upper arms bare. Her long, silky hair was loose with waves of chocolate-colored strands cascading down her back. She looked radiant.

I ran towards her and gripped her in my arms as I held her against me for the longest moment. Neither of us uttered a word, finding solace in each other's presence.

When we broke apart, I whispered against her ear, "Are you alright?"

She snorted, "Are you alright?"

I nodded my head on instinct, despite it being a lie.

"Liar," she whispered, and I laughed. I had never been able to get anything passed Emmerson since we were small children.

"You look breathtaking," she muttered.

"So do you."

"What's the plan?" she asked.

"I have a lot to tell you, but let's find a more private place to talk in case someone overhears us. Just promise me if you hear anything outrageous in there, don't react, okay?"

Emmerson nodded her head, willing to follow my lead.

"Ladies, if you will," Silas said, as he thrust his arm forward, directing us into the dining hall.

Instead of retaking his arm, I linked my arm with Emmerson's and strolled into the dining hall ahead of him.

As we stepped inside, everyone's gaze fixed on us. My attention was drawn to a dark-haired man at the head of the table. His hair was a shade darker than Silas's and the cut of his jaw was more angular, but you could see the resemblance.

This man was the King of Pyrithia, Silas's father.

Another man, seated to his right, bore a striking resemblance to the King, with matching hair color and distinct facial features. There was no denying who he was; Silas's brother, the man who thought to trap me in marriage and force me to carry his heir.

My hackles rose as I took him in, and I had to stop myself from snarling. A firm hand on my lower back pushed me towards the long dining table and the four vacant chairs that sat on the King's left. Silas pulled out my chair and waited for me to take my seat. Once settled, he took the vacant seat next to me while Emmerson filled the one on my other side, Cillian next to her. She gave my hand a slight squeeze underneath the table.

"Father," Silas started. "This lovely creature is Harlowe, Crown Princess of Valoren, and future Queen," he said with a wave in my direction. I inclined my head in a slight bow towards the King and he beamed at me.

"It is a pleasure to have you here with us, Princess." I wanted to roll my eyes. I would not be here if he hadn't sent his son to kidnap me, but it would probably be considered rude for me to bring that up at the dining table. So instead, I offered him a tight smile in response.

Silas waved a hand towards Emmerson and continued, "This is the Princess's companion, Emmerson. She is the daughter of the Captain General of the King's army." Emmerson just stared at the King as if she was bored. The King seemed to like this as he smirked at her.

"Emmerson is also the future Captain General of the Queen's army," I supplied, sipping my wine to hide my grin. Everyone stared at me as if I had denied the existence of the sun. So, Pyrithia was willing to have female soldiers, Cathal even, but just like everywhere else, they were skeptical when it came to women holding power. I intended to use every weapon at my disposal to throw these people off balance. My tutelage may be useful after all. Father would be proud.

"Well, this is a pleasure," he purred, and I noticed Cillian stiffen beside Emmerson.

"I wish I could say the same," Emmerson deadpanned, and I kicked her foot underneath the table.

The King just chuckled, not offended by her comment.

"I apologize for the manner in which you have both joined us here in Pyrithia. However, I am pleased to have you as my guests all the same," the King said.

"Guests," Emmerson snorted. "Is that what we are, your majesty?" I gave her another sharp kick, which she dutifully ignored.

"Of course," the King said, without hesitation. "And please, call me Leith," he smiled.

Darting my glance away from the King, I locked eyes with the Prince seated to his right. He was staring at me, his head tilted as he assessed me. I suppressed a shiver of unease as his stare lingered, making me uncomfortable.

"Where are my manners?" said Leith. "This is my son August," he said, pointing to the man staring at me. "And you already know my youngest son, Silas."

"Pleasure," August said huskily, and this time Silas was the one to stiffen. He snarled at his brother, who chuckled.

As I peered down the long table, I noticed Sienna seated a few spots away, glaring daggers at me. I returned the favor while I drank greedily from my wine glass. Silas glanced sideways at me, but I refused to meet his gaze.

The King began recounting all the beautiful sights he insisted Emmerson, and I had to see while in Pyrithia. I tuned him out, instead focusing my attention on August. He mistook my calculating gaze as interest as he said, "It would be my pleasure to show you around, Princess," with a cocky grin on his full lips.

"That won't be necessary," Silas said at the same time I replied, "Perhaps I'll take you up on the offer."

Silas swung his head in my direction, his stare burning a hole in the side of my face, but I kept my gaze locked on the Prince. I would have these two ripping each other to shreds and suitably distracted as I made my move to escape them both.

Servers emerged with platters overflowing with food, sparing me from having to meet Silas's stare. Everyone enjoyed their meal as they discussed the goings on of court and trading gossip.

"Have you heard the news, Princess?" Sienna gushed from her seat down the table. I glanced at her but remained silent.

"Silas and I are to be married," she beamed. Silas growled beside me.

"Congratulations," I said, my tone bored, although a jealous inferno was raging inside me. I would not give her the satisfaction of seeing that her declaration affected me.

"I am not marrying you, Sienna," Silas said through gritted teeth.

"Nonsense," she chuckled, ignoring his obvious agitation.

"We should throw a ball in honor of our esteemed guests," the King said, cutting through the mounting tension.

"A wonderful idea," August agreed. "It would be my honor to be your escort, Princess. I know my brother can be quite the brute. You likely think we are all uncouth animals," he laughed. "I would relish the opportunity to set you straight." The innuendo was clear in his tone.

Silas stood, his chair crashing to the floor in his haste. He slammed his palms down on the table and glared murderously at his brother. The room fell silent, everyone holding their breath, waiting to see what Silas would do next.

Silas stood to his full height and straightened his tunic. "I, for one, have had enough company for one evening," he said, his tone clipped. Turning to me, he stretched out his hand for me and said, "Come, Harlowe, we shall retire for the evening."

"I'm quite enjoying myself," I said sweetly, and Silas narrowed his eyes on me.

Silas thrust his hand closer to me before he gave me a pointed look, daring me to challenge him again. I wanted to, but I also wanted to play the long game. So I placed my hand in his and rose from my seat.

"Thank you for a lovely meal," I said to the King before offering August a small smile.

Emmerson and Cillian both rose from their seats and followed Silas and me out of the dining hall. Nobody spoke until we reached the doors outside Silas's chambers. Cian was still stationed there, but he kept his eyes trained straight ahead, ignoring our approach.

"Where are you staying?" I asked Emmerson, but it was Cillian who answered.

"We are in the suite next to yours," he said gruffly. Emmerson raised her eyebrow at his flippant comment that indicated they would share a room.

Cillian was blissfully unaware he had pissed her off. He would find out though, and soon.

"I will see you in the morning," I said to Emmerson, pulling her into a hug.

When I released her, Silas pushed his door open and pulled me inside behind him.

Chapter Fifty-Three

Inside his antechamber, Silas released my hand and stormed over to a small cabinet tucked behind a long black chaise. He picked up a glass and poured some liquid into it. Silas raised it to his lips and downed the contents in one go. He refilled the glass and repeated the process.

I watched him from my position by the door, intrigued to see this side of him. He was radiating anger that he could not control. It made him seem almost vulnerable. I pushed off the door, strolling over to him, and reached for his glass, refilling it. Then I lifted it to my nose, inhaling deeply.

Whiskey. Of course.

I took a small sip, reveling in the burning sensation as the warm liquid slid down my throat.

I started walking away from Silas, only for him to reach out and wrap an arm around my waist, pulling me back to him. He ran his nose along my throat to the shell of my ear, inhaling as he did so.

"You smell like sin Harlowe," he whispered huskily, and I had to force myself to repress the shiver that wanted to tear through me. "Tell me, Little Menace, what game are you playing?"

"What makes you think I'm playing?" I asked, as I lifted the glass to my lips and took another sip.

He chuckled darkly. "Tonight, when you entered that dining hall, wearing this," — he ran a hand down my stomach and then clutched the fabric of my dress — "every single male in there was imagining what it would be like to tear it off your body." He planted a kiss on the back of my neck before continuing, "This is the kind of dress that men would kill over, just for the chance to fall at your feet. Is that what you want, Little Menace? You want me to get on my knees for you?" he purred.

Liquid heat pooled in my core, and this time, a shiver ran down my spine without my permission. Silas chuckled against my neck, catching my reaction.

I took another sip of my whiskey to settle my racing heart before placing it down on the table next to me. I could feel my heart hammering against my rib cage, trying to break free of my chest.

Silas ran his hands lower down my stomach until he reached the junction between my thighs. He slipped his hand under the skirt of my dress, the long split up the side giving him easy access. He cupped my sex through my panties, and I moaned at the pressure.

"That's it, Little Menace. Show me how your body purrs for me," he praised. Silas slipped his hand beneath my panties and pushed a single finger inside me. He growled against my ear, finding that I was already wet for him. Silas worked his finger in and out of me, and I threw my head back against his shoulder, closing my eyes. His lips pressed against my throat as he inserted another finger.

My breathing picked up as I rocked against him, and he increased his tempo to meet my thrusts. I was panting now, and I knew I was close as I wrapped my arms around his neck behind me to steady myself.

"That's my good girl. Fuck my hand, Little Menace. Show me how your cunt weeps for me."

I cried out as his filthy words had me coming hard. He continued to pump his fingers inside me as I rode out my orgasm. When he withdrew them, he lifted the digits to his mouth and sucked them clean. The act made me shiver all over again.

As I lowered my arms from around Silas's neck, I turned to face him. I leaned down to retrieve my glass and took another sip as I placed my hand on his chest. I reached up on my toes to whisper in his ear and said, "Thanks," before lowering myself back down and turning away from him.

As I walked towards his bedchamber, I heard him snarl behind me, and my lips twitched upwards into a smirk.

"Harlowe," he growled, but I ignored him. Before I could reach his bed, he gripped my upper arm and removed my glass from my hand.

"What the fuck was that?" he hissed.

I raised an eyebrow in mock surprise before saying, "I thought it was pretty self-explanatory, Silas. I wanted to get off, so I rode your hand until you made me come. Is something wrong?" I taunted.

"Is something wrong?" he scoffed. Silas tipped my glass up, emptying the contents before throwing the glass into the open fireplace and smashing it.

"Don't fucking play me, Harlowe," he warned.

"Who's playing?" I purred, turning my back to him once more. I removed the circlet from my forehead and placed it on his bedside table. As I stepped out of my black slippers, I reached up behind my neck to undo the clasp of my dress. Large, calloused hands replaced mine, and Silas unbuttoned my dress, allowing me to step out of it.

Completely naked, I climbed into his bed, pulled his covers down, and nestled myself against his pillows. I reached up and unwound the braid on top of my head, letting my hair fall down my back.

Silas watched me from the side of the bed, my naked breasts exposed to his hungry gaze. I didn't acknowledge him once, which I knew was driving him wild with frustration. Finished with my tasks, I turned to Silas and found his heated gaze fixated on me, lust pooling in the deep brown depths of his eyes.

I raised a single eyebrow, challenging him to break the silence. He scrubbed a hand down his face as he exhaled. Silas lifted his tunic over his head and dropped it to the floor, revealing the hard contours of his muscled body. My gaze dipped to the deep Adonis belt of his hips as he untied his pants. The corded muscles of his arms flexed as he gripped his pants before yanking them down his thick thighs. He stepped out of them and stood before me, naked, his erect cock demanding my attention.

The gods themselves crafted the man; his body was created to be worshiped.

His toned physique was built for battle and right now, I was eager for him to go to war on my body. I resisted the urge to lick my lips, controlling my features to ensure I gave nothing away.

Or at least I thought I did. The smirk on his lips and the mirth twinkling in his eyes told me he knew exactly what his naked body did to me.

Silas pulled back the covers and slipped into bed beside me. He reached his arm out, clutching me, and pulled me to him. He tried to roll me beneath his body, but I pushed him back, not allowing it.

"And what do you think you're doing?" I asked huskily.

"I thought it was pretty self-explanatory Harlowe," he purred, repeating my words back to me.

"And what makes you think I'm interested?" I taunted him.

He ran his tongue up the valley between my breasts before trailing it back down to my peaked nipple.

"The fact that your nipples are hard enough to cut glass for one," he said as he sucked my nipple into his wet mouth. I gasped, unable to stop myself, and he chuckled darkly.

"I told you, Harlowe, you can lie to yourself all you want, but I'm done indulging you. You are mine and only mine. I own this body, and this cunt," he said as he ran his hand down my stomach, cupping me between my thighs. "When you come, you will do so while riding my fingers, my tongue, or my cock," he promised as he rubbed my clit with the palm of his hand, making me moan. "No other man will know the sweet sound of your whimpers, or the way you scream my name, because I am the only man who will be buried in your tight sheath ever again, Harlowe. Do you hear me?" he growled.

I ground myself against him, ignoring his words. He could think whatever the fuck he wanted. No matter how many times he told me he owned me, it would never be true.

With a swift roll, Silas had me pinned beneath him before I even realized he had moved. He thrust his cock inside me without warning, making me cry out at the invasion.

"That's it, Little Menace, be a good girl, and let me hear you sing for me." He set a punishing rhythm that had me playing catch up, trying to regain control of the situation. The sensation of him sliding in and out of me overwhelmed my senses, causing me to moan in pleasure.

"Yes Harlowe, that's it. Be a good girl and come for me." I forced myself to stop from coming by biting my bottom lip until I could taste the coppery tang of my blood. I would not let him dominate me and try to push me beneath him.

I wrapped my legs around his waist and flipped us until I was straddling him. Silas growled at me but made no move to unseat me. I rocked my hips against his cock, lifting slightly before dropping myself back down on his length, seating myself to the hilt. Silas thrust up to meet my movements, and I reached down to pinch my nipples.

Silas snarled, swatting my hands away as he cupped my breasts in his large palms. It was a battle for control, both of us trying to take it from the other.

Panting, Silas growled, "Ride me, Harlowe. Fuck your King until I come inside you."

"You're no king of mine. Now shut the fuck up, Silas," I said as I picked up my speed. He laughed, taunting me.

"Tell me who you belong to Harlowe," he demanded, his hips slapping against mine as our bodies battled one another.

"I belong to no one," I growled.

"Tell me you're mine, Little Menace."

"No," I hissed, seething, but too turned on to care much at the moment.

"Who owns this pussy?"

I continued to ignore him, refusing to give him what he wanted. He snarled when he realized I would not give in. He unleashed on me, pounding into me brutally. Then he fixed his hand around my throat, squeezing, but not enough to cut off my air.

I gripped his body with my thighs, hanging on for dear life as he used my body.

"Scream. My. Name." he growled, thrusting inside me, punctuating each word. Still, I refused to yield. No more, I had promised myself. I would make this man crawl to me if it was the last thing I did.

My orgasm tore through me, the brutality of Silas fucking me and my refusal to bow down to him, only heightening the pleasure. I wanted to slump against him, but his hand on my throat held me in place. He thrust upwards a few more times before he groaned and emptied himself inside me.

He lowered his hand from my throat, and I leaned over, resting my forehead on his chest as I sucked in air.

"You see Little Menace," he purred. "It doesn't matter what you say. Your body will always know who owns it. When I leave your tight sheath, you will feel me there for days after."

Sitting upright, I glared down at him, and he smirked, pissing me off.

I leaned back down to him and said quietly, "Who says that wasn't my plan all along?" I watched as his eyes narrowed on me and I continued, "You see, you and your family regard me as some piece of property to be owned and used, so that is exactly what you have become to me, Silas," I purred. "You mean nothing more to me than a good fuck, someone I can use whenever the desire takes me," I lied.

Leaning down further, I pressed my lips against his in a soft kiss. "Goodnight Silas," I said as I rolled off him.

He didn't move or say a single word.

As if he could simply fuck me into submission.

I smiled to myself. I was going to set this entire kingdom on fire, and then escape amongst the chaos.

No one would ever use me again.

Chapter Fifty-Four

Silas woke me up the next morning by entering me roughly, making me cry out. My eyes sprang open as he rocked his hips against me, his wicked smile the first thing I saw as he peered down at me.

"Good morning Princess," he said hoarsely, still driving his erect cock into my core as he continued to rock his hips against me.

"Silas," I moaned.

"Yes, Little Menace?"

I opened my mouth to respond, but I was cut off when he shifted his hips, thrusting into me at an angle and hitting that delicious spot inside me. I gasped, clinging to his biceps as he drove himself inside me.

"You were saying something?" I ignored him as I met him thrust for thrust.

"Tell me you're mine," he purred, picking up his pace.

"Never!"

"Or should I just use your body whenever I feel like it? Is that what we have become?"

"Quit whining and fuck me," I said, my voice thick with lust.

I was incapable of saying anything else as he continued his assault on my body. Pleasure engulfed me and I came all over his dick as he chased his own release. Silas grunted and buried his head in my hair as he reached his orgasm. For a while, we both lay there, panting heavily. Neither one of us spoke as we caught our breath.

Silas rose to his elbow and stared into my eyes for the longest time. Leaning down, he kissed me gently. Silas didn't do gentle. He made demands and took what he wanted roughly.

When he broke the kiss, he rested his forehead on mine, his eyes closed as he threaded his hand in my hair.

"Can we stop playing these games now, Harlowe?" he said, his voice low and hesitant. He lifted his head and searched my eyes.

"What games?" I asked, feigning ignorance.

"I get it. You're pissed at me, and you have every right to be," he started. "I fucked up. I know I did." He rolled off me, pulling me with him so we were on our sides facing each other.

"I honestly thought I was doing the right thing by you when I brought you here. I may have only been following my father's orders when I set out, but once I knew what your father and Kieran had planned, I knew I had to get you out of there." He sighed as if the weight of everything had become too much for him.

"I'll admit that I got a bit carried away in the Forest of Nightmares," he said with a sexy smirk on his lips. "I shouldn't have cuffed you. However, the thought of you being unprotected in that place was unbearable to me."

"It wasn't your call to make Silas," I pointed out.

"I know. I acted irrationally and out of fear. I fucked up, Harlowe."

"I said I didn't want to come here, but you ignored me. Now I'm at risk!"

He chewed on his bottom lip before answering, "I had no idea the plan had changed."

That just pissed me off. As if everything would have been alright if he kidnapped me under different circumstances.

He must have registered the change in my body language because he quickly added, "I know my intentions don't change the outcome. I shouldn't have made that decision for you. It is also wrong for my father to manipulate you into an alliance for our kingdom."

I just stared at him expectantly.

"I'm sorry," he said finally.

I fought the smirk playing on my lips. I had him right where I wanted him.

"You can't expect me to just forgive you and move on, Silas."

"No, not forgiveness," he said. "Just your cooperation. We're on the same side now, Little Menace. Stop fighting me and let me make this right. Let me help you."

"Help me do what?" I pressed.

"I'm going to get you out of here," he said. "As soon as I can find somewhere safe to take you."

I considered his proposal. My plan had been to rile him and his brother up, pitting them against one another, so they were too busy trying to outdo each other to keep a vigilant watch on me. And then, when the opportunity presented itself, I would slip away undetected.

It would be easier and more efficient if I had Silas on my side. I wasn't stupid, though. I knew I couldn't trust Silas. He had said and done too much for a few sweet nothings whispered in bed to undo everything. But I could accept his help, and at the first sign of trouble, I could cut him loose.

"I'm... listening," I said.

Silas smirked mischievously. "Oh, I know just how well you can listen, Little Menace," he said gruffly. I rolled my eyes at his innuendo, and he laughed.

The doors crashing open drew both our attention, and Silas grabbed the sheet, covering me with it.

"What the fuck do you think you're doing in here August?" Silas shouted.

Silas's brother was fuming. The vein at his temple pulsing with his anger.

"I should ask you that, little brother," August spat, his eyes darting to me.

"Don't fucking look at her," Silas snarled.

August crossed his arms over his chest and said, "And why's that? She is to be my wife, after all," he taunted.

I scoffed. August was delusional if he thought I would ever marry him. At least he was dropping the pretense of trying to court me.

"I struggle to see the humor in that, Princess," August snapped.

"There is no humor. It's simply not happening," I retorted, joining the conversation.

"I think you'll find you're mistaken," August derided, a cruel smile spreading across his lips.

Silas was up and standing over his brother before I could blink. He wrapped a hand around his throat and squeezed. "I already advised you and our father that Harlowe is mine. Whatever ideas you have about marrying her and taking over her kingdom end right here and now," he said, enraged.

August's face began turning a mottled red as he struggled to breathe under Silas's punishing grip.

Silas bared his teeth, his nose almost touching his brothers. "Now get the fuck out of my chambers before I end your miserable life." Silas shoved his brother back into the wall before releasing him.

"Our father will hear of this," August wheezed between breaths as he massaged his throat. "You disrespect him by fucking her against his wishes," he snarled. Silas was on him in an instant, slamming his head against the wall repeatedly, leaving a trail of August's blood in his wake.

I jumped up out of bed and rushed towards them, grabbing Silas's arm as I tried to stop him. If I was in any way a hindrance, it didn't diminish Silas's brutal attack.

"Silas you'll kill him!" I shouted, but he was beyond hearing me.

I scrambled onto Silas's back and wrapped my arms around his neck, trying to cut off his air supply. I had never seen him so angry, but I knew that if he killed his brother, there would be serious consequences for us both.

Relenting, Silas released his brother and his body slid down the wall.

"GET OUT!" Silas roared so loud I thought my eardrums might explode. His shoulders heaved and his entire body was trembling.

Holding a hand to his bloody face, August scrambled to his feet and fled from the room. Silas just stood there, trying to reign in his anger. He thrust his fist out and connected with the wall as his anger won out. The paneling on the wall crumbled under the impact and Silas reeled his fist back, hitting it again and again and again. When I thought he would never stop, he hunched over, cradling his fist in his free hand, and screamed his rage for the kingdom to hear.

I heard feet pounding right before Fionn, Cillian, and Emmerson burst through the doors. It was then that I remembered we were both stark ass naked. I grabbed a sheet to cover myself and tried to fight the flood of embarrassment that threatened to consume me.

Emmerson rushed to me, worry etched on her face, unable to make sense of the scene before her.

"Are you okay?" she rushed out. "What happened?"

"I'm fine. It's Silas who is injured." I looked over Emmerson's shoulder to see Cillian and Fionn both standing there awkwardly, unsure of what to do.

"Can you give me a second to get dressed and then we'll talk?" I glanced towards Cillian and Fionn and added, "Take them too. Get Fionn to retrieve a healer and I'll get Silas covered up."

Emmerson nodded and guided Cillian and Fionn out of the room.

I pulled on a shift and wrapped a robe around myself. I walked over to Silas and gripped his uninjured hand, pulling him towards the bed.

"Sit," I commanded, pointing to the bed. He obeyed without question as I scrambled around his chambers, looking for some pants. When I found a pair, I returned to his side and shimmied them up his legs.

"I told Emmerson to get a healer," I said as I finished with the ties.

Silas remained quiet as he ground his teeth together. I went to move towards the doors to call the others back, but his hand darted out and stopped me.

"If you believe nothing else I have ever told you, Harlowe, then believe this," he said, his voice low and edged with danger. "If another man looks at your bare skin again, I'll tear his fucking eyes out. If another man lays a hand on you, I'll fucking cleave it from his body. If I hear even a whisper of another man laying claim to you, I will end his fucking life in the worst way possible." His penetrating gaze bore into me, and I could tell he meant every single word.

"I'm no longer playing around when it comes to you, Harlowe. I am not a good man and I make no apologies for that. I deal in violence and death daily. Destruction is at the very core of my being. So when I see something I want, I take it without a single thought to the consequences. So understand that I mean it when I say I'd sooner slaughter every single person in this kingdom than give you up." He moved his hand to my chin, gripping it tightly. "If another man thinks to take what's mine, Little Menace, even the gods will tremble under my fury. My wrath will rain down from the heavens so violently, it will set this realm ablaze, burning it to the fucking ground until I get you back."

With that, he stood, crushing his lips against mine, sealing his promise with a devastating kiss.

Chapter Fifty-Five

I was left reeling from Silas's declaration, unable to sort through the plethora of emotions he'd evoked in me. It felt like he had shared a piece of his soul with me.

And it was black as night.

I was foolish for assuming I knew anything about Silas. My current circumstances were a testament to that. Despite it all, however, there had still been some underlying current that drew me to him. It made me feel like I actually knew him. And then he showed me a glimpse of the real Silas, and he terrified me.

I distracted myself from my spiraling thoughts by changing clothes and joining Silas, Emmerson, and Cillian in the antechamber. Fionn hadn't returned yet after going to get a healer as I had instructed.

Everyone was holding a glass of whiskey, sipping silently as the tension mounted inside the room. It was a struggle to drink the burning liquid this early in the morning, but I needed something to do with my hands.

Mercifully, Fionn returned not too long after Silas and I had left his bedchamber, followed by a young woman with chestnut brown hair and a welcoming smile. Her gray eyes were filled with ancient wisdom, telling me she was far older than her youthful appearance suggested.

Her gaze roamed over the room and landed on me, where it remained for an unnervingly long period before she glanced toward Silas. She tilted her head as she studied him, and then her scrutiny returned to me. I could not help but shift my weight from foot to foot under her assessment.

She blinked and then returned her gaze to Silas, her expression softening.

"Silas," she chided. "What have you done now?"

He didn't answer her, instead throwing back his glass and emptying its contents.

"It's his hand," I offered.

She placed the basket she had brought with her at his feet and took his hand in hers to look over the damage. She tsked when she saw the swollen, bloodied mess.

"Do I even want to know how this happened?" she inquired.

"Probably not," he shrugged, indifferent.

I rolled my eyes. The man was infuriating.

"He punched his fist into the wall," I informed her. Then added, "Repeatedly."

Her eyebrows knitted together as she looked at him. "Why on earth would you do that?"

"My brother barged into my room unannounced while I was in bed with my Little Menace," he growled, glaring back at me.

My cheeks heated, and I lowered my eyes to the ground, but not before I caught Emmerson lifting a single eyebrow at me in amusement mouthing, "Little Menace."

"He then let his eyes wander to places they shouldn't have." Silas spoke as if this was not the most mortifying moment of my life. I stared at the ground, trying to will it to open up and swallow me whole.

"Before announcing he had every right as Harlowe was to be his wife, despite the fact that I already informed him and my father that she was mine. So I choked him and slammed his head into the wall," he finished.

"What?" Emmerson questioned while Cillian groaned. Fionn just stared at us with a look somewhere between amusement and horror.

"I see," the woman said, and she made it sound like Silas's explanation was entirely reasonable.

I snorted, and all eyes turned to me.

"What?" I said, lifting my shoulders. "She made it sound like his response was proportionate," I defended.

"He's lucky he left with his life," Silas growled, and I folded my arms across my chest, tired of his antics.

"This will cause problems, Silas," Cillian warned.

"I don't fucking care," Silas snapped.

"I'm not saying you were wrong to do what you did. I'm just pointing out the reality. August, the coward he is, will rush to your father, who won't be pleased with what occurred here."

Silas grunted as the woman continued to prod at his hand. Satisfied, she began removing items from her basket.

"No man will ever escape unscathed if he tries to tell me I can't fuck what belongs to me," Silas snarled.

I tipped my head back towards the heavens. For the love of the gods, please just open up the ground and drag me down to hell. It would be an act of mercy.

Drawing my attention back to the room, the woman grabbed a pestle and mortar and began grinding herbs into a fine dust before retrieving a vial containing some kind of liquid. The woman emptied the ground herbs into the vial and began chanting to herself, moving her fingers over the concoction as she did so.

"You're a witch," I gasped, and the woman raised her head to look at me. She grinned before returning to her task.

"Arabella is an ally," Silas said. "She was not alive during the War of Witches, and I won't see her punished for something she had no involvement in."

A small pang of jealousy sparked to life inside my chest at the tender tone he used to speak of his friend.

"That's how you got the concealment spells," I said, narrowing my eyes on him, and he nodded.

"Drink this," Arabella said, passing Silas the vial containing the liquid. He thanked her and downed the contents.

"A healing elixir," she said for the benefit of the room.

With everything calmed down, Emmerson made her way towards me. "Fucking again?" she questioned. "I thought he was the enemy," she chided.

"I slipped," I said lamely.

Emmerson snorted, "And what? Landed on his dick."

"Not literally... it was metaphorical...." I inhaled to calm my agitation. "I'm sorry," I mumbled.

"Don't be. I'm glad one of us is getting dick," she sighed. "Just remember who and what he is," she warned, and I nodded in understanding.

While Silas may be on my side when it came to August and the King, his behavior this morning reminded me he was dangerous. He wanted to keep me at all costs, and that meant I couldn't trust him. He would remove any obstacle in his way, and he had already proven that included me.

Arabella finished up and repacked her items into her basket. She stood and turned towards me, a warm smile on her face.

"Princess, I wonder if you would be so kind as to escort me back to my chambers?" she asked.

"Of course," I said simultaneously with Silas's firm, "Absolutely not."

I narrowed my gaze at him, daring him to challenge me.

"August can't be trusted," he insisted. "You can't be moving about the castle unprotected."

"I'll go with her," Fionn offered, and Silas growled low in his throat.

"Thank you, Fionn," I said and offered Arabella my arm. She beamed at me as she slid her arm through mine.

"Do you know what an aura is, Princess?" she asked after a few moments of silence. I scrunched my nose and shook my head.

"It is an energy source, if you will, that surrounds your body, and each one is unique to an individual. The colors vary from person to person and mean different things."

"Can you see them?" I asked, curious.

"Oh yes," she replied. "It is most fascinating. For example, your aura is a brilliant blue color, which means someone is an independent thinker, intuitive and open-minded." I nodded my head, not sure if I believed her.

"Silas's aura is a deep shade of red. This suggests an energetic, strong-willed, and grounded individual," she said.

I grunted. Silas was anything but well-grounded. In fact, I was leaning more toward insane.

Arabella laughed at my side, "It may seem strange to you given his behavior whenever you're around, but most of the time, that description would very much suit Silas. He consistently displays reason, sensibility, and meticulous planning. That is until you came along."

"What is that supposed to mean?" I said defensively, raising my voice more than I had intended to. I looked back and saw that Fionn was still trailing behind us.

"Oh, I mean nothing by it, Princess. Just that Silas is different around you. It also explains what I saw happening with your auras," she said absentmindedly.

"I'm not following," I confessed.

"When I first entered the room, your distinct blue aura surrounded you, just like Silas's aura remained his usual shade of red. But when you moved closer to him, your auras reached out for one another, becoming a vibrant violet color that surrounded the both of you."

I glanced at her out of the corner of my eye, unconvinced by what she was telling me.

Unperturbed, Arabella continued, "Have you ever heard of twin flames, Princess?"

I sighed and said, "No, but I'm guessing you're about to tell me all about them."

Laughing softly, she explained, "Twin flames are two souls who mirror one another."

"Like soul mates?" I asked skeptically.

"Not necessarily. Soul mates infer a romantic connection. Twin flames do not have to be. They could be friends, lovers, or even family. Twin flames experience a deep connection with the other person's soul. The feeling could be one of familiarity, longing, or recognition. Twin flames could be complete strangers and once they meet, that sense of connection between the two pulls them both together, no matter what might push them apart."

I mulled over her words as a sense of unease crept along my spine.

"When twin flames first meet," Arabella continued, "there is an instant connection. A sense that something has been missing in their life until the moment they met. Understandably, this can make both of them extremely protective and possessive of the other. They become fearful of losing them and feeling that sense of loss and longing all over again." She gave me a knowing smile.

"Are you trying to tell me that Silas is my twin flame?" I scoffed.

"I'm not trying to tell you anything, Princess. I'm simply telling you a story." I doubted that. Arabella was hardly being subtle.

"Pretend that I believe you for a moment. What would happen if twin flames were pulled apart, or one of them left the other?" I asked.

"Oh, I imagine there would be very little that the other wouldn't do to be reunited with their twin flame. For having a twin flame is a gift, one denied to many," she said pointedly.

"Well, this is me," Arabella said as she stopped outside a door. "Thank you for walking me back, Princess." She smiled sweetly at me before darting inside.

Confused, I turned around to find Fionn leaning up against the wall, waiting for me.

"Shall we?" he said, gesturing with his hand. I nodded, and he fell into step beside me.

Lost in my thoughts, we made the journey back to Silas's chambers in silence as I tried to make sense of everything Arabella had told me. What she didn't say was clear; she thought Silas was my twin flame, and his erratic, possessive behavior could be explained away by his intense need to be with me.

That, of course, was bullshit.

Silas might be possessive, but he was in control of his behavior. And he had made choices that had hurt me.

More troubling than anything else, however, was the fact that I had felt a connection, a pull, towards Kieran. And the thought that he could be my twin flame horrified me.

Chapter Fifty-Six

My father had summoned me to his private chambers, which meant that he did not want anyone within the castle to witness the tongue-lashing he wanted to give me. It did not bother me either way. I could tell my father that Harlowe was mine and only mine, within the privacy of his chamber walls if he wished, or I could scream it for the entire kingdom to hear. The result would be the same.

My Little Menace belonged to me.

"I hate to say I told you so, brother, but I did fucking tell you so," Cillian muttered next to me. He had insisted on accompanying me to meet with my father, likely fearful that I would finish what I started this morning and snap my brother's neck.

I didn't bother replying.

"What's the plan here, Silas? Talk to me."

"The plan is, I tell my brother and my father to fuck off," I retorted.

"I'm serious," Cillian snapped as he pinched the bridge of his nose.

"So am I."

Cillian reached out and grabbed me by my arm, stopping me in my tracks. I whirled on him, snarling in anger. Cillian didn't back down though.

"You need to do better than that, Silas. Harlowe and Emmerson deserve better than you fucking winging this. We dragged them here under the promise of our protection. Shit's gone awry, and it's our responsibility to get them out. Your little chest-beating contest with your brother this morning just made that task more difficult."

"So what Cill, I was supposed to just let it slide?" I glowered.

"No," he said. "But I expect you to have a plan to rectify this situation." He stared me down pointedly.

I exhaled in frustration and ran my hand through my hair.

"I can't fucking think straight when my girl is anywhere near me," I confessed.

"Stop thinking with your dick and you might surprise yourself," Cillian scoffed.

"And you're one to talk?" I asked, raising an eyebrow in challenge.

Cillian, the formidable war hero of Pyrithia, feared by men across the realm, and respected by his allies and enemies alike, had been acting like a teenage boy experiencing his first woman. Emmerson had Cillian wrapped around her dainty little finger, and he very well knew it.

"That's different," he scowled, and I barked out a laugh.

"How so?" I challenged.

"I am not a princeling going against the wishes of his king Silas. What I do does not matter. What you do, however, has the potential to fracture alliances. If you push your father too hard, he will push back. And if that happens, it won't only be our lives and the lives of our charges that are threatened. It will be all Pyrithia. Kieran's hunting her, her father's desperate to get her back, and your father wants to marry her into the kingdom. One wrong move and this all comes crashing down around us."

I widened my stance, placing my hands on my hips, and planted myself in front of him. "What do you suggest I do, then?" I gritted out.

"Don't provoke him. Hear him out." Cillian held up his hand to stop me from interrupting before continuing. "I'm not saying you have to agree to his demands. All I'm saying is that you need to appear to be considering them. Buy us time, Silas. Then we'll figure out our next move."

"You want me to lie to my father?" I clarified.

"Not lie. Consider his wishes, even if nothing changes for you."

"So, lie to him," I reiterated, and Cillian sighed.

"You know what Silas, you've already fucked us. Why not fan those flames," he huffed.

"Come on," I said, laughing at his exasperated state. "Emmerson keeping you up at night?" I asked, changing the subject.

Cillian growled, "That woman is loyal to a fault. She's more pissed than Harlowe is about everything that went down. Now she hardly talks to me, and any attempt I make to get near her ends in violence. She even kicked me out of my own bed."

"And you allowed that?" I asked, surprised.

"I had little choice. She got hold of one of my daggers and threatened to cut off my balls if I so much as took a step towards it," Cillian grumbled.

I winced, believing Emmerson would not hesitate to follow through on her threat.

"Tough break," I said, consoling my friend.

"I think I'm in love," Cillian muttered, running a hand down his face.

"That's supposed to make you happy," I laughed, clapping him on his shoulder.

"What about Harlowe?"

I contemplated my answer for a time before saying, "She's still angry, but she seems to be coming around."

"That's good," Cillian said.

"It would be, if I could trust it."

"What do you mean?" Cillian asked.

"Last night, she told me I meant nothing to her. That my only value to her was a body for her to find her pleasure." Cillian winced.

"But this morning," I continued. "It seemed like I was getting somewhere with her. I even apologized."

Cillian whipped his head around to gape at me.

"Yeah, yeah, I know. I'm the prick who never apologizes. But there's something different about Harlowe, Cill. She consumes my thoughts every moment, of every day. I can't bear the thought of her leaving me or of anyone else taking her. I'm wild and unpredictable when I'm around her. And the more she refuses me, the harder I try to lock her down."

Cillian snorted. "I know, brother. That's what I'm trying to warn you about. And trust me, I get it, I do. But you need to keep your head about this, alright."

I nodded. "Anyway, I'm not sure where we landed because fucking August barged in and, well, you know the rest."

We slowed as we turned the corner leading into my father's hallway. "Just promise you won't inflame the situation any further," Cillian said.

"Not making any promises," I muttered. "August is a right dick! So, there is no telling where this will go."

Cillian just groaned beside me. Sometimes I felt sorry for my best friend. I didn't always make things easy for him.

I didn't bother knocking as I pushed the doors to my father's chambers wide. August was slumped in a large armchair by the window; his face was a swollen mess. The healers hadn't been able to do much, I noted, smirking.

My father was pacing the space in front of his fireplace, back and forth, as he seethed with rage. Hearing me enter, he snapped his head up and marched towards me.

My father pointed his finger at the middle of my chest and bellowed, "You've gone too far this time, Silas. Look at your brother. He is the Crown Prince of Pyrithia. I cannot tolerate any assault on him. Even by you."

I just stared at my father. I'd let him get his anger out if that's what he needed. It wouldn't change a damn thing, but he didn't need to know that.

"Well?" my father threw his arms wide. "What do you have to say for yourself?"

I diverted my gaze from my father and looked over at my brother.

"I would say that he got what he deserved."

"Silas," Cillian hissed beside me. I guess this was not what he had in mind when he told me not to fan the flames.

"Is this a game to you?" my father howled, leaning into my personal space. Spittle flew from his mouth and landed on my face.

"I could have you flogged for this, Silas."

I narrowed my eyes at my father. He could fucking try.

"I see that's got your attention," my father said, glowering at me.

"Your Majesty, if I may," Cillian said.

"No, you may not Cillian. This is a matter between a father and his sons. Stay if you wish, but do not interfere."

I clenched my hands into fists at my side. My brother was watching the show, a smug look on his hideous face. I wanted to rail against them both, but Cillian was right. I needed to buy us enough time to get Harlowe and Emmerson out of the palace undetected.

My father was quiet for a long time as he continued his pacing. When he finally stopped, a determined look crossed his features.

"Silas, this is how it's going to be."

My muscles tensed, not appreciating where this was leading.

"The Princess will move out of your quarters today. She will have her own quarters made up in the guest wing. The welcome ball will go ahead as discussed, and your brother will use the intervening period to court the Princess."

He paused, checking to see if I would interject. I kept my jaw locked as I gritted my teeth. "You will wed Sienna the day after the ball."

"That won't be happening," I said, finally reaching my limit.

"It will," my father stated. "Otherwise I will have you stripped of your position and command of the Cathal will go to your brother."

I laughed. A full belly laugh that left your muscles aching and had tears threatening to spill from your eyes.

My father watched me through the narrowed slits of his eyes.

"My brother," I drawled, "is not capable of leading the Cathal."

"He can learn," my father countered.

"August has no dragon, Father. He has spent his life being pampered inside the palace, learning the viciousness of politics. None of that would help him convince a dragon to bond with him."

"Perhaps Caolán would be interested," my father said, tilting his head.

"Caolán would not abandon me for that gutless piece of shit," I spat. "That's not how it works, father, and you know it. If something were to happen to me, there's no guarantee Caolán would choose another Cathal, let alone him."

"Nonetheless, Silas, disobey me once more and I will remove you from command. I know how hard you have worked for your position son, don't make me do anything you will later regret. Harlowe is a beautiful woman, but so is Sienna. You could do far worse for a bride, Silas."

I ground my teeth so hard I thought I might break them. I felt Cillian grab my arm and tug me back towards the door.

"The Prince just needs time to accept your wishes, Your Highness. He will obey your command," Cillian offered.

"Make sure that he does, Cillian. Otherwise, his woman won't be the only one removed from your orbit."

Cillian stiffened, the threat clear; get me to play along, or he would lose Emmerson. I wondered if my father knew who had sired Cillian's little hellcat. If he did, he was a brave man to be threatening the only daughter of Samuel Rosinthorpe.

We were out in the hall before I had registered we had moved.

Cillian released me as he paced outside the now-closed door.

"Fuck!" he hissed, running both hands through his hair. "That was the very opposite of what I told you to do, Silas."

Walking away from my father's chambers, I heard Cillian jogging to catch up to me. When he fell into step beside me, I said, "You knew there was a chance it would go exactly like that. I bet you even envisioned it going worse."

Cillian growled, which was answer enough.

"Nothing can happen to Emmerson, Silas," he said, almost pleading.

"If you don't comply, you'll give your father a reason to intervene. Once we're out of the way, who will protect them, Silas?"

"It won't come to that," I stated.

"Oh, how are you going to ensure that?" Cillian challenged.

"Easy," I said with a lazy grin. "We're leaving tonight."

Chapter Fifty-Seven

"Silas," a feminine voice called after me as I made my way back to my chambers. I gritted my teeth, not in the mood to be dealing with Sienna right after my meeting with my father.

"You go ahead," I told Cillian. "Ensure Harlowe and Emmerson are both protected. I'll be there as soon as I've dealt with this," I said, tilting my head back in Sienna's direction.

Cillian nodded and continued down the hallway. Sienna caught up to me just as he disappeared around the corner.

I spun on my heels to face Sienna and growled, "What do you want, Sienna?" Hurt flashed across her face for the briefest of moments before she plastered on the seductive smile that had men falling all over her.

"There's no need for that tone, Silas," she purred, placing her palm on my chest. I gripped her wrist, removing her hand. Undeterred, Sienna took a step closer, invading my space.

"I'll only ask one more time Sienna, what do you want?"

"I want to talk about us," she pouted.

"There is no us, Sienna," I barked.

"Your father seems to think otherwise."

I narrowed my eyes on her and took a step closer, closing the distance between us.

"Let me be abundantly clear, Sienna," I said in a deadly tone. "I don't care what deal you and my brother struck with my father while I was away. There is no chance in hell that I will marry you. You need to let go of any delusions of becoming the next Princess of Pyrithia, here and now."

"Why, Silas? We've had our fun in the past," she rasped.

I wanted to shake her. Sure, we'd tumbled around in the sheets plenty of times, but I never promised her anything more. I explicitly stated that it would only be about sex. Sienna's motivation to marry me, however, had nothing to do with her feelings for me. This was about power. Sienna wanted more.

"With all the scheming you and August have been doing, I'm surprised you haven't attached yourself to him. He will be king after all."

"Silas," she drawled. "Do you truly believe I am solely concerned with status?"

"Yes," I answered without hesitation.

"Fuck you!" she spat, pointing a finger at me. "Before that stupid little whore came around, you were content with your place in my bed."

My hand jutted out, my fingers wrapping around the column of Sienna's delicate neck.

"Be careful with your next words, Sienna," I warned. "They may very well be your last."

Sienna swallowed but held her glare. "You've changed Silas, and not for the better," she said. I tightened my grip around her throat as she continued. "It's all because of Harlowe. What is it about her that would make you forsake your kingdom? Your King?"

I pushed against Sienna's throat, forcing her to step backward until her back hit the wall behind her.

"I could tell you it's the way her tight cunt wraps itself around my cock, milking me while I pump in and out of her," I said.

Sienna narrowed her eyes, and it was at this moment I realized she was jealous. Well, I knew she was jealous of Harlowe, but I had thought her jealousy pertained to her loss of status or sense of importance within my command. The way she looked at me now, though, how she glared daggers at me when I spoke of Harlowe, it was clear she was jealous of what Harlowe meant to me. I still didn't believe Sienna cared for me, but she was possessive, and she didn't like Harlow playing with her toys.

"Or maybe it's the way she sucks my cock, making me feel like a king as she worships me on her knees," I taunted.

"But mostly," I said as I leaned in to whisper in her ear, "It's the fact that she's not you."

I stepped away from Sienna, noting that my words had hit their mark. Good. I wanted her pissed enough that she wouldn't pursue this marriage proposal she had concocted. Knowing Sienna, though, it would take more than a few callous words to deter her. Not that it would matter after tonight. I was taking Harlowe and getting the fuck out of here.

Her hand went to her throat where I could see small red marks forming, highlighting where my fingers had been. I held her stare, glowering at her for a moment before turning on my heels and leaving her there, reeling.

"She won't be yours, Silas," she called after me. "August won't allow it."

Fuck August.

"He wants her because she's yours, and he won't stop until he has taken her from you."

Halting in my tracks, I spun back towards Sienna. The look of fear that flashed across her face told me I reflected my fury in my expression.

"What did you just say?" I growled menacingly.

Sienna gulped.

I gripped her throat again and squeezed.

"I asked you a fucking question, Sienna."

"August," she whimpered, "he wants her because you do."

"I heard you the first fucking time. TELL ME WHAT YOU KNOW!" I roared.

"H-He was there when I told your father why I was sent home," she stuttered.

"And?" I growled, impatience creeping in.

"He p-pulled me aside after and wanted to know a-about your relationship with her."

"What did you tell him?" I snarled.

"That you were obsessed with her. That you had spent almost all your time with her, training her," she said, raising her voice, her anger winning out over her fear.

"And why would you say that?" I growled.

"Because it was the truth," she spat. "The minute you laid eyes on her, everyone else ceased to exist for you. You couldn't stay away from her. You made excuses to seek her out, and you excluded everyone else when you spent time with her. I wasn't the only one who noticed it, Silas."

"What did my brother have to say about that?" I snapped.

"He said he would take her from you. That he would show you the power he held over you and prove that you were beneath him. He might not be stronger than you, Silas, but he knows politics, and he knew just how to proposition your father to get him to change his mind about Harlowe. He wants to break her, and through her, you."

"And you gave him everything he fucking needed to succeed." I was fucking livid.

Sienna lifted her chin. Well, as much as she could manage with my hand wrapped around her throat.

"You betrayed me, Sienna. I was your commanding officer, and you fucking betrayed me."

"I did this for you, Silas," she hissed.

"Oh, my apologies. Please, tell me how this is for my benefit?" I mocked.

"She is a distraction. Your obsession with her is leading you down the wrong path. You're turning against your King, and for what? You could have any woman you wanted, Silas, and you're going to destroy everything you've ever worked towards for her." The venom dripped from every word she hurled at me.

"Because she is my beating fucking heart!" I screamed, pounding a fist to my chest.

Sienna's eyes widened in shock, and I inhaled a sharp breath, realizing what I just confessed. Sienna recovered quickly, narrowing her eyes at me as she snarled.

"August won't let this go," she said, her confidence growing. "He has seen for himself just how enamored you are with her. He will make her his if it's the last thing he does. His disdain for you is so prominent, so pervasive, he would stop at nothing to destroy you. She is his way of achieving his goals."

"You better pray to whatever gods will have you he doesn't succeed, Sienna. Because if anyone comes between me and my Little Menace, I will tear them apart with my bare hands. The same goes for anyone who helped them. Now get the fuck out of my sight before I decide to get started right now."

Registering the truth of my words, she hurried to get away from me.

"FUCK!" I bellowed as I raked my hand through my hair. A sharp pain spread along my scalp as I tugged at the strands.

Sienna had given August everything he needed to seek his petty revenge against me. And he intended to use my Little Menace to execute it.

The sooner we left, the better. My father would come around once we had the chance to talk without August's poisonous tongue. I just needed to remove Harlowe from the equation while everything settled down.

Resolve settled in the pit of my stomach, calming the flames of my raging fury. I'd take Harlowe someplace safe where no one could coerce her or use her in any way.

Isn't that exactly what you have done to her? The insidious voice inside my head whispered to me.

While true, I was done playing games with her. Everything I had done to Harlowe had been under the false promises made by my father. I thought I had been protecting her by bringing her here. Now I would protect her by setting her free. I would stand by her side, help her fight those who would threaten her, always protecting her back. She no longer had to question my loyalty. I had failed her once. I wouldn't do it again.

No. This time, I was all in.

Chapter Fifty-Eight

"If that's true Fire Heart, you are no safer here than you were in your palace," Misneach remarked once I had finished catching him up on everything that had happened that morning.

Silas's father had summoned him to answer for what had occurred with his brother. He was unfazed when he left, but Cillian had returned some time ago and Silas was yet to materialize.

"Which is why we are leaving," I reminded him. Cillian told me about Silas's plans. He instructed me to pack for the journey to... well... we actually hadn't gotten that far in the discussion. If it was away from Pyrithia, I didn't much care where we were headed.

Emmerson had left with Cillian to pack her things, which were in the suite nearest Silas's chambers. Fionn had disappeared after them, with Cian replacing him as my personal guard. Preoccupied with his own troubles, he had left me alone while I schemed with Misneach.

"I still don't trust the General," Misneach growled.

"Neither do I, so we'll leave him and his men at the first chance we get."

I believed Silas was genuine when he owned up to his mistakes, but that didn't make his treatment of me any less of a betrayal. While he might be committed to proving his word to me, the truth of the matter was that I no longer had the luxury of trusting him. I couldn't risk him changing his mind, or making some other decision he thought was in my best interests when he disagreed with my course of action. I couldn't put Emmerson in that position, either.

Kieran was hunting me. My father was doing the same, albeit with vastly different intentions. I was now convinced I was the target of the attack from the Kingdom of Vidyaa. And according to the Lost Witch, there will likely be more attempts on my life. I needed to sort through everything she had revealed, none of which I could do while trying to navigate whatever was going on between Silas and me.

"You also need to learn how to regulate your power. I can feel it growing through the bond, and it is of no use to you if you cannot wield it effectively."

"Can the other dragons sense it, too?" I asked.

"Yes," Misneach confirmed. I rubbed my temples, trying to fend off the burgeoning headache I could feel coming on.

"You also need to train in aerial warfare. Perhaps the General can be of use in teaching you before we relieve ourselves of his company," Misneach mused.

"Can't you teach me?"

"I can only teach you so much, Fire Heart. You will eventually require a Cathal to train you in the elements I cannot."

"Hmm."

I wasn't opposed to Silas training me. He indeed enhanced my hand-to-hand skills. However, I did not relish him having any kind of power over me while I remained undecided about what I intended to do about us.

A knock on the door pulled me from my ruminations. Cian made his way to the door before I could answer it.

"There are things I must attend to before we leave Fire Heart," Misneach said. **"I won't be far. I will come straight back if you need me."**

"What do you have to do?" I asked, curious how Misneach spent his time.

"Believe it or not, Fire Heart, I had a life before I met you," he scowled.

"Okay, okay. Go do... you."

Misneach huffed, but I could tell he had moved further away.

"I'll be right outside," Cian said, pulling my attention back to my current company.

Sienna stood just inside the doorway, her long brown hair hanging loose around her face, her caramel highlights glinting in the light of the fading sun. Her beauty was undeniable, yet there was a subtle edge to her. A desperation of sorts that warned me to tread carefully.

"Sienna," I said curtly. "What can I do for you?"

Sienna moved further into the room. Her gaze swept the space while her hand glided across the fireplace mantle.

"I once fucked Silas right here," she said, pointing to the space in front of the fireplace. "It was wintertime, and we spent the night curled up together, soaking up the heat of the flames, fucking like animals all night long," she laughed.

"Congratulations," I said dryly. "Is there a reason you're telling me this?"

"Silas made some interesting comments about you when I spoke to him earlier," she said, ignoring my question.

I knew her game. I knew she was trying to bait me. I also knew I would regret hearing whatever poison she was about to drivel, but I couldn't help myself.

"Please," I drawled, "tell me, Sienna. I am sure you intend to whether or not I care to hear them."

Sienna walked towards the settee. She sat down, making herself comfortable as she folded the skirts of her dress. When she was satisfied, she lifted her gaze to meet mine, a smirk playing on her painted lips.

"He told me how you like to get down on your knees for him. How you suck his cock like a common whore." I clenched my jaw but gave no other indication that her words bothered me.

"He told me how he feels like a king, standing over you like that, his cock pressed between your lips," she said.

This time I couldn't hide the flinch her words elicited. Hadn't he told me he was king inside the bedroom, right before he commanded me to drop to my knees? The only way Sienna would know this, is if Silas had shared our intimate moments with her.

What was Silas playing at? What reason would he have to share those details with Sienna?

With a glint in her eye, Sienna continued, "He told me about his meeting with his father. He has agreed to move aside for August."

"I don't believe you."

"Don't believe me," she shrugged nonchalantly. "We are still getting married the day after your ball, regardless. Then it will be your and August's turn."

I clenched my hands into fists. There was no chance I would ever marry August. At least marrying Kieran would have protected my kingdom.

"He hasn't returned yet, has he?" Sienna crooned, once again pulling my attention from my spiraling thoughts.

"Who?" I snapped.

"Silas," she grinned triumphantly. "He hasn't returned from his meeting with his father. You want to know why?" she asked, leaning forward.

I just stared at her, not trusting myself to speak.

"He was with me," she chuckled. "He came to inform me of his plans, and well, you know, one thing led to another, and before I knew it, we were naked between my sheets."

Jealousy curled inside my stomach, and I fought to keep it from showing on my face.

"He told me he enjoyed his time using your tight cunt, and how it wrapped around him, milking him as he pumped in and out of you."

Her words pierced my heart. In the midst of passion, Silas had said those very things to me. She could only know that if he told her. The image of them in bed, with him recounting what he did to me, made bile rise in my throat.

Sienna stood and then crossed the floor until she stood in front of me.

"I told you in Valoren you were just a way to pass the time. I said he would tire of you, and when he did, he would find his way back to my bed, where he always knew he belonged."

"You can show yourself out," I said in a bored tone. Sienna just smirked, victory gleaming in her eyes.

"I said get out!"

Cian opened the door and popped his head inside at the sound of my raised voice. "Everything okay in here?" he asked.

"Fine," I said, my eyes never leaving Sienna's. "Sienna was just leaving."

Before she could move, though, I grabbed her wrist and leaned in close to her ear. "He was also just a way for me to pass the time. And yeah, I played his dirty little slut, because I enjoyed the things he did to my body whenever I did. But he never had my affection," I lied. "Unlike you, Sienna, I know my worth. And I won't ever be someone's second choice. In case you haven't heard, men start fucking wars over me. I don't need to beg and plead for a man's attention. Nor would I ever lower myself to do so. If you want to be Silas's fall-back bitch, go ahead. I'm sure it's quite comforting to know that when he's done messing up someone else's sheets, he'll come crawling back to you... eventually."

Releasing her, I took a step back and smirked at the hatred I found plastered on her face.

Sienna wordlessly turned and marched out of the room.

Cian retreated once Sienna was gone, which left me little else to do but stew in my heartbreak that was rapidly turning to rage.

Chapter Fifty-Nine

The room darkened as I sat in the armchair overlooking the palace grounds. No one had returned to the room, and I lost track of time. I had no idea what was going on outside these four walls. For all I knew, everyone could have abandoned me. Well, that could have been true, had it not been for Emmerson in the room next door. They would have had to remove her forcibly, and I still would have heard her.

I often wondered how I got so lucky to have Emmerson as my best friend.

The door creaked as someone opened it, and I turned to see Cian stepping inside. His face was paler than usual, and he had dark circles under his eyes. The Cathal who had accompanied Emmerson and me to Pyrithia had been guarding us around the clock. It was no wonder it was showing.

"Princess," Cian started.

I rolled my eyes. "You don't need to call me Princess Cian. You and I both know it means nothing here, anyway."

"Harlowe then," he corrected. "I have something I'd like to discuss with you."

Sitting up straighter in my seat, I waited for him to continue.

"You and I have never been close," he said as he took a seat opposite me. "That is why I think I am best placed to have a frank discussion about your future."

I raised a brow but did not interrupt.

"Everyone is clouded by their affection for you. I have no such issue."

I barked out a laugh. "Please Cian, don't hold back on me."

Cian cracked a small smile. "I don't dislike you, Princess... Harlowe. All I'm saying is I'm removed from the situation, and I think that comes with valuable insight."

"Which would be?"

"Silas is not himself when he is around you. He is making decisions that place both you and our kingdom at risk." He glanced at me to gauge my reaction before continuing. "I want to help you."

"Help me how?"

"I'll get you out of here."

"Isn't that Silas's plan?" I questioned.

"It is. But that's problematic too. He can't abandon his responsibilities here for you." Cian shot me an apologetic grin. It was the first sign of emotion I had seen from the stoic Cathal.

"How would it work?"

"I'll take you to your dragon and the pair of you can leave right now. I have even packed you some provisions."

"I'm not leaving without Emmerson."

"I know. I've taken care of that. Teller is bringing her to a pre-arranged meeting spot."

"Does Teller know he is going against his Commander's instructions?"

Cian winced. "No," he admitted.

I had to give it to Cian; he was risking a lot by helping me. Of course, he thought by doing so, he was also acting in the best interests of his Prince and his kingdom.

This had been my plan all along; escape, and ditch Silas along the way. So why did the idea of doing that hurt?

Pushing my uncertainty down, I said, "Okay Cian. I'll go with you."

Without hesitation, Cian stood and offered me his hand. "Thank you, Harlowe." Emotion tightened my throat at the gratitude I found in Cian's gaze.

The corridors were quiet as Cian led me out of the palace, the sounds of our footsteps echoing off the stone walls around us.

"Where is everyone?" I asked.

"Didn't you hear?" Cian said, flashing me a cheeky grin over his shoulder.

"Hear what?"

"It's your official welcome feast tonight."

I scoffed. "Right. Perfect distraction."

Walking in silence, we turned a corner and entered an open courtyard through a wooden door. The night was darker than usual; the clouds casting an ominous haze over the grounds. I felt a prickling sensation crawl up my spine as though unseen eyes were peering at me from some concealed alcove. I stopped and peered around, unable to identify anything amiss.

"Everything all right?" Cian asked from up ahead.

"Yes, I," I started. I what? I feel... creeped out. I was being foolish. "Nothing," I replied, shaking myself out of my unease.

"We're meeting up ahead," Cian said, pointing to a structure in the distance.

As we got closer, I could see it was the storage shed the Cathal used for their training weapons. I knew this because we had passed it when we first arrived in Pyrithia.

Cian stopped ahead of me, peering around in the darkness. "So where is Emmerson?" I asked when I caught up to him.

"I don't know," he muttered, almost to himself.

"Well, well, well, isn't this a pleasant surprise," a familiar male voice sounded from within the shadows. I turned quickly and saw Kieran emerging from beside the small structure.

I took a step back and ran into a solid wall. Cian gripped my arm and pulled me behind him.

"Stay behind me, Princess," Cian hissed as he unsheathed his sword.

"Let's not get heroic," Kieran warned. "Bring me the Princess and everyone leaves here alive." Kieran held out his hand towards me as if he expected me to simply give up.

My heartbeat raced as Cian took a step away from him.

"Don't test me, boy," Kieran spat.

"How did you know where she would be?" Cian demanded.

"Misneach," I called desperately.

I'd promised myself that I wouldn't cower under the expectations of the men in my life. But coming face-to-face with Kieran again made me realize I was still shamefully afraid of this man. And I didn't want to face him alone.

There was a delay before Misneach responded. **"You're scared. What is happening, Fire Heart?"**

"Kieran is here in Pyrithia and he's going to take me."

Misneach snarled, and I swear I could hear it echoing around me.

Kieran growled and stormed towards me, but Cian extended his sword to stop him. Shadows swirled up Kieran's arms before they jutted forward and wrapped around Cian's throat. A sickening crack sounded in the still night air before Cian dropped to the ground, unmoving.

It took a moment for my mind to comprehend that Kieran had killed Cian, breaking his neck in mere seconds. Screaming sounded and I looked around to find the source before I realized it was coming for me.

Kieran's hand gripped my wrist just as the sound of beating wings filled the surrounding space. Misneach landed with a thud and the ground shook beneath my feet. Moments later, a second thud sounded, followed by a third. Caolán and Niamh flanked Misneach, both snarling and baring their teeth.

"We are with you, Daughter of Fire and Flame," a feminine voice sounded inside my head.

"What?" I blurted out loud.

"You hear me?" the voice sounded again. Niamh's serpentine eyes swiveled and locked on me.

"Yes," I breathed.

"She is ours," a rough, masculine voice said. It wasn't Misneach, so I figured it was Caolán.

"Caolán?"

The massive dragon took a step closer, and he lowered his head to the ground, a dangerous growl escaping him.

"Stay calm Fire Heart," Misneach said. **"We will not allow him to harm you."**

Given what I had just witnessed, I was not confident that anyone could stop Kieran from doing just that.

The cold bite of steel pressed against my throat as Kieran's hot breath fanned against my ear. "Tell them to stand down," Kieran growled.

"I don't control them," I spat, my heart hammering wildly inside my chest.

"Now, why don't I believe you?" Kieran purred.

"Fire Heart," Misneach rumbled.

"I'm okay, just..." Just what? What exactly was I doing here?

"Help is coming Fire Heart. Remain calm and we will keep his attention tracked on us."

"Okay." I released a slow breath, trying to calm my racing heart. Misneach came prepared. He had a plan. I just needed to keep my shit together and not get my throat slit in the meantime.

"Don't do anything foolish Kieran."

I turned towards the voice and saw Teller had arrived with Emmerson, who was going pale at the sight before her.

"You don't want to harm the Princess," he continued.

Kieran barked out a laugh, sounding unhinged.

"Is this boy serious?" Kieran whispered low enough that only I could hear. "No need to fret, little Bride. I'm not here to harm you. I'm here to take you home."

"I'm not your anything, and I'm not going anywhere with you," I sneered.

"Come now," Kieran crooned. "Is that any way to speak to your husband?"

"You're not my husband," I ground out.

"Not yet, but soon," Kieran purred. A shiver of unease rushed over me, and Kieran pulled me against him so I could feel the hard outline of his erection.

"You're getting me all excited, Harlowe. Your fear is intoxicating," he said, as he inhaled deeply.

"Misneach," I pleaded. Misneach growled and stepped closer.

"I wouldn't," Kieran said in a sing-song voice as he dug the blade deep enough into my flesh that a trickle of blood ran down my throat.

Misneach growled and stomped his feet. I could tell it was an effort for him to not lunge for me. Caolán snapped at him, and Misneach retreated infinitesimally.

"He is coming," Caolán's calming voice whispered through my head.

"Who is coming?"

"The Prince."

"Silas?" I asked, hoping he didn't mean August.

"Yes, Little One. We are but a distraction. He will come for you."

"Are you ready?" Kieran asked.

"What?" I responded, confused.

"They are trying to distract me, Harlowe. I'm not stupid. But they weren't the only ones buying time." I could hear the smirk in Kieran's voice, and my stomach churned as I waited with bated breath to see what was coming next.

Thick black shadows billowed around my feet, snaking up my legs towards my waist.

"What the hell are you doing?" I said, unable to hide the panic from my voice.

"I told you my powers were far more impressive."

Fear gripped me, closing around my chest and squeezing tightly. I couldn't breathe, couldn't calm my beating pulse. Everything that I had done to escape my fate was for nothing. Kieran had me, and he wasn't letting me go.

"HARLOWE," Silas bellowed, and Kieran snarled against my ear.

I whipped my head in his direction and saw him sprinting towards me, followed by Cillian and Fionn.

The distance was too great, and the shadows were nearly enveloping me. They wouldn't make it in time. Whatever Kieran had planned, he had been ahead of us the entire time.

The shadows crept up my throat as Misneach roared. I didn't have time to glance in his direction before the shadows had completely consumed me.

And just like the time Kieran had visited me in my chambers in Valoren, I felt our bond numb. I could vaguely sense Misneach and knew he was alive and close by, but I couldn't communicate with him. I couldn't tell him I was sorry for leaving him once more. I couldn't reassure him I would be alright, even though I wasn't sure I would be.

A powerful longing surged within me, compelling me to run towards him, embrace him, and never let go. I felt as though part of my soul was being ripped away from me. In such a short time, Misneach had become such an integral part of my being. A fact I only realized now that he was being torn away from me.

A small sob escaped me before I could stop it.

"Shh, Harlowe," Kieran whispered, almost gently. It shocked me enough to stop my impending meltdown. I couldn't see him with the shadows encasing us, but I could still feel his body pressed against mine. He had wrapped both arms around my waist as he held me tight.

"I will be everything you need from this moment on."

The knife. He was no longer pressing the knife against my throat. I could break free of his hold. I could...

The sensation of falling overwhelmed me, and I gripped Kieran's forearms instinctively. As quickly as it started, the feeling ceased, and my feet met solid ground. I swayed, but Kieran steadied me in his arms.

Lifting my gaze, I took in the monolithic castle before me. The gothic architecture of the castle created a foreboding feeling, made worse by the gloominess of the darkened night. The small sliver of moonlight that peeked through beneath the clouds cast an eerie glow over the structure, amplifying the unsettling feeling growing within me.

"I've waited a long time for this moment," Kieran whispered in my ear.

"Welcome home, Bride."

Acknowledgments

Writing this story has been something that I had only ever dreamed of doing and now it is a reality. I would not have been able to achieve this without the love and support of my family who encouraged me at every step along the way.

A special shout out to my husband Luke, for talking through all my ideas (sometimes on repeat) and giving me your honest and constructive feedback. I know just how busy you are and that your time is a finite resource, so I very much appreciate the many, many hours you poured into this story for me.

To my sister Sherrin, thank you for everything you have done to help me bring this story to life. From the weekends you sacrificed to help with re-writes, to the numerous phone calls when I needed to talk an idea or plot inconsistency through, and everything in between - Thank you!

To my beta team Billie, Savannah, and Corey, thank you for all the effort you put in to help shape this story and make it the very best that it could be. I truly appreciate your work.

Thank you to Nannie for pushing me to put my ideas down on paper. Without your constant encouragement, I am not sure this story would have ever been written.

To my children, thank you for reminding me how exciting it can be to let your imagination run wild. You inspire me to be a better version of myself every single day and I love you very much.

Finally, thank you to those who have taken the time to read my story. I hope you have enjoyed the ride as much as I have. The adventure continues in book two and I hope you will join me for the rest of Harlowe's journey!

K.J. Johnson

About the Author

K.J. Johnson is a fantasy and romance indie author who writes about headstrong heroines and morally grey men.

K.J. Johnson's debut novel, A Heart of Fire and Flame, is book one of the Fire
and Flame series.

After a lifelong obsession with reading and escaping into different worlds where anything is possible, she decided to let her imagination run wild and penned her debut novel - A Heart of Fire and Flame.

K.J. Johnson enjoys writing romance of the darker persuasion and you can expect plenty of spice, but check your morality at the door because it won't survive the ride.

In her downtime, she still enjoys getting lost in a good book and experiencing the world through the eyes of her favorite authors

Social Media Links

You can connect with me on:

https://kjjohnsonbooks.com
https://www.instagram.com/authork.j.johnson
https://www.tiktok.com/@authork.j.johnson
https://www.threads.net/@authork.j.johnson

Subscribe to my newsletter:
https://kjjohnsonbooks.com/newsletter

www.ingramcontent.com/pod-product-compliance
Lightning Source LLC
Chambersburg PA
CBHW070639310726
48982CB00001B/336
9781763682528